King of the Gulls

Stefan Scheuermann

Paul Alexander

"King of the Gulls," by Stefan Scheuermann and Paul Alexander. ISBN 978-1-63868-159-5 (softcover); 978-1-63868-160-1 (hardcover); 978-1-63868-161-8 (eBook).

Dedication

We dedicate this book to Clan Lindsay, its noble Chief, and its illustrious history.

Contents

Part One:

Vanora's King

Prologue

This story begins in May, 1587, in Kinghorn, a coastal village in Eastern Scotland. Mary Queen of Scots had been executed three months earlier. The Reformation was in full bloody swing, and vicious, covetous, sharp-clawed hands clutched at power. The people of Scotland were war-torn, battered to the brink by the ambitions of kings and queens and the zeal of religious extremism.

It was the first warm day of a cold spring. An old man, cloaked in heavy wool, dirty of dress and body, and smelling of the musky wild, walked through the fields outside of town, drawing the attention of everyone he passed. Few knew him. All knew *of* him. He was the region's seanchai, a minstrel, a storyteller and keeper of oral history. Where he had been, nobody knew.

He came rarely to Kinghorn, but walked with purpose on this May morning, turning his eyes neither left nor right, paying no attention to the hands that waved timidly at him as he passed. He walked past the ladies hanging the laundry, past the children at play, drawing a growing crowd in his wake.

His appearance was always a special event, one romanticized at every dinner table during the years of his absence. He stopped in the heart of town, standing like a dusty old statue. The prominent families greeted him there. The women took him indoors, stripped off his filthy robes, bathed him, groomed him, and untangled his knotted hair and matted beard. Free of his ample folds of heavy clothing, he was lean and sinuous, and covered from neck to ankle in gray hair. The women tended him well, for he was theirs and they were his.

Once he was cleaned and perfumed, they fed him and offered him a bed. The storyteller slept until late afternoon. When he finally rose again, he ordered a bonfire set on the beach. As the sun went low, every inhabitant of Kinghorn was gathered. The fire was lit, and the old man stood tallest among them. He hushed the murmur of lingering conversations with a raise of his hands above his head. The children gathered nearest, seated in the sand.

The light reflecting in the seanchaí's eyes from the fire was overpowered by the flame that shone from within. He cleared his throat in a deep and rumbling grunt that seemed to come from the sea behind him.

"Kinghorn!" he addressed them all, "In 1286, our King Alexander III died on this beach, on this very spot where I stand. You know this. You have all been told the story. But what you know is only a speck of the truth."

He bent down and took a pinch of sand between his thumb and index finger, held it up, then continued, "What you have been told is no more than a grain of sand. I have come to show you the beach."

He threw the pinch of sand into the fire. Whether from their imagination or from some power they could not understand, the fire appeared to double in brightness and warmth in a quick flash, then return as it had been. If it was imagination, it was one shared by all. They gasped together and squinted their eyes in unison against the brightness.

When their eyes recovered, their ears took their attention. Gulls gathered above in squawking, circling formations, increasing in number until they were as numerous as the eager people seated in the sand. The old man looked up and stared at them for several long and

4

awkward minutes, nodding to them while his lips moved in silent communication with the birds above.

He turned his face back to his eager audience and told them, "It is said that he died when he fell from his horse, that a drunken accident killed Alexander III."

One young woman yelled out, "How did he die?"

"You cannot understand how he died until you know why he died, and you cannot know why he died until you know how he lived."

He dropped his face suddenly to the sand between his feet, then raised it again, slowly, with his eyes wide and fiery. He drew a deep inhale, held it beyond its natural life, then released it as he spoke in a tone ruggedly aggressive, yet dulcet and comforting,

> Good evening my friends, find a rock to share
> Hear a tale of our people and land
> It's a story of faith and one of despair
> A tale I must tell you by sacred demand
>
> I will tell you of truths that are misunderstood
> But to me and a few have been shown
> I will speak of the things that very few could
> The words that I say may be cast into stone
>
> The night is young with a welcoming glow
> Of a fire we share on the sand
> Open your thoughts and learn what I know
> Let your hearts be altered before we disband
>
> This story is old and speaks of *our* past
> Of events that have formed who we are
> With hope formed anew and forever will last
> Like the light of a distant and twinkling star
>
> Thank you for your kindness and love from within

Eager ears and welcoming eyes
The gulls are now ready for our tale to begin
As they walk the beach and circle the skies

These are *their* verses, I speak for them now
As they have spoken for others
For on their wings the Heavens endow
The words of our fathers and mothers

Chapter One:

That Path You Draw

Tears of a child wishing,
Thunder is his cry
Pleading to the wind
For shelter in the sky

The penetrating chill of a specter's icy fingers ran down the boy's spine, waking him from what had been a warm summer sleep. The seven-year-old Prince of Scotland jolted up, every hair on his arms and neck standing erect, looking for the shaded figure that had spooked him. His eyes saw no specter. His skin felt only the July breeze floating spitefully through the window of his bedchamber. His ears heard only the call of his childhood companions — the gulls that circled outside.

"A dream," he declared to himself, "Only a dream."

He rose from his bed and shivered himself free of the lingering sense of dread. By the time he leaned against the window and fixed his eyes on his flying friends, his smile was bright and wide. There was energy in their flight, and Alexander knew them well. Their darting, diving circles and the rising pitch of their calls spoke of a coming storm.

At once, the gulls ceased their songs. They soared in silence. No sound came from the sky above, and nothing from the ground below. The natural world outside of his window had gone mute. Alexander focused his eyes on a single gull. He watched its muted flight in fascination, when a voice broke the silence. It echoed down to him from the sky above, or maybe from the ground below. He could not tell. It was a masculine voice, low, rich, simultaneously old and very youthful, and rolling as it spoke,

Oh seed of new light
With soil upon your hand
Make shallow the night
And foil the somber land

Seek boisterous thunder
That force from within
See truth and the wonder
Of darkness and sin

The clamor you hear
Is the storm that surrounds
Follow your fear
Learn what abounds

Your priest has been chosen
To show you the light
Your path is in motion
With gulls of pure white

Still fixed on the image of a single seagull, circling in an ancient dance with the wind, Alexander was struck with the realization that the voice he heard did not come from his sleepy imagination, nor from some arcane source beyond his window, but from a man, a real man. With a sudden, cold, and hollow sense of foreboding, he turned quickly, and there, at the threshold of his room, stood an old man.

Like his voice, the man was both old and youthful. As to his clothing, the prince could not have spoken, for his attention was seized by other features. The man was slightly hunched, as if under the weight of many decades of toil and countless miles traveled. The flesh around his eyes was dark and deeply weathered. But it framed the most magnificent pair of orbs.

In remarkable contrast to his face, his eyes were vibrant, like wild, tempestuous oceans that churned violently. They were still, and locked on the boy in front of them, yet they were in constant motion. Alexander could easily picture tiny ships being tossed about within the blue of those lively eyes. They were dark, but a light shone from beneath them, as if the sun had been removed from the sky and placed at the floor of the ocean to push its brilliance upward from within.

The man widened those eyes, and Alexander felt as though he might fall into them and drown. He turned his face to his feet in defense. An inexplicable draw brought his gaze up again, but the old man was gone. The prince ran to the door and looked down the hallway beyond. The passage was empty. He strained his ears for the burdened footsteps of a hunched old man. He heard nothing.

Echoes of the verses he had heard at the window rang through his memory, but not in vivid recollection, rather in a hollow, almost whispered version of the same voice. Suddenly, he felt a squeeze and pull as the fingers of destiny wrapped around him. Half-terrified and half-intrigued, he followed that pull in a full sprint down the hall. It was a dark passage, dimly lit as the tentative sunlight of the infant day managed to toddle its way into the adjacent rooms and creep shyly into the hallway.

He was in the Holyrood Abbey, an Augustine monastery with a royal residence wing. It was less than a mile east of Edinburgh Castle, yet it felt a hundred miles away. The spacious grounds and the solemnity of the monks gave the abbey a sense of seclusion. Alexander treasured his time there, because of the atmosphere, and because he was away from his spiteful mother.

His mother, the Queen Consort Maria de Coucy, was a cold and hard woman. She had been raised as a pampered child amid the aristocracy of Paris. Her heart was driven by two lusts — political ambition and lavish, regal pleasures. She viewed her son as the destroyer of both, and her resentment toward this little adversary began at the moment of his birth. In his mother's company, Alexander would have been too timid to race down a dark hallway in pursuit of a figure he was not sure was real. But at Holyrood, he was free to run like a child and chase fantasies.

The boy bounced down the hallway like a moth in search of a flame. In mid-stride, he opened his mouth to shout, but had no idea what name or title to call, so he just ran, and his rapid, desperate eyes darted in every direction, into every passage and doorway, and into nooks and crevices no old man could fit into.

His focused pursuit was disturbed by two of his royal guards. As Alexander passed them, they dropped to a knee and addressed him, "Your Majesty." It was a gesture and title reserved for his father. The oddity left his mind as quickly as it entered, and the search for the old man continued.

If there was one person in the young prince's life who could seize his attention *and* his affections, it was his nursemaid. Vanora was a short, broad-hipped, busty woman who had cared for Alexander since his first hours on earth. She had always been his only source of maternal care and nurturing. She loved the boy — truly loved him. And he loved her. Not a soothing caress nor tranquilizing lullaby ever came to him but through her. She was the only figure in all of his life who saw him, and treated him, for what he was, a boy; a sweet, generous, and compassionate boy.

His relationship with Vanora was intimate, their encounters casual and familial, so when he passed her in the hallway it was all the stranger when she, like the guards, dropped formally to one knee and addressed him as, "Your Majesty." The mysterious man from the bedchamber doorway fell entirely from his thoughts. He stared, perplexed, at his only human friend and the closest thing to a loving mother he had ever known. She remained on one knee, looking downward to the stone floor in front of her.

Alexander began a muttered protest, but only a single syllable escaped his lips before three knights approached and surrounded him. The famous warrior, Alan Durward, who Alexander knew and admired, who had entertained the child with thrilling battlefield tales over a feast just a few months earlier, stood to his right. Another storied fighter, Henry Baliol, framed the boy on the opposite side. Rigid concern dominated their features. Their jaws were clenched and their fists were balled tightly at their sides. They did not drop to a knee or address the child in any way, but stood in defensive postures that enveloped Alexander with a frigid sense of doom.

The third knight stood nobly in front of him. But he put off a very different air than the other two. His eyes were deep and penetrating, but bright and warm. Alexander had never seen him before that moment, but there was something in his presence that told the prince that all is well, or would be, as long as this man stood before him. He was David Lindsay, the King's most trusted friend and advisor. There was an uncommon duality in his features, chiseled like stone, with hard lines, yet there was a calm, refined gentility about him.

Lindsay knelt in front of the boy, but not in some subservient gesture. He lowered himself to look at Alexander, eye-to-eye.

"My boy," he began, "my dear and noble child, your father, the King, has died."

Lindsay waited to gauge Alexander's reaction before continuing. The prince was not yet eight years old, but the truth of the moment fell soundly on his little shoulders. His good father was gone from his life forever. He was well enough acquainted with his mother's character to know that frenzied, green ambition was swelling in her heart. Schemes and plots were being drawn in her mind.

Alexander stood in that hallway as the King of Scotland. His knees would have buckled beneath him from the sudden burden, if not for the strengthening presence of Lindsay. But Alexander did not want what David Lindsay, or any of them, had to offer. He did not want strength at that moment. He wanted nurturing reassurance. He did not get it from the three knights in front of him.

A deep-voiced flow of impossible expectations cascaded onto his head from Durward. Lofty words of unfitting reverence came from Baliol on his other side. Lindsay stood from his knee and silently looked down at the new King with more pity than supplication. Alexander drew his lower lip into his mouth and bit down on it. He lowered his eyebrows and wrinkled his nose, as his eyes began to well with tears.

"For heaven's sake, my Lords," came the scolding voice of Vanora, "He has heard enough for now. Don't say another word."

The knights all turned to her and immediately, obediently, closed their mouths tightly. Vanora's image transformed in Alexander's sparkling, innocent eyes. Her soft voice had an inexplicable authority over these powerful men. She owned the moment, and right then, right there, she owned the hallway and the young monarch within it. The knights would not refute her. She shooed them away. They bottled their words for later use, turned on their heels, and walked away from the king and his nursemaid.

When the thundering sound of the three marching knights had dwindled into oblivion, he turned to her. She threw her arms wide and he lunged at her, as if pushed from behind. She had no more than a few inches on him, yet she hoisted him into her arms like he was still two years old. She carried him into her bedchamber, and his panting breaths slowed and calmed with each of her quiet steps. She laid him across her bed and sat beside him. Rubbing his head, she sang,

> Rest your head
> On my breast
> Let the world beyond go to sleep
>
> Safe and warm
> Dream little one
> Your cares are the stars' to keep

Vanora's song worked as it always had. The sharp edges of Alexander's mind dulled and softened as if under the influence of a powerful narcotic. His eyelids tripled in weight, and he began to fall into that magical place between conscious thought and dream. But he was snapped violently from it when the song turned to a whisper, eerily reminiscent of the voice of the mysterious old man. His beloved Vanora repeated the words that had gripped him just a few minutes earlier and drew him into the hallway,

> Your priest has been chosen
> To show you the light
> Your path is in motion
> With gulls of pure white

Chapter Two:

The Storm that Surrounds

The Shadows of the castle
Darkened the humble sky,
Showing its force
As the entrance drew nigh

There was one week, seven furiously flowing days, between the death of the father and the coronation of the son. Alexander's life was fundamentally changing. His days and nights would never look the same. His very identity was comprehensively altered. Yet he did not have a moment of breath to contemplate the changes.

The expedience was necessary. Alexander was only seven and hardly cut a fearsome image. His father left Scotland in the midst of political and military complications that pushed against every coast and border. Some of the prominent barons feared that a child on the throne would degrade the precarious peace and invite invasion.

The notion was presented to them by the poisonous tongue of an ambitious baron who wanted anything but peace. Beolin Crymlyn of Clan Crymlyn was head of a family that had risen in the fog of war. His grandfather had been the petty laird of an impoverished community of Lowland farmers who found himself, quite accidentally, on the victorious side of consecutive clan battles. What began with luck continued by design. Beolin's father was an honorable man, but he was ambitious, and he instilled in his son and heir an insatiable thirst for political and social advancement.

By the time Beolin had a son of his own, his eyes were on the Scottish crown, if not for himself, then for his descendants. Peace made no sense to him. He had no patience for the slow progress of diplomacy when placed beside the rapid gains of warfare. He had opposed the treaties of Alexander's father. He opposed all treaties of peace when there was land, wealth, and prestige to be gained by the sword.

Beolin had an opportunity his father never dreamed of — a child, Alexander, precariously perched on the Scottish throne. This was the time, if ever there was one, to play his strengthening hand against one made suddenly weaker. Once the child sat on the sacred Coronation Stone and received the crown from the hands of the Archbishop of St. Andrews, it would be too late. The clans would lay their colors at his feet and he would be King. Beolin Crymlyn had to prevent the coronation.

He wrote a letter to the Pope in Rome, seconded and signed by other ambitious barons. In it, he laid forth his claim. He warned that the treaty with the pagan Norse would dissolve under the child-King, and Christianity would dissolve in Northeastern Scotland, even suggesting that the Scottish crown could land on a pagan head. Beolin affirmed his faith and loyalty, and outlined all he would do to keep Scotland in faith with Rome, were *he* to be crowned king.

Word of the conspiracy reached Henry Baliol the day the letter was sent. Baliol told Alan Durward, and the two of them took the matter to David Lindsay. It was three days after the death of the King. Lindsay kept his finger keenly on the pulse of the nobles. He felt the contention and foresaw civil war if the son of their dead King was not crowned quickly. When his friends told him of the Crymlyn conspiracy, "quickly" was not quick enough. He set the coronation date for four days from that moment. Lindsay, Durward, and Baliol divided the duties among themselves and made every arrangement.

A crown had to sit on young Alexander's head before the letter reached the Pope. Rome did not have the power to place Crymlyn on the Scottish throne, but if the Pope had declared it his wish before Alexander was crowned, Crymlyn would have the moral authority to resist the new King. Sides would be taken. Scottish swords would spill Scottish blood. What would be left of the Scottish crown would not be worth wearing. It was this, above all else, that Lindsay and his friends feared. A violent disruption of the order would cost them everything.

Beolin of Crymlyn did not content himself with sending the letter to Rome. He began a campaign to disintegrate trust in the royal bloodline and in all those who supported it. There were three men standing firmly in his way — Henry Baliol, Alan Durward, and David Lindsay. But that trinity of loyalists was no easy target. Between them, they held the respect *and the purses* of almost every high name in Scotland and beyond.

A cold war had begun, order against chaos, peace against bloodshed, tradition against divergence. The only thing that could prevent the cold war from turning hot was a crown — the Scottish Crown — on the head of Alexander!

Alexander's claim had to be strengthened at every turn. Lindsay, Durward, and Baliol thrust upon the new King everything that could signify his royal blood. This was not always easy to do. Vanora held the child tightly under her wing, and every step, every gesture, had to pass with her consent.

"Perception!" Baliol explained to her, "The boy's life will be in danger if he is not *perceived* as the King."

Politics was well outside of the nursemaid's talents, so she yielded to the knights on such matters. With Vanora's consent, Alexander wore the King's colors, the King's jewelry. He walked with the King's escorts, and at every turn, before every eye, Lindsay and the others boldly displayed their loyalty.

Those things that were the possessions of the King were suddenly Alexander's, and they were layered upon the boy in ceaselessly crashing waves. The King's horse, the King's colors, every insignia and accouterment of the crown was thrust on Alexander. In the chaos of those first days, all he wanted was his Vanora, and he could not have her. There was no room for a nursemaid amid the swarm of nobles and advisors, and a king could not be seen in need of his childhood caregiver.

Vanora's presence in Alexander's life was diluted, and he did not understand why. In the hallway outside of his room in Edinburgh Castle, Lindsay tried to explain to him all that was happening, but Vanora appeared and stopped him short.

"Do not put such weight on the child's mind!" she demanded.

"My dear woman," Lindsay answered, "He is no longer a child. His childhood ended with the last breath of his father."

"Sit down, Lindsay," she ordered.

Lindsay looked to his left and his right. There was no chair in the hallway.

She pointed to the floor against the wall and repeated, "David, sit down."

A knight of less wisdom would never have taken an order from a nursemaid. He could have dismissed her from her duties for simply calling him by his first name. But Lindsay was a man of vision. He saw what was not apparent to most. Vanora had no rank, no title, yet he saw she carried a spiritual authority that was not to be contested.

Lindsay obeyed and sat on the floor with his back against the wall. The much shorter woman stood over him and explained, "I know little of your politics. I know nothing of conspiracies and warfare. I yield to you on those things. I know motherhood, and I know this child. I know what he needs and what he does not. Trying times are ahead of us both, and we will need each other. Manage your arena, and I will manage mine."

While she spoke, he maintained eye contact with her. When she finished, he nodded his head, then lowered his eyes to stare at the floor between his feet.

Seeing that she had won the moment, she yielded, "No doubt, sir, you can make him a strong king, and he will need to be. But is strength the only trait of a good king?"

Still looking downward, he shook his head.

She added, "I know enough of kings and enough of men to know what makes them bad. I will not let that happen to this boy, my boy…, my Alexander."

He nodded again and looked up to her. She gestured her permission for him to stand and continue his efforts — but without telling the boy more than his young heart could handle.

The late King had had little time for domestic matters, and his knights had even less. Lindsay had only met Alexander twice when he was very young. No doubt, he encountered Vanora at the same time, but there was nothing in a homely nursemaid, with her stunted stature and awkward figure, to turn a knight's eye. He remembered only two encounters with the woman, both in a hallway with young Alexander.

The two brief incidents in the hallways laid a firm foundation for a relationship, the dynamics of which would sculpt the history of a nation. A man of staunch mental strength and physical prowess, and a woman whose spirit towered over the highest peaks in the Highlands and seemed rooted to both the earth and the sky — these two figures had Alexander in their hands, and in this unlikely unity, they had to find common ground on which the child-king could stand.

Vanora dismissed Lindsay from the hallway with a slight gesture of her wrist. The knight felt such a strange duality of spirit that he caught himself grinding his teeth in indignation for the impertinent manner in which he was addressed and commanded by a child's nursemaid. But he felt saturated to the marrow in the power of her presence. He obeyed her and walked away. When he cut the first corner, he stopped and listened, not as a suspicious spy for his kingdom, and not from jealousy. He could not have explained the enigmatic spiritual tether that was attached deep inside and prevented him from walking farther, but let there be no doubt at all that it held him in place.

Lindsay listened intently as Vanora told Alexander, "If I could follow the wishes of my heart, I would take you away from here, my lovely, away from castles and away from knights, and never release you from my arms. But Sir David and the others have a claim on you that I do not have. You are the King, my darling. There is no escaping that. That man will guide you as you need to be guided, but you also will need guidance of a different sort, the sort no knight can provide. And for that, dear child, you will always have Vanora."

Alexander's eyes began to well with tears, and he asked her, "Will I, Vanora, will I always have you?"

She lifted a subtle smile, kissed his head, and answered, "In one form or another, my sweet child, you will always have me. For you are my sweet child and will always be, no matter how you grow, what you learn, or what you may be forced to do, the sweet child in front of me must always stay at the heart of you, and within that heart, within that child's heart, Vanora will always be."

There was depth in her meaning that Alexander could not yet understand. But he understood what he needed to at the time. Vanora's love for him was all encompassing, and not just of the child in that hallway at that moment. There was timelessness to her love, and that, he *did* understand.

Vanora took Alexander by the hand and led him down the hallway, away from Lindsay. Lindsay overheard the entire exchange. By the time he heard their united footsteps walking away from him, his jaw was unclenched. His shoulders settled calmly, and a strong sense of rightness settled over him. He looked around the corner and saw an innocent child walking hand-in-hand with his mother, not the Queen Mother, Maria de Coucy, but his real mother.

As he watched them, he saw in Alexander what Vanora wanted him to see — a young King, his sovereign, but also a child. And he saw in Vanora the authority of a mother over her son.

The sound of the gulls
And their cries from above
Are now just a whisper
Within Vanora's love

Chapter Three:

Your Throne Has Been Chosen

The Stone so cold
With past underground
Shows him the flame
Where truth will abound

The final leg of this week-long journey was a formal procession from Edinburgh Castle to Scone Abbey, two miles north of Perth. Scone had been the seat of Scottish Royal Authority since the middle of the ninth century. Alexander was first placed on the King's horse, a light gray Garron with majestic lines. The beast was too large for him. It made him look puny, particularly beside the tall knights in the procession.

The solution came from David Lindsay, who suggested they place the King on an Eriskay pony. A white one was procured for the occasion. It was thick and shaggy, with short legs and a stout neck. Alexander sat regally upon it. The pony had a name, one that is lost to time, for the King renamed it that day. He called the pony Sir Walter. It was only a pony's name given by a child. He intended no royal action, but in granting the title, he knighted the beast. It was his first act as King, and the pony's life was never the same.

With Alexander looking larger upon the dwarfed pony, the only thing remaining was to reduce the dimensions of the accompanying party. For this, Lindsay gathered the largest Clydesdales to be found in the area. He painstakingly set the procession with Alexander at the front, tall upon his pony, and the trailing nobles behind, riding two-by-two, appearing like children atop their massive horses. It worked. To those viewing the procession, little Alexander looked larger than any of the grown men being pulled behind in his royal wake.

There was one exception to Lindsay's plan. The widowed Queen would ride behind no man. She rode on a Highland pony even smaller than the King's. An ever chilling presence, Maria de Coucy rode beside her son, now as the Queen Mother. It was a title with no exercisable authority, and one that rang distastefully in her ears. She could not stand the sound of it, and each time she was addressed in that way, she shivered with gurgling resentment.

She mumbled with disdain about the child she hated, "So this is The King, this boy who knights a pony. This is who they place on *my* throne."

This, and many comments like it, were heard by many as they proceeded. They were meant to be heard. She had never had a love for Scotland. She had no affection for its people, no more than she had for the sweet boy beside her. With each clop of a hoof beneath her, she was increasingly persuaded to leave Scotland. Her ambitions there were dead. All that she had hoped for from her marriage evaporated when this boy sprang from her womb seven years earlier.

In France, she would never have made such a ride on horseback. In her youth, she never traveled more than fifty feet without a plushly upholstered carriage. She was not in France. She was in Scotland, and the party paraded to Scone Abbey in the Scottish tradition. She had no choice. She must be at her son's coronation. Even her family back in France would have demanded it.

In the courtyard of Scone Abbey was the Coronation Stone, or the Stone of Destiny, as it was referred to by the old mystics. Every Scottish monarch since the earliest dynasties was crowned at the stone. It was yet another burdensome tradition, maintained by her burdensome son, in the increasingly burdensome country into which the Queen Mother had been married. Robbed of her first lust by the ascension of Alexander, she sought her second. She longed for the lavish lifestyle of the French nobility. And with her Scottish ambitions amputated, she bided her time miserably and scornfully until she could flee the rustic and rugged ways of the Scots and plant herself amid her father's ample riches.

Despite the chill from the Queen Mother, Alexander looked up to a clearing sky and a warm, direct sun. He did not have Vanora, but he had his only other childhood companions. The gulls joined the procession high above, as if Lindsay had placed them with care. They squawked, not haphazardly, like birds in the wild, but with a steady poetic meter. The rhythmic sounds from above were strange for creatures of the wild. Alexander twisted his neck around to look at the riders behind him. None of them noticed. Not one of the galloping nobles turned an eye upward in astonishment. As the beaked verses grew louder, the king turned back more frequently. Still, nobody looked up at the curiosity hovering over their heads.

"It is for me," Alexander thought, "They sing for me alone."

He could consider no other explanation. Such tightly concerted and rigidly metered noises existed nowhere in nature and surely would have drawn the attention of others. The sounds did not pass through the Scottish air, but directly into Alexander through some means he could not guess. The song of the birds was bright and celebratory, but with ominous undertones that sounded more like a warning of hardships to come than a lament for what had already been suffered. The gulls continued on in that way until they reached Scone Abbey, then they scattered and disappeared from view, as if they did not condone the events to come. Alexander pondered the loss for only the briefest moment. The gates were opened and the regal caravan rode into the courtyard.

As the King was being paraded through the courtyard, with all of the pomp and circumstance befitting the occasion, his attention was drawn from his duty by a solitary figure to his left. Hunched over the Stone of Destiny stood a cloaked and hooded figure, chanting in a deep, hollow voice that sounded like it was in a large, empty hall, rather than out of doors. Alexander marched Sir Walter forward, the boy's puffed chest pointing the way, but his neck contorted to watch the cloaked figure. He could not turn his head forward. It felt as though the hand of his own destiny was holding him by the chin saying, "Young man, don't you dare look away."

As his angle on the figure improved, he saw a long, gray beard peek from beneath the hood. The chanting continued, but it was not the chant, nor the beard, that fixed the young king's eyes so relentlessly. It was the rocks. Three small rocks rested ceremoniously on the Coronation Stone. It seemed to Alexander that the rocks were the recipients of the prayerful chanting. This notion was confirmed when the bearded man bowed low and lifted the rocks from the stone with reverence and care. The moment the rocks were in his hands, the man's chanting stopped. Just as the figure turned toward Alexander to reveal his face, the king snapped his head forward, as if that same hand of destiny turned his chin and said, "You have seen enough for now."

The procession dismounted and continued into the palace, away from the old man, away from the Coronation Stone and the gathering nobles, and away from the gulls above. Alexander strongly felt Vanora's absence. He was strangely and disturbingly untethered. Baliol arranged the coronation party according to tradition. The Queen Mother stood to the King's right, with a sour, puckered face that hid all of her natural beauty. Lindsay stood opposite of her, in firm but gentle contrast. The rest of the party trailed behind in forced grandiosity, with their chins high and their chests puffed out.

The law demanded that Alexander be knighted before being crowned. The issue of his knighthood needed to be resolved before they proceeded into the courtyard. The very next glimpse the barons would have of their king would be one of a new knight. David Bernham, Bishop of St. Andrews took his place at the head of the procession, with his back to Alexander. He turned suddenly, holding up in his right hand a braided belt of knighthood. The knighting of the boy was a political necessity, meant to dissolve the only legitimate challenge to the coronation of the child-prince. The Bishop wasted no time on ceremonial grandeur. He simply bent low, wrapped the belt around Alexander's hips, stood tall and domineering, and declared Alexander a Knight of St. Andrews. The necessary deed was done and the coronation could commence.

Kinghood terrified Alexander, but knighthood enthralled him. To him, the emphasis was on the wrong noble title. The rushed lack of ceremony for his new knighthood frustrated him. When the Bishop turned his back to him and took his first step toward the courtyard, Alexander sighed sharply.

Lindsay heard the airy outburst. Himself a doting father, he stepped firmly toward the Bishop and interjected, "Not yet, Your Grace! The belt of knighthood carries no authority until it holds a sword at the hip of the new knight. In our rush to commence, we seemed to have forgotten."

There was no truth to Lindsay's words. The belt was enough to serve its purpose. But Lindsay had said it, so nobody contradicted.

"Does the boy have a sword?" the Bishop asked impatiently.

Alexander answered timidly, afraid of being scolded from one direction or another, "I have no sword of my own."

"You *have* a sword, my King," Lindsay spoke in a deep, slow voice.

David Lindsay unfastened his own sword from his hip, held it sideways, as if about to set it on an altar, dropped to a knee in front of Alexander, and presented the sword. It was magnificent. It was the Lindsay hereditary sword, come to Scotland with the family from Flanders many generations earlier. The value of the gift, given so freely, was lost on nobody. The guard flared out from the blade and split into points at the end, like the forked tongue of a snake. The handle was wrapped in braided wire. The pommel bore the Lindsay crest, a swan seated upon a crown. Carved beneath the crown was the Lindsay motto, "Endure Fort" (Suffer Bravely).

Baliol, ever steeped in tradition, reminded Lindsay, "That is your hereditary sword. It belonged to your fathers and it should belong to your sons."

Never turning his eyes from the King, Lindsay answered, "I have been meaning to forge another."

He may have answered flippantly, but the sword was clearly dear to Lindsay. He kissed the pommel like a faithful son kissing his father before handing the sword to the boy. It was heavy, but not burdensome. For the pride that rushed through his limbs, the gangly arms of Alexander could have held a full-sized barrel filled with salty sea water. Lindsay's sacrifice did exactly what he intended it to do. It aggrandized Alexander's knighting, exactly as the romantic-minded boy needed.

The Bishop was visibly impatient with an interruption he viewed as unnecessary. It was not because Lindsay had commandeered the knighting of the King, but because the barons waited in the courtyard, and he feared they would see the delay as an omen. He cleared his throat loudly, but Lindsay ignored him. He took the sword from Alexander and fastened it to the belt of knighthood around the child's narrow hips. He raised the belt high on the boy's waist, to lift it from the ground.

It was a futile effort. The sword stood every bit as tall as Alexander. There was no way to fasten it to prevent it from dragging on the ground behind him. Lindsay twisted his lips to the side in thought, grunted quietly, then unfastened the sword and handed it to his sovereign.

Thinking quickly, he suggested, "I think you should carry the sword, my King, so it may be seen equally from all sides of you."

Alexander nodded in agreement, and Lindsay returned the nod reverently. Once he stood and backed away, what remained was a small knight with a sacred sword in his arms and the courage to face the daunting duties in front of him.

On Lindsay's command, the ceremony began. The pipes rolled and the drums rattled, and King Alexander III of Scotland began his manicured march to the Stone of Destiny. He was still a gangly youth, but he carried himself well, regally, nobly, kingly — just as Lindsay had instructed him. As he breached the threshold of the courtyard, he drew the admiration of everyone in attendance except for his mother.

There may have been admiring eyes on Alexander, but that is not how the child experienced them. As he marched with his regal brow pointed forward, his eyes rapidly volleyed left to right and back again, contrasting in the extreme with every other pair of eyes within range.

The weight of their collective gaze crippled his young mind. Sweat beaded on his forehead. But other than that subtle indicator, nobody would know, for his body performed its duties. His legs stepped with the courage of a warrior marching to battle. His breaths were deep, calm, and steady. His arms held a large and heavy sword in front of him and appeared to have twice their natural strength. Oh, he was the vision of a tiny king well worth admiring, but within that shell was a wounded and tormented child that would have drawn pity in an equal degree, had it revealed itself.

All other eyes seemed to disappear when Alexander locked his on the Bishop of St. Andrews. He was such a stern man, an impatient man, and one who never felt himself beneath another. The fact that the Bishop towered so high over Alexander, and pointed to him with long, spindly fingers, made his harshness all the more vicious to the child.

He beckoned Alexander with a curl of his finger. The boy obeyed and broke from the procession. Lindsay and the rest of the procession joined the others in attendance, while the Queen Mother sulked in the shadow of the courtyard wall.

The Stone of Destiny held an inexplicable arcane power but the Bishop swallowed it in his dark shadow. He gestured for Alexander to sit, and the young King climbed upon the Stone like he was hopping on Vanora's bed. The moment he settled in place, he felt as if hands had extended upward from the Stone to hold his narrow hips firmly in place. Of course, nothing came from the Stone and nothing held his hips, yet the young King was immobilized nevertheless, seized by some spiritual grasp he had no chance to escape from.

This unnerving sensation dissipated with the hollow, echoing, ringing of a voice in his inner ear. Like the rhythmic gulls before, he alone heard it. It was not a

28

frightening voice, yet not remotely soothing. The tone was calm but scratchy, deep and bellowing, like a large rusty bell in a spire too tall to see from the ground.
It spoke to his innermost being,

The kingdoms of old are all present
They show their faces at night
Each King and Queen and Peasant
With Force and Bloodshed, with Triumph and Might

Follow the truth to see what is due
To release them and fill them with Light
You were born for a throne
Not of wood or of stone
But of wings that have not taken flight

Follow the Gulls that will guide you
Hear the voice of the breezes beside you
Take the love that the Queen has denied you
To the people who wallow in fear and in spite

Whether the verses echoed in his head or repeated, he could not tell. But they seemed to lock him in a motionless chill, as if he were embedded in a glacier. When the voice withdrew, and he regained control of himself, when the natural sounds around him returned to his senses, the crown of Scotland was already on his head. He had no interest in the lofty words of the Bishop, and that is just as well. Alexander heard none of it. He experienced none of the coronation rites, as he was embedded in the cryptic verses.

He turned his head sharply in each direction, hoping to catch a retreating glimpse of whomever or whatever recited the verses. He saw nothing, but one clear vision returned to the forefront of his memory — the cloaked man who had stood chanting over the very stone upon which Alexander sat.

The blessings had been recited by the Bishop. The crown had been placed on his head in front of the barons of Scotland. Alexander was King. This was a fact that had not yet dawned upon him, as he scanned his eyes frantically across the figures in the courtyard, searching for the cloaked man. His attention was brought back to the ceremony when the first of the barons stepped forward.

The proud baron wore a wool cloth fastened over his shoulder with a brooch. It was of his family colors, his family make, and it represented the loyalty of his entire clan. He unfastened his wool and laid it on the ground at Alexander's feet. The young king had no idea of the symbolism behind the gesture, no notion of what was to be said or done in response. Had the coronation not been so rushed, he would have been taught these things, but as it was, the child-King was painfully ignorant.

As the baron walked backward away from Alexander, another stepped forward in his place. He too unfastened a similar plaid wool, but of different colors and design, and laid it at the King's feet, directly over the first. One baron at a time, each featuring the distinct and signature design of their clans, placed their family colors in front of the Coronation Stone.

David Lindsay was the last of them. He did exactly as the others, laying the red and green fabric of the Lindsays atop the others. But Lindsay dropped to his knee and set his colors down with reverence. He did not kneel in homage to any emblem of his prestigious family, nor in supplication to his King. Like in the monastery hallway, he lowered himself to Alexander's level for Alexander's sake.

He winked at his new sovereign as if to say, "You are doing well, my boy. Soon this will all be over."

That is how Alexander read it, and that is how David Lindsay meant it. The grinning wink settled the King enough for him to realize he had not been breathing. He drew a deep and desperate inhale, followed it with a slow exhale and drop of his shoulders, and he returned Lindsay's wink.

Once the loyalty of the clans was sworn by the laying of the colors, the coronation procession reassembled. Alexander took his place at the tail, and they all marched into the throne room of the palace. Once before the throne, the procession split into two lines, forming a human corridor. Alexander walked slowly, still carrying the Lindsay sword, through the corridor, to the high, ornately sculpted, deep brown, wooden throne. He leaned the sword against one side, and he sat on the throne of Scotland, the crowned King, eternally affixed to a destiny he could not yet understand.

Some other child, some other young king, may have reveled in the experience, putting on royal airs, raising his nose above all others, and assuming the childish notions of kingship. But Alexander was not some other child. Like every event of his life, minute and grand, he internalized the moment. His thoughts were inward, his eyes and ears were inward. He would have traded it all for the warm arms of Vanora and the playful squawk of his gulls.

Distant as his mind was, he had more duties to perform. The time came for the presentation of gifts. Each knight and baron walked reverently to the throne and placed before the child symbolic gifts, the inner-meaning of most Alexander could not discern. The poor boy's senses were in a state of shock.

Through all the formal addresses and oaths of loyalty, through the cascading accumulation of trinkets poured at his feet, Alexander strained his ears for the sound of the gulls outside. There was nothing familiar and comforting taken in by his eyes. His sense of touch was burdened by the lavish and luxurious folds of a newly crowned king's clothes. His nose sought the nurturing scent of Vanora, which was, of course, entirely absent. So, his ears reached for their old friends.

At times, he thought he heard them. Whether their circling call from high above the palace managed to cut through the walls and roof of the stately palace, through the clamor of gossiping nobles, to the physical ears of an overwhelmed child, or his mind conjured what his senses could not reach, may never be known. What is certain is that only the tiniest portion of his attention was paid to the event at hand.

Even Lindsay brought little comfort, little escape from the rigid, enclosing confines of the affair. Relief came from an unlikely figure. Alexander had nearly forgotten the cloaked man who had so tyrannically seized his attention as he first passed the Stone of Destiny. Suddenly, there he was. After all others had presented their gifts, the old man appeared as if rising from the cracks of the stone floor, shoved from the deep earth below to represent all that is ancient.

Everything and everyone around Alexander seemed to disappear. The noises of the room muted, like being heard through hands cupped over the ears. How zealously his attention was held. The old man approached the throne, and Alexander saw his face clearly. It was a face that had haunted each of those few quiet moments in the last seven days, the same face, the same old man who had spoken his mysterious verses outside of Alexander's room at the Holyrood Abbey.

One line the old man had spoken rang through Alexander's head, as it had repeatedly since he chased the mysterious figure down the hall.

Your priest has been chosen
To show you the light

He heard it resoundingly as the bearded man approached him, not from the old man, nor from any of the fading figures in the room, but from some source more internal than external.

The man did not bow, kneel, or curtsy, but walked up and stopped, knee to knee with the king. He reached his cloaked arm forward, turned his palm upward, unfurled his finger, and there, on his palm, were the three rocks he had taken from the Coronation Stone. One was pure and purple, clear, seeming to magnify the man's hand beneath it. He could not have said why, but it reminded Alexander of Vanora. One of the rocks was pristinely white and opaque. It appeared to shine its whiteness on and through the other two. The third was rough and porous, gray and jagged. Alone, it would have been nothing to behold, but the presence of the other two gave it value, and in some strange way, it gave value to the other two.

Before he knew what he was doing, Alexander reached his hand forward and turned his palm upward to receive the gift. The old man seized his wrist and put the rocks in his hand.

He forced the boy's fingers shut, leaned in, and whispered, "I am your great grandfather, and I am his father. You asked for my help on this journey. I will be your guide. When you see me again, you will be shown life's truth. Always remember this, there is a reason that darkness is abated by the light of the moon... follow that light. The wings will guide you home."

Alexander was suddenly aware of the others in the room. All talking had ceased. All eyes were on the throne. Lindsay stood defensively, ready to thrust into action. But there was no danger there.

The old man drew a sharp inhale, pulling Alexander's attention back to his lips. He expelled that breath in verse,

Your clansman I am
From lands long ago,
I bear you these gifts
To keep as you grow

Take these three stones
And this ring from my hand,
To brighten your path
When the dark has command

This ring is a symbol
Of what will become
Of a heart that will break
But will never succumb

Your home will be shown
As bright as the sun
Among all the gulls
When the fighting is done

When the man finished speaking, he removed a ring from his little finger and handed it to Alexander. It was of a metal, deep and black, like the center of the eye. Affixed to it was an image of a gull's wing, in the finest detail. Each feather of the tiny wing appeared soft, though it was of the same metal. Alexander half-expected it to flap itself free of the circle and fly from Scone Abbey to the coast. The old man stepped back from the throne, and Lindsay and the others came forward. Out of defensive curiosity, they surrounded the King, obscuring from Alexander's view the one thing he wanted to see — the old man, who seemed to disappear back into the floor from which he appeared, back into the earth.

The crown sits heavy
On the brow of the King
But carried less weight
Than the black, winged ring

Chapter Four:

Bound in Old Leather

The love of a mother
Was the love of a wife
And the fuel for the fire
Of a passionate life

After the coronation, the position of the Queen Mother was uncertain. She was not well-liked among the nobles. She had never embraced her adopted country. She rejected it more demonstratively when she realized she would never rule her late husband's subjects. She had harbored spiteful bitterness for her son from the moment his name was declared. The crown on his head embittered her further.

There was nothing in Scotland to tempt her to linger. The languages and dialects, the clothing, the raw and rustic manners, the food, everything about Scotland disgusted her, and she wanted out, at any cost. That cost would be heavy.

Beolin Crymlyn was among the nobles to lay his colors at Alexander's feet on Coronation Day. Before departing Scone Abbey that day, he sought her out. "I can get you to France," he promised, "and in exchange, I will have the support of your family when I need it." He arranged her passage back to France in exchange for her oath.

Although hers were the only ears that could hear him, he dared not speak directly of his future *need*. The very breath to speak it was treasonous. There was no reason to speak it. She understood what he wanted. He wanted the crown of Scotland, and she would have seen it on the head of a pig over that of her own child. The deal was struck, and Maria de Coucy was bound for France before the end of the week. Her absence from Edinburgh Castle when the entourage returned was felt by nobody, except that the air was a little sweeter and easier to draw.

The weeks following the coronation permitted few wandering thoughts. It was a frenzied storm of obligations to set the new reign firmly in place before forces could dishevel it. Alan Durward was the keeper of the royal schedule. Alexander hardly had time for a private thought. He was bounced from one Lowland palace or monastery to another, from Edinburgh to Glasgow, from Dundee to Dumfries.

He learned little in the chaos. Lindsay was eager to begin training him in all a Scottish King must know. Alexander yearned for the quiet times that dominated his early life. He did not miss the Queen Mother. Let us be perfectly clear about that. In fact, he had not given her a single thought since he rode beside her to the coronation. But he missed being ignored. He missed having his mind and thoughts entirely to himself. And he missed Vanora.

After two weeks of ceaseless travel, with his buzzing head never resting on the same pillow for three consecutive nights, he became listless, dazy, and often unresponsive. Durward, Baliol, and Lindsay were always within an arm's reach of him, but Durward had his eyes ever on the itinerary. Baliol played the diplomat and spoke for the King to all the nobles and clerics they visited. Lindsay tagged along like an unused appendage, waiting for his opportunity to begin the training and, all the while, inserting what quips of understanding he could pass in one quick breath.

Only Lindsay's eyes were constantly on the King, so only Lindsay's eyes noticed his spiritual decline. Between Thornhill and St. Andrews, he broke from the royal entourage and rode his horse with haste to Edinburgh Castle to fetch Vanora and take her to St. Andrews. He found Vanora in her room, scribbling away in a book. The book was bound in old leather, with a worn leather strap that marked the page. The writing was clearly in verse, with regimented meter. It was no ledger and no woman's diary. *That* he could see clearly. Along the border of the pages were lush, colorful illustrations, and there, on the table beside the book, were dishes of colorful inks and a variety of pens and brushes. Vanora was the author and the artist of whatever sort of book it was.

"Who is this woman?" Lindsay thought to himself, as he approached her silently from behind, "These are the skills of the monks, not the pastimes of a nursemaid."

As he continued to stealthily watch over her shoulder as she worked, he was bludgeoned in the gut by a memory. The penmanship, the border illustrations — upon intent inspection, they struck him as familiar and dragged from the depths of his memory images both sweet and rancid. They were of the same hand as another book he had come to know well.

In 1235, Lindsay fought in defense of the Crown in the Galloway Revolts. During the conflicts, a soldier served under him, a memorable man of deep thought and abounding spirituality. His name was Ulchel, and above all others who fought beside him, this man's face and this man's voice haunted Lindsay. There was nothing particular about Ulchel's face and nothing peculiar in his voice that would adhere him to the memory of a noble.

Ulchel fought with furious passion, and saved the lives of many of his countrymen, but he accepted no praise at the end of the day. When the initial revolt was defeated, Lindsay went to him and asked him what fire fueled such fierceness. Ulchel spoke of his wife and young child. He spoke of nothing else, as if they were a tiny island on which the man's heart and mind lived.

"A soldier who fights for love...," Lindsay pondered.

While speaking of his wife, Ulchel showed Lindsay a book. It, too, was leather bound verses with ornately illustrative borders. It was a book of scriptures. It was prefaced by a poem composed by Ulchel and penned into the book by his wife. Ulchel read the poem to Lindsay, with eyes bedewed and a voice choked by extreme emotion. The verses were magnificent in their expressive beauty, and they struck a deep chord in Lindsay.

Later that same year, the exiled leaders of the Galloway Revolts returned. Lindsay and his army were dispatched again. The night before the battle, Lindsay found Ulchel and asked if he still carried the book. Such a romantic soul would never be without it. He handed it, with pride, to his leader. Lindsay read the poem again, and again, and several more times before sleeping. He set it to memory, hoping its impassioned verses would light a similar fire in him. Ulchel died in battle the next day. After the victory, Lindsay buried him on the battlefield, placing his wife's book on his chest before covering him with earth.

Ulchel's welling eyes and faltering voice remained with Lindsay, as did his intense love, and they served as his moral watermark ever since. The longer Lindsay stood and watched Vanora work, the more clearly his images of Ulchel polished in his memory, and the more certain he was that Ulchel's book was penned by the same hand he watched scribbling away in front of him.

Still looking down on Vanora from behind, he silently mouthed, "Ulchel's wife?"

He made no sound, but Vanora turned to him as if in response.

"Sir David?" she asked, "Is my child with you?"

Suddenly remembering her place, she amended, "The King…, I mean to say, is the King with you."

"No," he answered, "Your child is not with me. I came to bring *you* to *him*."

Nothing else was spoken between them in her room. He dared not ask about books, poems, impassioned lovers, or children. Neither did he let it go. He had no doubt the truth of the matter would be his in time, and he pocketed it for a later encounter. He escorted Vanora to the stable. As he prepared his horse to carry two, Vanora rode up behind him on her own horse. It was no maid's mule, but a pony of pure breeding and professional training, and it obeyed her every twitch.

Not for the first nor the last time, Lindsay asked himself, "Who is this woman?"

He nodded reverently to her, mounted his horse, and led her from Edinburgh. When they arrived at St. Andrews, the royal entourage was already there. They were all in a panicked uproar. Alexander stood at the window of his room, staring into the sky, speaking in whispers to the gulls above, and responding to nothing spoken or asked of him by the nobles and clerics who grasped at his attention.

Baliol met Lindsay at the gate and briefed him on the King's condition. He suggested a number of elixirs and tonics.

As Lindsay stepped from his horse, he answered, "I have brought the only tonic the King needs."

He gestured to Vanora and instructed Baliol, "Take her to the King. I am weary from travel."

Baliol, believing Vanora to be *carrying* the aforementioned tonic, obeyed and took her to Alexander's room. They walked together, and together they found the

King as he had been, staring out the window, whispering to the sky. The nature of the tonic revealed itself. She did not pull a vial from a hidden purse or pocket. She pulled her arms from her sides and extended them to the boy with only a quiet hum to announce her presence. Revived on the spot, Alexander turned with new color and vigor.

"Vanora!" he shouted, as he ran the few necessary steps to plunge himself headlong into her nurturing embrace.

Baliol could not understand what he was witnessing, but it was enough for him that Lindsay understood, and that his sovereign was again himself, and the business of the Crown could resume.

In the morning, with Alexander fully revived, Lindsay sequestered his student for a lesson in the courtyard. He forbade any interruptions, even by Vanora. For the first time since the coronation, Alexander was eager to learn. He was enveloped by love, and he gave a warrior's passion to the lesson. Armed with sticks, Lindsay taught the child swordplay from dawn well into the afternoon. They stopped when Alexander's attention took wing.

"We are done for the day," Lindsay told him, "Your mind is no longer with me."

Alexander hardly waited for him to finish speaking before bolting from the courtyard in search of Vanora. But he was not yet hers, not until he passed through the hands of Durward and Baliol. The following days were similarly passed, training in the morning with Lindsay and walking the manicured steps of a monarch in the afternoon with Durward and Baliol.

The first weeks of Alexander's kingship had been toiling and trying. Under Lindsay, he was more warrior than king, and under Durward and Baliol, he was more king than child. Balance came at the end of the day, in the loving arms of Vanora. But Vanora was more than mother to the child. Her fingers were already rooted deeply into his future and into his destiny. She planned and plotted, and she foresaw much more than Lindsay, Durward, or Baliol knew, more than Alexander knew.

The calendar paid no mind to the age and readiness of the King. Events that mandated Alexander's attendance arose. Alan Durward kept the royal schedule, and he reminded Lindsay of the Braemar Gathering. It was a centuries-old Highland tradition. The strongest warriors in the Highlands gather at the base of Creag Choinnich, in the craggy, shrouded heart of the Highlands, and race to the top of the mountain. Alexander's great-grandfather, Malcolm III, attended the race in 1065, and awarded a prize to the winner. Every year since, the King of Scotland attended the event and awarded the prize.

Durward was all too aware that the slightest deviation from royal tradition could weaken Alexander's claim on the crown. Lindsay agreed, and the arrangements were made. The young King would go to Creag Choinnich, watch the race, and reward the winner.

"I must clear this with Vanora," Lindsay told Durward.

Durward tilted his head and cocked an eyebrow. His eyes turned sharply to one side and he strained his memory to place the name to a face.

"His Majesty's nursemaid," Lindsay reminded him.

"The nursemaid?" Durward asked, hardly believing his own ears, "If he is still tethered to a nursemaid, then that tether must be severed immediately. For the sake of the country, send that woman away."

"No... no...," was all Lindsay could say. He could not find the words to explain this woman's power, her wisdom, and her profound importance in the life of the child-King.

Durward stared at Lindsay, awaiting some intelligible response. None came.

Lindsay simply stiffened his posture and commanded in a deepened voice, "Make the arrangements, Alan. I will discuss the matter with Vanora."

Durward sighed, shrugged his shoulders, turned on his heels and walked away. Lindsay remained where he stood, internally continuing his effort to place Vanora's existence into words, knowing it was not the last time he would have that conversation.

Lindsay approached Vanora very tentatively. He knew Durward was right. Alexander had to go to Creag Choinnich. But he also knew the child could not be pulled away from the mother by force. He found Vanora in the garden, laughing with the King at the bumbling antics of the bees. He called Vanora aside and explained the important symbolism of the race.

"My dear man," she answered, "Do you think I am unaware of it? I have been with the Royal Family for decades."

"Yes…, of course…," Lindsay stumbled, "so you must see why we have to take him."

"Of course, he must go. I've already discussed it with him. We could not keep him from it if we wished to. He is so excited to race."

"Oh no," Lindsay corrected, "The King will not race. He only observes, and rewards the winner."

"But he wishes to race."

"My dear woman, Creag Choinnich is perilous for the mighty. He could never win. He would never reach the top."

"No, he will not win. He must not win, but he will finish. His destiny depends upon it."

Lindsay pictured the hill in his mind, and could not imagine a child surviving the ascent. He had seen men of storied prowess fall in the effort. But Vanora had spoken, and in doing so, muted any protest that might have been trying to find traction in Lindsay's head. This child, still

43

laughing at the bees, would soon run against fierce Highland warriors twice his size, up a mountain that was determined to destroy the fragile.

"I pray she is right," Lindsay mumbled to himself as Vanora returned to her son, "For his sake, for my sake, for the sake of us all, I pray she is right."

This boy in the garden
A mere child in age
Must clash with the mighty
And the warriors' rage

Chapter Five:

Honor Their Love

The gulls are all faint
Obscure where they fly
It is time to look forward
To what is under the sky

The royal entourage traveled to Aberdeen. It was the last necessary stop on the post-coronation tour. Vanora took an inconspicuous position among the servants. It was enough for Alexander that she was with them, that when his heart yearned for her, he could turn his head and see her. To most others, she was invisible, an understated accessory of a royal caravan.

Nobody told Vanora to assume such a humble post. She knew, as did Lindsay, that her place in Alexander's heart afforded her a prestigious position at the hip of the King. The woman had no vanity. She contented herself perfectly with the simple conversations of the simple-minded people traveling beside her.

Aberdeen afforded Alexander more time to work with his tutors. His hours with Baliol, poring over ancient texts of historical Scottish peerage, perusing maps and studying the dress, traditions, family colors, and mottos of each significant clan under his rule, dulled his wits and numbed his every sensation. When Durward took his turn with the King, he taught the skills of diplomacy, the rules of regal oratory, and the crafty tools of politics. This was more interactive than Baliol's books, but still could not keep his attention.

Alexander spent his mornings craving his time with Lindsay, where he learned swordplay and military strategy. It felt much like playing to the child, and to Alexander, Lindsay began to feel like a playmate, albeit a tall, forceful, and often scolding playmate.

On their last day in Aberdeen, the tutors tried to prepare Alexander for the event at Creag Choinnich. Baliol explained who would be there, and made certain Alexander could identify each participant by the colors he wore. He provided tidbits of knowledge that a king should be able to drop among such people. Durward prepared a script for the King to recite at the gathering, keeping it rigidly within the confines of tradition.

Of the three of them, only Lindsay knew the boy would compete. He was still gnawed deeply by skepticism. But his faith in Vanora's judgment grew with every encounter, and with every revelation about this extraordinary woman. He kept the King's perilous involvement in the race a secret from his fellow knights. They would find out soon enough, and Lindsay felt neither the strength nor means to explain it to them.

In the last week of August, they were again on the road, traveling west to Creag Choinnich, directly into the heart of the Highlands. Alexander had spent his entire life in the polished palaces and monasteries in the Southern Lowlands, and along the picturesque eastern coast, always among the same sort of people — those manicured nobles and clerics, and well-tailored merchants. He had never been on a mountain, and he had never encountered the mountain people.

It would be an exaggeration to say Alexander was frightened of the new experiences that awaited him, but enough trepidation thinly coated him for him to demand Vanora's company. She took a position far more befitting her station, and rode with Alexander in a carriage. Her company warmed him throughout and emboldened him to embrace the rugged Highlands and its people.

Vanora told him legends of the Highlanders, mysterious, arcane tales that severed all ties that bound his mind to his immediate surroundings. His eyes went glassy, and his head drifted dreamily to the side. He could never have recounted what she or anyone else might have said after that. She may have listed the items in her cupboard for all he knew. She continued to speak. He continued to hear her voice, and that was enough to hold him in his distant daydream.

His eyes drifted to the sky beyond the carriage window, and fixed mindlessly on the scavenger gulls that followed the caravan. His neck twisted awkwardly, as his winged playmates seemed to lock in place like figures in a painting, bound in oils long-since hardened. It snapped him from his stupor. The carriage had stopped. Lindsay rode beside the carriage, casting his large shadow over the window.

He was a polished Lowland noble, but he knew the Highlanders well. He had commanded them in battle, fighting beside them, eating and drinking beside them, hearing their stories by the fire, and learning what fueled their hearts. They did not want to see their King riding into their rugged country seated upon a pillow inside of a carriage, keeping the company of a nursemaid.

Lindsay dismounted his horse, opened the door, and informed his student-King, "A carriage is no place for a king, not here, not to these people. We must show them the King of the Highlands, whose carriage is a horse's back and whose throne is the mountain."

Alexander obeyed his teacher without question. Sir Walter, the knighted pony, awaited him at the front of the entourage. After a few friendly words spoken directly to the beast, the King mounted. Lindsay and the other knights rode beside and around him, the Highland way, not subserviently behind.

Alexander still could not walk with the Lindsay Sword dragging from his hip. But he could ride with it, and that is exactly what he did. Not by the recommendation of David Lindsay or any other, but of his own command, he attached the gifted sword to his knight's belt. It looked as long as a spear as it sloped down the side of the horse. But the image did not dwarf the boy in appearance. It aggrandized him! What is more, Alexander knew it, and it swelled his confidence, puffed his chest, and raised his chin. By the time they reached the hills, he authentically led them, and they authentically followed.

They were met by Sir Colban, a Highland laird who had fought beside Lindsay. Sir Colban was surrounded by a band of eighteen of his clansmen, all of them on foot. To Alexander, they seemed to spring straight from the Highland legends Vanora had just told him. They had none of the polish that had always surrounded the boy. They were rugged in the extreme, with feral whiskers that seemed to cover every inch of their skin. Even their hands and knuckles had beards of their own. They stood in support of their laird, who stood in defiant posture before the entourage.

Alexander's imagination was never bound by the stone of any castle. It lived perpetually in the wild, and these wild men suited the child just fine. While the southern palace maids gasped at the appearance of the Highlanders, Alexander was ready to run beside them through their native mountains. He was ready to race, but not as their king. Oh no…, he wanted to discard all of the royal insignia, the capes, the robes, the crown itself, and run as one of them. As it was, he still carried the accouterments of the King — this child on a pony. Had the

Highlanders been able to see into his heart, into the imagery of his mind, they would have adopted him as one of their own, and the loyalty on display would have been rooted to something much deeper than national allegiance.

Lindsay flung himself from his horse like a man half his age. He took one bold step toward Sir Colban, who returned with a bold step of his own. The two men stared each other down, raising a strange tension in the air.

"I have won, and you owe me," Colban demanded.

"Well," Lindsay responded, "a bet is a bet, and I am a man of my word."

He unfastened the iron pin that held his wool at the shoulder. Upon it was the same family crest that was on the Lindsay Sword. He handed it to Colban with a mock-formal bow, as he said, "I know when I am defeated. I yield the contest to you, Sir Colban."

The incident between them was for them alone to know. Nobody else, not even Durward and Baliol, understood what was happening. What was clear to all was the mock-formality. Their childlike smiles hid poorly behind their rigid vocal tones. In the absence of his pin, Lindsay tied his wool in a knot at his shoulder, and as he lunged forward to hug Colban, despite his manicured beard and regal posture, he looked rather rustic, and fit quite well within the company of Highlanders. He had rubbed elbows with them before, under the sort of circumstances that bind men tightly to one another in faith and affection.

The moment needed nothing else to draw Alexander more deeply into his mystic imagination. Yet Lindsay's transformation was not complete until he began speaking to the Highlanders in their own dialect. Not one word out of eight was recognizable to the King. In response to Lindsay's strange syllables, the Highlanders looked at

Alexander with reverent surprise. With wide smiles on shocked faces, they bowed to him.

The foreign conversation was brief, and Lindsay returned to his horse. Before he mounted, he walked by Alexander and gave his student a wink. The boy could not have winked back if he wanted to. His eyes were held wide by a force beyond his control, by unfettered wonder.

Once Lindsay was back on his horse, Alexander stuttered in bewilderment, "That…, that was…"

"That was a Highland dialect," Lindsay finished for him, "and you *must* learn it."

Alexander repeated in a contemplative trance, staring at the rugged men before him, "I must learn it."

Lindsay snapped him back to the moment, "Your Grace, lead us forward at your will."

Alexander ignored him and returned to the subject that gripped him, asking, "What did you say to them?"

"I told them about their King. I told these men, who once served *me*, about the young man *I* am so eager to serve. And I told them you will run beside them at the Braemar Gathering."

In the words of the mountain
A King introduced
And the men of Creag Choinnich
Impressed and amused

Chapter Six:

For Dust Char Not My Thunder

The stones at his side
Glow as hot as embers
As he hears the echoes
Of long-past Septembers

A gathering space had been prepared at the base of the mountain, with tents and tables, trinkets and refreshments. Tremendous casks of ale, large enough for Sir Colban to have fit comfortably inside, were lined in a row. He would have been comfortable indeed in such a chamber, for the ale was his, a product of his own lands and his own hands. To Alexander, the casks seemed like they were there for the gods, for despite the crowd of beastly Highlanders, he could not have imagined such a volume being consumed. For every cask at the base of the mountain, there were three at the top, but we will get to that later.

There was still a formal distance between the King and his subjects. Alexander and his tutor-knights stood under a tent, with servants and squires framing them in a half-circle behind. Vanora took a humble position among the maids. It was meant to be an understated spot, obscure amid the grand nobles who clustered in front. But she was made conspicuous by Alexander's steady glances back to her, each one returned with an encouraging smile. There is nothing Vanora could have worn or carried that would have pronounced her authority more clearly than the King's obvious need for her love.

Baliol whispered in Alexander's ear, "It is time for you to begin the gathering by announcing the race."

He was near enough to Sir Colban's keen ears, and the host declared loudly, "Oh no! The King cannot announce the start of the race. I'm afraid I must do it this year."

"You?" Baliol asked indignantly, "With all respect and gratitude, the King always announces the race, and you, sir, are not the King."

Lindsay began nervously chewing on his fingernails. He knew what Colban would declare next, and he had a good idea how Baliol, deeply steeped in tradition, would react. Vanora also anticipated the coming surprise, but she delighted in it. She simply smiled and crossed her arms in front of her.

"I make no royal presumptions, my Lord, but the King cannot announce the race from among the warriors competing."

"Why," Baliol challenged, "in the name of Our Lord, would he announce from amid the challengers?"

"Because he will be running against them," Colban thundered with a half-laugh.

He followed the announcement with a hearty slap on the King's back and a roll of rich, deep, oily laughter. He knocked the air from Alexander's lungs, but when the small boy regained his breath, he returned the laughter, not deep, rich, and oily, rather like a sneezing cat, but it carried the same jovial feelings.

Baliol and Durward were stunned witless. The climb was perilous. The competitors were large, rugged, fierce, and often brutish men. Durward feared for Alexander's safety. Baliol feared for the traditions of the gathering, for who would dare defeat the King? He visualized the

Highlanders toddling frightened and tentative behind Alexander, scared of overtaking him by a single toenail. Lindsay shared the fears of both — Vanora of neither.

"You make certain," she leaned forward to command Lindsay, "that those men run their hardest. If the child defeats a single one of them..."

"I know, I know," Lindsay answered.

There was only one way he could ensure her wishes were fulfilled. Lindsay would have to race. He took Alexander by the hand to lead him into the midst of the competitors, Vanora slapped his hand free of the King's. Lindsay looked back sharply and received a scowl that reduced the mighty man to the proportions of a child.

He turned his subservient gaze from Vanora to Alexander, and humbly suggested, "After you, Your Grace."

Alexander was like a young stallion at the gate, and Lindsay's words opened that gate. The boy shot from the tent with speed that impressed his fellow racers. Lindsay followed behind him and took his position for the beginning of the race. Alexander thought he had fallen into a hole and dropped from the world he had always known, into a land of unearthly legends, one of giants and ancient, magic, living land.

There was beating of chests and slaps on backs, war cries and hollers, and Alexander would have drowned amid it all if not for the buoyant swelling of his pride and excitement. Since the coronation, he had been a king and he had been a student, but he had not much been a boy. Rough and rugged as the men surrounding him were, there was playfulness in the atmosphere, boys being boys, bonding as boys, ready for the rough and tumble play of over-sized children.

The deep voice of Sir Colban boomed and echoed through the clamor, silencing all. He was no Durward. He had not trained in the skills of oratory, nor did he have the vast well of expression that the more refined knights could boast. It was all for the best, for they were in the Highlands, amid the Highlanders, and Colban's words suited the environment and the occasion perfectly.

As Colban roared on, Vanora walked stealthily behind her son. She placed her hands on his shoulders, bent down, and spoke into his ear, "This will be no race across the lawn, my sweet child. Turn your thoughts within yourself. Run with these men, but do not run against them. Do not run against the mountain. Run against the pain. Run against your fear. Run against the demands of your own body. The other men, the mountain, and Scotland herself want you to succeed. Allow your spirit to be pulled forward by them, for they will always be in front of you and never behind you."

She leaned closer still and whispered,

Oh son of mine
Show your colors true
Seek the gulls from within
To guide your way through

Set down your crown
And let it be still
Prepare your thoughts
For toughness and will

Her final poetic, whispered word was punctuated by the blast of a horn. The race began, but nobody moved. Nobody spoke. Hardly anyone breathed. Lindsay broke the awkward moment, giving a battle cry that stirred the hearts around him. He ran forward, upward, toward the top of Creag Choinnich. His eyes were ahead, but his mind was on the child behind him. He heard the footsteps of younger, stronger men, but none of them overtook him. None of them gained.

"It is as I feared," he thought to himself, "They are afraid to defeat him."

He circled back, behind Alexander, among the other racers, telling them a few at a time, "Don't you dare lose to this boy!"

"But, Sir David," one of them argued, "He is the King."

Lindsay answered, "And you are his warriors. What will he think of you if you cannot defeat a child? What will he think of himself if he beats the best of us?"

"I can't—" the man continued.

Lindsay interrupted threateningly, "Win this race or deal with me at the top!"

Once he convinced them all to race their hardest, Alexander was quickly left behind. He pushed his legs as he saw the backs of hollering men dwindle up the mountain in front of him.

For the first few minutes of the race, Alexander ran quickly, but he tired as the hill got steeper and the trees thickened. Soon, he was alone, well above those nobles and servants still at the bottom, and far beneath his fellow competitors. He slowed, but he did not pause. His run turned to steps that kept the steady rhythm of his heartbeat, which he could feel and hear pulsing within his ears.

He pushed on at this rate, watching wildlife, and even the breeze, race past him as quickly as the Highlanders had done. Vanora's words bounced inside of his head like a chanted prayer through an empty cathedral, "Show your true colors." It gave him little strength to push forward.

Her words continued to ring vividly through his inner-ear, "Seek the gulls from within."

He looked up and could see no gulls. The voice that had been ringing in his head suddenly seemed to resound in his chest, "the gulls from within." He turned his eyes from the sky, patted himself twice on the chest, as if knocking on the door of the spirits within him. He turned his eyes forward, up the mountain, and new vigor surged through his limbs.

He ran for what seemed like hours, though the sun moved slowly across the sky. With eyes forward and upward, he caught his foot on a root, dropping him forcefully to a knee. He fell onto one elbow and knocked the side of his head on the trunk of a tree. He drew a deep inhale, the purpose of which was to push forward a cry. But he held that breath within him, until the whimpering cry turned to the roar of a warrior, and it was in that form that the breath left his mouth.

He stood where he had fallen and leaned a hand against the tree that had struck him. His tiny hand held to the birch, and he could feel his pulse in his palm. His mind was taken away to the many years that had passed, the many Braemar Gatherings over two hundred years. The yells of his fellow competitors were high above and gone from his senses, yet he heard the cries of racers.

The tree he held, the rocks beneath him, the very breeze that whirled around him, told of the glories of past events. Whether they spoke aloud and would have been heard by others, were they around him, or they spoke directly into his heart, or were the product of a weary mind and vivid imagination, he could not say and he did not care. He felt like a part of something bigger than one day, bigger than one king, old and mighty as the mountain itself, and the power of warriors past, present, and future pulsed through his legs.

With his palm embracing the tree, vibrations passed from the bark, into his hand, up his arm, and into his heart, where it echoed in words clearly stated.

> The trees knew the men
> Who ran here before
> Two hundred years
> Of warrior lore

Your feet tread the path
Your hand holds the tree
That speak to you now
Through the rock and the bough
Of what you must be
Both the seed and the plow

Alexander became aware of all that he was — child and king, son and sovereign, fragile and powerful in both extremes. His eyes focused like a hawk's, and the highest tree on the mountain appeared mere steps away. He climbed with new vigor, one step at a time, at the pace of a child, but with the heart of a warrior.

What began as a rhythmic grunt, pushed from his feet with every step, and bursting through his lips, grew too gradually to notice into a war cry, with the pitch of a child's throat, but with the tone of a man who held the memories of the mountain in his heart. On and on he went, step by step, hour by hour.

The nobles and servants who had gathered at the bottom rode on horseback around the west side of the mountain, up a gentler slope, and arrived at the top before the racers. Such a welcoming party they were. The King's inclusion in the event mixed curiosity, excitement, and fear into an intoxicating brew that seasoned the high mountain air. Conversations were low in anticipation, but they combined to sound like many swarms of bees, swirling in clusters across the peak of Creag Choinnich.

The Highlanders obeyed Lindsay. They raced with all that their sinuous muscles and Highland hearts could muster. The first to breach the peak was a man named Ludan. He was tall and thinner than most, with long, wiry, black hair that he wore behind his head like the veil of a bride. The race had not been easy for him either. His knees showed evidence of every stumble. His elbows bled from being yanked down from behind. His face was bruised from the many blows that struck him in the heat of the fierce competition.

Ludan should have been the recipient of uproarious applause. But this race was like no others. All thoughts were on the King. Ludan did not strut around in victory, nor did he seek the soothing refreshment from the casks of ale. He turned on the spot and stared down the hill. Others joined him, a few racers at a time, many still pulling and punching on each other to gain one last advantage. But each, upon reaching the top, turned his eyes and attention down the hill.

They saw other racers weaving between the trees and fighting to finish, but saw no sign of Alexander. Lindsay reached the top around the middle of the pack. He did not sit. He did not rest. He hardly drew breath. Like the others, he stared down the hill in silence.

It was a successful race. Every competitor had made it to the top, all but one. After nearly an hour with no sign of the King, concerned mumbling turned to conversations, and conversations turned to panicked speculation. Where was Alexander? Was he safe? Was he alive? Had he given up and returned to the base of the mountain?

The tent from the base had been struck and re-pitched at the summit. Vanora waited under it with Durward and Baliol. Lindsay joined them there. Durward locked Lindsay's eyes in a glare of contention and blame. Lindsay did not shy from it, nor did he engage it. He simply stared back, unable to hide his concern behind the wrinkles around his eyes.

Lindsay turned his eyes to Vanora, drawing the glances of the other two with them. Such a placid expression rested on her, something between confidence and pride, as if the boy King was already safely at the top and standing between them. Durward and Baliol excused the look as the ignorance of a servant. But Lindsay saw much more deeply. This was the look of understanding, of knowledge beyond that of those who surrounded her.

The strange moment was disturbed by a shout in the familiar voice that had initiated the race. Sir Colban caught a glimpse of Alexander between the trees, and he shouted, "The King! Huzzah! Huzzah!"

The racers all turned their attention down the hill, and at the sight of the brave child, they echoed, "Huzzah! Huzzah!"

Alexander slogged forward, staring down at his feet, with no idea how near he was to the top. His feet were unnaturally heavy, like two anvils attached to his ankles. His skin began to burn with a searing heat, right where the stones in his pocket touched his leg. The heat did not come from the stones, but from deep within his leg, reaching outward from beneath his marrow.

His mind left his pocket and became aware of the sounds from the summit. They shouted again, "The King. The King. Huzzah!"

Their voices thundered down to Alexander, whose anvil feet were replaced with wings. Some shouted in words Alexander did not know. The words may have been strange, but the sentiment was clear enough. They were effusions of patriotism, of frenzied loyalty of the highest order. Their cheers so lightened Alexander's spirit that his weary feet hardly knew they were touching the rocks beneath them. He ran with more excited energy than his first fifteen steps of the race, and the Highlanders continued, "Huzzah! Huzzah!"

Vanora stood near Lindsay, too short to see over the excited clansmen. She reached to her side and took Lindsay by the hand. When Alexander reached the top, he was swept into the hairy, sweaty arms of the Highlanders, who hoisted him and tossed him, ceaselessly shouting, "Hail the King! Huzzah! Huzzah!"

Alexander's childish, high-pitched giggles pierced the deep voices surrounding him and found the ears of Vanora and Lindsay. Lindsay pulled his proud eyes from the celebration to stare at the wise woman beside him.

"How did she know?" he silently mouthed, and again asked himself, "Who is this woman?"

As he stared at her, she continued to hold her eyes proudly to her son. The look of pride, the gaze of familial love, struck him as distinctly familiar. It was the same expression Ulchel had when he spoke of his wife and child.

"This must be," Lindsay thought, "This must be the wife of Ulchel. But she has no child, no son nor daughter she has either shown or spoken of."

Amid the boisterous celebration, in the shadow of the roaring Highlanders tossing Alexander in the air, catching him, and shouting their praise, Lindsay mustered the courage to raise the subject.

"This moment reminds me of something," he began, drawing her attention and gaze toward him, "It brings me back to the battlefield and the most remarkable man to ever serve me in war. His name was Ulchel."

At the mention of the name, Lindsay looked for any subtle indication that she might have known him. She gave none, but locked her eyes to his in full attention.

He continued, "The man fought like no man has fought. He saved many lives, including my own. After our victory, I asked him what could fuel such fierce fighting. Love. He told me of a wife and a child, and that every swing of his sword was for love of them."

At this, Vanora winced, as if pinched deep beneath the skin.

It was a small indication, so Lindsay continued, "He had a book he kept with him, scribed and illustrated by his wife. It was prefaced by a poem he had composed for her, one she had written into his book."

Lindsay turned his eyes upward, shut them tightly, drew a long, exaggerated inhale, and released it into the mountain air with the words he had long ago set to memory. He began,

To the wind I give the stars
Oh still be the forests composure
To the sun be our keeper
And night our time of peace

With eyes thickly bedewed by swelling emotion, Vanora joined her voice to his, reciting in unison,

For dust char not my thunder
And bring forth stillness to reign
As the sun hovers over the sea
So shall your beauty

The stars align and share your wonder
For God is of the midday sun
The same as the stormy night

To the trees give my thanksgiving
And to the love I share with you
So we glow
For pause is my glory
And wonder shows my force

I declare to the age that I understand
As I give blessings for the touch of your hand in mine

At the conclusion of the verses, they both held their breath, neither sure how to proceed. Finally, Vanora answered what he already knew, "Yes, Ulchel was my husband."

She placed a hand on his shoulder and added, "It brings me a strange comfort to know he fought with you. Did you see him…, were you with him when…"

She could not bring herself to finish the words. She had no need. He answered her, "Nobody was nearer to him when he died. He died bravely. He died proud. More importantly, he died in love. When the battle was over, I held him. His face was peaceful. There were no signs of anguish on him, nothing of fury…, only love, and the sort of peace only true love can bring."

Vanora sighed in a stupor of deep reminiscence. Lindsay's words brought her comfort that ignorance had kept from her. Her imagination had pieced together a fiction that was hard to live with. The truth was infinitely easier on her heart.

With the question of Ulchel's wife answered and confirmed, there was still one question that burned, and Lindsay wasted no time addressing it, "Ulchel spoke of his love for his wife, and for their child…,"

It was an uncomfortable topic, and Vanora spared him from continuing. She interrupted, "Yes, our daughter, Beigis. She was not yet two years old when Ulchel joined you the second time. She never understood that her father had died, for I lost her only three weeks later."

Lindsay was unaware of his own surging compassion, until it escaped him in the form of a cry that popped from his nostrils, unable to leave through his tightly pressed lips. He cupped his hand behind Vanora's head, bent downward, and kissed the crown of her head.

The bubble inside of which their conversation had occurred suddenly burst, allowing back to their senses all of the sounds of the scene before them. They heard the hearty Huzzahs. They heard the faithful cheers of loyal countrymen. They heard the high-pitched giggle of a child piercing it all. The sun was lower in the sky, but any day's radiance that had faded was replaced by the gleaming smile of a proud child.

Vanora took Lindsay's hand and they both turned their attention fully to Alexander, as she said to him, "Look, David. Look at our boy."

The tears of a mother
Watching her son find his crown
Water the garden
Where fruit will abound

Chapter Seven:

Show Us Your Brush

Her voice held firm
As the regents enforce
The plans of the King
For her to endorse

Durward, Baliol, even Lindsay, could not have foreseen the success of the Braemar Gathering for their young king. It doubled their motivation to teach the child, and to embark on his education with their full energy and attention.

Vanora knew. Somehow she knew, and Lindsay's confirmation of her identity, and the strange connection between them, made her presence in his life, and in Alexander's, seem nothing short of Providential. There had been a great deal of uncertainty. It still lingered, but in a muted form, like a thin residue of something that once coated the skin thickly. Durward and Baliol reveled in the unexpected success of the race, while Lindsay relished a sense of national confidence he had never truly experienced until he stood beside Vanora, reciting her husband's poem, while mighty Highlanders tossed his delighted little king jubilantly in the air, shouting praise.

The royal entourage rolled south, completing its whirlwind tour where it began — at Edinburgh Castle. Alexander did not roll. He trotted. His slight frame bounced a full inch off the saddle with every proud step of Sir Walter. The pony seemed to sense his rider's pride. The humble little horse raised his head like a show horse on a victory lap. Alexander did not win the Braemar race. In fact, he finished an hour after the other competitors, but to him, and to all those who rode triumphantly behind him, it was very much a victory lap.

The King's tutors rode in a supportive half-circle behind him, with Lindsay on the right, Durward on the left, and Baliol directly behind. The three knights appeared like a chalice, holding within it the sacred blood of their country. To them, that is exactly what they were. Vanora did not ride in a carriage. Had she done so, she could not have savored the sweet air Alexander's pride left in its wake. She was the only mounted woman, but she rode so naturally that, like a knight in her own right, quite commanding of the beast beneath her, it struck nobody as peculiar.

Word of the success in the Highlands had already reached Edinburgh Castle by the excited scribbling of Sir Colban. It was late morning and all the staff and residents of the castle greeted the entourage in the courtyard. It was not at all the raucous reception Alexander received at the top of Creag Choinnich. It did not speak of a triumphant moment, but of a new and optimistic state of being. At the command of Durward, it disbanded quickly, and the castle went about its common business.

"Take an hour, Your Majesty," Durward said as he and Alexander dismounted simultaneously, "Bathe and change, and meet Sir Baliol in the study. We embark immediately on a new journey, a journey of the mind."

Lindsay nodded in agreement and added, "Three hours in the study, then to the map room with Sir Durward. In the evening, you will be ready to swing a sword in the courtyard with me."

"Oh no, no, no," came the scolding voice of Vanora from behind, "You have not scripted his day with work."

"We have, and we must," Durward answered, "and every day for the foreseeable future. Enough diversions. There is much for him to learn."

Lindsay rolled his lips into his mouth and bit down on them, awaiting Vanora's response.

"You will not bury his triumph so quickly beneath books and maps," she answered before turning to Lindsay and adding, "And you will not lacerate it with a sword."

Durward's shoulders rose in indignation. He drew a sharp inhale through his nose and parted his lips to make way for a blistering rebuke. But he was interrupted by Lindsay.

"What do you recommend?" Lindsay asked her.

"Were this an ordinary day," she railed, "he would take this entire day to recover from travel and contemplate all that has happened to him in the past months. But this is no ordinary day. He will take the rest of this day and all of the next."

"Why?" Baliol asked, "What is special about this day?"

Vanora calmed her voice and posture, and she answered, "Gentlemen, your King turned eight years old as we traveled to Creag Choinnich. The day passed as it needed to, not as I would have had it. But now he is here, in his home, and the child will have his birthday celebration. Today he belongs to himself. Tomorrow, he belongs to me. Surely, gentlemen, the delay of thirty-six hours will not doom the nation."

Durward began one last protest, "The King needs—"

Vanora interrupted with the authority of a bishop, "The child needs to celebrate his eighth birthday, as a child should celebrate. Join us if you wish, but keep your books, your maps, and your swords in their place."

Durward and Baliol stood stone-still, not sure how to respond. Lindsay gave Durward a hearty slap on the back and suggested, "Come boys, let's clean and eat, and prepare for the day after tomorrow. Right now, the King..., the child..., belongs to her."

Durward parted his lips one more time for a timid protest, but nothing came. He dropped his chin, more in admitted defeat than in agreement, and the three knights walked shoulder-to-shoulder into the castle, resigned, if not content, to allow Vanora her time.

Durward and Baliol were true to their form. They sequestered themselves within their stone, academic sarcophagi, and settled the nerves Vanora had rattled by furiously preparing their first lesson. Lindsay, much more in the form of a thoughtful father, spent the afternoon and evening at his desk, writing into a journal all that had happened since the death of Alexander's father. The effort brought forth thoughts and feelings that had been buried shallowly beneath the bombardment of events that followed. They brought, in almost stinging sensations, thoughts of his own family — his wife Margaret, and his two sons, Alexander and William — and their home, Byres Castle.

He thought strenuously of the child-king in his care, about how the death of a father so violently overturned the life of a son, and he thought about his own boys, painfully placing them in Alexander's shoes, tormenting his own imagination with theoretical disasters. Intense familial affection swelled in him, and he determined to see his own family, his own estate, his home.

In the morning, Lindsay found Alexander in Vanora's room. They were playing a word game, finding rhyming terms that described the people they knew. He listened from around the corner as they exhausted the words that described Baliol. As they began the rhyming adjectives for Lindsay, he stepped into the room and brought the game to a halt. He presented Alexander with a gift, a journal of his own. He kneeled before the boy and handed him the leather-bound book.

"I am going away... home, to my own family. I will miss your birthday celebration. This is for you to write your thoughts and feelings, to keep them for yourself, and if you wish, to share them with others."

Much more like a father than a knight, he kissed Alexander's cheek and continued, "I will be gone for two weeks. Listen to Vanora. Listen to your mother. But pay attention to Durward and Baliol. In very different ways, they love you too."

With that, he nodded to Vanora, left the room, mounted his horse, and rode east in haste. Byres Castle was only eight miles from Edinburgh Castle. Lindsay rode it in half the normal time, but it seemed like a full day to him, as his imagination placed his wife's arms around him, and he could almost feel the hair of his boys run through his fingers.

Lindsay was gone from Edinburgh, in body and spirit. It was his intention to leave no thoughts of himself behind, and in that, he succeeded. Durward and Baliol remained entombed in their efforts, and Alexander was comprehensively Vanora's.

Vanora had been preparing this day in her head since just after the coronation. She went to the kitchen and ordered all the food she would need to give Alexander the birthday of an eight-year-old child. There were fruits, meats, and breads. The culinary highlight of the day was a cake. It was a dense, heavy, sweet bread, coated in a sweet berry glaze.

There were other children in the castle. They were the sons and daughters of servants. The children of nobles were rarely brought to the capitol seat of the monarchy. Vanora roamed the castle looking for fellow celebrants for the royal birthday. She did not have the authority to relieve servants of their duties, and the social divide between the child-king and the children of servants was cavernous. Vanora took Alexander and the food to the forest southwest of the castle, for she knew the day had to be theirs and theirs alone. Of those left in Edinburgh, only she saw the child within the monarch, and only she could give him a child's birthday celebration.

It was an intimate party of two, a fact that pinched Vanora's heart. She imagined playmates for her boy, envisioning him laughing, running, jumping, and playing in wondrously imaginative adventures with children his age. Yet there they were, alone together in the woods, celebrating a birthday. Alexander would have had it no other way. It was only in private company with Vanora that he felt like himself, like a child, free to be a child. He was free. He was silly. He flitted around trees, mimicking the sounds of wild animals the moment the trees hid them from the world around them.

Whether by chance or in response to his carefree squawking, the gulls appeared, quadrupling the size of the party. They announced themselves with sound, then appeared in the gap of the forest canopy above, flaunting their skills in swirling and diving aerial acrobatics. Alexander looked up and seemed to answer them in their own language. There was an undeniable intimacy between the boy and his feathered playmates, and Vanora was grateful to them. But she still regretted the absence of other children, of a sibling to bicker with, or a best friend to compete with, and any of the thousands of tiny contributions other children could make to his childhood.

She had what she had, and she delighted in it. She sat against a tree and watched Alexander grab twigs in each hand, reach his arms to his sides, and flap like a gull. He ran in circles, turning and swooshing and squawking, while his flying friends danced above him.

Vanora spoke under her breath,

My child of light
Your hands filled with glee,
Show us your kingdom
Where gulls seek the sea

Your crown will rule
In this world you draw,
Show us your brush
And paint what you saw

Your hands know the beauty
Of sunlight and sky
And your heart knows the power
Of the light in your eye

Draw with this light
A castle anew
Paint with God
On His canvas of truth

You are my child
And forever will be,
My little seagull
Happy and free

When Alexander finally settled his attention on his only human companion, her smiling, maternal face was the warmest, brightest thing in his world. They ate and they played. There was no talk of wars or swords, no crests or crowns, no training or study. There was an eight-year-old boy and his doting mother. They played a game of sticks and rocks. Both chose a stick and a rock and tried to knock the rock along a determined course in as few hits as possible. Around and between trees, they hit their rocks and laughed. In one exaggerated swing, Alexander lost grip of his stick and flung in several feet behind him, and they laughed. Vanora accidentally struck a tree with hers, breaking the stick in half, and they laughed.

It was in no way an athletic competition. It was a game, with laughter as its primary point. They lost count of their strikes. Nothing could have been of lesser importance. It did not end when one of them completed the course, but when Vanora wound up and swung her stick, losing her balance and falling to the ground.

"Are you hurt?" Alexander shouted in authentic concern.

"My score is hurt," she responded, "but how could I win? How could I expect to defeat the warrior who reached the top of Creag Choinnich?"

The moment her smile lifted the edges of her mouth, he dove on her, and the two of them rolled on the dirty ground in a delightful mix of wrestling and tickling. The sticks, the rocks, the games were over, and they settled into a picnic with all the scrumptious treats Vanora had packed. They ate all but the cake. It was a surprise and saved for the end of the party.

She silenced him in a moment suddenly austere. All of her concerns for him swelled within her. The absence of playmates, the structures of his royal title, the slicing and portioning of his time among all the full-grown concerns of a monarch, all cascaded upon her head in full force. Her own wishes for him were a burden she would not place atop the rest. Seated across from a child who, at that moment, was in every way a child, she handed him his piece of cake, placed a hand on his head, pulled him to her chest, kissed his head, and blessed the boy and the day in verses that flew from her heart with the unguided freedom of the gulls that still circled above,

Oh son, my son, I give to you
A hope of your flight over the storms that brew

You are my child and always will be
I give you my heart, an island at sea,
Take this and grow and share what you learn
A gift without fear and one that you earn

As she spoke, Alexander looked down, focusing on a single stitch of the blanket beneath him. He drew one, slow, long inhale, as if trying to draw all of her hopes for him through his nose and into his heart. When she finished, he looked up to her flooded eyes and saw in her what she had always been — the hardest pillar to which he was anchored, and the softest surface on which to land when he falls.

He clapped for her verses, and in response, she clapped for him, "My Alex turns eight, hip hip huzzah."

He stood and bowed to her, then leaped onto her as he had done before, wrestling and tickling until it was time to return to the castle.

So much has happened
And what is his fate
The mother applauds
As her young King turns eight

Chapter Eight:

Where Love Finds Its Trail

A man finds his way
A mother sheds a tear,
Our King finds a friend
While his parents stand near

Byres Castle was as cozy a family home as could be found in all of Scotland. David Lindsay arrived on a warm morning. The garden was in full bloom. His boys, still awaiting their tutor, swatted sticks playfully at each other in the throes of imaginary battle, shouting their gallant cries and noble declarations in defense of their fair mother. Lindsay's wife, Margaret, divided her attention between the flowers she picked and the delightful antics of her sons.

Lindsay had changed. He did not yet know how much. The loss of his dear friend, King Alexander II, set off a chain of events that swept him through a strong current of revelations, personal growth, and new understanding. At the core of it all were two figures that had quickly burrowed their way to the very core of him. The first was to be expected. The new King was a responsibility he was prepared to assume. His role in young Alexander's life had long been discussed and secured. The other figure to alter him was entirely unexpected.

Lindsay was a kind lord, generous with his servants and protective of the poor and downtrodden, but never on familiar terms with those of a lower station. The mysterious Vanora was an enigma his rational mind could not dissect. In a very short time, she transitioned in his eyes from a nameless nursemaid to the only true mother his King had ever had, linked to his past by the haunting memory of a fellow soldier who had forever changed his notion of conjugal devotion. She wielded tremendous authority over Lindsay, royal authority, but that power was held in soft, nurturing hands.

When Lindsay entered the garden, he saw his wife and children very differently from the last time he had been with them. Vanora had placed the clear and lucid lenses of love over his eyes, and it was through them that he viewed his wife and children, his garden and home. His heart was, simultaneously, lighter than the few, sparse clouds above, yet burdened by tremendous weight.

The children dropped their sticks and abandoned their imagined quests when they heard their father's thundering steps running to greet them. Margaret was drawn to her husband, but frozen in place by the sight of her laughing boys flinging themselves into their father's arms. Her eyes wanted to watch from a distance, but her legs had other plans. They conspired with her arms to place her quickly in the embrace of the only man she had ever loved.

They had been apart for two months. The boys were not noticeably taller. Margaret's features were exactly as he had left them. Yet to Lindsay, under the color of his new vision, they were *all* brighter, lovelier, and more radiant, almost too radiant to bear. They had all suffered much longer separations. They had, many times, been divided by war, uncertain of ever seeing each other again, and then been reunited. But it was this sunny reunion that drew tears from David's eyes, and from his wide open mouth, a giggling, full-throated cry.

Mother and children did not know how or why he was altered, but *that* he was altered was as clear, warm, and delightful as the sky above. For a third of an hour they remained in the garden as a tightly wound, intertwining, laughing, crying, squeezing, and kissing cluster of familial bliss.

When they finally entered the castle, the tutor arrived to sweep the children into their daily routine. Lindsay took his wife to the bedroom, where they re-committed to a union of body, mind, and spirit. In the evening, before sleep, when David and Margaret were again alone together, they shared their experiences of their months apart. Margaret knew well of Ulchel, of the journal and the poem, and of the remarkable devotion that burned so fiercely inside of him.

The revealed identity of Ulchel's wife, this ideal of love and devotion, as the nursemaid of a prince, then the mother of a king, and finally a sage of subtly poignant wisdom, was as astonishing to Margaret as it had been to David. But Margaret gave the details little thought. It was Vanora's effect on her husband that drew her wildest amazement. Whoever this woman was, whatever title she bore or role she fulfilled, she had managed to put a sparkle in Lindsay's eyes that kept the night as bright as the clear day had been. His touch was tenderer, his kiss more expressive of his passion, and his gaze so much more filled with glorious wonder — and for that, she was grateful beyond expression.

In the morning, Lindsay arose early. He isolated himself in his study with a heart laden with regret and yet charged with determination. He pondered without pause. He thought of his boys, and he thought of King Alexander. He reminisced about his own childhood, of his father, and his older brother. Amid these thoughts, he was suddenly burdened with great pity for his child-King, a boy without a brother and without a father.

"Thank God for her," he said out loud as he thought of Vanora.

She was right. She had been right all along. Alexander was a child, and he needed a childhood. How clearly Lindsay saw it now! His two weeks at home went quickly, but lovingly, with his children — children with a father, children with a brother. He felt fleeting guilt as he considered how he would have contributed to the boy's troubles, dragging him prematurely into a tragic adulthood, if not for the vision of Vanora.

The eight-year-old King was still the King. He still had to be pushed into shoes he could not possibly fill. He would grow up before his time. That could not be avoided. But there could be balance. There must be, if the boy-king were to become a good king. Of this fact he was entirely convinced, and he was determined to wield the full force of his influence to see it happen.

He was expected back at Edinburgh Castle that day, but he could not fight for the needs of Alexander while ignoring those of his own family. He decided to stay home for three more weeks, providing a father to his own children, while securing a mother to his King. He wrote to Durward, informing him of the delay in the King's training, but giving no explanation.

"Leave him in Vanora's care until I return," he wrote, "Make no effort to interfere with them."

He poured a bright fragrant wax on the letter and sealed it with the Lindsay crest, securing his desires with the weight of his family name.

He decided to settle his two sources of guilt in a single move — to take his son, William, with him to Edinburgh Castle, to serve as a playmate and training companion of the King. There were two maternal figures he needed to consult. He pitched his proposal to Margaret.

"Why William?" she asked, "Why our youngest? Should you not take Alexander?"

"And have two Alexanders running about the castle?" he jested before sobering the moment, "Our Alexander is nearly fourteen. He will soon make his own way, leaving William without a companion. Any such action on his behalf would interfere with his future. He has no need of the sort of schooling the King will receive. William could flourish as an older brother to the King, and his own skills will progress. His Grace is only three years younger, and they could be very good for one another."

"More importantly," he continued solemnly, "though I will be only eight miles away, my days will be full and my time not my own. I want my son..., and my wife."

Her sour grimace lifted from the corners of her lips to raise her entire face.

"Our Alexander can run the estate for a week at a time, and you can stay with us in Edinburgh."

After the groping kisses that followed his proposal, Lindsay had one more letter to write, and one more woman's permission to gain. He wrote to Vanora. He would not dare introduce his son into Alexander's life without her blessing. He returned to his study and stared at empty parchment, juggling, adopting, discarding, and returning to words in a frenzied cycle, until he finally cleared his mind and wrote,

My Dear Lady,

Your words and your deeds have done much to alter my opinions on the one subject of our shared devotion — your Son and my Sovereign. After deliberations with my able wife, I have decided that both of our interests would be best served if I bring my son, William, back to Edinburgh, to serve as schoolmate, companion, and counselor to your dear boy. In my mind, I have listed the many wise benefits of the idea. I could provide them to you if you wish. I suspect you will have no need of them. Your maternal wisdom will see, as my wife sees, that a brotherly figure in Alexander's life could balance the perils of his title with the normalcy of childhood and give him that which you have been fighting to give him.

I confess a degree of self-interest in my wish for the company of my own child, but I suspect this too need not be explained to you. My wife, Margaret, will be more often in Edinburgh, and our example of familial connection can only serve our King well. I would not dare put the scheme into action without your blessing. Alexander is, as I have come to realize, first and foremost, your son.

Please return a response at your convenience, as I intend to return with my son, William, in three weeks.

All Blessings to You From,

Your Humble Servant,

David Lindsay

A servant was dispatched before the wax seal hardened. The letter found Vanora as Lindsay had left her, alone with Alexander. Before breaking the seal, she grinned, held the letter to her chest, and told Alexander, "You will have a new young friend, my love."

"Really?" he asked eagerly, "Who? Who is coming?"

"One of Sir David's boys."

"How old is he? What's his name? Is he very tall?"

Vanora pulled the letter from her chest, looked at it without opening it, turned her eyes to Alexander, and answered, "I'm not certain. Let's find out."

She opened the letter and confirmed what she already knew.

"William," she said, "his son, William. He will come back with his son, William."

Alexander's look of delight turned to one of puzzlement, as he asked, "How did you know?"

"Your friend Lindsay is many things. He is the lord of a wealthy family, a knight and warrior, a politician, a loyal patriot. But above all of these, he is a moral man and a good father. In teaching you, he thinks often of his own children. He loves you, although he might not know it yet. He will remain true to you. But he would never abandon his own family. Of course he will bring his son here. His heart decided before his mind considered it."

Such lofty thoughts flew just over Alexander's head, but they were moral seeds, planted to be fertilized and cultivated later. What mattered most was clear enough — Alexander would have a new friend, a playmate and schoolmate, a big brother, and a father figure, standing tall, noble, and heroic above them both.

Vanora handed Alexander some papers to read, poetry of her own composition and by her own hand, to occupy the boy while she wrote her response to Lindsay's letter. She responded immediately, as Lindsay had requested, not because he requested it, but because she knew he could not focus on his wife and children as he should until the matter was resolved.

Vanora's response was in Lindsay's hand three mornings after he dispatched the request. The delay was not from a disrespect for his feelings. She took an entire afternoon framing her words with exquisite art. Colorful images of flora and creatures from long forgotten myths wove and danced along the border of the pages. She responded in verse, both mysterious and poignant.

The letter read,

A father I see
In those heart-filled eyes,
A soldier you'll be
Until your demise

Show them your path
Where love finds its trail,
Charges through wrath
A sword without fail

One boy of your seed

And one of no chord,
They two are brothers
By design of the Lord

Raised by a force
Above what you can see
You are his father
Raise him with me

The Teacher of Gulls
From now until death
The wisdom of God
Will spring from your breath

The letter had every effect Vanora intended. It was plain enough to give the relief of an answer, yet enigmatic enough to churn his mind in contemplation. It had been many years since Lindsay was a student of any kind. He felt like a student as he lowered the letter to his lap and pondered the layered meanings. With all of his skills, all of his experiences, this new teacher of his dangled an unfamiliar brand of wisdom in front of his face, just out of his reach, demanding that he take steps forward to obtain it and to deserve it.

Lindsay smiled, thrilled by the challenge, but content to let it sit for three weeks. He set the letter down and committed whole-heartedly to what Vanora knew he was, a doting father and mentor to his children, a husband and faithful lover to his wife.

His brother is coming!
The gulls declared
His mother smiled
At a childhood shared

Chapter Nine:

The Melody of Love

The heart of a child
As bright as the sun
Warmed the stone castle
As the two became one

David Lindsay was a warrior, a statesman, a scholar. Alexander had plenty of those in his life. What he needed was a father. Vanora was mother to Alexander and mother to Lindsay. She sculpted David into what she knew her child needed. The change in Lindsay was apparent to all in his circle. When he rode back to Edinburgh after three more weeks at home, with his son William wrapping him from behind with loving arms, he was, above all else, a father. And he was finally ready to assume his proper role in the young King's life.

When Lindsay rode into the courtyard, Alexander was with Durward. He called for the King. Excited to see Lindsay and meet William, Alexander ran the corridors, too fast for poor Durward, who was perturbed by the disruption to a lesson that had waited three weeks to resume. He burst into the courtyard to see William dismounting the horse. Durward was not far behind.

Lindsay wasted no time introducing the boys to each other. William was older by two years, yet they bonded instantly and ran together to play in the woods that surrounded the castle, as if they had been raised together from the crib. Lindsay pressed no agenda, not immediately. He watched with a light heart and a wide smile as the boys ran from his sight. Durward began a panicked protest, but was shushed by Lindsay's quickly raised hand.

Vanora watched in stealth from behind a half-opened door. She was proud of Lindsay. His actions in the courtyard were evidence of her influence over him, and of his readiness to take on the role of father in Alexander's life. Durward retreated to his study, mumbling his disapproval under his breath.

Lindsay sought Vanora. A new life was beginning for Alexander, and Lindsay wanted the counsel of the one person who would be the base of that new life. He found her in the corridor and escorted her to the dining hall, where they talked and laughed on topics personal and spiritual for a full hour, getting to know each other before mentioning Alexander.

They spoke of Ulchel and of Margaret, of memories from their childhoods, of personal triumphs and heartbreaks. It was exactly what needed to happen, *when* it needed to happen, if they were to be the twin pillars that upheld a king and kingdom.

Lindsay admitted, "I admired your husband while he lived, but after his death, I came to love him."

"How so?"

"He spoke of you with the passion of a fiery lover. I admired him for that, but I didn't understand it, and I never compared it to my own life, to my own marriage. It was, I am sad to confess, something I thought beneath me. But something in his love for you was branded deeply into me when he died, and it has remained in my blood, something I could feel but not describe, sense but not identify... until recently."

He lowered his eyes from hers and winced in contemplation.

"Go on, David," she urged.

"I cannot account for this change in me. It is as if that part of Ulchel has finally awakened in me. I burn, Vanora. I burn for my wife. I feel connected to her, and this distance of only eight miles pulls on my ribs and restricts my breath. I tell you, I have loved…"

She continued his thought, "But *now* you are *in* love."

"Yes. It is embarrassing… to think that I cannot be eight miles from my wife without pain. What does that say about me, about a knight?"

Vanora smiled at him with the eyes of an approving mother, then she answered, "It says that you are more than a knight. You are more than a father and more than a husband. You are becoming a man, everything a man should be, and everything Alexander must become. You are exactly what you must be, where and when you must be."

They stared at each other in silence for several minutes. When they began to speak again, they were strictly on topic. They discussed and debated the upbringing of the child-King. By the time they departed, Alexander's immediate future was scripted, with a balance of childhood frivolities and dynastic considerations, of play and study, of love and duty.

To the delight of Durward and Baliol, Alexander's lessons surged forward with full force the following morning. The itinerary included play time, personal study on subjects of Alexander's choosing, prayer, nature and exercise, and of course, time with Vanora each evening, when the lessons of the day were filtered through her signature sensibilities. William was at his hip most of the day, studying, playing, sparring, and praying. In the evenings, when Alexander joined Vanora, William joined his father, where he was cherished by a suddenly swelling heart.

Alexander's tutors were not the only ones to fill his head each day. The Church took its seat at the table. A rotating carousel of friars and scholar-monks seized a fistful of hours each week for the learning of scripture. It was a deeply Christian country. There were no differing opinions battling for Alexander's faith. His holy tutors spoke with the confidence of clerics and the support of everyone with concerns in the young King's life.

There was no greater advocate for Alexander's spiritual training than Vanora. Their evening hours together were filled with prayer and scripture. Vanora knew every line and every quotation the clerics knew. But she supplemented the scriptural wisdom with other words, words from other books, and with passages that did not exist in writing, but had been passed on, tongue-to-ear, for countless generations.

With each line Alexander quoted from the Gospels, Vanora was quick and ready with spiritual quotations from other sources, sources outside of Christianity, ancient wisdom that had been rooted in Scotland since before recorded time. The young King had learned the Bible well. He knew the Gospels and could quote them on command. He spent his earliest years moving from monastery to abbey, from church to chapel. His early tutors, well before Durward or Baliol, were monks and friars, and he was steeped thoroughly in theology. Vanora's cryptic quotes did not overtly contradict his scriptural schooling. It complimented it. It enhanced and enriched it.

More enthralled than confused, Alexander asked, "Where am I to find the Word of God? Is it in the Bible or in other places, places you have been taught and I have not?"

Vanora answered without a breath of pause, "Christianity is a young religion. Truth existed before the Bible, and God existed before truth."

The young child had no concept of the distant past. Vanora spoke of swaths of time far too great for a little boy's comprehension, and his puzzled look showed it.

Vanora placed it into a metaphor he could visualize, "Christianity is the fresh new leaves on a tree. The leaves are beautiful. They dance in the breeze. They shade us from the sun in the summer and shelter us from the freezing rain in the winter. They provide a harbor, a sort of house, under which we can gather. But the leaves do not stand high above us on their own. They are held by twigs. The twigs are supported by older branches, unaffected by the wind. The branches connect to a single trunk, old, firm, and implacable. We can rest against the trunk. We can lean our weight against it when we are weary and it will never tumble. But the trunk does not stand alone either. It is held in place and nurtured by roots, which go deep and mysteriously into the unknown earth."

The metaphor should have been well beyond the comprehension of an eight-year-old child. But Alexander followed it. Oh, he understood it exactly as she wanted him to. He sensed the full weight of it. His eyes were opened to an ancient past he could not have fathomed before that moment. It would be an exaggeration to say that he gained new wisdom, but he gained an understanding that truth exists that is older than anything he had ever read, and is rooted to the very depths of the earth.

An insatiable thirst enlivened inside of him, and he began peppering Vanora with questions. They came too quickly for her to answer, and she realized that his mind was too ravenous at that moment to consume and retain understanding. She calmed him with a song that both settled and liberated his mind, lulling his body to sleep while untethering his mind to roam freely through dreams of its own making.

Oh son of the sea with roots in the sand
Hear the calm voice of the gulls and the land
Sing softly the true melody of love
Fulfill our wondrous creator's demand

The following morning, Alexander awoke surging into a new identity. He was expanding on three fronts. Durward and Baliol were developing a king. The friars and monks enriched a faith. At the head of this trinity were Vanora and Lindsay, who expanded Alexander in a more personal way, not as a king and not as spiritually faithful, but as a man, as one human among many, with all of the signature traits of his species.

Lindsay spoke openly and emotionally about his newly inflamed passion for his wife and family. He could not help himself. It saturated every morsel of his being. Vanora, too, cried on Alexander's shoulder as she told him stories of her husband and the child they lost. Lindsay became more interested in his student's commitment to his loved ones, and less in his ability to swing a sword. Vanora refined the boy's compassion, so Lindsay yielded more of his training time to her.

After a month of studying with teachers, playing with William, laughing and crying with Vanora, and growing outward in every possible direction, Alexander's fate was designed in a late-night meeting. Durward, Baliol, and the week's resident monk, a man named Gordell, gathered in the study to plot and plan the next generation of Scottish royalty.

Durward began, "If we are to secure the support of the clans, the King must marry. Even if he cannot yet produce an heir, the first step must be taken."

With moderately offended sensibilities, Gordell protested, "But he is only eight years old. The Church may not support…, surely another year or two…"

"No, no," Baliol leaped in, "Durward is right. The dynasty is fragile. We must give the people the hope of continuity."

Gordell looked suddenly to his left and right, back to Baliol, then asked, "Where is Lindsay? These discussions should include him, should they not?"

Durward and Baliol looked at each other with a blend of guilt and deception.

After an awkward pause, Durward answered the question in meticulously chosen words, "Of course, we will need Lindsay's blessing for anything concerning the King. But we dare not present Lindsay with speculations and theories, or he will shoot the idea in the nest before it takes wing. Let us form a plan, find a match, and go to Lindsay with a fully developed scheme."

Baliol kept the family tree of every prominent surname in Western Europe, and he offered, "I will compile a list. We will choose the best matches and then present a short list to Lindsay. He will have the final say, but not before we form our list and our argument."

It was agreed, and Baliol committed his long nights to searching the books and scrolls, and the storied lineage of every noble girl from Amsterdam to Glasgow. In six days, he had his list. He met again with Gordell and Durward. The three of them scratched names from the list one at a time, until only six names remained. On the seventh morning, they invited Lindsay to their gathering. They presented him with the well-rehearsed scheme, prepared for any possible reaction — any but one.

Lindsay did not immediately reject the proposal, but responded calmly in a manner they did not foresee, "This is a good list. There are some fine families here. But Alexander will not marry a family. He will marry a girl, an individual girl with her own traits. How can we choose who Alexander will love?"

"Love!?" was Durward's astonished response, "We are speaking of a queen, the mother of our next King. Why do you ask about love?"

Lindsay lifted a subtle grin, like an adult observing the actions of a child. No good could come from explaining his concerns to Durward and the others. To them, Alexander was a commodity of the country. Of the men in the room, only Lindsay saw the boy behind the crown. Only Lindsay knew the child for all that he was. And only Lindsay invested in the human behind the King.

He astonished them further with a proclamation they would never have considered, "Nothing more can be decided on this matter without Vanora. I will take your list to her. She will decide what happens next."

"Vanora?" Durward asked incredulously, "The nursemaid, the servant? You wish to take the affairs of men to a servant-woman, to place the future of the dynasty in the hands of someone who could not possibly fathom the stakes?"

Lindsay turned suddenly solemn, and scolded Durward in a dramatically deepened voice, "Vanora is his mother and much, much more. I do not turn to her because she holds the maternal rights. I turn to her because she knows best. I seek her counsel on many matters, and you, gentlemen, would benefit from doing the same!"

He snatched the list from Baliol's hand and stormed from the room. If his strong, paternal voice had not already cowered them into submission, his thundering boot steps that echoed back at them as he marched away would have been enough to silence any further protest.

Lindsay made no stops and hardly a pause between the study and Vanora's room. By the time he sat beside her, his demeanor had changed entirely. He was not a statesman in her presence. He was not a knight, not the lord of his estate. He was a man, and he was a loving and concerned father. He would not show her the list, not yet. It seemed too transactional, and he feared her reaction. He brought up the topic of a royal marriage, informing her, as if she did not already know, that plans were already being drawn up and debated.

With thoughts much more heavily on Alexander's health and happiness than the affairs of state, these two pillars of the young King's life discussed and debated the future of their shared child. Marriage would happen, and would happen soon, too soon, but Vanora and Lindsay would see that it happened their way, focusing on the boy more than the King, on a heart more than a crown, and on a bride more than the product of some lofty lineage. The list would wait for the following morning.

A bride will be chosen
Who loves our fair king
A mother turns ill
As gulls form one ring

Chapter Ten:
The Gulls Form a Ring

Scared and Afraid
Our King shakes with fear
He looks through the trees
And sees gulls flying near

In the morning, Lindsay wasted no time bringing the proposed marriage to Vanora. She was in the garden, squatting in the dirt, caressing the moss that grew on a stone, speaking to it in ancient words, long forgotten by all but a very few. Lindsay stood unnoticed and watched her. He did not know her words. He did not need to, the sentiment was clear enough. It was the voice of a caregiver whose heart was fully committed to the silent recipient at her fingertips, not as a mother to a child, more like a very old friend coming to the aid of a loved one in need.

As Lindsay studied her, intrigued beyond measure, his mind tried to grasp at the unreachable phenomenon before him. Vanora's words turned melodic and took the form of a song with the strangest arrangement of notes, incongruent with one another, yet quite comfortable in the company they kept. There was something simple, even elementary in the way she sang and rubbed the moss, yet it was still beyond him, both beneath him and above him in ways that titillated and tormented his brain.

Although Lindsay made no sound and remained out of her view, she suddenly stopped the song, turned her head from the stone, but not enough to have seen him, and she spoke, "David, you have something to show me?"

With Baliol's list in hand, he walked gingerly and reverently toward her, like stepping to the altar of an empty cathedral, or working his way between the headstones of a sacred cemetery.

Again she seemed to read his thoughts and encouraged him, "It is a garden, not a graveyard. Come."

She stood, turned to him, and gestured her hand to a nearby bench. They sat together, and Lindsay told her about his meeting the night before.

Vanora reached for the writing in his hands and said, "I suppose Baliol made you a list. May I see it?"

He handed her the list, but before another word passed on the subject, a servant from Lindsay's estate stumbled into the garden, weak from a strenuously fierce ride and hardly able to catch his breath.

In clear distress, he stuttered, "Lady Margaret..., your wife..., my Lady..."

"For Heaven's sake, man," Lindsay scolded, "tell me! What has happened to my wife?"

"She is ill, very ill."

Lindsay stood sharply and ran from the garden, as the poor servant tried to continue, "The priest is with her. He... he..."

Lindsay sprinted to the stable, mounted his horse without a saddle, and rode at full gallop toward his home. Vanora looked to the mossy stone, gave it one pleading request in its ancient tongue, then commanded the winded servant, "Get William. Bring him to the stable, and I will meet you there."

The servant found William reading to Alexander. He blurted his news with more strength but no more composure. He took William to the stable as Vanora had commanded. She had already saddled a horse and led it by the reins. It was a tall horse, and Vanora would have struggled to mount alone. With no words or gestures between them, young William helped Vanora onto the horse and mounted in front of her. With a spur, a crack of the reins, and a holler, they were off to the Lindsay estate.

Alexander had seen Margaret Lindsay, but had never spoken to her. Still, he felt an intimacy with her through his love for Lindsay, and through Lindsay's flamboyant love for his wife. The blurted announcement of the servant and William's hasty departure sent Alexander's mind into swirling torment. He did not know what to do. He ran left and right, back and forth down the halls, to no thoughtful destination, picking up speed in proportion with his panic.

His mind cleared with a moral mandate that fell on him suddenly and spoke to him in lucid terms of the heart. "Go to them!" it demanded. Vanora was gone. Lindsay and William were gone. The other tutors were buried in their own affairs. No eyes were on Alexander, so nobody of authority saw him march with focused determination to the stable. Guards bowed to him as he passed, then returned their eyes and attention to their posts. By the time Alexander stood beside his friend and pony, Sir Walter, nobody in the world knew exactly where he was.

As he saddled Sir Walter, he explained to the beast where and why they were going.

"I do not know the way," he explained, "I will need you to take me there."

He spurred Sir Walter from the stable and into the field beyond, with a child's misguided trust in the animal that raced away with him.

When David Lindsay arrived at his home, there was an eerie quiet about the place. No servants buzzed here and there on their daily duties. The kitchen was quiet. The fires were not yet lit. The entire house was in a state of silent fret, which fell upon poor David the moment he broke the threshold. It anchored itself to his heart and pulled him to depths he had never known.

He ran directly to the master's chamber, where every servant in the house lined the walls like dramatic statues at an exhibit, each eye focused on the fevered matriarch struggling to breathe on the bed. The fear for Margaret's life was real, but so was the fear of contagion. There was a broad perimeter around the sick woman. David pierced it like an arrow. He ran to the bed, kneeled upon it, and wrapped his wife's face in his cupped palms.

Her true peril dawned upon him as he felt the unnatural heat radiating from her skin. Her lips were white and chapped. Her eyes were dark and sunken. She had deteriorated so suddenly and in such a short time, and there was little hope in the household of her recovery.

David scanned his eyes across the room, at each servant lining the wall. Finally, one of them had the courage to say, "We have called for the priest, My Lord."

Lindsay understood the purpose of the priest. He was no healer. He was summoned to grant the final rites to a dying woman, to ensure the safety of her soul. Lindsay returned his focus to his wife, and for the first time, considered a life without her. The thought broke his poor mind. He collapsed upon her and wept, grasping at her and shaking her, screaming and grunting an incoherent barrage of blurted syllables. To the others in the room, he was the very portrait of a man gone mad. The chaos in his breaking heart swelled to consume his mind and every other part of his being. Had he been seen in that moment by the men he had led on the battlefield, or the nobles he had addressed at court, or by his own children, they would not have recognized him as David Lindsay.

The sight of the noble master of the house, so altered by despair, so broken into pieces, was too much for the servants. They trickled out one at a time, in whimpering tears. As the last one left, she was replaced by the newest arrivals. Vanora and William entered the room, still out of breath from their rigorous ride. They met the eldest Lindsay child in the hallway, William's brother, Alexander. He had been kept away from his mother for fear of her illness. Vanora took him by the hand and dragged him into the bedroom.

There they stood — the ever maternal Vanora, and the Lindsay children. David turned to them, and his wits were regathered by a slender string of hope. Such familial love flowed at him from the three newcomers to the room. The boys had never seen their father cry in such a state. David had no pride left in him. He looked to his boys and invited them into his arms with a fresh torrent of tears. Vanora released their hands and they ran to their father and mother.

They were a family in mourning, despairing an inevitable loss, an unspeakable tragedy. Vanora was less certain of Margaret's demise. She hushed the concerted crying of the three male Lindsays with a calming, nurturing, and hopeful, "Shhhhhhh."

It turned their faces to her in pleading gazes, but the moment was shattered by another entrance. The local priest entered the room, with two friars at his side.

"Sir David!" the priest scolded, "Get yourself and your children away from the dying woman!"

"Their mother," Vanora softly responded.

The priest looked at her as if she had spat on him.

Vanora continued, "Her name is Lady Margaret, and she is their mother."

"Leave this room, servant woman," the priest directed, "There is urgent work to be done, God's work, the work of the Church, my work."

Lindsay softly and shakily spoke, "I would like her to stay."

"For what purpose? There is nothing here to be cleaned…, not yet."

Vanora said nothing in her defense. This was not the time for such a stance. She simply looked to David with the supportive eyes and maternal expression he needed.

The priest turned his eyes from Lindsay to Vanora and back again, and demanded with his expressive eyebrows that the servant woman be removed.

Lindsay, with cheeks glistening with salty tears, turned suddenly stern, and spoke to the priest with the authority of his title, "Do what you have come to do. Vanora stays!"

With that order, the humble woman in the corner disappeared entirely from the priest's thoughts. He pulled a book from some deep pocket hidden within the ample folds of his robe — and he began to read. He read of death not life. He read of Heaven and Hell, and of Purgatory, of sins to be atoned for. The room took on the air of a funeral, of a ceremony for the dead. But Margaret still breathed. Her heart still beat. She heard and at least partly understood the dark, final rites being given to her.

With each word, Vanora's jaw clenched more tightly, and her teeth grinded in her mouth. Finally, she interrupted, "What are you doing? This mother, this wife, is not dead. She is ill, and there are things that can be done."

From the moment David felt the fever and saw the sunken, withered features of his wife, he, too, had assumed her death. But with such a proclamation from such a woman, a seed of hope sprouted its first leaf. David's eyes darted to Vanora and clutched her calm face in their intense focus.

The priest, irritated by the impertinence, turned to her, leaned his head over her as if from the pulpit, and thundered, "Do not interrupt me, woman. You do not know what you are saying. Go! Leave this poor family and do not torment them with false hope."

Lindsay looked at Vanora with the face of a child, and with deep pleading in his broken voice, he said, "Vanora?"

The priest began another protest, but Vanora raised her hand to his face and demanded, "Shush! I am speaking to Sir David."

The fury of the priest is hard to describe. His deeply reddened face stared at Lindsay, demanding his interference. It did not come. Lindsay kept his eyes on Vanora and pleaded again, "Vanora?"

Vanora took one step forward, standing between the priest and the bed, and she told David, "Your wife is very ill, very ill indeed. But she is not dead. There are things that can be done, things we can try."

With the innocent curiosity of a child, Lindsay asked, "Things?"

"Yes," she calmly responded, "There are remedies in nature, power in the touch of healing hands. We need not resign to the worst until we have tried."

Lindsay stood from the bed, not as a hopeless widower, but as the husband of a sick woman. The priest and his assistants had all but evaporated from his attention. He was squarely focused on the encouraging words of Vanora. Lindsay and Vanora, with two stout and loving boys beside them, formed an imposing alliance, and the priest did not stand so tall in their united shadow.

With timidity never before heard from him, the priest asked, "Sir David, your wife's soul is in peril. Will you please discard this woman from your home? There may not be much time."

Lindsay turned to the priest, grateful for his presence, but much less certain of his role in the matter.

The priest continued, "And there is more. You may purchase an indulgence for your wife, shorten her time in Purgatory, hasten her spirit into the hands of our Lord."

"How so?" Vanora interrupted.

"Yes," William added in support, "How so?"

The priest began a long-winded recitation of the rites of Holy Indulgence, until Vanora asked in mid-syllable, "Money in your purse will bring Margaret sooner to Christ? How so?"

The priest gave one last appeal to the faith of Sir David, with a forceful gaze into his eyes.

"Thank you for coming, Father," Lindsay spoke with authentic gratitude, "but I need you to step outside while I speak with Vanora."

The priest drew a deep inhale in obvious preparation for a stately protest, but David stopped him short, adding, "She has things to say, and I will hear them. This is my wife, my love and my life, and if she may be saved..."

The priest looked to Vanora with disbelief. She simply turned her eyes to the floor and pointed to the door. The priest scoffed, turned on his heels, and marched from the room like he was leading a procession. Once the door was closed behind the clerics, what remained in the room was an equal blend of familial affection, true fear, and blooming hope. What was conspicuously missing from the room was despair.

The priest was closed in his thinking, but his heart was true. He remained faithful to his vocation and stayed at Byres Castle, rarely venturing beyond the master hallway. His most ardent prayers for Margaret's soul flew in constant procession from his lips, in the form of a whisper, barely audible beyond the reach of his arms. The two friars, equally committed, hung from his sides like purses.

Vanora meant no personal insult when she decried the suggestion of an indulgence to the Church. She knew the priest was not a greedy man. He earnestly believed the payment would benefit Margaret. But Vanora's vision was sharper. It cut through superstition like a gull through a light breeze. Vanora was focused on the perils at hand. She had already forgotten the encounter. The priest had not, and he added to his whispered prayers an appeal to God for Vanora's salvation.

The house was filled with an eclectic cast of characters like it had never seen before. That evening, another was added to it. A ferocious banging on the front doors echoed suddenly through a house that had been prayerfully holding its breath for hours. The reddened knuckles behind the banging belonged to Durward's personal squire. He came with a message as urgent as the banging suggested. He was led to the hallway outside of Margaret's room, where the trembling priest tried to extract the urgent news.

"I am to give the message to Sir David," the faithful squire spoke with a reverent bow.

As he rose from his bow, Lindsay walked from the room. With the door ajar, and Vanora peering curiously through the crack, Lindsay demanded, "I am here. Give me your master's message."

"His Grace, the King…,"

Vanora's voice rose from the inner room, "What of the King?"

The squire turned his eyes briefly to the room, then quickly back to Lindsay, and he asked, "Is he here?"

Lindsay shook his head as his jaw clenched and his teeth grinded.

"The King is gone," the squire continued, "It appears he left in pursuit of you, My Lord, but he is nowhere between there and here."

Lindsay's spirit was gripped on opposing sides, in a tug-of-war between two desperate mandates. His eyes darted back and forth as he considered what to do. The danger to Alexander was not exaggerated, not while he wandered unguarded through the countryside. There were any number of ambitious barons who might seize the opportunity. Beolin Crymlyn would crush the boy's skull as soon as look at him, were he to find him riding the wilderness alone. That was the reason for the expedient search for a bride. Until Alexander was married, with his own healthy child suckling robustly at the breast, claws of many colors would be scratching at his crown. The terror of the moment was duly warranted.

A hand rested gently on Lindsay's shoulder from behind, followed by the nurturing calmness of Vanora's maternal voice, "Go, find our boy. Leave your dear Margaret to me."

Until that very second, he never truly understood what it meant to trust. His faith in the little woman behind him was unreserved.

He turned to her and said, "My family and my home are in your hands."

She responded, "And my son is in yours."

The priest began a half-witted protest, but Lindsay cut it well short of completion, asking him graciously, "Please, return to your church and light a candle for my wife and for your King. My household is not in need of you right now."

The priest began one last objection, "But that woman —"

Lindsay shouted, "That woman is the master of this house and the chief of my family until I return and relieve her of that duty."

He softened and continued, "There is much you can do for us from within the church, services only you can provide. Please, light the candles and pray."

The words had softened, but he spoke them with an arm extended down the hall and a finger pointing to the door. With equal portions of indignation and obedience, the priest left the house with the two friars clinging to his hips.

Lindsay turned back into the room and saw Vanora already recommitted to her charge. She sat on the bed beside Margaret and, with one hand on the fiery forehead, she hummed. Lindsay sat beside her. With one hand, he held his wife's shoulder. The other held the back of Vanora's neck.

Vanora's hum rose in volume and lowered in pitch, then transitioned into a chant in these words,

Darkness be dim
And fade from our sight,
You are as weak as a whisper
And healed by the light

Release what is not
And mute what is foul,
I see through your veil
With the eyes of an owl

I reach to your depths
With hands unafraid
And take hold of this woman
The heavens have made

Sleep now my child
And dream of the sun
And the green, rolling hills
Where the primroses run

The words and the tone coupled to untether Lindsay from his wife's bedside. He kissed the top of Vanora's head, then bent down to Margaret and placed his lips on her lips. He held there through a long inhale, as if trying to draw her into his heart through his nose. He withdrew with the subtle smack of a tender and devoted kiss, gave one squeeze of Vanora's shoulder that spoke a thousand words of faith and gratitude, then marched with determination to find his missing king.

Lindsay called to arms every one of his clansmen within the county. Search parties of four and five assembled and began hurried, unorganized, and haphazard, patternless rides that flew from Byres Castle like bees from a shaken hive. Lindsay was the head of a party of five, but in his panicked determination, he outrode them all. Before he knew it, he was alone, guided by nothing more than instinct.

When Alexander left the Edinburgh stable, he asked Sir Walter to take him to Lindsay. With the naivety of a child his age, he trusted the pony to do just that. With the crack of the reins, Sir Walter turned west. The cardinal directions meant nothing to the child. He could have been riding directly upward to the sky or downward into the earth. He hardly would have known the difference. Yet he did not feel lost. He looked to the sky and saw a flock of gulls. As he watched, their random flight patterns began to form into a circle of flawless symmetry.

"Lady Margaret," he declared to his pony, "They must be circling Lady Margaret."

He spurred Sir Walter forward, toward the circle of gulls, until his view of them was obscured by thickening branches. He had entered a dense patch of forest south of Linlithgow Castle, and with the distance obstructed by a cruel collaboration between the thickening trees and the darkening sky, the boy began to despair. When his surroundings blackened entirely, he felt caged, afraid, and helpless. With shallow, quickening breaths, he dismounted Sir Walter. When the pony laid in a narrow space between trees, Alexander curled against him and cried himself to sleep.

Waking fears and horrid dreams wove together into a terrible mental tapestry, as poor Alexander dipped and rose in and out of restless sleep. Stiff-legged and miserable, he awoke in the morning to the heavily filtered sunlight that managed to slither beneath the forest canopy. His fear for his own safety was real, but it shared only half of his troubled mind. He still worried for his friend and teacher. His love for Lindsay and his desperation to help him slammed in competition against his own peril, making a bloody battlefield of the child's heart.

Sir Walter stood and huffed, apparently ready to continue to God-knows-what destination the beast had in mind. Alexander lost faith in his four-legged navigator, and he held the reins in place. The trees around him, which had felt like the bars of a cage during the dark night, gave the secure comfort of protection, and he hid behind them from the world beyond. For hours he stood with the reins in his hand, alternating between heavy sobs and meandering thoughts on countless topics, thoughts that were as lost of direction as he was.

Without eating, drinking, or sitting, Alexander remained as he was until dusk. When the dark of another night began pushing the day into the dirt beneath him, Alexander's despair hit its zenith. He chose a direction without contemplation, and pulled Sir Walter forward, desperate to get free of the wooded tomb that had encased him all day. Sir Walter was reluctant, and he pulled with much greater strength against the child's paltry force. Alexander screamed at the horse, then screamed even louder to the sky, to the gulls that had led him there, scolding them, and begging for their guidance, sending a shrill beacon echoing off the tree trunks, reaching innocently and dangerously toward any passing ears.

His scream was hushed by the sound of clopping hooves, which seemed to speed as his yelling stopped. A wave of chills ran across him. He was an intelligent boy. Many times he had heard the whispered warnings of treachery that were not meant for his ears, and as the approaching hooves grew louder, he cursed his own voice. He would have cowered behind a tree if it would have done him any good. But the King's fat pony was well-known and could not be shoved into a pocket and snuck away. Alexander held firmly to the reins like a sweating statue.

Sir Walter seemed eager for the company, and he neighed and huffed in jubilation, declaring their location. The steely silhouette of a manly figure dismounted his horse and drew his sword. Alexander's fear turned instantly to elation, for he would have known that fatherly figure in half the light. It was David Lindsay.

Alexander began a gleeful greeting, but Lindsay stopped him, "Shush! Not a word!"

The command carried weight. The King, the two horses, even the breeze, obeyed him. In the silence of the following minute, Lindsay turned his keen ears right and left, up and down, in random patterns, trying to pick up any sound around them that might indicate they were not alone. Once satisfied, he relaxed his posture, sheathed his sword, and gave Alexander an embrace befitting such a reunion. When he released his student from his arms, he did not scold. He did not interrogate. He handed Alexander a flask of water and instructed him to drink.

While Alexander poured the water ravenously down his throat, Lindsay removed his horse's saddle and laid the saddle blanket on the ground. He gestured for Alexander to take a seat.

"Shouldn't we be leaving this place?" the boy asked.

"The dark is ideal for an ambush," he instructed calmly, as if safe in a classroom, "I can guard you better *here* until morning."

Lindsay gave him a pouch with dried meats. Alexander sat and ate, then laid and slept, while Lindsay stood firm at his wooded sentry post until the shattered rays of another morning weakly lit the forest floor. When the time was right, Lindsay woke Alexander from a deep sleep and led him, on foot, southeast out of the forest, away from the uncertainty of Linlithgow Castle. Once clear of the woods and under the bright but gray sky of a cloudy morning, they mounted their horses and rode toward Byres Castle.

They were not led one by the other, like a teacher and student or a king and subject, but side by side, like old comrades returning home from a shared adventure. They rode without conversation for several minutes, until Alexander finally blurted, "Your wife!"

"Vanora is with her," was all he responded.

Nothing more needed to be said, not to Alexander, who sighed deeply at the news. From that point, they spoke of light topics. Alexander asked to see the new Lindsay Sword, recently forged. Lindsay showed it as he told stories of the battles he had commanded. Alexander received them with enraptured attention. They rode with urgency, but not desperation.

As they passed south of Edinburgh, Alexander asked, "Aren't you taking me home?"

"Do you want to go home? I rather thought you would like to come home with me, to be with Vanora."

Alexander smiled his consent, and the two rode quietly together until they reached the Lindsay estate. Once in the castle, Lindsay wasted no time sending servants in each cardinal direction to inform his clansmen that the King had been found. He sent his faster rider to Edinburgh, to relieve Durward and Baliol and the many concerned members of the King's court.

Having concluded all business in the matter of the missing child, he returned his full heart to Margaret. With a thundering pulse that knocked against his veins with increasing force at every step, he walked to the bedroom. He entered a scene both strange and delightful. Margaret was sitting up in bed. Her eyes were as wide as her smile. Her complexion was rosy and seemed to put off a light of its own. Vanora stared at him for some indication of

Alexander's condition. He relieved her with a simple wink and smile.

There was a pungent aroma in the room, which would have been unpleasant had it not been so peculiar. It wafted from a steaming mug on the bedside table. Lindsay looked at it and winced.

Margaret told him in a voice still weakened and in recovery, "It is a tea of sorts, something Vanora made me from roots and herbs."

Lindsay bent toward it to take an exploratory sniff. Vanora, from her chair beside the bed, could see Alexander peeking through the door.

"My child!" she screamed.

Lindsay stood tall and turned to him, inviting, "It is all right. Come in and see."

Alexander took two tentative steps into the room, glancing curiously at Margaret, then he turned his arms and his legs to Vanora. He leaped at her and wrapped his gangly, adolescent arms lovingly around her neck. Oh, what a reunion it was. Old Scotland had never seen such a warm and joyous room. David kissed his wife repeatedly, creating a concerted rhythm with the furious kisses Vanora laid on Alexander's head. William entered, ran to Alexander, pushed the back of his head teasingly, then patted him on the back.

By the following morning, a royal entourage of soldiers, scholars, and clerics arrived at Byres Castle to take the King back to Edinburgh. With the authority of his crown, Alexander sent them away. Where Vanora was, where Lindsay and William were, was home, and he would be nowhere else. Durward and Baliol tolerated the King's wishes for one week. In their misguided imaginations, they visualized intense schooling in the Lindsay courtyard and library. No such thing occurred. In that week, Byres Castle was the home of a family, not the school of a monarch.

By the end of that week, Margaret was on her feet, not simply on her feet, but with a fine swinging step and lively rocking hips. The Lady of Byres Castle was in full vigor. There was a crispness in her voice and a keenness in her eyes, as if much more than the recent illness had been removed from her. It was in part, no doubt, from gratitude, after having so nearly brushed the grave.

But there was something else, something neither she nor her husband fully understood. A new brand of vivacious power was instilled in Margaret during those late night nursing sessions. The roots, the herbs, the songs and prayers, the compassionate touch of an affectionate hand — these were not the only things Vanora had brought to the sick woman's bedside. Through some method, either intentional or not, she endowed Margaret with an old, feminine strength, the same strength that pulsed through *her* with every beat of her heart. Margaret was not only recovered, she was reborn — a newly radiant form of the same wonderful woman.

Margaret was not the only one affected. David Lindsay's recently inflamed passions swelled further. His wife's hand was almost constantly in his. His lips pressed to her head, cheek, or lips with every third breath he drew. The image shone on Alexander with an unfamiliar light. In Lindsay's home, in the week after Margaret's recovery, the young King discovered a new definition of marriage, one entirely absent from his earliest years.

At the end of the week, impatient in his faithfulness, the ever-dutiful Durward arrived at Byres Castle with six Royal Guards. He insisted that Alexander return with him, return to his lessons, to the neglected affairs of state, and to the safety of Edinburgh. Vanora nodded her consent and expressed her intention to join them, leaving the Lindsays in the intimate peace of their immediate family.

Before she left the castle, she pointed to David and Margaret, and whispered in Alexander's ear, "That, my son, is a husband. Take a long look and remember what a husband looks like."

Durward led the procession back, with six mounted soldiers trailing formally behind him like the train of a wedding dress. Alexander and Vanora took up the rear. Their moods contrasted comically against the others. They rode back to Edinburgh under a much happier sky than the one that had escorted them away. Their hearts were united in all matters but one. Alexander did not know his wedding was being plotted, and Vanora had a ponderous decision to make.

Lindsay remained at home for another four days. On his last morning at home, he walked into his garden and found Margaret kneeling in a flower bed, toiling away. Never had normalcy been such a delight to him. As he walked toward her, he noticed her singing. He stopped his approach and listened to the words dance gracefully with the melody,

Let the ocean sing its song
While the gulls form a ring
As the stars fill your heart
And Luna starts to sing

Let her voice heal your heart
Telling darkness to comply
For she is our light
Our healer in the sky

Receive all that she gives
With her soft silvery light
You are now of truth
For you share the Heaven's sight

David kneeled beside her and asked, "What is that song?"

"I'm not sure. I believe Vanora must have sung it to me. It is the first thing I remember thinking about when I came out of my fever, and it has stayed with me since."

It was a mystery, but one they were both content to leave mysterious. They went inside, cleaned up, and savored each other's intimate company before David left for Edinburgh. He kissed his vibrant wife and left his home in her capable hands. He returned to Edinburgh in the late morning, while Alexander was in lessons with Baliol. He went directly to Vanora's room to thank her for the great service she had provided to his wife.

The moment he made eye contact with her, she said, "Margaret."

"Oh, she is quite well, my dear friend. You made well certain of that."

"No, no," she corrected, "Margaret of England."

"Margaret of England?"

"Come now, Sir David, you don't think I will have forgotten my duty, or Baliol's list. I have decided. Our boy will marry Princess Margaret of England, King Henry's daughter."

The matter had been violently pushed from Lindsay's thoughts, and its return fell on him rather heavily. He stuttered, "Margaret.. Yes, King Henry.. Yes, yes, I agree. They are close in age. Politically, it is the perfect match."

"To Hell with all that," she scoffed, "Margaret is a warm, gentle, but strong and faithful girl. They will be very good for each other."

Lindsay had one foot in each of two extremely different worlds. He was the primary regent for the King of Scotland, but he was also a doting father and family man. After a lifetime embedded firmly in the affairs of state, Vanora had dislodged him with a soft but firm hand, and pulled him into the realm of the heart. Vanora's decision suited both of those realms. Margaret of England would soon be a royal bride of Scotland.

With parents at his side
And illness has withdrawn
He wonders what is to come
With a new and brighter dawn

Chapter Eleven:

Cherish His Tears

A beautiful sky
Filled with gulls upon blue
Swaddles the nations
With the marriage of two

The rocking and rattling of the English Royal Carriage was a rugged serenade to the wild dreams of Margaret of England. She knew nothing of the country she was being married into, nothing of the Scottish King who would be her husband. She was eleven years old, on that strange and awkward bridge between girlhood and womanhood. Her mother had prepared her with all she needed to know. She was going to marry the Scottish King, to bear his children, to produce an heir that would bind the kingdoms in kinship.

The Scots! Her image of them and their country ravaged her dreams with coarse violence as her sleeping head bounced on the inside wall of the carriage with every rock on the frozen rustic road. She dreamed of the husband she had imagined when she was awake, the one described to her by ladies-in-waiting back in London — of an old, gray-bearded, hairy, smelly Scotsman, monstrously bulky, with a mug of provincial brew in one hand and a rusty ax in the other, ordering her into his bed in some language he shared with the wild animals.

When she awoke from her dreams and found herself still riding north, into colder and wilder lands, the truth was no pleasanter than the nightmares, so she believed. The wedding was set for Christmas Day, a day her memory had gilded with warm memories of lavish gifts, indulgent meals, and parental affection. How very different this Christmas would be! Try as she might, she could not place a leash on her savage imagination — Christmas night in the bed of a Scotch warrior-king!

She had an academic understanding of her wedding night with the kilted troll she imagined. She knew just enough to terrify her. She would do her duty. She had no choice, but traveling from Southern England into Yorkshire, where the wedding was to be held, she felt herself passing from her life into some hellish afterlife.

York was the halfway point between London and Edinburgh. It was an apt metaphor for the balanced equality of the marriage she would someday enjoy, but she could not have known that while she bounced around the carriage, driven from all she had ever known and loved.

York Castle was in her country. The fact made it no less foreign to her as she reached the bulky, gray gatehouse. They passed into the courtyard where the Scottish Royal Entourage waited. The carriage that carried her from London represented the last of her old life. Stepping out of it, into the courtyard, to meet her brutish troll of a husband was almost more than she could bear.

When they cleared the gatehouse, into the open courtyard, young Margaret was greeted by a scene of surprising delight. It was Christmas Eve, and the inner walls of the courtyard were lavishly decked in garlands and wreaths, and sprigs of berried branches. There was no hairy troll awaiting her, but a boy, as nervous and uncertain as she was frightened. He did not fear. How could he? He was squeezed against Vanora's side by the protective arm of a mother, and standing in the shadow of David Lindsay, while the three of them, and everyone else within the castle, waited to see the renowned beauty step into sight.

The moment Margaret's face came into view, Alexander knew her to be his bride. Margaret darted her eyes frantically across the courtyard, back and forth several times, trying to identify the beast that would drag her north to Scotland. There were no monsters in the courtyard, no hairy warriors with mug and ax. There were well-groomed Scottish nobles, clerics in their robes, and well-pruned servants. Margaret's mother led her to a tight cluster of handsome people. Durward, Baliol, Lindsay, and Vanora stood framing Alexander from behind.

"My love," the English Queen told her daughter, "this young man is your groom."

Lindsay stepped forward, bowed low and reverently to the English Queen and Princess, rose from his bow, and introduced his sovereign, "Your Highness, may I please introduce you to King Alexander III of Alba, King of the Scots."

Alexander was thoroughly besotted at the very first glance. He did not respond. There was no formal bow of his gangly, adolescent figure. He simply smiled widely through a deeply reddening face. Margaret was indeed a remarkably beautiful child. Her fear and nervousness had turned her face ruddy. The relief in seeing her wild Scottish brute transformed into an innocent, doe-eyed, tender little boy, right in front of her face, lit her ruddy complexion aglow. Oh, she was a radiant sight, an angelic vision of royal feminine beauty, as if she had been dipped in a sunrise and still sparkled with the radiance of that unreachable heavenly treasure.

The Scottish entourage bowed in unison. When she rose from her bow, Vanora leaned forward and whispered into Margaret's ear,

This is your groom
This boy on my arm
Cherish his tears
But do not alarm
He sees your beauty
For I do as well
Love will be plentiful
Of this, I can tell

Vanora pulled away from her with a slightly lifted grin and a subtle wink. There was such a flow of nurturing warmth in the verses she whispered, that Margaret's blushing sparkle began to put off a soft warmth that heated the frozen December courtyard, or so it seemed to those nearest to her. Vanora's words completed Margaret's transition from a nightmare to a blissful dream that she embraced with her body and soul.

The connection between Alexander and Margaret was intense, instant, and obvious to all who witnessed their introduction.

Lindsay leaned into Vanora and admitted, "Again, you were right. These children *will* be very good for each other."

It would be an exaggeration to say that Alexander was in love. He was ten, and his notions of romantic love were not yet those of a man. But it would fall far short of the profound truth to say he was merely drawn to her beauty. There was a sudden and strong, almost tyrannical, spiritual grip on him the moment he saw her face, as if destiny herself wrapped her finger around him, pointed him in Margaret's direction, and tethered her to him with some invisible ribbon connected to his innermost self.

The keep of the castle had recently been renovated into a royal suite. The English entourage settled there, while the Scottish King and his countrymen settled into the lower quarters. When Alexander was pulled from his fiancé and taken to his room, that ribbon was pulled taut, and the strain on his spirit was severe.

For the next few hours, he asked almost constantly, "Where is Margaret? What is she doing? When can I see her?"

It would have both pleased and relieved him to know that she felt similarly and asked similar questions. She had known love. She had known care and kindness. But she had never seen a face so gentle, so innocent, and so eager to adore her. His brief company in the courtyard stirred in her feelings she had not yet known. Not yet a woman's desire, but more than a child's fascination.

The dull hours of the afternoon were finally broken by the arrival of King Henry. Margaret's father, King Henry III of England, did not travel from London with his daughter. He had been in Flanders and arrived in his own country by ship, landing in Hull and proceeding under heavy guard from there. Upon his arrival, even the sleepy stones of the castle were awakened to full vigor by the blast of the horns and the march of the grand procession. Henry was a good King and a much better father. He would pursue none of the formal reverences due to him until he first checked on his daughter, saw to her spirits, and emboldened her with his paternal affection. Only after that paramount effort was complete did he greet Alexander and his regents.

The sun set shortly afterward, and large tables were set outside of the castle gates and lit warmly by dozens of torches. King Henry and the Archbishop of York stood side-by-side, overseeing the efforts. A horde of tattered revelers in poor, dirty, worn out clothes, rounded the castle wall, raising an uproarious clamor. Lindsay and

Durward grabbed Alexander, fearing they were under attack, but calmed when they saw no fear in King Henry or the Archbishop.

Baliol was well-versed in every tradition on their grand old island. He took Alexander by the hand and whispered to him, "Watch this. Watch this and learn."

The raucous crowd settled calmly at the tables. They chanted in unison, "Bring us meat. Bring us bread. Bring us drink."

The demands were not threatening, but jovial, more sung than shouted. The air was cold, but did not bite at the skin. It was fought and soundly defeated by the high spirits of the Christmas revelers. The Archbishop raised his hand, and robed clerics hustled from within the castle walls, pushing carts filled with lavish food, food fit more for the royalty within the castle than the rabble without. When the carts were in place, Henry and the Archbishop each took a loaf of bread and ceremoniously served it to a rugged serf at the table.

Baliol repeated to Alexander, "Watch this. This is a tradition that speaks to what a king really is, what he must be."

After the King and Archbishop delivered the bread, they backed away and returned to the nobles that stood in attendance. The clerics that had brought the carts continued what the King had started. They served the poor industriously, breaking heavy sweats in the cold night air.

Alexander's face was lit by the glow of dirty, lowly people receiving such royal treatment. He turned his head to his left and saw Margaret. Her substantial smile betrayed her delight in the scene before her. Acting on instinct alone, Alexander broke from his regents and ran to her. He took her by the hand and pulled her forward to the carts of food. There was no need to instruct her. They were of the same mind. Simultaneously, they loaded their arms with food and, side-by-side, they served the poor of Yorkshire on Christmas Eve.

The two children worked like mules, pushing themselves beyond their natural limits, powered deeply within by the spirit of the sacred day and the authentic gratitude of the region's poor. They were observed. Oh, they were closely observed. King, Bishop, barons, and regents, guards and soldiers on both sides watched in delighted astonishment, as the betrothed youths embraced the tradition and all it stood for. The wedding was the following day, but it would be safe to say that the children were tied to each other that evening, under the orange glow of torches, in the aroma of the feast they served together.

Margaret Lindsay could not attend the wedding in York. She was again away from her husband on the sacred holiday. After the feast of the poor, David sequestered himself behind the thick, dark stone of his chamber in the castle, and he wrote to his dear wife,

My Precious Lover,

The eve of our Lord's birth brought me much to move my spirits. Our King's bride is everything we prayed for in a Queen. The children are very similar. Their hearts were united in charity, as I watched them feed the poor of Yorkshire, toiling like servants in the open night air.

I tell you, my love, what I witnessed tonight is the perfect prelude to a royal marriage. Vanora was right. They will be good for each other and good for Scotland. I see in them a new kind of King and a new kind of Queen, the likes of which have never been seen in our country or any other.

This child King of ours is altering me, much more, I believe, than I am altering him. The evening sent my mind to spin, but of all the thoughts it evoked, love dominated, my love, my love for you. I am filled with such duality of spirit — resentful of our separation, yet brimming with gratitude for my most precious possession. It is you, my dear wife, always my dearest, as I remain eternally,

Most Faithfully Your Husband,

David Lindsay

Christmas morning was particularly bright and warm, or so it seemed, as the region still basked in the benevolence of the previous evening and the anticipation of the royal wedding. The most regal procession was formed to carry the betrothed children from the castle to York Minster Cathedral. It had all of the pomp and circumstance of two kingdoms being united in marriage. English horns and Scottish pipes found kinship in their unlikely pairing, just as an English princess and a Scottish king found it in theirs.

Riding at the head of the procession, on a pristinely white horse in gilded dress, was the Archbishop. A train of clergy in their Christmas vestments walked in solemn prayer behind him. King Henry rode behind them on his magnificent stallion. Princess Margaret and her mother followed in a stately carriage. The Scottish took up the rear. Alexander sat alone in a carriage, but a few yards from the castle, while the procession was in motion, he climbed from the carriage and stood on the coach seat, beside the driver, straining his eyes forward to catch any glimpse of his beautiful bride.

"Your Majesty," the coachman warned, "It is bad luck to see her before we arrive in the church."

Alexander was deaf to superstition. The despotic demand of his heart brushed the warning aside, and that is how he traversed the distance, perched like an eagle atop the coach seat, straining his young eyes for a glimpse of a shoulder, for a sight of that auburn hair, for that face that had so thoroughly spellbound him at first glance.

The cathedral was magnificently decked for the holiday. It seemed that every candle in England was lit inside and stood in blazing eagerness for the grand event.

Once all were settled, they began Christmas Mass. Monks from the nearby monastery chanted Christmas hymns. In the large cathedral, their voices seemed rather to descend from heaven than billow from the altar. With all of the splendid decorations, the vast arches of the cathedral, and the echoing hymns of the monks, Alexander's attention had only two masters — his radiant bride in full blush, and the old man, the very same from his bedroom in Holyrood Abbey, the one from his coronation, who gave him the stones he still kept in his pocket.

At the conclusion of the mass, Alexander and Margaret were brought forward. From the very back seat, they could both be seen shaking. Such an excess of swirling fears and excitements could not be contained within their small frames. Neither quite understood what was expected of them as husband and as wife. But they both found calmness at each other's side, for whatever would become of them, it would come to them both, together.

A sudden hush came over the murmuring attendants. The Bishop began administering the vows. He began with Margaret, who responded on cue with, "I will and I shall."

To the shock of most, the dismay of a few robed clergy, but the delight of Vanora and the old man, Alexander interrupted the Bishop, and blurted loudly in a raw, impromptu, but vivacious effusion from his swelling heart,

As long as the sun rises and the stars shine above
You are my partner to have and to love

Through joy and sorrow, through comfort and pain
My love for you will always remain

Please take my hand as I hold to you
I am now yours and you are mine too

Princess Margaret was also in shock as the interruption began, but by the time Alexander ended his spontaneous vows, everything else, everybody else in the world had disappeared. He alone stood near her and he alone mattered. Her blush reddened further, and glossed like polished porcelain under the flow of her tears. With his final word, this husband of hers had completed quite a journey, from troll to sweet boy, and now to the noblest of young men, whose poetic words, though belted through a child's voice, bore the ageless dignity of love.

With his long-scripted formula demolished by the interruption, the Bishop did not quite know what to do next. He placed a hand on each of their heads and blessed the marriage with a mumbled prayer, then raised his hands high and introduced to the Heavens and all in attendance the groom and the bride — King Alexander III and Queen Margaret of Scotland.

The procession returned to York Castle much as it had left, but with one obvious exception. The Scottish royal carriage, rustic in comparison beside its English counterpart, led the splendid caravan. Its passengers were a young king and queen. Such was the notion of all that surrounded it. Inside the carriage was a very different truth. They were a boy and a girl, two children just beginning to open their eyes to the delights of love, drawn to each other's similar hearts. It was first and foremost a friendship in that wooden carriage, a new friendship that felt eternally in place, with the excitement of newness alloyed strangely with the comfort of long-hardened affection.

By the time they dismounted and walked hand-in-hand into the castle, they felt as old friends recently reunited. They were both mostly blind to the glamour of the celebration. Only two things were vibrantly in their senses — the sight of the other's smiling face and the feel of the other's tightly held hand.

A gluttonous feast was served, like a Christmas dinner and wedding feast were brought consecutively. When the remnants were removed and the tables were cleared away, music and dancing followed. As the festivities wound down, Durward approached the King.

"Your Majesty," he began softly, "The evening has been about you and your bride. Tonight is about your country. You have a duty to perform."

Lindsay was nearby. He interrupted, "Sir Alan, I know what you would say, what you would have them do. But think of this first. Tonight we have taken a large step in securing the dynasty. Is that not enough for now?"

Durward turned his eyes sharply to Lindsay and said, "You see the eyes of the barons. They look for the strength of the crown, and they look for the weaknesses."

Lindsay began a rebuttal, "The people—"

"The people look where the barons look. Many of them have strong, grown sons, continuity to their lines. Until our king has that..."

"Look around you, Alan," Lindsay replied in protest, "We have the most powerful families in Scotland and England. We have the Church. You are the King's Durward, the Hostarius of the Crown. Are you not enough?"

Durward was offended, and he did nothing to hide it in his scowling expression as he answered, "I am the keeper of the King's property, first among which is his crown. Are you questioning my loyalty?"

"Oh no, Sir Alan. You are the faithful Usher. Your loyalty is beyond reproach. I question your sanity."

Vanora heard the men arguing and pieced together the gist of the confrontation. She stepped gracefully to them and interfered, "My Lords, there is merit to both of your arguments, but Sir David is right. You cannot make a dynasty until you have made a king, and you cannot make a king until you have made a man. Look at them. Neither is ready for what you demand."

They had all but forgotten about the young bride and groom, who stood staring at the argument, still hand-in-hand. While their night and their future was being debated, one thing was evident as they stood shoulder to shoulder, each gripping tightly to the other. Whatever they were forced to do or not do, they were prepared to go through it together.

Durward gave a fleeting glance to the children, but turned from them back to Vanora, and he began, "Dear woman, it would be wise of you to..."

He bit his tongue, for just as his loyalty was beyond reproach, so was *her* wisdom. The fiercely defensive face of Lindsay put a sudden halt to Durward's line of thought.

He turned his eyes from Vanora to the Bishop. "Your Grace," he implored, "surely you must see what I see."

The Bishop, looking down on the innocent and united children, answered, "The Church understands the expediency of the wedding, but I tell you, the Pope would never condone the consummation of this marriage until the children are of age."

The voice of the Church was final, and the tightly clustered debate broke up and disbanded among the other guests. Alexander and Margaret took the high throne at the head of the room, and the noble guests took their turns bowing and blessing the newlyweds.

In a reflection of the coronation, the old man came last. Alexander and Margaret stood from their thrones and held hands. The mysterious sage took their free hands in his, leaned forward, and spoke his blessing in a gruff whisper,

Children of light, bringing warmth to the cold
Shine forth with your joy, let it ring bold

Follow your hearts and give shelter to all
To the ship, be the hull
To the head, be the skull
To the beach, be the gull
With the primeval call

He turned from them and walked away. As he diminished from their view, the newlyweds pondered the words deeply, while each subconsciously rubbed the other's hand with their thumbs.

The old man walked into the courtyard and through the gatehouse. He looked up to the swirling gulls. They danced in the cool sky, in celebration of the day. The wrinkled old sage smiled at his swirling friends, and spoke aloud,

Thank you my friends
For sharing the skies
Allowing my thoughts
To see with your eyes

Show me his soul
So I freely can see
This pathway of light
To the King's destiny

Part One Epilogue

The old storyteller, the seanchai, stood tall and lean, his eyes wide and his posture erect. With the final line of verse, he released a long exhale, and with it, all tension in his muscular figure. He slouched before his captivated audience, looking much more like an old man. He stared at the sand between his feet. The people of Kinghorn froze in anticipation of his next words, of a continuation of the story. Even the flame of the dwindling fire seemed to hold still, as if painted onto canvas.

He did not continue the story, but humbly requested lodging for the night. Many rooms were offered — the best rooms in the best houses. He accepted the humblest room in the tiniest house. As he followed his host away from the gathering, the rest of the town sat spellbound and dumbfounded. They had expected knowledge. They had expected history. They were unprepared for the swell of emotion that accompanied the story of Alexander III, and they knew there was much more to be told.

Before he left the beach, the seanchai turned and saw the townspeople frozen in contemplation. He took one step toward them, drawing their attention back to him, and he told them,

We are all but one
As many can see
We share one thought
To love and be free

Take these words
I have shared tonight
To follow the gulls
And learn of their flight

Come back after dawn
With your minds prepared
And I will continue
This story I've shared

The boy becomes man
Amid mystery
Through faith and fear
And great treachery

Part Two:

Bug-Bane and Heather

Prologue

In obedience to the seanchai's request, the people of Kinghorn returned to the beach after dawn, well, most of them. Many came before dawn, having awoken before the sun with images of Alexander, Vanora, Lindsay, and even Sir Walter haunting their dreams. They came to the remnants of the previous night's fire, starving for the rest of the story.

The sun was fully risen and the old man was still not among them. With little conversation to pass the time, they stared toward the town, twitching at every movement to catch their eyes, from the sway of reeds in the wind to the passing of a bird.

At last, the family who lodged the seanchai arrived at the beach. The old man was not with them. They had not seen him all morning. Servants were sent back to town to fetch food and drink from the many households in attendance. There was no sense of propriety among them, not as they gathered on the beach. They were united by the story, unified into a single family by the storyteller and their shared national history.

By the time the feast was set, it was nearly midday. From along the north side of the beach came the sound of the gulls, flocked more like birds in migration than the scavengers of the coast. In equal step beneath them was the old man. He joined those gathered and shared in their feast. The gulls that had escorted him did not fly away, nor did they circle above. They landed among the townspeople in full expectation of being fed. These scavengers were not seen as a nuisance, not by the people of Kinghorn, not after all they had heard the night before. The squawking flock was treated as honored guests and fed by each hand in attendance.

The meal was not all about the food or the drink. They were impatient for a different sort of sustenance, for any slight morsel of the story to come. When they prodded the sage for a hint, he replied only with nods and smiles. When the feast was cleared away, the people gathered in a semi-circle around the ashes of the bonfire, staring silently, yet screaming with their gestures and leaning forward with pleading faces.

The seanchai let out a long sigh, drew his next breath, and released it into the salty wind, saying,

I thank you all
For your presence here
My friends have come
To join in the cheer

It is they who keep
This story I share
And asked me kindly
To pass it with care

This cliff above us
And the trees by its side
Are all included
As well as the tide
So let us begin
With our eyes opened wide
And learn what becomes
Of the King and his bride

Chapter Twelve:

Shouts from the Skye

As the chapel cleared
And the clans stood by
A message was shown
From the Isle of Skye

Riding to York with her mother, Princess Margaret dreaded Scotland. After meeting her young husband and all who accompanied him, she could not wait to ride north to her new home. A five day stay in York was planned, then a royal procession of the newlyweds that mimicked Alexander's travels after his coronation.

Alexander and Margaret had bonded instantly, and by the day after the wedding, they did not want to part from each other. They could not be alone together without a chaperon. This role was filled in rotation between the King's regents. It was a far cry from their normal routines. They did not teach, nor did they study. They simply sat and watched as the children talked.

On the third day after the wedding, Lindsay sat in the highest chamber of York Castle, while the giggling whispers of his King and Queen rolled half-noticed around his ears. His mind was adrift through romantic memories of his own wedding, and of all the moments since that had stitched his own dear wife so tightly to his soul.

131

The children were playing a game. It was Margaret's favorite and had been presented to her by her father as a wedding present. A large tapestry rolled out flat on the floor. It was a map, with castles and forests, dungeons and caves, dragons, wizards, and every sort of misadventure upon it. The object of the game was to roll your marbles safely from point to point across the map, avoiding the dangers, battling the marbles of your opponent, and arriving safely on the other side with the most marbles still in play.

Lindsay was lulled into an imaginative trance by the clicks of the marbles against each other and the friendly banter of the two young competitors. As he sat at the window, staring into oblivion, his mind was snapped back to the moment by the sight of Vanora in the courtyard below, speaking with flamboyant gestures to the same cloaked man from the coronation and wedding.

He could hear nothing being said between them, but the language of their bodies spoke loudly. Something was wrong! Lindsay abandoned his post and ran down to the courtyard. As he reached the final corner, and daylight filled his eyes, he was halted by strange words in a deep and gruff voice.

The old man continued,

Thoir leat e
Gus bleed agus ionnsachadh
Airson claidheamh na fala
Is e sin a dh'fheumas e a chosnadh

Lindsay remained around the corner, out of view of Vanora and the old man. He listened as they held hands and chanted together,

Hear the gulls

Shouting down from the sky
Scáthach demands
Her knight to comply

The Sword of the Picts
Waiting under the Isle
Will give him the force
To conquer the vile

Hold the Firbolg
With the weight of the slain
For the sword of Dún Scáith
Will defeat evil's reign

Lindsay watched in stealth as the mysterious sage walked away. Vanora returned to the castle and found Lindsay dumbfounded in the hallway. He stammered, "That man... he's the one... those words. I did not understand all of them."

Vanora placed a hand on his shoulder and calmed him with a quiet "Shhhh", soothing him enough to gather his wits and ask, "Something is wrong. I could see that clearly. What is it? What did he tell you? What is it you know about our King?"

Vanora translated the old man's message into verse he could understand,

The storm is near! The gulls have warned
The clouds are moving
And fortune behooving
The one who is quietly, wretchedly scorned

Bring her the man the gulls hailed with a cry
Fly to the castle
Escort the vassal

To the mystical matron on the Isle of Skye

She is the keeper of the ancient blood sword
Now the regent must bleed
If we hope to succeed
The Mistress of Shadows must grant his reward

The danger is present, a sinister dread
To keep the unseen
From the King and the Queen
The Swan must carry the weight of the dead

Lindsay let out a sharp sigh and asked, "So our King is in danger…, and the answer is on the Isle of Skye? But his parents cannot help him. His father is dead and his mother has returned to France."

"Oh David," she answered, "those are not his parents. They never really were. It is you, my dear man, you and I."

"The Swan," he recited from the last line, "the emblem of my family. So we must go to the Isle of Skye. What waits for us there? The Norwegians are there. It is their island. How can it help protect our King…, our son? I heard something about Dún Scáith , about the Picts and a sword. Please Vanora, tell me what you know."

"We will have plenty of time to talk while we travel. For now, there are two children at play together. Return to your post and I will make the arrangements for our journey."

With many more questions than answers, Lindsay obeyed and dragged his troubled mind back to the game of marbles and the two innocent children. When he entered the room and saw Alexander and Margaret still at play, his urge to act on their behalf grew desperate. There was a stark contrast between the light hearts at play and the one brooding on the chair by the window. Their giggles were accompanied by the grinding of Lindsay's teeth.

When the game was finished, and the children separated for the day, Lindsay sought Vanora. She was not in the castle. She was not in York. True to her word, she was securing all provisions needed for the strenuous journey to the Isle of Skye. Lindsay was surprised how the thought eased his mind. He could not have explained his trust in her to anyone who did not share it. He had no idea what the following weeks would bring him. But he praised God that night that Vanora would be at his side.

The following morning, the Scottish entourage was preparing to return to Edinburgh. Vanora was still gone, and there were too many more questions than answers. How could he explain to them or to their English hosts that nothing could be done until the King's childhood nursemaid returned. He made no excuses and gave no explanations, but simply declared that they could not yet depart. The word of David Lindsay carried just enough weight to secure obedience.

For Alexander and Margaret, the following day went much like the previous. They talked and played with little mind for anything but the warm and delightful company of the other. Lindsay's anxiety rose in steady, hourly increments, until finally, just before the sun set, Vanora returned.

She joined them at supper, and when the hall was cleared of all but the two of them, Lindsay told her, "I am ready. I will follow where you lead me, do as you command me. We will leave for the Isle of Skye tonight."

"We will do no such thing," she answered with mock sternness, "I do not believe it is so very urgent. We will see our children to their beds, rest well tonight, and in the morning, you will go home."

"Home?" he asked in surprise, "to Byres Castle?"

"Yes…, to your wife and eldest son. Spend a day there, then meet me in Edinburgh, where you can give your love to William before we set out."

The thought of holding his wife under his own roof took much of the jagged edge off of his fears and uncertainty, enough for him to rest soundly and leave in the morning with greater confidence. Uncertain of what unknown dangers beckoned him so far away, he asked if Alexander and Margaret could stay in York until his return. It was agreed, and Durward and Baliol sent for all they would need to school the King in a foreign castle.

Lindsay rode in a frigid winter rain. It took him twenty hours of fierce riding in terrible conditions. He stopped for a few hours in Blyth, then followed the coast to Dunbar, where the weather cleared. By the time he entered his own estate, the air had turned quite warm, enough for him to enjoy a day of leisure walks with his wife, followed by a night of intensely devoted passion.

Margaret was desperate for answers that were not David's to give, so little was spoken of the journey ahead. Of the countless separations the couple had suffered in their years of marriage, the one that took place the following morning stung most piercingly. It was the sharpened edge of uncertainty that cut them both so deeply. When he had gone into battle, she could envision him in battle, and form her prayers accordingly. She could not picture his journey ahead, nor the nature of the trials he would face. They would be separated by more than the miles between them. When David parted in the morning, it was a blind separation, and it pinched at Margaret cruelly.

Vanora poured her love on Alexander and his child bride before leaving for Edinburgh, telling them nothing to trouble their minds or sour the infancy of their marriage with fear. She left quietly, with only a single Scottish soldier as escort. By the time she arrived in Edinburgh, all was ready for the journey, all but David Lindsay, who appeared the following day with fresh and vigorous determination.

Lindsay gathered a few of his clansmen to accompany them, but Vanora turned them away.

"This is a journey," she told him, "you and I must take alone. We cannot take a band of our countrymen and remain unseen by the Norse. And when we reach our destination, you must face her alone... all alone. I cannot be with you."

There was so much mystery swirling around the event that Lindsay's mind could not form a question. He simply clenched his jaw tightly, took a deep inhale through his nose, followed by a sharp exhale, mounted his exhausted horse, and trotted through the gate. Lindsay on his horse, Vanora on hers, and a beast of burden to carry their provisions, turned west alone, and rode toward the darkening sky of a threatening winter storm. Vanora was fueled by her trust in an ancient wisdom passed down to her from centuries beyond measure. Lindsay was driven by loyalty to his King and country, by gratitude for all that he held precious, and by a strengthening trust in the short, broad little woman riding beside him.

Lindsay was like an infant in Vanora's arms. He knew nothing of the details of their journey. He had never been to Skye or any of the Western Isles. He had never been so far from his home, but he knew enough of maps and legends to know there were many miles of wild, rugged country to travel. He held none of the logistics. All of that was in the hands of the little woman riding beside him.

He remembered her saying, "I will make the arrangements for our journey."

In the silence between conversations, he wondered at his own peace of mind, how the company of this woman could cradle his spirits like a mother.

They rode toward Stirling against a strong, bitterly cold wind, slowing them to a crawl. But the dark clouds covetously held their moisture. The travelers remained dry. It took six hours to arrive at Stirling Castle. The castle had long been a favored royal residence, and Lindsay had every reason to expect a warm welcome. In his mind, he composed and rehearsed a reason for his strange and surprise visit.

There was no need. Before she left York, Vanora dictated a letter to be written in the King's hand and marked with the Royal Seal. At the gate of Stirling Castle, she presented Lindsay with a letter from Alexander that would secure them royal lodgings at any castle along the way.

It simply read,

Sir David Lindsay and his companion travel

on Royal business. They act for the King and will

receive all Royal accommodations.

King Alexander III

Stirling obeyed. The castle was under Lindsay's command for the two hours they spent warming and refreshing themselves. They were provided fresh horses and resumed their journey under a warmer, clearing sky.

David rode tall
While haunted within
And Vanora beside him
With a confident grin

Chapter Thirteen:
This Air Where We Meet

She's here!
Declared the gulls above shore
The teacher of shadow
Our lady of lore

The voyage to the western coast provided little to distract Lindsay's thoughts from the mysteries that awaited him. He begged Vanora to fill the hours with all she knew about Dún Scáith, the Fortress of Shadows, and about the legendary Shadowed One, Scáthach. She told him a tale that would have offended his high logic two years earlier. But she was a very different woman in his eyes than the one he thought he knew when this story began. He received her tale with the innocent faith of a child.

With a voice broken by the hearty clops of the hooves beneath her, she instructed, "Before she was known as Scáthach, when the earliest people shared the land with those who came before, they called her the Warrior Maiden. She was brought to Skye from Ireland by the demigod, Cú Chulainn, the son of Lugh, to train him in the art of war. He built for her the castle Dún Scáith, where she has remained ever since, training the warriors who are chosen and sent to her."

"And you think I am one of those warriors?"

"Not I! I did not choose you, though I would have for the dangers ahead. No, no, *she* has chosen to teach you because you, and you alone, can serve her purpose. It is your hand that will be needed, your hand that will wield Firbolg."

"What is Firbolg?"

"It is a legendary sword, forged by the Picts in the fires beneath Skye. The task ahead of you must be difficult and important if she offers you Firbolg. But do not think she will hand it easily. Expect your time at Dún Scáith to be challenging."

That was all she taught him by the time they reached the cliffs of Glenelg. They camped near the cliff until sunrise. They abandoned their horses and all of their supplies, and scaled the cliffs to a small boat and the robed man that awaited them.

Lindsay began to bargain with the sailor, but there was no need. Vanora nodded. The man nodded back, stepped aside, and gestured for them to board. From the shore of Glenelg to the rocky edge of Skye was 1,500 feet, which the robed sailor traversed quickly with a single oar. Not a word was spoken between them. Lindsay and Vanora stepped from the boat, and no sooner were their feet firmly on the ground when the boat and its silent captain pushed away, turned north, and dwindled into the distance at an unnatural rate.

The hike to Dún Scáith took several strenuous hours. They were tired and they were hungry, but they reached the castle in the late afternoon, and the sight of their destination lightened them of all physical discomforts. The stone fortress sat on a high outcrop of rock off the shore. During low tide, it connected to the main island by a narrow path of earth. In high tide, only a precariously thin and worn stone bridge anchored it to Skye.

The tide was in when they arrived, and Vanora led Lindsay to the mouth of the bridge. She gestured toward the castle, and he took a few tentative steps onto the bridge. When he looked back to her, she had stepped away.

"I have not been called to her," she reminded him, "This encounter is for you alone."

He turned his attention back to the castle. It appeared as abandoned as the wilderness that led them there. There was no bustle of guards, no castle staff carrying things to and fro in their duties. The only things he perceived were the sounds of nature and the foreboding sense of dread that seemed to shout from the stones. If there was a legendary warrior in the castle, she kept no company and made no sounds.

Fear pushed Lindsay's faith beneath his reason, and he whispered to himself, "What am I doing here? Nobody could live so long."

With increasing frustration, he mumbled on, "There is nobody here, no Scáthach, nobody but the two fools who came here today."

His raspy words came from a tiny portion of his mind, a cynical little chamber he usually kept shut. But it opened its door on that bridge and commandeered his thoughts. That cynical chamber may have held his lips, but his faithful heart kept control of his legs, and he continued to walk gingerly across the bridge as the high towers of the fortress grew in perspective with each step.

Finally, his devotion to his King and country overwhelmed all doubt. He turned back to Vanora, but she was gone. He his eyes scanned quickly in all directions around him. She was nowhere to be seen. He called to her, but when she did not answer, his obedience to her swelled within him, and he took the several bold steps needed to finish crossing the bridge and stand at the decaying archway that led into the main chamber of the castle.

There was no doubt, it was long abandoned. A slender ray of sunlight shot through a hole in the chamber ceiling.

There were no furnishings, no heirlooms decorating the walls. Whatever had once filled the castle had long been plundered away or decayed to dust. What remained were lonely stones that spoke of a distant grandeur long-past.

Lindsay explored every forgotten room in the dreary old building, each adding more weight to his doubting heart. He returned to the main chamber and sat against the north wall.

He puckered his lips hard to one side, bit on the inside of his cheek, pressed a clenched fist tightly under his nose, and spoke loudly, "I have come to you as you have commanded. This is your castle, is it not, Shadow Woman? Your Dún Scáith? So where are you? I am tired. I am hungry, and I am in no mood to be toyed with."

His complaint went unanswered, and the wind and waves that rambled in jovial conversation with each other outside seemed to be mocking and taunting him. The sun did not remain as witness. It kept its course and time, diminishing its contribution to the fortress interior until the hole in the roof where it had stabbed through revealed a small cluster of brightening stars.

Those few stars did nothing to illuminate the room. Lindsay strained his eyes to make out the deep lines between the stones. There was nothing but darkness, as if he had been placed into a tightly latched trunk. His eyes yearned for anything to embrace, so he turned them upward, to that small hole and cluster of stars. He was more angry than frightened — but at whom — at some mythical legend who may or may not have been based on a real person long dead?

Still seated as he had been in the cold, dark chamber, he alternated between doubting the existence of Scáthach to cursing her for her tardiness. His thoughts went suddenly to Vanora, unaccompanied and God-knows-where on the dark and wild isle. He began to stand to go in search of her, but managed only a twitch before the tiny twinkling of those few stars disappeared and returned, as if a large hand had passed over the hole. It froze him in place, staring upward.

He released a long, slow sigh when the phenomenon repeated itself, and he knew it for what it was — a bird. A bird, or perhaps several, circled above the fortress, passing over the hole in staccato patterns. They announced themselves formally with a single squawk, which was echoed by another, then accompanied by many.

What began as a delicate song of gulls in dulcet concert with the sound of the waves, grew piercing and shrill. Louder and shriller it rose.

"There must be thousands of them!" Lindsay yelled, but not loudly enough to hear himself over the riotous scream from the sky.

The noise turned painful. He stood, buckled over, and cupped his ears with his hands. As he did, and the hovering chaos muted, it began to transition in tone, or so he imagined. It transformed slowly from the united squawk of a thousand gulls to a voice, a feminine, melodic voice, seeming to hum an ancient lullaby. He removed his hands from his ears, expecting a painful resurgence of noise, but the noise was gone, and the feminine song remained.

The song came from above him, from the circling birds, as if they had been possessed by a thousand angels sharing a single voice. No light came through the hole in the roof. The gulls formed a flying curtain that shut out the heavens. But in the complete darkness, David Lindsay felt like he faced the brightness of paradise. Such was the intoxicating effect of the song.

The voice seemed to descend, to saturate the fortress and echo from the deep cracks between each stone. It moved up and down mysterious scales, with notes that would have been incongruent with one another had they come from a less heavenly voice. The hummed melody began to take the form of syllables, of consonants and vowels that danced so comfortably with each other that they blended seamlessly. When those syllables became language he could understand, it chilled poor Lindsay to the bone.

"Scáthach?" he whispered timidly.

Echoing simultaneously from each stone in the fortress, the voice spoke,

This floor where you now stand
This air where we meet
Is not of this world
Or for worldly feet

You are of sun
Presented in time
To learn of the truth
And see the sublime

The council of gulls
Has carried me here
To show you the ways
Of facing this fear

You are the one
Chosen from love
To carry the sword
Of the lion and dove

As the echoes of the final verse died away, a striking realization settled on Sir David. Scáthach, the gulls, the Pictish ancestors of the island, Vanora, and the old man at the coronation — there was a strong connection between them. He could see that clearly, but the nature of the connection was still out of his grasp. He suddenly swelled with pride in being the one man, of all the noble lords of Scotland, to be in that cold, dark fortress, to be part of this intimate circle of arcane understanding into which he was just taking his first steps. There was no more anger, no frustration or fear, only loyal determination and open-hearted obedience.

He dropped to one knee and declared himself her willing disciple.

"Rise!" she answered.

As he returned to his feet, the room brightened just enough for him to make out the dark cracks in the opposite wall — and a shadow! The chamber was still very dim, and the shadow moved so fluidly that he could not discern where it ended and where the darkness of the room began.

"Please hold still, Scáthach," he begged, "I cannot make out your form."

The voice went deep and stern, and echoed more reverberating, as if in a hollow chamber four times the size.

These shadows you see
Are not from above
They are enemies of old
Trapped outside of love

This castle you see
Is not of this land
For it holds the truth
Of light and of sand

I am with you
But not in this light
I fly with gulls
Where all is in sight

Chills ran across every inch of his skin as he drew his sword.

He waved his weapon haphazardly in front of him, then declared, "But I see only shadows, and not the figures that cast them."

Do not fear
These shadows at hand
For they are outside
The ways of the land

Follow the gulls
And seek their high call
For they are the path
Beyond shadows and wall

Despite the lesson, he winced his eyes, straining to see what was not there. Without warning, Lindsay felt the steely strike of an armored fist across his cheek. His knees buckled beneath him, but he did not drop. The invisible attacker was no phantom, the pain, no trick of his mind. Blood ran from his cheek and dripped from his jaw onto his shoulder.

Scáthach repeated,

Do not fear
These shadows at hand
For they are outside
The ways of the land

"Yes!" he said, "I understand. I must not seek with my eyes what is apparent *to* the eyes."

Do not strike at shadows

Nor swing at the air
But at the darkness that cast them
Aim your blade there

Lindsay sheathed his sword and darted forward to the wall. Facing the wall, he shuffled to his side until his own body covered the elusive shadow on the wall, then he turned, drew his sword, and thrust it forward. A hideous, screeching scream rang out. The shadow fell onto the floor and disappeared, as its pitiful holler turned into the normal squawk of a gull above.

"The gulls and the spirit," he thought to himself, searching for a connection.

He began a question he could not finish, "Are the gulls a sort of —"

He was struck in the back. The blow felt as if it slashed him deeply. The sting swam through his blood to saturate everything beneath his skin. Again, he did not fall. He hunched forward slightly, drew one quick breath, then stood erect and sought the shadows, with no thought of the figures that projected them.

Lindsay swallowed his reason. He pocketed his logical thoughts and gave way to his instincts. His hands and feet seemed to act on their own, as if controlled by a puppeteer high above him. His sword flew with wild precision, not at the shadows on the walls and floor, but at the invisible phantoms that cast them. One shadow after another fell into the floor and disappeared, and each wretched scream turned into the normal call of a very normal bird. As each fell, another appeared. Scáthach allowed no break for rest or instructions, but struck him with damaging effect each time he paused or took a wrong step.

For endless hours it went on, and when Lindsay thought he could not raise his sword to the level of his waist, the first rosy brush of the morning's light stroked across the wall opposite of the archway. The shadows dissipated. The gulls scattered. And David was left with an empty fortress, the sounds of the waves, and more bruised and bloody wounds than he had ever suffered.

He dropped his sword, collapsed against the wall, and cried, not from the physical pain. That was nothing to him. It was the surge of understanding, the sudden and violent opening of doors in his mind that swelled his emotions beyond containment.

With the shadows gone, he dared to ask, "The shadows are not simply targets for my training, are they? They are the spirits of the treacherous, of scoundrels and betrayers long dead, which you have brought here with you, through the gulls!"

In a self-congratulatory tone he asked, "Am I right?"

No answer came, nothing. As the new day continued to brighten the crumbling interior of the fortress, not only did it look empty and sound empty, it felt empty. Lindsay was, again, alone in an abandoned castle, with a body that demanded sleep and a mind that refused to give it.

He leaned his head back, closed his eyes, and pondered everything he had experienced that night. When he opened his eyes again, he noticed a small plate and a cup on the floor, against the opposite wall. The cup was filled with a thick, syrup-like nectar that was sweet but biting on the tongue. As he swallowed the first sip, the sting on his tongue traveled down his throat, into his belly, where it traveled through his hips and down his legs, across his shoulders and along his arms. It dulled the pain of his wounds and slowed the trickle of his blood.

On the plate was a piece of flatbread and some dried meat. Lindsay tried to remember the last time he had eaten. It seemed like weeks ago. The food went down with hardly a breath between bites. He washed it down with the rest of the nectar, and his eyelids tripled in weight. In a half-dreaming stupor, he lifted the plate. Beneath it was a bandage and a note in Vanora's familiar handwriting. It read,

A tear I share with you alone
A mothers heart, a friend's kind words, a servant's faith
Is always shown

Keep safe your scars, let them heal
For your heart is pure, and stout, and calm
But full of zeal

Your teacher is wise and loves you as well
Let her show you the light, the sea, and the sky
Where all the gulls dwell

He wrapped the bandage over a gash on the back of his head, stepped through the archway into the direct sun, collapsed to his side, and fell asleep.

He awoke near midday with few physical pains, and spoke to himself, "The wounds, like the shadows, were not real."

When he pulled the bloody bandage from his head, he knew otherwise. Although unnaturally healed in so few hours, every cut, gash, and bruise was still on him, and very real.

He stood quickly and looked around for Vanora. When he could not see her, he crossed the narrow bridge and marched a full patrol of the area, not daring to place his own voice into the sacred air by calling for her, opening his eyes and ears widely, with increased sensation. His eyes saw farther, and his ears discerned the break of individual waves from the opposite side of the fortress outcrop.

Vanora was not there, yet he felt strangely observed and cared for by her. With Vanora's well-placed meal still satisfying his belly, he gathered his courage to re-enter Dún Scáith and face the eye-opening torment of another lesson. The fortress was much like he had found it the day before — empty. There were no vicious shadows, no voice echoing verses from within the stones.

The scene may have been the same, but Lindsay was very different. His arms ached and his wounds throbbed. The voice of Scáthach still rang in his mind like the reverberations of a giant bell that had just stopped swinging. But she was only in his head. His ears heard nothing of her. His eyes saw nothing more than the mossy stones of a long-abandoned castle. He walked the passages from one dilapidated room to another, straining his eyes and ears for any sign of his mystical tutor. But he was alone. Not even the gulls sought his company.

He returned to the main chamber, drew his sword, and reenacted the lessons from the previous night, repeating aloud the words of Scáthach, "Do not strike at shadows nor swing at the air, but at the darkness that cast them, aim your blade there."

He did not forget the cryptic warning of the old man. Some danger waited crouched in the shadows, with eyes on Alexander. Lindsay grew impatient, as the sun slowly trekked across the sky.

"Scáthach," he shouted, "I am ready to continue, to take what you give me and suffer what I must. Come to me now, for I have duties to perform."

His words echoed back to him, as the only other inhabitants of the fortress.

It was the dead of winter, and the days were short. The light through the hole in the roof took on the blush of another sunset.

"Finally!" he declared aloud, "The shadows of night return."

The sky went black, and only the silvery cast of moon and stars seeped through the hole in the roof. Lindsay stared upward, waiting for the wings of the gulls to again disrupt his view of the heavens. It came exactly as he expected, beginning with the faint squawk of a distant bird, joined by another and another, and rising in clamor as it approached.

The silvery light was blocked by the crowded skies above. Shadows swirled around the dark walls, and the holler of the gulls softened again into the feminine voice of Scáthach.

The shadows of Skye
Are not yours to command
Nor the birds in the air
Nor the men on the land

You are here because
Of what swells in your heart
You must suffer to learn
What sets you apart

Forget the hour
The month and the year
Focus your thoughts
On facing your fear

Dún Scáith will keep you
As long as it must
Should the mountains wear flat
And the sea turn to dust

Follow the gulls
And seek out their way
Give yourself freely
To the need of the day

The anxious impatience of his long day of waiting still clung to Lindsay like a sticky sap, coating him inside and out.

He challenged his teacher, "Are there no shadows during the day? Can the sun not provide the same service as the moon and stars? You speak of months and years. Our situation is desperate, and our King sits in a foreign country without me and without Vanora. Can you only come to me at night? Must we waste the hours of the day?"

The voice of Scáthach harshened back into the scream of gulls above, and Lindsay regretted his words.

"Forgive me, teacher," he shouted upward, "Do not leave me now."

The gulls suddenly silenced. Their sounds were replaced by a fierce wind that rushed from room to room within the fortress, creating a thunderous sound much louder than the gulls. It was an angry, scolding howl that swirled around Lindsay as the wind pushed his strong body side to side, as if he were a boy of six years.

"Forgive me!" he shouted again, as he dropped to his knees.

The wind died along with its howl. The language of the gulls returned to the sky above, then again softened into the voice of the Warrior Maiden.

This is not a place
Where strength is a fight
For the gulls in the air
Will be your true sight

Submit now, my child
To the kingdom above
You reach for their sword
Their force and their love

Release this fear

This source from within
And all will be free
A new life will begin

There was such relief in the return of her voice. The sticky sap was washed from him, and he returned his thoughts and his ambitions entirely to the lessons of the moment, careless of the passage of time. He drew his sword, ready for another long night of violent battle. But no shadows came at him. No dark fists struck him. The voice of Scáthach left the walls of the fortress and inhabited the inner walls of Lindsay's skull.

The lessons of the night were not of defense, but of understanding. His eyes shut, but not by his own control. It felt as if soft fingers brushed his eyelids and held them closed. A tender hand pushed on his shoulders, escorting him to a seat against the wall. Although his eyes were closed in a dark room, he perceived a bright light. A blinding, piercing, almost painful ray that stabbed into his head. It softened, and what replaced it was a warm, summer scene that felt as real to him as any he had witnessed. He stood on a muddy path, at the entrance to a poor, crumbling village. He looked down at himself. The arms at his side were not his. He was shorter and wearing the tattered clothes of a stranger.

With an open heart full of questions, Lindsay asked, "What is it I am seeing? I do not know this place. I do not know this body I am wearing."

In a whisper into his right ear, the voice of Scáthach answered,

The boy you revere
Is more than your King
The crown on his finger
The black winged ring

It is the symbol of that
Which he always has been
What you must help him
To be once again

You cannot become
What he needs you to be
Without the things
You now hear and see

The pains of the past
That suffer and mourn
Have reached to the future
To teach and to warn

See through their eyes
And take what they give
Through the lives of the past
I must force you to live

It was clear to Lindsay. He witnessed a moment of some distant past, through the senses of one who lived it. He knew there was some lesson to be gained, and he resigned himself to gain it. He perceived everything. The smells, the sights and sounds, even the thoughts and fears of this man, felt to Lindsay like his own.

He walked to a rugged hut and saw the door was already open. Fear surged through him. The fears of this past stranger. Inside was a hooded figure with his back to the entrance, hurriedly taking things from the shelves. Lindsay felt the full weight of the panic. Before he knew what was happening, a club was in his hand, bludgeoning the stranger's head. With his free hand, he pulled the blood-soaked hood to reveal the man's long lost father.

He dropped to his knees and released a horrid scream, begging the corpse for forgiveness and professing a son's devoted love through broken, coughing sobs. Lindsay felt he would suffocate from the crushing guilt and strangling despair. The desperate gasps for air faded along with all other senses. The world went black, and Lindsay felt like he was falling. When the falling sensation stopped, brightness returned to his vision.

He stood in a dress, walking through a field where a battle had been fought. It was not the dress, nor the feminine whimper from his own mouth that told him he was living a moment in the life of a woman. It was the strange feeling in his heart, a feminine sensation entirely new to him. He was a mother, searching the bloody field for her son. The wailing of other women was all around. Some were young lovers. Others were daughters in search of their fathers. Lindsay felt the full force of a mother's heart, a heart beginning to lose faith.

At the glimpse of a familiar orange shirt, half-submerged in blood-dyed mud, there was no doubt. This was the son. Lindsay felt a surge of strength he had never before known, as the mother ran to her boy. She turned him, and the glossy gaze of lifeless eyes stared back. It felt as if a fire had been lit inside of this woman, which burned everything under her skin with searing destruction. It was the sort of pain only a mother could feel and only a mother could endure. Lindsay lived the full force of the moment, feeling everything experienced by the mother.

The bloody battlefield went dark, and the mother's torment subsided. Lindsay's eyes opened again. This time, it was his own eyes, the eyes of David Lindsay. He sat in the darkness of Dún Scáith, with the gulls calling in concert above him.

He shouted, "Enough!" then stood sharply and pleaded, "Enough, please! I cannot take any more."

He felt the same soft fingers of Scáthach press his eyelids shut, while firm hands pushed down on his shoulders, returning him to a seat against the wall. He cried, knowing he would return to the memories of the past. In a transition that took mere seconds, the sound of his own cry became the voice of another horrid moment in the life of another miserable soul with a lesson to be learned.

In some, he lived only minutes, only a few piercing debilitating minutes. In others, he experienced several days, weeks, and many, mournful months. In each case, the sorrow of a human life was sewn to him, stitch by stitch. These were the lessons of life that were earned the hard way by those who lived them, and learned too late to help them. One at a time, he was placed into the lives of countless people, of kings and paupers, men and women of all ages, from past eras, distant and near. He lived the moments of their lives, seeing what they saw, suffering what they suffered, feeling what they felt, and most importantly, learning what they learned.

Each sickening loss, each sensation of rage and betrayal, love and jealousy, fear and despair, all coursed through David Lindsay with the same intimate rawness as they had through those whose lives he was shown. Poor Lindsay was subjected to them all in relentless succession, with no chance to recover. It was more consecutive, compounded misery than any human was meant to bear.

He had experienced more than two years of sorrows before he opened his own eyes again. The sunrise on the solitary fortress was a tremendous relief. His body was still tightly clenched from the last desperate moment he had endured. He was both hungry and nauseous, but one question dwarfed all other thoughts. How long had he sat there, living day-by-day, week-by-week, in the worst moments of suffering people?

He had a strong urge to feel the sun on his own skin, in his own time, and to occupy his mind with matters of his own life. More than that, he wanted to see Vanora, to have her comfort him and answer all the questions Scáthach would not answer. With more physical strength than he expected to have, he walked through the grand arch and out under the open sky.

He intended to shout for Vanora. He drew an inhale and parted his lips, but saw, on the wall of the bridge, at the far side, another plate. There was no food or bandages, just a flask and a note beneath it. It read,

My Dear Man,

I know what you endure so bravely, but I also know why you must. Drink this elixir. It will help you recover and help you prepare.

This battle you face

Is not of your own

It is of a sweet child

With a heart free and wild

Facing the world alone

This sword you seek

Is not for a sheer heart

It is of an ancient light

Twice as dark but just as bright

As the images now tearing you apart

You are now ready

To face what most would flee

A test that will not break you

A quest that will take you

Across the land and the sea

Soothe yourself for now

But remember what was learned

All their lives have been you

Keep their souls within you

Those who fought and fell and those who

lived and burned

Yours in Admiration and Affection,

Vanora

Lindsay was disappointed there was no food on the plate. His mind expected hunger after so long, but his stomach was still. He uncorked the flask and drank the elixir. It was thick and bitter, but with a sweet aftertaste that pulled a warm sense of well-being in its wake. He prepared himself for another long and idle day of waiting. No such day came.

He replaced the flask and took two steady strides across the bridge when an inexplicably large wave broke against its base. It crashed and sprayed seawater across the narrow passage. But it did not pass and fall in a natural way. It lingered in front of Lindsay in the form of a heavy mist. As the sun struck the mist, it illuminated the form of a woman — a watery woman, small and elegantly formed, unclothed and shimmering like polished armor under the direct sun. Her skin looked soft and supple, yet hard as steel.

Lindsay's eyes were tyrannically fixed by her magnificent beauty. His heart begged him to speak to her, but his mind and his tongue could not coordinate. It would not have mattered. She gave him no chance to speak.

In a delicate voice, but a sharp tone that was somehow muted, as if being shouted from behind a closed door, she told him,

I am Uathach
My mother you know
This is her castle
And you are its foe

I am the sentry
Who stands on the wall
Defeat me and live
If you fail you will fall

The sword of Cú Chulainn
Resides where you train
You must conquer my army
To fully obtain

The sword must be earned
To wear at your side
Show it your strength
Fight your way inside

Remember your teacher

Keep this your one thought
To defeat this castle
With what you were taught

The slight-figured woman of water should have been no task at all for a warrior of Lindsay's prowess. He took one step across the bridge and was halted by a sight that both bewildered and terrified him. Ten foot, fifteen foot, twenty foot waves crashed with thundering, human-like screams against the base of the outcrop, each sending the same mist into the air. As each settled into the same unnatural stillness, they formed into other women, until a dozen watery war-maidens lined the wall of the fortress.

Lindsay wanted to shield his eyes from their fierce beauty, but he could not look away. He would have faced a thousand vicious night-shadows rather than one of the fortress' misty sentries, with their bare, watery flesh and their warrior scowls. But he thought of his young King and Queen, and he knew that, come what may, he must see this challenge to the end.

He thought about his own wife and children, about their despair should he be vanquished, never to return. But then he thought about Vanora, and he said aloud, "She would not have brought me here to die."

With that assurance, he lunged toward the feminine blockade. The sun off the mist was blinding, and he struggled to make out the form of his enemies. He did not know where one ended and the next began. A flash of light rippled across the space in front of him, making the familiar sound of steel against steel. He was slashed across the shoulder. The cut was not deep. It was a warning that told him, "Do not take this challenge lightly!"

Lindsay drew his sword and went into a fierce battle. His weapon passed right through its targets, who seemed unaffected by it. When he struck at them, they were a mere mist. When they struck back, they were flesh and steel.

The battle raged for hours without pause, neither side yielding an inch and neither gaining an inch. Lindsay would not be driven back across the bridge, nor could he gain a position on the archway. When he could no longer lift his sword to the height of his own hips, the shimmering beauties fell against the ground like the splash of a normal wave. They were gone, and Lindsay knew it was time to rest.

After an hour, he rose to his feet. The waves crashed. The mist sprayed. The bare, watery flesh of the fortress defenders appeared again before him, and the battle continued. As the sun began to set, they disappeared as before. He dared not enter the fortress until his victory was earned, so he crossed the bridge and laid himself on the cold, hard, damp winter ground.

The following day, and the several that followed, went on similarly. On the fifth night, while his aching body begrudgingly embraced the frozen ground, gulls circled above him. Their shrill cries were not unwelcome. It soothed him, and he drifted in and out of sleep.

He could not have said if it was a dream or the voice of his old friend speaking through the gulls, but he heard his late sovereign, Alexander II, teach him, "Why do you strike against the mist, and why do you continue with a futile strategy? The farmer does not push the water with his hands, nor does he slice it into portions with his sword. He channels the water's own power to his will. Then it knows he is its master, and it serves him."

If it was a dream, it was one that stuck vividly to him. The words rang clearly in his memory as he engaged his opponents on the sixth day of battle. The nearest one flashed a misty sword toward his head. Rather than setting his sword against it, he held it to his side, in the direction of the swing. His guard was down, and he braced himself for a slicing blow. The mist ran along his sword, concentrating into large drops, until it dripped from the tip like any ordinary drop of seawater. She was gone, and he turned his attention to the others.

One by one they flew at him in beautifully seductive violence. When he received them, rather than resisting them, each fell from the edge of his sword in quiet, delicate drops, and returned to the sea. Only Uathach remained. She swung her misty blade at him with the war cry of a thousand voices. Lindsay held out his hand. When the blade reached him, he received it in his hand with a large, swooping motion. His hand was wet, but not from his blood. Uathach's sword was a small puddle of seawater cupped in his palm. He looked up to her. She smiled at him. She did not say a word. Her eyes demonstrated her delight. She closed her eyes, lowered her head, and burst into a thousand droplets in every direction.

The fortress was his to take, and Firbolg, the Sword of Cú Chulainn, awaited its new master. He entered through the large arch, into the main chamber, and there, at the base of the opposite wall, was a large stone he had not noticed. A stream of shimmering water ran along its outer crevices, declaring it boldly as the way to his prize. He pulled on the stone. It was surprisingly easy to move. Behind it was a passage running downward. It was little wider than Lindsay, but he squeezed through the opening and crawled down it with blind faith. Twenty, thirty, maybe forty feet at a downward angle he crawled, until the hole opened into a larger tunnel.

No light entered. It was absolute darkness, but he could hear the echoing squawk of gulls muffled at a distance. He followed the sounds until the tunnel turned into a cave, the dimensions of which he could only imagine. He marched without trepidation, remembering the words of Scáthach, "Follow the gulls."

In the complete darkness, the sound of the gulls suddenly silenced, as Lindsay brushed his feet against a mound. He bent down and grasped blindly over the knee-high mound, until he felt something familiar. As sure as the features of his own face, it was the hilt of a sword. He pulled it easily from the soft, clay mound, yet it sang out as if scraping against hard stone.

This was no Celtic claymore, long and bulky. Although he could not make out its every contour in the darkness, it was a full twelve inches shorter than his own sword. The blade was narrower than a long sword and wider than a rapier. Yet it was not so easily wielded. It weighed three times what a sword that size should weigh.

Lindsay had little time to ponder the peculiarities of the ancient weapon. The gulls called out again. As their sound reached his ears, a fresh sea breeze brushed his face from the same direction. He followed until his eyes perceived a speck of light, growing in size with his quickening steps until he reached the mouth of the cave. He stepped onto the rocky beach, and there, standing beside the beached boat, was Vanora and the same crusty old sailor.

With no thought for the sword in his hand, Lindsay ran to Vanora and asked, "How is our King? Is he safe? How old is he now? Do they have children?"

Vanora answered in contrasting calmness, "I imagine the King and Queen are exactly as we left them two weeks ago. They are still in York, getting to know each other under Durward's watchful eye."

"Two weeks?" he questioned in a half-whisper, "It feels like a year or more. How can that be?"

Vanora smiled and shook her head, kissed his cheek, and gestured toward the boat. They boarded the small boat, and left the Isle of Skye without another word passed between them.

A knight of the kingdom
Now knighted anew
By the Warrior Maiden
And the daughter he slew

Chapter Fourteen:

Loves True Home

The King and Queen are home
The crowns are stored away
It's time for innocent children
To roam, discover, and play

Little was said between Vanora and Lindsay as they retraced their path back to Edinburgh. There was much to be discussed and debated, and those topics would be thoroughly canvassed later. But while they traveled, Lindsay's thoughts were too mired in the improbable experiences he had undergone on Skye. First among them was the passage of only two weeks. He recounted in his head the many months he spent living the moments of past tragedies, the days spent fighting the shadows, and the relentlessly long, stretched hours in combat with the women of the mist.

Vanora would have insisted he spend some days with his family at Byres before traveling to York, were it not already understood between them. After one night in Edinburgh and one shared breakfast in the morning, they went their separate ways. Lindsay went home. Vanora also went home — to the house she shared with Ulchel. It sat empty for most of the year. Vanora's duties kept her in the residences of the Crown. But she visited from time to time, to tidy up and reminisce of her starry-eyed youth and her passionate husband.

The home was buried in a dense forest, only a couple of miles southeast of St. Andrews. The area was called Dunino. A narrow stream called Dunino Burn ran along the southern edge of the property. There was a sizable field facing the front of the home, but the home and the field were ensconced within thick and ancient woods. The house was less than fifty years old, but Vanora and her people had lived on that plot of land since long before recorded history. It was a ten hour ride on horseback from Edinburgh to Dunino, but the land was beautiful, and Vanora could have ridden it blindfolded.

The home was nestled near an ancient grove, a place of sacred significance to the few inhabitants of the area. It was a spiritual site long out of common use, an old Druid Den, whose few remaining caretakers tended to it lovingly. To the handful of loyal practitioners, Dunino Den maintained every bit of its early glory. What remained of it was only the smoothed stone floor, in the center of which remained a large pit, once used for ritual purposes long forgotten. Vanora was very rooted to it, and her visits home were more about the sacred grove than the house.

This particular trip was not for reminiscing of her marriage or reconnecting to her spiritual ancestry. She wanted to prepare the home and grounds for a more patriotic purpose — to bring Alexander and Margaret there, and provide them with a place to grow in understanding and love, away from regents and tutors and all the distractions of state. With the one servant who accompanied her from Edinburgh, she spent three days preparing a quaint and secluded little winter paradise, with plenty of logs for the fire, and a pantry full of rustic cuisine. Vanora glowed in anticipation, to once again be the mother of children in that house.

When the house and grounds were brought to order, there was just one crowning addition to make. Vanora found a plank of wood, carved upon it the following verse, and hung it over the front door.

Welcome to our home built of pure love
Surrounded with light with hands from above

With the home prepared for the children, Vanora sent the servant back to Edinburgh and began her journey to York alone. She rode to Hexham and secured lodgings in Hexham Abbey. At the dinner table that evening, she placed an extra setting beside her and kept it clear in waiting. Lindsay arrived half an hour later with Firbolg hanging at his hip.

She stood, gestured to the chair beside her, and said, "I have saved you a place. Come and eat with me."

Lindsay's jaw hung open. They had coordinated no rendezvous. Just two hours earlier, he did not know where he would stop for the night. Yet there she stood, as if fulfilling an appointment. Prior to Skye, the enigma would have haunted his contemplations, but he had learned well to accept such things as beyond him, and feel more gratitude than bewilderment. He kissed her cheek, thanked her, and took his seat at the table.

Over dinner, she told him about the home she had prepared for the children. She told him how often they would be taken there and how long they would spend. Lindsay bit the inside of his lip, not because he was hesitant to remove Alexander from his lessons and duties, but because he would have to explain to Durward and Baliol the necessity of it.

After dinner and a comfortable night of sleep under the care of the monks, Vanora and Lindsay rode from

Hexham together, speaking of little but their one shared devotion — Alexander. They arrived at York in the early afternoon and entered the castle to the great relief of all within.

They were peppered with questions that Lindsay did not know how to answer, and Vanora felt no obligation to respond. Lindsay dared not speak the truth, yet some explanation had to be given for their month-long absence. He told them that he spent the month in intense study, preparing himself to guide their King through his minority. This much was true, but the details of his experience on Skye would have made him ridiculous in the eyes of Durward and Baliol, and suspicious in the mind of the English Queen. When pressed on the matter, he told them honestly that he learned swordplay, studied history, and practiced the art of siege warfare. They were content with the answer, but their meager understanding fell immensely short of the fantastic truth.

When Lindsay set his eyes on Alexander, the child appeared different. He was not taller, nor more muscular. His facial features had not chiseled into a manly figure in the weeks apart. The difference was not in a deepening voice or the sprouting of lonely adolescent whiskers from his chin. It was not physical at all. Lindsay could not place his finger upon it, not until he saw Vanora and Alexander in the same glance, then it struck him. Alexander, Vanora, the old man, the gulls, Scáthach and the misty maidens, the ancient Picts — there was something that bound them together, some intangible kinship. As he pondered the connection, the words of Scáthach surged through him in reverberating memory.

The boy you revere
Is more than your King
The crown on his finger
The black winged ring

It is the symbol of that
Which he always has been
What you must help him
To be once again

Whatever the connection, it was just out of his reach, and something forbade him to ask Vanora directly. He locked it away in a private chamber in his mind and committed himself to the matters of the moment.

After a month of waiting stagnantly in York, the Scots were eager to return to their country. The Queen of England was needed in London. York was abandoned to those who called it home. Edinburgh was keen for the monarch's return, and the procession into the castle was almost as grand in its reception as the pageantry of the wedding a month earlier.

Once settled in Edinburgh Castle, Durward and Baliol were impatient to resume the King's education. Lindsay had the unenviable obligation to inform them of another delay.

He gathered them in his office and told them, "My Lords, I know you are impatient to press forward. I share the feeling. But the King's education must include more than what is taught by any of us."

He paused to recall the words of Vanora, then continued, "If he is to be a good king, he must first be a good man. If he is to be a good man, he must first be a boy. The King and Queen who will govern our country together must get to know each other..., as children..., before they can perform the duties of adults."

The facts presented were difficult to refute, so, reluctant as they were to yield more precious time, the regents set their lessons aside. Lindsay gathered a few of his clansmen and escorted Vanora and the children to the loving home Vanora had prepared for them. The Lindsays camped on the outskirts of the grounds, keeping a watchful but distant eye. Vanora took the children inside, for this was *her* home, and these were *her* children.

They stayed for two weeks, playing games as a family, reading to each other, going on long walks beside the frigid creek that ran along the property. A mother, a young king, and a girl outside of her own country, grew together in calm, comfortable affection, with no obligations upon them but to unite.

On the second to last day, Vanora sent them outside alone, without chaperon, to talk and play unguided. She observed them from a distance, curious of how their dynamic would bloom in isolation. They were very like one another, these two children. They fell quickly into a shared fantasy, conjuring in unison the same imaginary giants to defeat, villains to escape, and mountains to ascend. They quickly became as Vanora prayed they would — friends — childhood friends at play, bonding irrevocably in common sensibilities and character.

After hours of rigorous play, where active young imaginations spun wild adventures, Vanora called them inside. They were cold. They were sweaty. They were dirty. They were hungry. Vanora remedied those conditions in order, then sat them on a bench, one on either side of her. They leaned their heads against her opposite shoulders with clean clothes and full bellies. The warmth of the matriarch radiated outward from her body and her spirit in equal proportion.

The tired children nestled in tightly to the nurturing love, which they framed like bookends. As they dozed shallowly in and out of a comfort induced stupor, Vanora began to speak. Her verses slowly took a playfully melodic form, turning seamlessly to song, as she recited,

Oh children of mine
With faces so pure
Your vines will grow

And love will endure

Grow wise in your mind
Stay young in your heart
Grow into each other
And you never will part

These vines of new love
Will bind you both fast
And form into a tree
Of the future and past

This tree of new light
Will stand firm and tall
And serve as both warning
And gathering call

My King and my Queen
Still fresh as the dawn
I love you both dearly
In this life and beyond

The next day, the children went out to play. Oh, how they moved about the surrounding woods. Lindsay and his clansmen had quite the athletic challenge to keep a watch on them without being noticed. Margaret led the way, seizing her playmate by the hand and yanking him about.

Her surroundings were very different than her life in London. She had never played in the woods, never been allowed to run wildly with a playmate. She led Alexander to a creek.

"Look!" she shouted, pointing up the narrow stream, "Our enemies attack!"

Alexander was aware of the dangers of his life, just aware enough to think she was in earnest. His eyes fretfully followed her pointing finger. The only thing that moved toward them was a swarm of tiny, gnat-like bugs called midges. When he turned back to Margaret, her grin displayed her playful mood, and he joined her in her fantasy.

"Come!" he shouted in return, "We will make our escape along the river."

They ran downstream away from the midges, when Alexander stopped sharply, pulled on Margaret's arm, and drew her attention ahead of them, where a small cluster of midges hovered over the edge of the stream.

He yelled, "My Lady, we are surrounded!"

He released her hand, grabbed a stick from the ground, lunged at the bugs, and swung the timid little twig at the swarm. It passed through their ranks with a high-pitched whistle.

"There are too many," Margaret declared, "Run!"

They continued their escape along the stream until they came across a large oak tree with a hollowed trunk.

Margaret yanked Alexander to a stop, pointed to the tree, and declared, "Finally, the safety of our castle."

"Our castle?" Alexander asked.

"Of course. You are a king and I am a queen, and this is our castle."

He needed no more coaxing. He threw his arm over her shoulder and escorted her into the hollowed trunk. It was a dark old oak, with thick, cavernous bark, but not in the eyes of the children. In their shared fantasy, they saw the same magnificent fortress, complete with stained glass windows, high turrets, and over-sized banners hanging in radiant colors from the highest ramparts.

What their imagery did not include was much of the real world around them, including Vanora, who, curious of their adventures, had followed them at a stealthy distance. She leaned against a tree and strained her ears to hear what the children were saying. Suddenly, a hand rested on her shoulder. It seems Lindsay's curiosity was equally insatiable. Lindsay had left his clansmen behind and followed the children in their escape from the villainous midges.

Vanora turned, startled, but when her eyes beheld Lindsay, she placed a finger over her lips and gave a quiet, "Shhhh."

Lindsay began to open his mouth. Vanora placed the same finger over *his* lips and gave him a stern gaze, as if to say, "Don't you dare interrupt them."

Lindsay's grin went ear to ear as he nodded his obedience. They both squatted behind the tree and listened. The children wove their united minds through a series of imaginative scenarios, from mundane household matters to the wildest of adventures, all within the confines of their glorious castle. Vanora and Lindsay listened intently, employing the extent of their self-control not to burst into laughter.

At last, it was too much. Margaret informed her King that it was time to collect the taxes. She ordered him into the "courtyard" to receive tributes from their subjects. Alexander stepped out of the trunk, looked left and right, then back to Margaret with an inquisitive gaze. She waved her hand forward, urging him to go on. He took two more steps, with no idea what he was supposed to do.

He turned back to her again and asked, "What are taxes?"

At that, the parental voyeurs behind the next tree could no longer contain themselves. They erupted in simultaneous laughter, startling the children, but not pulling them from their fantasy.

Margaret yelled from within the tree, "Who goes there?"

Vanora and Lindsay stepped from behind their hiding place. Alexander, mere feet away, looked directly at them and shouted, "State your business if you value your lives."

Vanora and Lindsay dropped to their knees, and Vanora answered, "We have come to pay our taxes."

Margaret stepped out to face them, and with a stern face, still thoroughly encased in the fantasy, informed them, "You may pay your homage and your taxes to your king and queen."

Lindsay patted his empty pockets, then looked at the ground around him, trying to find something to pay. Vanora reached into some deep pocket, buried beneath the ample folds of her dress, and pulled out a single coin. It was newly minted — the first of the coins to commemorate the coronation of King Alexander III. She kept it as a mother's proud memento. If she were ever to part with it, this seemed like the perfect situation.

She reached the coin forward and said, "We are but poor farmers, my King. Please accept this humble tribute."

Margaret walked past Alexander, took the coin, and replied, "The King and Queen are pleased with your gift. Return to your farm with our royal blessing."

Somehow, Vanora kept in character. She lowered her head in reverence. Lindsay, on the other hand, could not contain himself. He chuckled in irregular bursts that popped through his nose while he bit his lips shut. He pretended his giggles were cries of gratitude, wiping his eyes and thanking their most royal majesties for their graciousness.

Vanora and Lindsay rose to their feet and backed away, behind the woods and out of sight of the children. Alexander turned toward the hollowed trunk, and there, between the children and their oaken fortress, was a cluster of their arch-nemesis, the vile midges.

Alexander clapped his hands together in front of him, smashing three of the insects in a single blow, and sending the rest scattering to regroup.

Margaret leaped at him and threw her arms around him, praising him, "You vanquished our enemies!"

Alexander puffed his chest. Margaret gave him a tender kiss on his cheek, which turned his pale face the deepest crimson.

Margaret pulled her lips from him and parted them to declare, "You are a hero, and you need a hero's name."

After a thoughtful pause, with her eyes straining off to the corners of their sockets, she returned her gaze to her hero and said, "You are Alex Bug-bane, savior of the kingdom."

He squared to face her, swelling with authentic adoration that flowed beyond their fantasy and into his true heart. He took her hands and deepened his blush even further. Margaret could not remember a happier moment. She had never lived one.

She threw her arms around Alexander, squeezed him tightly, and in a whimpering cry not strong enough to contain her swell of emotion, she spoke into his ear, "I am so happy here with you.... I love you... Alex Bug-bane."

The nickname broke the sobriety of the moment and set them both into laughter. He released her, pulled away, and looked to the brush between the trees for some token to present to her. There was a bunch of wiry heather, whose early pink blossoms were just beginning to bud. He picked it, escorted her back into the hollowed oak, placed a sprig of heather behind each of her ears, stroked her cheek with his thumb, took one step backward to admire her more clearly, and in a tone resembling Vanora, he said to her,

Queen of the fields

Blowing in the wind
With wondrous heather
As shown in your skin

You are my Queen
Of heather so fair
May I be your King?
And mind to your care?

I'll call you by name
Of heather and breeze
You are Queen Heather
Of beauty and ease

Vanora and Lindsay heard the entire exchange from their hidden position behind the trees. But it did not induce laughter. It was tears that found an escape from the proud and doting parents. They snuck away in different directions. Lindsay rejoined his clansmen, camped at the outskirts of the estate. Vanora returned to the house and yelled to the children from that distance that it was time to come in and eat.

When the young adventurers walked through the door, they were greeted and directed, "Queen Heather, Bug-bane, wash up. It is time to eat."

The children grinned at each other, squeezed the other's held hand, and obeyed their benevolent matriarch.

Our King and Queen
Shared joy from their day
As the hot stew warmed them
And love found its way

Chapter Fifteen:

The Storm Grew Fierce

A childhood paused
By forces unclear
Shining the light
Of a love so dear

At the end of two weeks at Dunino, Lindsay and his men escorted the King and Queen for the ten hour trot back to Edinburgh. Each pause along the way provided them with a loyal greeting, a hearty meal, and plenty of good-humored welcome. But among such company, they were King Alexander and Queen Margaret, not Heather and Bug-bane.

They performed their regal pleasantries with rigid formality, and were kept at a chilly distance from one another. They would hardly have been recognized as children, certainly not as the same two children who battled midges and made a narrow escape through the gates of their oaken fortress. They both missed Vanora terribly. They missed Dunino, and silently, secretly wondered when they would return. It was only on the road, with no company but Lindsay and his clansmen, that they were able to laugh as children, to call each other's nickname, and to continue to tighten the bond that formed in the trunk of that blessed old tree.

Their return to Edinburgh stripped them entirely of their innocent, adolescent banter. Alexander was whisked away from map room to library to armory to stable, in rigorous training that was intent to make up for lost time. Queen Margaret was placed among the women of the court to draw, sing, and embroider, to perfect all the feminine skills designed to please a husband and household.

The children were permitted one hour a day together, under the tyrannical supervision of clergy, when the only words allowed were prayers and quoted scripture. For three tense and lonely weeks they went on in this way. Alexander engaged his training with an open heart. But it was only with Lindsay that he felt more like a son than a patriotic project.

There was not a moment in Edinburgh when Margaret felt like a daughter to anyone, never like a friend, never a child or playmate. The vivid imagery of recent memories painted her dreams at night with vibrant colors, and each night her spirit went there — away from the royal castle in Edinburgh to the muddy banks of Dunino Burn, the worn provincial furnishings of a rustic old home, and to the arms of Vanora.

After three weeks, Vanora returned. She assumed the chaperon duties from the local clergy, turning at least that one hour a day into something the children both cherished.

Vanora and the regents argued and debated for hours, but at last, they formed a schedule for the indefinite future, one that included a week every couple of months, for Alexander and Margaret to join Vanora at her home and grow as children are meant to grow, to allow the slow growing vines of a maturing love to wrap and intertwine.

Baliol saw the merits of Vanora's argument, but was reluctant toward anything that would delay Alexander from taking his rightful place among the monarchs of the world. Durward struggled to see any benefit at all. His loyalty was fierce, let there be no doubt at all about that. But his love was for the dynasty, and not so much for the boy who carried it.

Lindsay's heart was comprehensively with Vanora, but his mind could not afford to be. As a co-regent, matters of state weighed heavily on him, and Durward's argument had merit of its own. The previous year of his life was one that saw matters of the heart swell to overpower the objections of the head. Each time he looked into Vanora's eyes, the coast of Skye reflected back. The rustling of her dress reminded him of the spraying mist of Dún Scáith. Her frustrated sigh echoed back as the whispered voice of Scáthach, and through her grimace he saw the broad smile of a mother delighting in the playful antics of her children. The objections of Baliol and Durward did not stand a chance. Two weeks later, Vanora, Lindsay, and the children were packing for a return to Dunino.

They maintained the bargained schedule, returning to Vanora's home for one week every two months, returning to laughter and play, to familial affection, and to the only place fertile for the growth of a childhood friendship into the love of a man and a woman.

In August of that year, 1252, Alex Bug-bane and Queen Heather were again children at play, engaging in some chivalrous competition outside of their hollowed tree. It was a warm afternoon, and Alexander had drenched his shirt in sweat. He removed it and jumped into Dunino Burn. When he rose from the water, he shone very differently in Margaret's eyes. He was a week from turning eleven. She was twelve and a half. But his training with heavy swords had turned him muscular, and for the first time in her life, Margaret felt the allurements of physical attraction.

Alexander felt nothing of the sort. He tried to resume their childhood fantasies, making-believe as they had been. She turned silent and awkward. Try as he may, he could not coax her back. She stared at him in blushing contemplation of her own strange feelings. His failure to pull her back into the game brewed frustration. By the time Vanora called them back to the house, he did not call her Queen Heather, but simply Margaret. Over dinner, she stared at him in silence. He refused to make eye contact. It did not take long for Vanora to place her finger on the cause.

After they ate, she gathered them beside her and recited the sort of adventurous tales certain to seize Alexander's attention, introducing elements of romance, of marital romance, that would soothe Margaret's discomfort, and shine a light on her that Alexander could not help but notice. By the time they saw each other the following morning, there was a new dynamic between them. They were again Bug-bane and Heather, but knotted together by a different string, a deeper string that neither yet understood.

Vanora managed to tie that knot tightly, and it is good that she did. Within two hours, they were riding back to Edinburgh. They returned to news that would put the integrity of their new bond to the test. Using his daughter's new title, Margaret's father, King Henry of England, made a political claim on Scotland. A messenger arrived at Edinburgh Castle mere minutes before they returned. He carried a note written to Alexander, demanding a vow of loyalty to the English King.

Many feelings reverberated through Edinburgh from that small piece of parchment. Fear and uncertainty, patriotic defiance, incensed outrage, all battled for supremacy. Each regent had his own feelings, with his own demanded response. But no decision could be made without consulting the King. Margaret was quickly separated from Alexander and isolated like a prisoner of war.

The regents gathered in the map room. Alexander was escorted into the room by eight armed soldiers. The gravity of the situation was clear to him, but the nature of it was a mystery. Durward read the letter to Alexander, and the three regents began peppering the boy with advice and scenarios, strategic possibilities and political solutions.

Alexander interrupted them, asking, "Where is my wife?"

Baliol began to answer, "The Princess—"

"That is an English title she no longer holds!" Alexander scolded, "She is the Queen of Scotland and her place is here, in consultation with us!"

The stern, kingly authority from this boy of nearly eleven sent proud chills across the skin of the regents, and rallied patriotism from their very depths.

Baliol answered, "Of course," then turned to the guards and ordered, "Get your Queen. Bring her here."

Not a word was said among them until Margaret joined them in the room. Upon Alexander's insistence, Baliol read her the letter. There was a tense pause, waiting for her response.

She stepped to Alexander's side, stood staunchly against his shoulder, took his hand, interlacing her fingers tightly with his, and she said, "Scotland is not my father's and never will be. Our country is not England's, it is ours. Her hills and valleys, her streams and her coasts, her people are of Scotland and will never be called English."

While Alexander's words rallied their individual patriotism, Margaret's bound them together. King Henry expected to play his daughter as a game piece, but she was no longer at his fingertips. Henry had no hand in Scotland, not Margaret's, not anybody's.

In his surging zeal, Durward unfurled a map and began to advise military strategies. As he spoke of men, of Scottish lives in terms of numbers, Lindsay was pinched deeply in the gut, and he remembered his lessons on Skye. He was pulled in full force back into the lives he was forced to experience, particularly that of a woman, slogging through an abandoned battlefield, looking for her son. Suddenly, the numbers of which Durward spoke had faces, and for each one of them there were many more, tearful faces, mourning faces.

He swiped his arm across the table, sending the map across the room, yelling, "She hurts! Oh, God, she hurts!"

With the staring gasps of the others, his mind returned to the moment. He was again himself, in the map room in Edinburgh Castle, and astonished faces surrounded him. He could not explain the nature of his outburst. Margaret, sensing the intensity of his pain, though not understanding its source, began to cry for him.

Only one person could understand him, the one person whose advice was conspicuously absent from the room, and he mustered the courage to demand her, "Where is Vanora? She should take part in this."

Whether Durward or Baliol would have protested will never be known. Alexander gave them no time to form a thought. He answered, "Sir David is right. This matter needs her wisdom."

Within two minutes, Vanora had joined them. It did not take her long to sense the room. It was ripe with the aroma of war and conflict. Lindsay read Henry's letter to her. She took it from him, read it with her own eyes, studying each pen stroke, searching beneath the words, into the heart of the man who wrote them.

She placed the letter calmly on the table and said, "The loving heart of a father cannot live beneath the same ribs as the vicious heart of a conqueror. A father's hand wrote these words. It will not come to war."

Baliol began an academic list of conquerors who had fathered children. Vanora shushed him with a quick raise of her hand, looked to Alexander and Margaret, and instructed them, "Write back to him. Refute his claim. He cannot know how you have united."

She turned her eyes directly at Margaret and continued, "It must be in your hand, in your words. Write as his daughter *and* as the Queen. Sign it together."

Durward began, "Simply telling him no will not—"

"Henry will not wage war on his daughter," Vanora interrupted, "not when he sees how she has grown, who she has become. I tell you, he will be filled with more protective pride than ambition."

She patted the table twice in front of Margaret, nodded, and told her softly, "Write the letter, my dear, and put it before a father's eyes."

Vanora walked out of the room without another word or glance. Lindsay scrambled to provide ink and parchment, while Margaret thought of her loving father and composed the words in her head. It was as Vanora suggested — the tender effusions of an affectionate daughter, lined with the unyielding resolution of a queen in defense of her country.

The letter was dispatched immediately and could not have taken very long to reach London. Still, three weeks brimming with fearful energy passed without a response from Henry. The fear was not paralyzing. Scotland was abuzz, preparing for whatever might come, rallying the clans, seeking the support of the French and Dutch.

Alexander was in constant motion, bouncing between his teachers, learning the skills of diplomacy from Baliol, the fortifications and men at his disposal from Durward, and the practical skills of battle from Lindsay. Vanora was nowhere to be found. She left Edinburgh the moment Margaret's response was sent. There were ancient places to visit, people to consult, and wisdom to be garnered before the perils ahead.

Lindsay was not sure if he had acquired Firbolg for his own hand or Alexander's. He laid before the boy a selection of swords, from prince's swords, slightly longer than a dagger, to claymores that stood as tall as the King. Centered among them was Firbolg. Visually it stood out from the others. It was much shorter than the long swords. The handle was thin and wrapped with forest-green strips of some unknown material. It felt like a sponge in the hand and seemed to grip the palm of the wielder. The pommel was small and narrow, little more than a decorative coin, providing no counterbalance against the heavy blade.

The blade was of some dark, long-forgotten alloy, much heavier than any known metal. Naturally, Alexander's eyes went straight for Firbolg. He gripped the handle, but could not lift the sword. He touched the blade, and his eyes rolled back in their sockets. To Lindsay, the child looked possessed by a demon.

Alexander turned his head suddenly and fiercely to his teacher, the whites of his eyes still dominating his ghostly gaze. He opened his mouth, and a voice that was not his own came forth from his lips — lower of pitch, scratching and aged, but somehow familiar. Undoubtedly, it was the old man, the same old man whose mysterious appearance seasoned the coronation and wedding with an arcane aroma. Alexander's brow contorted, and his eyes opened wide and glowing white. He spoke directly to Lindsay.

Scáthach chooses who carries the sword
It is not yours to give, and not yours to hoard
This child did not see the things you were shown
Did not battle the shadows, was not cut to the bone

Firbolg was placed where Firbolg must be
By one who is older than you or than me
And there it must stay secure in the hand
Of the one she has chosen from all in this land

Lindsay could not be certain from whom the message was sent, but one thing was clear — Firbolg was for his hand alone, until it returned to its home on Skye. Alexander's eyes rolled back to normal. His facial features softened. His voice was once again his own. He had no notion of the poetic exchange that had just occurred. He reached for Firbolg.

Lindsay snatched it quickly, saying, "Not this one. Choose any other."

Alexander chose a long sword, and the lesson began. The Lindsay family sword that Sir David had gifted to him at the coronation was not an option. It sat mounted on the wall of Alexander's bedchamber, as a cherished personal heirloom.

Lessons with the sword were not the only war preparations required of the young King. The soldiers at the Crown's disposal could never defeat a force from England. The warrior clansman of his whole country would need to be called to arms. To do so, Alexander would need to rally them himself.

One week after the letter from Henry, Baliol plotted a course of travel — by ship along the east coast to every town and castle between Edinburgh and Aberdeen, then by horseback to Inverness, southwest along Loch Ness, then across the rugged heart of the Highlands, back to Edinburgh. Letters were dispatched to every clan chief along the rigorous route, demanding the reception of the King and the dedication of men, arms, and money in defense of Scotland.

With only Lindsay and a small company of soldiers, Alexander took to the sea. The refinements of court were replaced by creaking boards and salty sailors. The danger of the excursion did not come from the rugged Highlands, nor from the treachery of ambitious barons. It came from the sea. Sailing between Dundee and Arbroath, their small ship was swallowed by a storm. Even the seasoned sailors were terrified, and prepared their souls with vulgar prayers shouted in desperation.

In the chaos of the sudden storm, the soldiers went below deck. Lindsay remained above with the sailors, assisting as he was able. He looked to the bow, and there, to his astonishment and terror, was Alexander, with his fingers wrapped around the rail.

The ship was pushed to every angle by the raging waters. At one moment, the bow pointed directly to the gray sky above. At the next, it aimed straight to the mysterious deep beneath them. Up and down the small ship rolled, while the child King of Scotland clutched to the open rail.

Lindsay fought the wind, the tossing of the boards, and the violent waves crashing across the deck to get to his King. But it was not the King of Scotland in his eyes. At that moment, that was not how David Lindsay viewed him. In fear for Alexander's life, the boy he fought to save was his very own child, the only son of his friend and brother, Alexander II. The sort of desperation that can only surge from familial love took hold of Lindsay's muscles and pushed him to the bow.

He stopped short of reaching Alexander, not because of the wind or waves, not because of the tossing of the ship, but because of the boy himself. Lindsay was frozen in amazement as he drew near enough to hear Alexander. The child shouted outward. There was no fear in his voice, no despair. His clutch of the rail was not from fear of being tossed into the sea, but from the swell of a different emotion. Of this, Lindsay had no doubt.

Lindsay wrapped his arm around the rail and watched and listened. Gulls swirled above in amazing feats of aerial acrobatics, shouting their gull voices into the wind. Lindsay heard only the yelling of birds. What entered Alexander's ears was very different. Through the voices of the gulls, he heard from his late father, speaking directly to him.

In a voice undoubtedly his father's, piercing the wild, thrashing sounds of the storm, Alexander heard, "Alexander! Are you there? Are you there son?"

Alexander shouted upward, "Father, is it you? I hear you!"

Another large wave beat the bow, nearly dislodging Lindsay from his desperate grip. Alexander released the rail, but he did not slip. He did not fall. He simply stared upward and repeated, "I hear you! Is it you?"

He was stopped in mid-breath, as his father's voice returned down to him from the wild patterns of gulls in the storm.

I am here, my son
Your father is here
There is no need to worry
There is nothing to fear

I am proud of you
In all you have done
In all that you are
My marvelous son

This kingdom is yours
A lifetime to lead
For all is now calm
I have settled the greed

Listen to Lindsay
Follow his lead
He will make you the man
Our country will need

Tell him I miss him

This brother I see
This friend at your side
As he had been for me

He's your new father
He loves you as I
And will never leave you
With danger nearby

The poisonous tongue
Is now closed in its mouth
You have nothing to fear
From our friends in the south

Go back to your bride
With her you should be
Oh, she would have been
As a daughter to me

The voice of the former King turned back into the sharp and piercing yell of the gulls. The birds scattered into the storm, leaving Alexander shouting to nothing but the vicious wind and the savage waves, which still conspired treasonously against him.

The mastery of the sailors was put on flamboyant display. They brought their King through the storm, clear of the treacherous shoreline to their left and the open ocean to their right.

When the weather was dangerous, Alexander had stood on the bow. When it calmed, he hid in a corner below deck. His father's words set his mind on his friend and bride, on his Queen Heather. He thought of the stream beside Vanora's house, of the fields and the rooms that were their shared playground — and he missed her terribly. How very different was his current setting and company! He cried, and he whimpered her name.

Lindsay, never far from him, observed the boy's tender heart and loved him all the more for it.

They docked safely at Arbroath. The ship required repairs, and provisions had been lost. Lindsay secured accommodations for two days, at which point they would embark again and continue their mission.

Lindsay settled quickly and wrote a letter to his wife. It read,

My Beloved Wife,

I send this letter south by horse, while I travel north by sea. Your tender heart must understand what a desperate thread of connection it is to me. But I do not suffer alone. My torment has company in our beloved King. The boy burns for the company of his wife. Each day, he earns my admiration and pity in equal measure.

We survived a terrible storm. Of all the swords that have swung toward me, none of them put me in such fear for my life. Alexander was altogether different. At the height of the danger, he stood at the shaking bow, seeming to speak the jargon of the tempest, in a heated but respectful debate with the wind and waves.

But as stout as he is, he is equally fragile in matters of the heart. He misses Vanora and speaks openly of it. What he keeps to himself is his longing for Queen Margaret. I often find him crumbled and shattered, crying for her. I have seen love in many forms, both authentic and artificial. It is a rare and pure form I see in our young King. I tell you, he loves her. It is not a childish infatuation. I recognize it as the same sort of fire that burns in my own chest and always will, as I remain eternally,

Most Devotedly Yours,

David

The ink had hardly dried when Alexander tugged on Lindsay's sleeve and told him, "We don't need the sailors. We can take a carriage home."

"Home?" Lindsay asked, trying to make sense of the boy's words, "We sail to Aberdeen. We will not face another such storm. Do not fear that. The journey is safer by sea."

"No, no, you misunderstand me," Alexander continued with a calm and confident manner, "We have no mission. There will be no war with England."

Lindsay had seen enough of the mysterious to pause before correcting the child. He stared into Alexander's eyes, waiting for the voice of another to whisper a mystical message through the child's lips. But the King's voice was his own, and his eyes did not roll back. He simply stared at his friend and teacher with an innocent and faith-filled expression.

Lindsay asked, "Why do you say that? Have you heard news that I have not?"

"No, no, not news." He looked down to his feet and pondered how to place his thoughts into words, then looked up and continued bluntly, "I spoke to my father…, and he spoke to me. He said…, oh, how did he say it? He said there is nothing to fear. This kingdom is mine, a lifetime to lead. He said I can go home to my wife. We should not fear England. How did he put it? Something about a poisonous mouth now closed. Yes, that was it. So you see? We can go home now."

"When did your father tell you that? You have not seen him since well before he died."

"It was not before he died."

Chills ran through Lindsay, from scalp to toes and back again, then he asked with unsettled nerves, "When did you hear your father?"

"Today, in the storm."

There was no deceit in Alexander's face. What he said, he truly meant. But the stakes were high, and the royal regent could not act upon the faith of his heart, nor upon his love of the child before him. He served the Crown, the Crown that once sat upon the head of Alexander's father. Lindsay kissed the boy's head and left the room to dispatch the letter. Many silent debates shouted within his head, but when he returned to Alexander, he was resolved. The mission would continue. They must prepare for war.

They embarked for Aberdeen as planned. The sea was placid and the voyage uneventful. When they arrived, they were met with a letter from Edinburgh. It was written in Vanora's hand, and spoke of the events that had occurred in their absence.

King Henry had replied to Margaret's letter. He apologized for any distress he had placed upon her, begged her forgiveness, and stated his pride in her, using the most eloquently devotional words in the language. He confessed that his earlier demand was not his own idea, but placed into his ear by a poisonous tongue. He cursed his own weakness, but refused to identify who had influenced him. He referred to the man only as "a Scottish nobleman, one I had long trusted."

It appeared the danger from the south was over. Lindsay considered the news and could not help but recall what Alexander had told him in Arbroath.

He faced Alexander, took him by both hands, and said, "I am sorry. I should have believed you, and I should have obeyed. You truly spoke to your father, didn't you?"

Alexander squeezed Lindsay's hands and answered, "I did, and there is more. You did not give me a chance to tell you."

Lindsay's lungs seized in anticipation. He neither drew nor expelled air, but waited with widening eyes.

Alexander continued, "He told me to listen to you…, that you are my father now. You love me and will never leave. He called you his brother. He said he misses you."

The only motion on Lindsay's stone-still face was the free and steady flow of tears that made easy work of his chiseled cheeks. He did not realize he cried until the tears fell from his stately jaw and crashed upon his forearm. He stared at the son, but his thoughts were on the father, and he found himself jealous of Alexander's opportunity to hear his voice.

But all tenderness returned to the boy when Alexander asked him, "Was he right?"

Lindsay shook his head subtly in confusion.

Alexander recited his father's words, "He loves you, and will never leave you. That's what he said."

Lindsay pulled him into an embrace and told him in a struggling voice, faltered by the swell of emotion, "I love you as my own. That is true. I cannot promise to always be with you. But my love will be. It will never leave you."

They shared a long, tight, and still embrace, disturbed only by an occasional shake of Lindsay's chest, as his breath found its only escape through the giggles and sobs that blended seamlessly into each other.

Between the collaborative words of Vanora and Alexander, there was nothing left to consider. Lindsay arranged a carriage back to Edinburgh. They traveled with the utmost haste to return the King home to his mother and his bride.

A father is shown
To our child King
As the gulls surround
Guiding his ring

Chapter Sixteen:
Honor This Union

As children at play
Their love formed and grew
Growing together
With parents in view

The enigma of the poisonous tongue that had whispered into King Henry's ear, this unnamed, treasonous Scottish noble, was like an itch on the inside of Lindsay's skull. It could not be scratched, and only increased in irritation as he dwelled upon it. Some evil eye was focused on Alexander, some Scottish eye, and one of means and enough influence to steer the behavior of the English King.

It seemed the forecasted dangers that sent Lindsay to Skye and placed Firbolg at his hip were closing in. He felt unprepared and, as he rode back to Edinburgh, the sky itself felt like it was pushing down on him, thickening the air, making it difficult to breathe. In contrast, Alexander's mood was light. With each mile, the images of Queen Margaret's hair in the sun and the feel of Vanora's lips pressed against his forehead reverberated more vividly in his memory.

But Alexander could not revel in his excitement. The tender-hearted boy felt too keenly the weight upon Lindsay's poor mind. For most of the journey back, the carriage rode hollow, while its only intended passenger rode beside the driver, as near to Lindsay as he could be without joining him on his horse. Had he only looked to his young King, Lindsay would have been lightened by him. But he did not. His mind was on his hip, on the mystical sword, the acquisition of which had once made him feel powerful. It had the opposite effect at this moment. It felt heavy, too heavy for him, as did the unknown responsibilities that came with it.

Lindsay returned his King to the protective confines of Edinburgh Castle, but how safe was it? In every hand that passed near Alexander, Lindsay expected to see a knife. He even caught himself entertaining suspicions of his friends and fellow regents, Durward and Baliol, for which he chastised himself severely. He longed for the provincial innocence of Vanora's home, where the only other people within shouting distance were Alexander and Margaret, Vanora, and a few of his own Lindsay clansmen.

It was a refuge not at his disposal. November came and brought with it the coldest air and sharpest wind to curse the Lowlands in a decade. It was no time to travel, not around the Firth of Forth. They hunkered down in Edinburgh for a paralyzing winter. Heavy rain turned to pelting sleet. It was impossible to cross the courtyard without getting soaked or assaulted. For two months, it seemed like the very same clouds hovered overhead, spitting down as they spewed forth a dark, long-winded tale of misery.

Despite the weather, Margaret and Alexander were happy. Oh, they wished for the outdoors. The sun was an old friend they missed very much. But Margaret's response to her father's letter, her resolute defiance, gave her a certain celebrity within the walls of Edinburgh Castle. Her name was shouted between patriotic songs in the dining hall. With much of Alexander's training shelved by the weather, she found herself more in his company. For this, she thanked every snowflake that fell.

David Lindsay was often away. Travel was miserable and often perilous, but he took the opportunity to visit the estates of his fellow nobles when they were most certain to be home. The identity of the treasonous tongue haunted him more deeply with each day that passed. He visited his own home only once between November and March. He was greeted warmly and well cared for wherever he went. But to his increasing frustration, he learned nothing.

He spent days and weeks at a time under the frigid open air, eating little and sleeping less. He slept in rain and awoke under snow, only to rise and press on in his quest to discover the danger to his King. A weaker man would have perished, either from exposure to the winter air or from lack of sleep and nourishment.

David's son, William, took much of his father's responsibilities as teacher. He was no seasoned warrior, but he was well-taught, and he was quite adept at transferring that knowledge to Alexander. In that long winter, their friendship grew into a brotherhood they both cherished. William and Queen Margaret grew to be as brother and sister. They were so mutually protective of each other that one might have thought they were brought up together in the same crib.

It was not until mid-March that the sun pushed out from behind dark clouds for more than a few hours at a time. When it came with the spring, it came with a vengeance. The air warmed dramatically in just a few days. The ground dried. The sky was filled with the romance of birds. The smell of infant blossoms wafted through every window. And Edinburgh Castle emptied. The cell door flung open and the months-long captives escaped.

Among them were Alexander, Margaret, and Vanora. It felt to them like the sun escorted them personally to

Vanora's old home. Lindsay was away, so it was William who gathered the Lindsay clansmen and set their sentry post in the woods that enshrouded the house. The boy commanded his father's men admirably. They created a safe shell, inside of which friendship and romance could bloom.

They spent three weeks there. Each morning, Vanora fed the King and Queen, and sent them outside to live within the fantasy worlds they created together. Each evening, they returned to the house, tired and sweaty, with heads full of imaginative adventures, treacherous villains and daring rescues, monstrous, flying beasts, and an oaken castle by a stream, where they could always find safety from attacking bugs.

On the last full day before returning to Edinburgh, the morning was rainy. When the clouds broke, the sun shone upon a wet field and muddy paths. The bugs were out, and Alex Bug-bane sprang in defense of his Queen Heather. He chased one particularly large bug, but was out-raced.

Margaret teased him, "My hero, perhaps you are growing too old to serve me. I must find a new knight to protect me."

He answered, "Give me a challenge to prove myself."

Very quickly, she shouted, "Catch me!" Then she turned and ran in the opposite direction.

Had he greater romantic awareness, he would have let her escape him, chased her down, and taken her into his arms. He had no such notions. In four strides he caught her, and the chase died in its infancy.

"Give me another challenge," he demanded.

"Well," she answered, "it is clear you can pursue, but can you escape pursuit?"

With a teasing smirk, he dared her to catch him. She took one step toward him, and he turned and ran away. The chase was on. He was taller and stronger, and she was in a heavy dress. He could have easily lost her, but this was a game he did not want to end too early. He maintained an intentional pace that kept her two strides behind him. They ran across the field, through the heather, and beside the stream.

They ran through a muddy puddle. Alexander's foot threw mud upward behind him. A thick glob hit Margaret in the face. She screamed and stopped her pursuit. The scream frightened Alexander. He slid to a halt and turned to her. She was not injured, as he had feared. She stood with a dirty, pouting face of artificial displeasure. Despite her efforts, the grin she tried to hide managed to show itself in sly glances from the corners of her lips and in her smiling eyes.

Margaret began to wipe the mud from her cheek, but Alexander stopped her, saying, "You should keep it. You are the Queen. Everything the Queen does is fashionable. Soon, every woman in Edinburgh will be wearing mud on her face."

Margaret's hiding grin burst free in absolute freedom. They both laughed, never breaking eye contact. Alexander's laugh stopped suddenly, and his face sobered in an instant, not from fear, pain, or sadness, but from beauty. His skin tingled from a strange, energetic surge that came from his very depths. Her face was blushed from the running and the laughter, giving her a glow that contrasted deeply against the mud on her cheek.

He walked to her slowly, cupped the side of her head with his palm, and wiped the mud from her with his thumb. Her face was the softest thing he ever remembered touching. An energy flowed from her, through his hand, and down his arm to fill him entirely. It was such a new and strange sensation to him. She had long been his playmate, through many games and imaginings. He had long loved her, but this was different. He saw in her the girl at play, but also the stout young woman who had stood firmly against her father, in defense of her husband and country. Those two sides of her were wrapped like a gift inside of magnificent physical beauty.

His mind was desperate to do or say something. He had battling urges to shout his affection or to grab her or to run away. Or all three. But what to shout or where to run, he did not know. That mental debate did not last. It was interrupted when his body took control. Margaret parted her lips slightly to speak. Before either of them realized what was happening, he had leaned forward and set his lips to hers.

It was no one-sided kiss. Their lips embraced like old friends reunited after a long separation. He kept his soft grip on the side of her head. She placed her hands on the front of his shoulders, then softly wrapped them around to his back. The childhood friendship had been slowly evolving, blooming just under their notice. When their lips reluctantly pulled from each other's, with an almost silent smack, the evolution was complete.

They stared at each other with wide smiles, still every bit the same friends who played marbles on a tapestry. But gilded over that friendship was an electric romance, not an adolescent infatuation, but a noble love based on mutual admiration, like-mindedness, and fiery attraction.

They said nothing to each other. There was nothing in the realm of language that could outspeak the kiss, no words from any poet that could say more as they continued to stare into each other's eyes. They took hands and walked side-by-side back to the house, with their eyes locked together, glancing away only briefly to note their path.

Vanora greeted them as they came into the house. She knew exactly what had happened. She would have noticed the difference in them had she been blindfolded. She kissed them both through her smirk, sat them down at the table and served them refreshments.

They did not go to their separate beds that night, but fell asleep on a settee, Alexander leaning against Vanora, and Margaret against Alexander. The Queen fell asleep with a firm grip on Alexander's arm, and her head nestled snugly into his neck. Had Vanora noticed nothing else of their maturing love, this would have said it all. They had been married as strangers and children. Now, they belonged to one another.

Vanora leaned her cheek against Alexander's sleeping head and gave the children an ancient blessing of blossoming love, the same words whispered to her and Ulchel when they were very young lovers.

Sweet child of mine
Your love blossoms new
Honor this union
This binding of two

Let her eyes and yours
Follow paths of true light
Growing in love
And finding your sight

Your armor is forged
From Heaven above
Crafted by gulls
And led by the dove

The next day, the atmosphere of the morning air was entirely new. The children still giggled with each other. They still conjured and shared the fantastical imaginings of children. They were, after all, still young children. But they spent more time in quiet conversation than in rigorous play. Vanora watched from a window, while Alexander and Margaret sat in the front field, facing each other with legs crossed in front of them, so near each other that their knees touched lightly.

They told stories of their earlier years, truthful accounts of their successes and failures. Sitting in the field that morning, they came to know each other, and the adolescent love that had been in slow and steady bloom aged into something rich and succulent. And it was only the first of many such conversations.

Their union was the reverse of most. Their marriage came before their courtship. When the courtship finally came, it came sweetly. It brightened the world around them and made beautiful everything that passed before their eyes. It has long been said that love is blind. In their love, Alexander and Margaret were not blind to each other, but to the ugliness of the world around them. Jagged rocks seemed soft and welcoming. Stinging insects appeared as sailing swans. Their love had placed colorful lenses over their eyes.

It was only in this way that their love reflected their young ages. In viewing each other, they saw truth. Their long, deep, honest, and personal conversations put them bluntly in each other's hands. Their affection was not based on sensual attraction or on ignorant assumptions that could later be proven untrue. Their long friendship, gradual romance, and constant communication secured a mature love that rooted them together at the core.

When they left Vanora's home and returned to Edinburgh, the courtship continued. None could help but notice the difference in them. In the breaks between lessons, and between the short journeys Alexander had to take, they were inseparable. They belonged to each other. This was as clear to the casual observer as the clothes they wore.

Their happiness was soiled by one haunting concern. Their dear David Lindsay was long-absent, wandering who-knows-where on his quest to find the treasonous noble. They heard occasional word of him, as he stayed at one notable castle or another. Each consecutive report was more frightening. Word came of a hollow man, gaunt of face, withered of figure, gallivanting restlessly in rusting armor, from Inverness to Oxford, from Swansea to Norwich. Rumors traveled that he had gone so far as Ireland. He sent no letters, not even to his wife at Byres. Many had assumed his death.

In Edinburgh, Lindsay's absence was conspicuous in the extreme. A pall of worry for his welfare draped heavily over the entire city, nowhere more than in the heart of Edinburgh Castle. While there, Alexander's happiness came in tiny morsels, savored very briefly then gone. The only time he felt consecutive moments of joy was when he was at Vanora's house, with his mother, and with his sweet love. His passion for Margaret swelled with every day he grew older and every hour they spent together. More than a year was spent in this way, passing between different worlds, studying and worrying, then relishing bliss.

On 4 September, 1254, Alexander turned 13 years old. There were two things he wished for. One was out of his reach. He wanted his friend and father-figure, David Lindsay, by his side again, to see him safe and healthy, and gain from his company all that could be gained. The other was gladly gifted. He wanted to be with Margaret and Vanora, at the house where his love blossomed. Vanora took them there, with no guards, no Lindsay clansmen, just the three of them. They rode tightly together, Vanora on her horse, Margaret on her own, and Alexander atop Sir Walter.

It was a warm afternoon when they arrived. Vanora went indoors and the children set immediately to play. Something strange was in the air, nothing that could be seen or heard, nothing to smell or feel. The children both sensed it, but neither could put the sensation into words.

Lindsay was not with them. He had not been with them all year. In his long absence, as scarce reports of him trickled in, his image became more legendary than tangible. He was spoken of daily, but none could visualize him. In no way did the few descriptions to reach Edinburgh resemble the David Lindsay they had always known and loved.

Lindsay was a man driven beyond reason, in constant travel. He sought faith in any venue that offered it. He prayed in the monasteries, attended mass, received the Holy Eucharist, then visited ancient sites of spiritual significance, left behind by the cycling ages of the distant past, all in search of the guidance that eluded him. Nothing seemed to speak to him. Nothing gave him answers. On and on he pushed himself. Three horses had died on him, pushed, like Lindsay himself, through exposure, exhaustion, and malnourishment. Yet, Lindsay lived on, driving his fourth horse like he drove himself.

He remembered the old Druid gathering place near Vanora's home. At the first thought of it, he was driven by something both deeply within him and as distant as the stars. He pushed his withered and weathered body at full speed until he arrived. It did not occur to him that Vanora, Margaret, and Alexander might be there, a hearty shout from where he was. He sat on the smooth stone, begging the earth beneath him to speak.

His desperate quest disconnected him from what had been his world. He had no notion of the calendar, no idea it was Alexander's birthday. He did not know that three people he loved dearly were just down the stream from him. He sat on the rocks at the Druid site and looked to the sky for gulls. There were none. There were no birds of any kind. The only life he witnessed was the local flora.

He slapped his hand on the rock and spoke in frustration, "I went to Skye. I did what I was told to do. Where is the magic, now that I am asking for it?"

An answer came immediately, but not from gulls or stones, not in the form of a shadowy sage or misty warriors. It was the scream of a girl he heard, and not any girl. It was the terrified cry of his Queen. He believed it, at first, to be some spiritual sign placed directly into his heart by the ancient wisdom he sought. When the scream came again, he knew it to be a sound heard by his mortal ears — a horrible, threatening sound. He sprang his aching bones upright and ran toward the open field.

Many horrific images passed through Lindsay's mind as he ran. None were as terrible as the truth. A band of men stormed the homestead. They wore their clan wools, but they had been dyed black. The pattern of the plaid could be dimly seen, but no colors. There was only one reason for such a disguise — to obscure the identity of a clan as they perpetrated something vile.

Sixteen men ran from the woods beyond, into the open field. Several had swords drawn. All had a vicious hunger in their eyes. Their aim was clear. Their eyes were set firmly on the King, in disregard for everything else around them. They charged at Alexander, but whether to kill him or abduct him, there was no way to tell. That answer would never come. Within one minute of Margaret's scream, Lindsay appeared like a rusty hero in some ancient Celtic legend.

Such a sight he was. Firbolg swung above his head as if it flew by its own power. The mission against the King was abandoned by most of the attackers. The raspy, rugged cry of the charging Lindsay took their full attention. Only three remained on task, and went for Alexander. The remaining thirteen converged on Lindsay. Firbolg flew with the fury of the ages. Each time Lindsay withdrew it from an enemy, the blood upon the blade did not drip or coat, but was absorbed into the weapon, consumed by it, adding weight to the heavy sword.

While the fight ensued, the unarmed Alexander ran in defense of his teacher. The three remaining attackers did not pursue him. Watching their clansmen fall two at a time to Lindsay and his sword, they dared not approach. Alexander was little more than an ignored nuisance. The attackers were focused on Lindsay, and all thirteen of them were dead within two minutes.

Whatever was the plot of the attackers, it did not go as planned. The remaining three altered course. They went for Margaret, catching her easily and hoisting her upon Vanora's horse, one of the three mounting behind her. They had come with no horses of their own. The two others took Margaret's horse, and they rode away with the Queen of Scotland. Her shaken scream drew Alexander's attention. He looked up to see his best friend and bride curled over the shoulders of a retreating horse.

Lindsay was focused on the corpses of his slain enemies, inspecting them closely, still intent on discovering the identity of the danger. Vanora had run out of the house at Margaret's first scream. She watched the horror in a paralyzed trance of disbelief.

On instinct alone, Alexander ran in pursuit of Margaret. He took no more than ten strides before being met by his faithful pony. Sir Walter, as if summoned by his master's call, ran beside Alexander, who mounted the beast and rode at full sprint into the woods, guided only by the diminishing cry of his Queen.

Lindsay's attention was taken away from the slain by the desperately pleading cry of Vanora, "David! Get our children!"

Lindsay's horse was in the opposite direction. He had left it at the den, untied and wandering God-knows-where. There were no remaining horses. Lindsay's gaunt and leathered face turned away from the dead, toward Vanora, who pointed in the direction of the abducted Queen and pursuing King. His shaking legs pushed his gangly frame and rusty armor forward with inhuman speed, into the woods on a hopeless errand — to catch by foot three sprinting horses, find the King and Queen to whom he had long sworn his allegiance, and save the children he loved so dearly.

With sweat on his brow
And force in his eyes
David pursued
While watching the skies

Chapter Seventeen:

The Lives It Now Bears Are Carried By You

A snake in the forest
A lone royal horse
Firbolg in chorus
With the blood at its source

Lindsay ran without pause, over hills and around trees, leaping streams like a creature of the forest. It is hard to imagine what fuel propelled him. It was nothing of this world, certainly nothing from within his emaciated figure. To anyone he may have passed under the lowering sun, he must have appeared like some bony woodland spirit from fables of the distant past.

His burning legs shoved the ground beneath him without navigation. He could have been running anywhere, or nowhere at all. His instincts served him well. Within an hour of running from the scene of the attack, he found Sir Walter. The pony stood alone among the trees. He appeared agitated, darting his eyes from side to side and huffing in frustration. It seemed that, like Lindsay, he sought his King.

But why were the horse and the King not together? As Lindsay soothed the royal beast, he closed his eyes and imagined what had passed. Alexander must have caught up with the men who took Margaret, or they turned and took him when they realized he was in pursuit of them. How very fortunate they must have considered themselves. They failed to take the King when they attacked Vanora's home. They retreated in defeat. Yet, their intended prey sought *them* out — alone!

Lindsay could not know in which direction they had gone. He could not know, but Sir Walter could. He mounted the dwarfed horse, patted him on the shoulder, and ordered him to ride to Alexander. Sir Walter took a few steps forward, stopped, made a quarter turn to the left, took a step forward, then one backward, and huffed a whimpering neigh.

Lindsay ordered sternly, "Take me to your master!"

Sir Walter took no steps, but whinnied in a sorrowful tone.

Lindsay scolded, "Ignorant creature! Move, damn you!"

Sir Walter dropped his long head and huffed again. Lindsay lowered his cheek against the horse's neck, softened his tone, and spoke, "Please, my friend, remember. If you cannot seize your own memories, share them with me so I may lead us."

With his cheek still pressed against Sir Walter's neck, he clenched his eyelids tightly shut, cleared his thoughts, and tried to see in his mind what the horse beneath him had witnessed. Nothing came into his mind, but something familiar came into his ears. The sound of gulls above him rang clearly through the darkening space between the trees. Lindsay looked up. The canopy above was too dense to reveal anything above it. Had it opened a passage for his eyes, it would not have mattered. The day was late and the first stars were beginning to wink down at the world beneath them.

The gulls did not circle above. This much was clear. They moved. Their sound traveled to Lindsay's right. Any traces of the former Lindsay, that politician and military commander, that noble of high reason, were long evicted from within his rusted armor. Without a single consideration, he turned Sir Walter toward the traveling gulls, and trusted the fate of the King to those winged guides.

The sun fell completely. It was so dark, Lindsay could not see the ears of the horse he rode. He committed his safety to Sir Walter and his direction to the gulls, not knowing what he would encounter or when he would reach his destination. At last, a flickering light appeared between the trees. It was soon accompanied by the sound of horse's hooves and the creaking swing of a lantern on a pole.

A single rider approached him calmly. It was Beolin Crymlyn, Chief of Clan Crymlyn. It was strange to find a man of his prominence riding alone in the dark woods, but then, no stranger than finding David Lindsay in the same woods, riding in rusty armor on the King's horse. Crymlyn did not appear astonished to find him so. In fact, he was quite calm.

"Sir David," Crymlyn spoke softly, "You do not look well at all. Follow me. I will bring you to shelter, food, and rest."

Those were tempting words, yet they were strangely delivered. Crymlyn did not ask why Lindsay was in the dark woods without escorts and without a torch. He made no comment on the royal horse, no inquiries about the King. This would have been suspicious, and had Lindsay been in a normal state, with his wits fully about him, his sword would have been drawn, and the interrogation would have been rigorous.

As it was, Lindsay was pulled in opposite directions by the two polar aspects of his being. The gulls called his spirit straight forward, and Crymlyn trotted away to his right, beckoning his body to physical comforts he had not known in more than a year.

"Come, my noble friend," Crymlyn continued, "Whatever is your care, you should rest and recover. There is a home nearby, where you can eat and sleep in comfort. Tomorrow…, yes, tomorrow, I will assist you in your quest."

"My quest…," Lindsay mumbled before turning his gaze to Crymlyn and raising his voice loudly, "The Queen has been abducted. I must find her."

"And you will, my friend," Crymlyn tried to calm him, "I have no doubt you will, and I will help you… after we eat and sleep."

"How can you speak so calmly? We cannot know her peril."

"The King is with her. As long as they are together, they will get by."

At Crymlyn's last words, Lindsay held his breath. He did not want the sound of his own breathing to disrupt the thoughts in his head. He had not mentioned Alexander. How could Crymlyn know they were together? There is only one way. He had seen them, or knew of the abduction and pursuit. Perhaps he had planned it. A younger, more thoughtful David Lindsay would have chased Crymlyn down, arrested him, and used all political influence at his disposal to secure the release of the King and Queen. But it was not a young and thoughtful David Lindsay sitting on Sir Walter that night, but a man whose mind had given way to his feelings.

The sound of the retreating gulls was fading. Desperate to maintain their guidance, Lindsay lost all notion of Crymlyn. He spurred Sir Walter with a desperate cry, and the horse and regent tore through the trees in pursuit.

The gulls flew in an unnaturally straight path until they came upon a castle. Lindsay knew it. He had been there before. It was the home of Beolin Crymlyn. The treachery he suspected was confirmed. The gulls landed on the roof of the main hall. When Lindsay came to the gate, they dispersed and assumed the natural behavior of wild birds.

Lindsay no longer needed their guidance, but he found himself alone, in the dark, with an imposing structure to breach, who knew how many men to face, and the lives of two precious children to save. There was one thing he knew for certain — Beolin Crymlyn was crafty. He had men at his disposal and enough wealth to arm them well.

The walls in front of him were daunting, and Lindsay may have been discouraged if not for his training on Skye. His eyes saw the dark, shadowed stone of Castle Crymlyn, but his mind saw Dún Scáith and the walls he had to ascend to conquer Uathach, take the fortress of Dún Scáith, and earn the sword at his side.

The castle was still and quiet. Whoever was holding Alexander and Margaret, they were hunkered inside, and the walls of the castle were unguarded. Lindsay scaled the wall without interference, and found himself in an eerily empty courtyard. There were only two doors from the courtyard into the castle. The main entrance was sealed by large, thick double doors, with tremendous iron hinges. The bolts of the hinges looked like large eyes that stared at Lindsay, as if to dare him to enter. A smaller door was on the tower to the right. It appeared less imposing, and far less of a challenge to breach.

Any tactician with a drop of sense would have advised a stealthy entrance through the smaller door. Lindsay gave that no thought. He drew Firbolg and stepped toward the thick double doors. With each step, the weight of his sword doubled, until finally, it became too much for Lindsay to wield. The tip of Firbolg dragged on the ground, while Lindsay tried to pull it along. At last, he could no longer pull it.

With all of his strength in full employment just to keep his grip on the handle, Lindsay looked down at the blade with a wincing, pleading expression. He asked the sword, "Have you come this whole way with me just to abandon me now, when I finally need you?"

Suddenly, all the blood that had been absorbed into the sword in its centuries of use appeared to flow like a crimson stream down the blade. In a flash of a moment, Lindsay could see the faces of every person ever slain by Firbolg, staring wide-eyed back at him from the rippling red current that still waved across the sword. It grew heavier and heavier, and the powerful warrior's grip began to fail.

Lindsay looked directly upward, to the stars above him. They offered neither help nor discouragement. He spared just enough of his strength to whisper upward, "Scáthach."

Down from the sky, up from the ground beneath him, from his right and his left, a voice rolled onto him like waves. It was a familiar voice, a challenging yet comforting voice. Clear as the sky above, it was the voice of his teacher, Scáthach. It spoke to him in a tone that simultaneously soothed and agitated.

The sword in your hand has fought far and wide
From the nearest hills to the distant seaside
Now it bears the pain
Of the men it has slain
It drained what it gained from those men as they
died

And now those lives are carried by you
You see it run red with a deep morbid hue

You can see their wet eyes
And hear their lost cries
And you wonder what strength will help you get
through

Let go of your weakness and allow me to lead
For you are my child and this is *my* deed
You know what death brings
Both to peasants and kings
And you brandish my sword without hatred or
greed

Go, David Lindsay, Carry it tall
Find the boy and the girl who bring hope to us all
The lives you must end
Husband, father, and friend
Have chosen their fate and the place they will fall

Lindsay's attention was comprehensively on the voice of his teacher. By the time the last word finished echoing inside of him, he realized that the tip of his sword no longer cut into the ground at his feet, but shone and sang above his head. Lindsay held the sword high. It was still very heavy, heavier than any other sword he had ever held. But it was not too much for him. He bore it with ease. He bore it with pride. He bore it with confidence and the blessing of its true master.

He was not alone in that courtyard. The strength and courage of many surged from the handle of Firbolg and into the bones of his hand, where it traveled to the far corners of David Lindsay, united and swelled within him, and found a release through a battle cry that rang from his lips as he charged toward the thick double doors.

By the time Lindsay's rushing legs had carried him to the door, Firbolg was in a full and forceful downward swing. The mythical sword cut through the dense oak like paper. Splinters flew into the castle with a thunderous sound. The might of the sword had not been exaggerated by the thousands of lips that had spun its tale.

Such a terrifying sound it must have been to those inside. Retreating footsteps accompanied panicked voices that scurried down every hallway from the main chamber. A dozen torches lit the room brightly, exposing Lindsay to any number of unseen doorways and passages.

He swung Firbolg over his head, and a swooshing, whistling noise flew outward from it. The sounds turned to vocalized howls, all aimed at the torches in the room. With the gale of an ocean storm, they extinguished the lights. The howling sounds traveled down each hallway, under doors, up stairwells, and through corridors. Lindsay watched in amazement from the threshold of the courtyard as the light from the passages and windows high above dimmed with every extinguished torch. They found every flame in the castle and turned the fortress as dark as Dún Scáith at midnight — an environment David Lindsay knew well.

He had spent countless consecutive months wondering why he had been taken to Skye, why he held the miserable memories of people long dead, why he was slashed and bruised by shadow and water. Since the day he sailed from the island with Vanora, he had been searching for purpose in all he had done and learned. Here he was at last, again in a fortress of shadows, well trained for the moment, and seething in a furious fit of desperate devotion. As he marched forward, toward the nearest corridor, Firbolg waved in front of him, as light as a child's toy, as if it charged to duty under its own power.

It was absolute darkness within, yet Lindsay moved through narrow archways, around sharp corners, and up steep stairs as easily as running through an open field at midday. As he turned a corner, he heard the sounds of a blade cutting through the thick air. It sang to him unnaturally, clearly announcing itself. Lindsay dodged it easily, and Firbolg cut through its wielder in a single, subtle swipe. As the enemy fell to Lindsay's feet, the blood was absorbed into the blade, and Firbolg grew heavier. A flash of memory projected clearly on Lindsay's inner eye — not his own memory, but one belonging to the man at his feet, a soft memory, a kind memory.

In the voice of Scáthach, words echoed the flashing memory like thunder after the lightning.

Where breath once stood
Now without voice
David, be humbled
At what was your choice

A life once stood
Now a weight on the floor
David, look to the stars
Before you look to the door

Clear your thoughts
Declare to the sky
Then Scáthach is here
Your friend and ally

Give me your pain
I will share it with you
And carry the stain
Of all that stains you

In the highest chamber of the tallest tower, two of Crymlyn's men stood in the dim, silvery light of a partial moon that only half-heartedly cast its light through a narrow window. Two frightened children were on the floor beside them. Alexander and Margaret were bound tightly at the ankles. But the pain of the bindings was no consideration. Neither knew the purpose of the abduction, nor the intentions of the abductors. Crymlyn was right about one thing. The children were together, and they each drew strength from the sounds of the other's labored breaths.

One of the two men guarding them was frightened. The other, a coarse, dim-witted fool named Brody, was driven by feelings more sinister. In the darkness, he groped at Margaret, yanking on her dress and patting and palming her from knee to shoulder.

Margaret screamed at him with furious defiance, "Take your hands off of me!"

Brody's breath huffed from his nose like an animal on the hunt. He chuckled at Margaret's demand and continued to grope her.

"What are you doing?" his wiser clansman asked.

Brody grunted, "We have her. She is ours to take as we want."

"Are you mad? This is the Queen, the daughter of King Henry!"

In a mindless, animalistic frenzy, Brody yelled, while his hands continued to have their way with Margaret, "She is mine! She is mine!"

Although it was dark, Alexander knew well what was happening to his best friend and bride. He worked his way to his feet and threw himself on Brody. The boy was little nuisance against the devious instincts of the fool. Brody knocked him back to the floor without pausing his depraved self-pleasuring.

Margaret screamed repeatedly, "Stop touching me!"

Alexander followed, yelling, "I will kill you! I will kill you!"

Brody's comrade was appalled, but his fear of the mysteriously swooshing winds and the extinguishing of the torches overpowered his disgust. He did nothing in Margaret's defense. The screaming of the children was carried down the corridors by the very same wind that had flown from Firbolg. It reached Lindsay's ear as if mere feet away from him.

All thoughts of the man he killed left Lindsay. He marched loudly toward the children's screams. Nine armed men were between Lindsay and the highest room of the tallest tower, cowering against the walls in fear. They heard Lindsay's thundering approach and, one at a time, swung their weapons at him. One at a time, he cut them down. Each extinguished heartbeat sent flashing visions up Firbolg, through the handle, into Lindsay's bones, and directly to his eyes. Soft memories of quaint family moments from the lives of these men haunted poor David with the tragedy of death and all that is lost when a man is killed. By the time he reached the last thick door between him and his sovereign, Firbolg was as heavy as a full barrel of ale.

The heavy sword made easy work of the door. The only light in the room was the dim silver film of star and moonlight that managed to crawl through the window. Lindsay stood tall and fierce, and appeared like the ghost of a warrior giant to the man cowering in the corner. Brody was unshaken by the booming splintering of the thick door, or the tall, dark figure that towered over him as he remained crouched over Margaret, grabbing, fondling, and tugging ravenously at her.

He also failed to notice the sudden silence of the children. Their eyes and full attention were on Lindsay. Before Brody knew what was happening, he was skewered through the ribs and hoisted into the air on the tip of Firbolg. A pathetic wheezing whimper bubbled through his gurgling mouth. Firbolg held him up with little effort from Lindsay.

The gasp of the other man drew everyone's attention to the corner. Firbolg let go. Brody dropped to the floor, dead. The sword was too heavy to wield. Lindsay fastened Firbolg to his hip, took one last glance toward the shaking, cowering man in the corner, hoisted the children, one in each arm, and ran from the room, down the bloody corridors of mangled bodies, into the courtyard and through the gatehouse.

He marched forward as if intending to carry the children all the way back to Vanora, until Alexander yelled, "Sir Walter!"

Yes. Sir Walter was still in the stable. Lindsay set the children down, ran to the stable, fetched the royal pony and returned to his King and Queen. Margaret mounted first, high on Sir Walter's shoulders. Alexander sat behind her in a single, effortless leap. He held her like he was holding his own breath deep under water, as if releasing her would end his life. Lindsay squeezed the bridle and led them into the forest, guided by a line of gaily squawking gulls.

In the deep, dark, wee hours before dawn, fretful Vanora walked from her house. She had not slept. She had hardly sat for more than ten consecutive seconds since Lindsay had run in pursuit of the children. In a skittish stupor, she wandered across the field, into the woods, and along the stream to Dunino Den, the old Druid gathering place. She sat exactly where Lindsay had been seated the previous day. She buried her face in her hands, and through her cries, she begged her ancestors for help and guidance. The sunrise breached the horizon, and a single radiant ray made its way between the trees, to Vanora's face. She dropped her hands and looked upward. Two doves hovered above her. Vanora heard a descending reply.

It's her!
It's Vanora!

She looked up and saw the doves descending, and she whispered, "Mother, is that you?"

It is Us
We are always around and above
Your father and I
In the form of a dove

We're here
Here to help
And guide you, our child
To speak to your heart
Through the free and the wild

We are so proud
Always with you
In the rocks where you sit
In the trees that surround
In all that you touch
Between the sky and the ground

The gulls in the distance
Leading three from above
Back to your arms
To your garden of love

Go to them now
They are in need of your care
In the field of our home

And its succulent air

Vanora bounced to her feet like a child one quarter her age. She turned to the sound of the gulls and knew they were guiding her children home. She ran along the stream, and when she breached the threshold of the woods, there, on the opposite end of the field, were four stout hearts in triumphant return — loyal Sir Walter, loving Queen Heather, brave Bug-bane, and one weathered, leather-faced knight in rusty armor.

They all rushed to the center of the field in a reunion like no other. Their arms intertwined like the roots of a single tree. Such feelings abounded! The grasses and the wild flowers seemed to stand erect and lean inward, eager to absorb the energy that flowed outward from the cluster of tight embraces. There was one dark flower among them, one life in that field that could not soak in the sun. It was Lindsay! He could not enjoy the reunion as the others did.

Firbolg hung oppressively on his hip, tugging on his belt as if it despised his company.

He pulled from the others and declared abruptly, and in a voice scratchingly incongruent with the mood of the moment, "The children are safe in your arms, Vanora. I must go back to Skye and return Scáthach's sword to her."

Vanora waved her finger in his face and scolded him like a child, "You will do no such thing!"

"But I wielded Firbolg. I saved the children. I no longer need it. It is no longer mine."

"Firbolg is yours as long as it wishes to be, and it will return home as it sees fit. Now, you must return home. You need the healing hands of love, and there is only one place you will find them. Go home, David. Go to Byres. Go to Margaret. After so long away, her obligation is to you, as yours is to her."

"But the sword is too heavy. It wants to be away from me."

"If it wanted to be away from you, you would no longer have it! You are meant to feel the weight, and feel it keenly. Do not dare release yourself of that burden in a decision that is not yours to make."

Lindsay had thought that the story was written, that everything he suffered on Skye and since had come to its peaceful conclusion. Vanora said otherwise. His weakened body despaired. His legs buckled beneath him, and he dropped to his knees.

Vanora sent the children to the house. When the door closed behind them, and Vanora and Lindsay were alone in the field, she bent down, caressed her cheek against his, and whispered into his ear,

This weight that you carry
Is harder than stone
For I feel it too
You are never alone

This burden is ours
To us both it has blown
We carry this together
In the heart and the bone

It is time to recover
To heal from your woes
To rest your poor arms
From the blood of your foes

Go now David
And be with your bride
She is your home
And to her you must ride

The journey to Byres would be easily made by a stout man with little to burden him, but that was not David Lindsay. Vanora would not dare send him on his way until he was refreshed and could tolerably bear the effort. She took his hand and led him to the house. Sir Walter walked behind them like a protective chaperon. In the house, Vanora did as Vanora does. She cooked and served, bandaged scrapes, and sang ancient songs in forgotten languages that seeped into them and healed them all like soothing ointment.

In the morning, Lindsay was visibly brighter, his posture more upright, even his armor seemed less rusted. He kissed and embraced his three beloved ones and walked to Dundee, where he secured a horse for a calm, slow, and uneventful ride to Byres Castle.

Lindsay sat on the beach
Of the River of Tay
Looking up in wonder
As the gulls flew away

Chapter Eighteen:

This Young Man to Whom You Have Given Me

As safety is shown
And peace endures
A queen sees her king
Observing love as it matures

Word of the abduction and rescue traveled quickly to Edinburgh, across Scotland, to London and beyond. Vanora had enough understanding of the vengeful hearts of men to fear an attack of retribution from Clan Crymlyn. The terror of the abduction from the field soured the milk of a homestead that had long been a place of nurturing joy and comfort. Vanora and the children shared equal portions of spine-stiffening anxiety. Without a word shared on the matter, they all prepared to leave the home and return to the safety of Edinburgh as quickly as possible.

By early evening, they were packed. Sir Walter was the only remaining horse, and he served as a beast of burden for their belongings. They embarked on foot, and braced themselves for a long voyage. They were little more than a mile from Vanora's home when they were taken into the welcomed arms of Alan Durward and an outfit of forty soldiers, marching double-time to secure their King and Queen.

There were horses to ride and a wall of shiny-armored men surrounding them. Despite the abundance of horses, Margaret rode behind Alexander and held him so closely it felt like her arms were wrapped twice around him. Vanora rode behind Durward, sharing a saddle with a man who had never understood her. But as her arms gripped him, he felt what others had felt. He came to understand what Alexander, Margaret, and Lindsay knew well — there was a magical sense of well-being in her arms, a profound truth radiating through them from deep within her and beyond. He could not have put the sensation into words, but as they galloped along the roads, he thanked God for Vanora.

The walls of Edinburgh Castle were every bit the protective bosom they expected. In response to the abduction, knights and soldiers volunteered, and were conscripted, from every clan between Creag Choinnich and the English border. It was not fear that salted the air of Edinburgh, but a fierce and defiant sobriety of mind. The King and Queen were whisked away to their respective chambers, torn from each other like children who needed protection, not like a young man and woman whose recent experience served to mature them beyond their years, and tightened and fertilized a growing, arduous, mature love.

For the first day, their separation was a mild frustration. There was much work to do and many people to correspond with. Margaret wasted no time writing to her father. Before she cleaned and refreshed from the journey back, she sat at her writing desk and reached out to her father with the heart of a doting daughter. She wrote,

Dear Father,

Please do not fear for my condition. I am well now, and it might surprise you to read, I was well before being rescued from my captors. I must tell you about this child I have married. As you know by now, *I* was the one taken from the field, not he, not until he charged in pursuit of his wife, with no regard for his own safety. But his actions that day were a small part of his heroism.

Locked in a dark and damp chamber, he had no stores of despair in his heart, while mine felt like iron in my breast. Nor had he any rosy delusions. He was fully aware of our peril. But danger had no authority over him. He lifted my spirits with his stout faith, and he threw himself, bound, at an armed man in defense of my honor. Despite the circumstances and his youth, I had never felt more safely situated, not since I was in your arms, dear father.

You and mother taught me to love, and I know you want me to be happy, so I am certain it will please you to read that I love him. I truly love this young man to whom you have given me, my husband, my King. I praise God for the Wisdom of

Providence, which placed me beside Alexander in that terrible room.

My beloved father, sleep well under the assurance of my happiness, and under the oath of my eternal love and gratitude for all you have done for me.

Eternally Yours,

Queen Margaret of Scotland

The letter reached a furiously anxious King and Queen of England and did all it was intended to soothe their hearts and minds. It reached Henry the morning after another letter, one from Beolin Crymlyn. In desperate fear of Henry's wrath, Crymlyn spun a tapestry of words excusing his crimes. He claimed that Margaret was unsafe in Scotland, that Alexander and his regents planned to kill her and marry Alexander to someone else. He warned that the Scots were planning war with England, and Margaret's murder at the hands of the Scots was to be the catalyst, baiting Henry into a doomed attack.

Henry was torn. Crymlyn was a reputable noble. His name and his clan enjoyed the prestige of many valorous ancestors. Henry had already called for his war council when Margaret's letter arrived. Had Margaret known the extent of Crymlyn's plan, she would not have ended her letter so abruptly, not without telling all that she knew. The letter sewed a vibrant seed of doubt, and Henry wrote back immediately.

In his letter to his daughter, he explained all that Crymlyn had warned. He confessed that it was Beolin

Crymlyn that had convinced him to stake his claim on Scotland. He begged her to reveal what she knew with the utmost candor and honesty.

Crymlyn rode to England shortly after sending his letter to Henry. By the time he crossed the English border, Henry had already given orders to arrest him. Word of the orders reached Crymlyn just before Henry's men. Crymlyn made his escape and took refuge in the castle of a distant cousin, near Ayr Scotland, on the West Coast. To all involved, the treasonous criminal disappeared without a trace. Most assumed he was dead, or had sought a new life overseas. Beolin's father had been a man of high repute, a man of impeccable nobility, whose irreproachable character was universally admired. It was only for the memory of the father that the son was not pursued.

Margaret replied to Henry's letter. She wrote of the heroics of David Lindsay, about Durward's arrival with forty soldiers. She described, in dramatic detail, the hordes of knights and soldiers conscripted into service for her protection. When she wrote, weeks had passed since her return to Edinburgh, since she had been so defensively sequestered from all that was warm and loving. She felt safe, no doubt at all, but comfort in that safety teetered precariously on her heart with growing frustration. Never before had she so deeply loved. Never had she so ardently desired, and the object of her desire was kept from her, kept hard in study and training, being thrusted headlong into a newly fevered rush to prepare him for a treacherous world.

The letter began what became a steady correspondence between Margaret and Henry. They connected between many miles more tightly by the pen than they ever had been in each other's company. With each letter, they were less a father and daughter and more a woman and man — the King of England and the Queen of Scotland. Despite the maturity of their relationship, part of Henry's heart always held her as his little girl. As Margaret's frustration with her separation from her husband grew intolerable, her feelings found vivid expression in her letters to her father, and that part of Henry's heart was pinched cruelly with paternal affection.

The days flew quickly for the regents, and the day Alexander would come of age to assume his full authority rushed at them faster than they wished. There was no greater priority. Margaret's time with her young husband and hero was sparse and brief. Two years of letters between Margaret and Henry flowed. Each letter from Margaret was written in greater frustration, until, despite Margaret's insistence, Henry wrote to Durward. While yielding to the authority of the Scottish regent, he suggested that the children had come of age. Alexander and Margaret were fifteen and sixteen respectively, and even the Bishop of St. Andrews agreed — it was time to consummate the marriage and secure the monarchy with an heir.

Alexander and Margaret had not seen each other in three months, and only four times that entire year. In late September, 1256, the King was taken back to Edinburgh from a voyage to visit the Countess of Flanders, Margaret II, to sew connections both political and economic. He was travel-weary, yet he had grown much in his time away, both in masculine stature and in mature understanding. To Queen Margaret, to his Queen Heather, when they reunited in the courtyard, he appeared as a dreamy version of the boy she knew. If not for the familiar child-like grin that beamed from him when he saw her, she would have shuddered at his touch.

Alexander was pulled by the hand by Baliol, who now stood a full four inches shorter. Alexander tugged his hand free with ease.

"Nothing now, John!" he demanded in a deep, manly voice that reverberated off the courtyard walls with proprietary authority, "I have not seen my wife these many months. There is no more urgent need."

Alexander knew why he had been taken back, what decision had been made in his absence. Margaret did not know. Alexander rushed to her, hoisted her into his arms, and whispered his devotion in words that caressed her ears with intoxicating excitement.

Baliol interrupted the moment, informing his King, "The chamber is prepared for the consummation. Come, my King. The time has finally come."

Any plans Alexander had to present his bride with the news was shattered by Baliol's unceremonious proclamation. Alexander turned to Margaret with an apologetic expression, only to see her in the deepest blush.

A voice came from behind, closing in at the pace of short, stubby, but determined legs, scolding in the voice of Vanora, "John Baliol! What is wrong with you? For Heaven's sake, man, you have declared open war on romance!"

Vanora took Alexander and Margaret by the hands and pulled them to her own room, where she prepared them for the monumental moment ahead of them with the tender, assuring words of a mother. This was no act of state she prepared them for, but the next step in a continually developing relationship that had been, unfortunately, stunted by separation.

Seated together beside Vanora, they were again Heather and Bug-bane, and yet so much more. Their maturing bodies coursed with the desires of a man and woman, but so much more than that, their hearts and minds overflowed with the fruits of a ripening romance based on firm mutual respect, an intimacy of knowledge about each other's innermost selves, and shared experiences that bound them together at the deepest levels.

Memories of Vanora's house, of the field, the woods, the stream, and the hollowed tree, were still darkly tainted by images of the attack. Horror stains deeply, but much less deeply than love. There was little discussion on the matter. The act so heartlessly plotted by Baliol, this deed that belonged to Alexander and Margaret alone, could wait for a setting equally their own.

They waited two more days until Lindsay could join them. He was very much his earlier self, full and stout of figure, neatly groomed in polished armor, but with every one of his toils residing in his dark eyes. They traveled together to Vanora's. During the trip, both King and Queen received all of the advice, all of the warnings, and all of the love from Lindsay and Vanora that parents could give. When they arrived at the house, Alexander and Margaret dismounted their horses, took each other by the hand, stared into each other's eyes for a full minute, then, with no adolescent lust within them, they walked hand-in-hand to the house and through the front door. The evening was nothing more than the next appropriate step in a romance for the ages.

Still staring at the closed door of the house, Lindsay said to Vanora, "Last time we were here together, we watched over a boy and a girl. Although only two years have passed since, we are now with a man and a woman, with the noblest King I have ever known, and with a Queen who commands my loyal affections with regal authority."

Vanora looked up to his dewy eyes, leaned her head against his arm, and replied, "Yes, I, too, am very proud of them."

"But not surprised," he continued, "Nothing surprises you. You have vision, where I am destined to blindness."

She pulled from him and turned him to face her before saying, "Yes, you suffer from blindness, as we all do. But you have shown that darkness does not inhibit you. You are capable of more in blindness than others are in sight."

She was speaking of his heroics in the rescue, and of much more. He felt the full weight of the compliment, which burrowed to the deepest chamber of his heart. The brightness of his blush compensated for the lowering sun.

Once they were certain the Royal Couple was secured in the bed chamber, they went inside and recited poems and legends to each other until they fell asleep in their chairs. When they awoke, Alexander and Margaret were already seated among them. The young couple had taken a strong step into adulthood, yet they maintained their innocence. Vanora and Lindsay were awakened by the childlike giggles of two people who were both young and old, light of heart yet sober of mind. With the full pride of a mother and a father, Vanora and Lindsay basked in the noble virtues on display in front of them.

They spent three weeks at the house, the four of them, and by the time they rode toward Edinburgh, they were as much a family as any four people had ever been.

As the King and Queen grow
Ever more in love
Our eyes are drawn
To the gulls high above

Part Two Epilogue

As he finished the day's portion of the tale, the old seanchai's eyes lit bright and fiery. In the breath that followed, his animated gestures and bright eyes subdued simultaneously, reminding his audience that the ageless figure that had spoken with youthful vigor all day was, in fact, an old man who needed to stop for the day and rest for the night.

The crowd on the beach sat still and stared at his next several breaths. He lifted his eyes to them and, in a tired voice, he spoke.

Our story of a boy you did not know
You have listened and learned and watched him
grow

As he becomes the man the gulls foretold
Please prepare for what will unfold

It is time to pause this story of our past
We'll gather at sunrise to finish at last

For what is to come you may not believe
Keep your eyes wide and prepare to receive

He did not wait for the offering of a bed and roof. He walked into the town and into a home of his choosing, not knowing whose it was. He helped himself to the pantries.

The proprietors entered behind him and watched in surprised pride as the day's celebrity helped himself to the master bed.

Part Three:

The Sandy Beach of Heaven

Part Three
Prologue

On the third day, nobody waited for the old story-teller. He was up before anyone in the humble household that hosted him. He strolled the beach for miles in the dark. By the time the eastern horizon began to blush, he was already back where the ashes of the previous night's fire silently and somberly held its secrets.

The first of the townsfolk followed shortly behind the sunrise, not expecting to see the object of their collective fascination standing like a mossy statue, exactly where he stood the day before. Word spread quickly. Breakfast was grabbed hurriedly or foregone entirely. Before the sun exposed its whole face to them, the people of Kinghorn were gathered once again, with hearts that had been opened widely by the dreams they had awakened from.

Beginning in a hushed voice, looking down, as if speaking in confidence with his own toes, but growing slowly louder and clearer as his chin raised, he said,

Our king grew tall, brave and strong
With his parents keeping watch to help him along

With his wife at his side
And a child on his knee
Love became stronger
In abundant degree

His duties were large
But filtered through light
Showing peace to the land
And clarity of sight

But what is to come
Your stories don't share
For this is our truth
Of which few are aware

Thank you for coming
At the rise of the sun
For in a way our story
Has only begun

Chapter Nineteen:

Where Life Finds Its True Sight

Love flew high
As high as a bird
The children grew older
Their romance matured

On a Monday morning in early March, 1261, the vibrant scents of the season rode through a narrow window high in Edinburgh Castle, and for the first time in nearly twenty years, Vanora held a baby to her bosom. The royal blood of Princess Margaret of Scotland blushed her infant cheeks and cast its glow onto Vanora's proud face. The child was beautiful! How could she be otherwise? She was the firstborn child of Bug-bane and Heather, and she looked to all as if she were hand-sculpted by God on his finest day.

Vanora's joy was resplendent, but a tinge of apprehension lurked in the shadowy recesses of her mind — not a vision of doom, nothing so distinct, but a low-humming, distant sense of dread tugged gently beneath her buoyant spirit. The child would know glory, of this she was certain, but tremendous sorrow lurked in the distance, casting a disturbingly deep, silvery-blue hue over the child's angelic face.

To Vanora's dear heart, the child was as much her own as any infant had been. No sooner did she hoist the baby into her arms than words flowed from her spirit to the child's ears. With the pungent aroma of Spring flora saturating the room, she sang,

Oh child of light
So precious and pure
See with these eyes
Let your vision endure

For your child-eyes see
What most have forgotten
As the world to many
Turns vicious and rotten

For darkness invades them
And begs the removal
Of the Heavenly space
Where all find approval

I pray as you age
May you see with love's light
For this is where life
Finds its true sight

Vanora's heart was simultaneously light with love and heavy with a spiritual weight that remained just beyond her recognition. The child in her arms carried a dark aura, but one of magnificent beauty. Vanora could not foresee the source of the darkness. Something burning deeply within the child's future days awaited, some wretched sorrow, some breaker of hearts. Vanora consulted every guide at her disposal, but none could give her a precise warning.

Whatever it was, it was well into the child's future and not the concerns of an infant, nor of a mother and father so deeply in love. Love, not tragedy, was the order of the day. Princess Margaret felt no dark doom hovering over her. She was comprehensively cocooned within the doting love of her father and mother, of Vanora's abundant heart, of the Lindsays and all who delighted in the child's radiant beauty and abounding spirit.

She grew under such care, flourishing in body, mind, and spirit. When she was eighteen months old, she toddled with her usual laughter into the throne room of Edinburgh Castle, grabbed her father by the knee, and looked lovingly up to him as he received the full authority of the King of Scotland. It was September 4, 1262, Alexander's twenty-first birthday. The regency of the child-King was ended, and the power of the throne was handed to Alexander in an unceremonious event.

The three who had served as regents, Lindsay, Durward, and Baliol, attended with Queen Margaret and Vanora. The Bishop should have been there, but he was with his dying mother. So the regents stood in line before the King, and, along with a few recited words, transferred their authority to Alexander. Durward removed the ring of royal authority, last worn by the previous King, and slipped it onto Alexander's finger. There was no oath, no declarations, only handshakes and embraces.

In truth, the event suited the occasion. Alexander's wisdom had grown steady and strong in the years after his abduction. His opinions had long carried the weight of a king's. The transfer of authority was more symbolic than practical, and Alexander was the sort of man that would continue to heed the advice of his former regents. Nothing really changed.

The first recommendation of a former regent was rejected. Baliol suggested that the seat of royal authority be moved from Edinburgh back to Scone. To Baliol, tradition was the foundation of strength. But to Alexander, love was. Edinburgh was where he learned to be a man and king. It had been his home. He consented to outfitting Scone palace as a permanent royal residence, but had no intention of moving his household.

After the subtle ceremony they shared a small feast. Princess Margaret bounced from lap to lap, as she had since her birth, receiving an abundance of love from each hand to hold her.

Near the end of the feast, Alexander announced, "People will expect to see me. They deserve to see me."

Durward asked, "What are you proposing?"

"I must tour the Kingdom, show them the sort of King they have."

"Oh yes!" Baliol agreed, "A grand and glorious tour to announce your coming-of-age."

"No," Alexander refuted, "not grand, but simple... no gold flashing in front of them, no rich robes, no crown."

Baliol began a protest, "You should show them a King, regal and resplendent."

Lindsay interrupted, "His Grace is right. They do not need to see a King. They need to see a Scot, to see that they are led by one of their own, by the same boy who raced up Creag Choinnich, now grown into a man... stout, brave, and in love with his wife and his country."

There had been a habit, long in place, when Lindsay stopped speaking to look to Vanora for approval. This moment was no exception. As Lindsay drew his next inhale, all eyes went to Vanora. She simply smiled and patted Lindsay three times on the shoulder. It was her signature seal of approval. With that, it was done. It was decided. Alexander was to tour his kingdom as the humble leader of a proud but humble country. The precise details were left to the former regents, now the King's diligent advisors, except for one surprising proclamation.

Alexander announced, "I must tour the entire Kingdom, all the way to the northern shores."

"No, no," Durward objected, "The north is occupied, and a fragile peace keeps the King of Norway from marching south."

"Yes," Alexander answered, "a fragile peace procured by my father, and I will finish what he began."

Lindsay interjected, "Are we planning a tour or a war?"

"No war!" Alexander assured them, "We bring no soldiers, only a handful of royal guards. We do not invade, but the King of the Scots will visit the Scots… all of them."

Vanora rarely pushed an unsolicited opinion, but she ventured one in defense of the plan, "Our King is right, there are people to see in the far north…, people and places."

The former regents recognized the futility of further objection. The feast broke, and King Bug-bane, Queen Heather, and their precious little treasure retreated to the royal chamber.

During Alexander's childhood, Vanora had done much to keep the King humble and instill in him the spirit of a servant, despite Durward and Baliol's extravagant efforts to the contrary. She saw his tour of the Kingdom as the perfect opportunity to put her guidance to the test. Alexander would see his share of castles and grand estates. He would also see dirty farmhouses and impoverished villages. Much would be revealed about the sort of man and king she had raised, and she prepared for the journey with equal portions of pride and apprehension churning within her.

The tour would also be a test for Queen Margaret, who, although spending the happiest days of her youth at Vanora's humble home, was born and brought up in the lavish confines of Windsor Castle. How would the daughter of the English King respond when filthy, rough and crude, illiterate people grasped at a chance to touch their queen? When she and Alexander were together, they seemed blind to all riches but those of the spirit. Vanora pressed the limits of her authority to ensure the King and Queen traveled side by side, as Heather and Bug-bane, the same playful children who wallowed in the mud together.

One week after Alexander came into his power, a small and simple entourage gathered in the courtyard. Baliol had drawn a map, marking clearly all of the homes and families that must be visited.

Vanora pulled Lindsay aside and begged, "Have you seen Baliol's map? Speak to him, David. You know well that a tour of affluent families is not what is needed. Neither do I need to tell you that Alexander and Margaret are unlike any king and queen that have ruled this country or any other."

"Yes," Lindsay replied, "We must drag them through the dirt and see how well they wear it. Leave it to me."

If Lindsay said it, it was as good as done. Vanora gave the concern no more thought. She turned her mind and her efforts to a book she had been binding by hand all week. Its pages were blank. Her intention was to fill them as they traveled with stories and pictures of the tour, for Alexander, for his children, and for posterity, imagining it would someday serve as both documentation and as a manual for future kings.

Much of Alexander's time during the preceding week was spent with Lindsay, learning the basic greetings and pleasantries of each isolated culture from Dumfries to the Northern Hebrides, intently studying each of the diverse languages and dialects under his rule, including those of the Norwegians who occupied the north and west of the island.

Lindsay instructed him repeatedly, "You cannot know a person without understanding the culture, and culture is sewn tightly to language. There is also no greater sign of respect than to speak to them in their own words. This is essential," he repeated, "*This is essential.*"

The opulence of Alexander's mind was on bold display in those lessons. He absorbed and reproduced language with uncommon ease. With each new word or phrase, he felt a stronger connection to the faceless strangers who spoke it. His sense of responsibility to those countrymen he had not yet met wrapped more tightly around him each time he spoke one of their words — and he could not wait to speak to them face-to-face.

It was a cool and rainy September morning and four plain, understated carriages were filled with the travelers. Only four lightly armed guards were permitted to accompany them. The entourage was ready to roll, Vanora, with her bound pages empty and ready to fill, Baliol, with his map newly marked by Lindsay with poor farms and villages to visit, Alexander, with his head full of words and phrases and an itching eagerness to put them to use, and Queen Margaret, with a toddler on her lap and a deep longing for greater intimacy with a country she embraced fully as her own.

A journey to take
With eyes opened wide
Our family will grow
And learn from the ride

Chapter Twenty:

Sharing Water from the Stream

As Vanora stared in wonder
At Scotland's King and Queen
Her thoughts were drawn to the ancient walls
Of a legendary scene

The Royal Entourage traveled southeast along a small river they called *Watter Gala*. Along the way, they encountered no towns or villages. Occasional hut clusters hung from the river like small fruits on a vine. Alexander wanted to stop at each, embrace his countrymen, and hear stories of their lives. To Durward's delight, even Vanora admitted that they could not visit every Scot in the country.

There was another reason Vanora was eager to press on. Where the *Watter Gala* drained into the larger *Watter O Tweid*, near the tiny village of Galashiels, was an ancient and abandoned settlement. In its Bronze Age glory, 2,500 years earlier, it had been a sacred site, the religious capital of the Kingdom of Maetae, people of early Pictish ethnicity. All that remained were the mounds and ditches of the old earthen work fortifications, not recognizable by any passer-by as more than a natural landscape. When

Vanora ordered the carriages to a stop, nobody knew why. Only she saw the subtle landmarks for what they were.

Vanora knew the site well. Not only had she been there many times as a child and adult, but she could visualize the temple that once stood there. Her mother had described it to her, as it had been described by *her* mother, and back through the women of her family, through centuries beyond record, to a Pictish priestess who presided over the temple and surrounding villages.

The effect of the place on Vanora was obvious to all. Her eyes lit widely. She hummed some ancient chant that reverberated in her chest and seemed to amplify in volume, as if a tiny chorus of mystical singers stood upon each of her ribs. She kicked off her shoes and kneaded the grass and dirt beneath her with her toes, in pulsing, rhythmic embraces of the sacred earth beneath her. She walked among what appeared as natural grassy ridges to everyone else as though she were walking down the halls of a holy cathedral.

The curiosity of the onlookers held very different flavors. The guards watched in bewilderment. They knew well *of* Vanora. The inexplicable authority of this servant woman was obvious, and it confounded them. They could not understand why the King, the Queen, and three of the most highly decorated nobles in Scotland obeyed her command to stop, and watched her with reverence as she meandered a trance-like walk around an unremarkable patch of land outside of an ordinary little village.

Durward and Baliol understood enough to know that whatever Vanora was doing, it was beyond them, not beneath them. They watched with intrigue, like children watching a magician prepare for his act. They waited for her to grow in size, or conjure some scaly creature from the dirt to march along beside them in their journey.

Between those two extremes sat Alexander, Margaret, and Lindsay. They knew of Vanora's lineage. Each in their turn had been the blessed recipient of her wisdom, wisdom passed to her through her maternal line, back, back through the ages, back to the very temple grounds upon which they all stood. Alexander expected no magical conjuring from his mother, but a new installment of arcane wisdom, sung to him in the form of a lullaby, or whispered to him in verse.

As they all stared, Vanora dragged her bare feet in slow, small steps along the inside of what had become clear to them all as the ancient remains of a settlement. It looked like the strange dance of an old woman. Alexander, Margaret, and Lindsay saw it for what it was — Vanora's reluctance to disconnect her skin from the dirt beneath her, as her body and spirit communed with the past.

For more than an hour, the guards sat on their horses and watched. Queen Margaret dismounted and sprawled out on her back amid the high grass, clenching the soil with her fingers, trying to see what Vanora saw. Alexander walked at a distance behind Vanora, as she dragged her feet in dozens of laps through the site. Lindsay had one advantage over the others. He had been to Skye, to an ancient fortress. He had witnessed the mystical firsthand. He had battled the water sprites, fought the shadows, held and wielded the sword that carries the blood of its vanquished. It felt to him like he was back on Skye, dwelling among the unearthly. With his eyes wide open, he visualized the Pictish Priestesses strolling in conversation beside Vanora.

Of all who witnessed the day, Lindsay's vision was nearest the truth. Vanora walked among the sages of the distant past. Birds of conflicting breeds mingled above her and around her. Gulls, of course gulls, but also doves, house sparrows, and three dark-brown owls, all contributed the signature sounds of their breed to the natural noises around her. To each, she nodded or shook her head, smiled and winced, as if the concerted sounds of the birds took her through a wide and varied conversation.

Vanora had indeed conversed with the priestesses of the past, sought their advice, and received their ageless wisdom. When she finally put her shoes back on and mounted the carriage, a new light seemed to rise from her deepening wrinkles, giving her aging features a look of timelessness. It was clear to her dearest ones among them that they rode away from Galashiels bearing more than they arrived with, and it was held inside of Vanora.

Before a dozen rotations of the wheels, Vanora was scribbling away in her book. Queen Margaret sat beside her and strained her eyes to spy just one little tidbit of the mysteries taking the form of written words, as the pen of Vanora vigorously scratched the pages. Whatever she wrote, it was not meant to share, not just then. She closed the book and stuffed it into a bag.

They continued southwest, deeper into the land of the Britons. The people were Scots by nationality, but ethnically, linguistically, and culturally were foreign in the extreme. They stopped in a rain-soaked, muddy village called Mauchline. The prominent feature of the area was an abbey, built and run by the Cistercian Monks of Melrose. The surrounding settlement was of poor farmers, providing crops for the abbey and for the pilgrims who visited.

The abbey rose from the horizon as they approached, a glorious testament to God and to those who dedicated their lives to the Church. Baliol was delighted. He had much to discuss with the monks, academic and religious points that tapped naggingly at the inside of his skull. To his dismay, Lindsay directed the entourage right past the luxurious abbey, to the poor farmhouses beyond.

They stopped beside a young man named Owain, who struggled to pull his plow through the muddy land. His young wife, Eira, filthy to the waist in mud, joined his efforts. They did not notice the caravan beside them, not until Alexander leaped from a carriage and ran to assist them. It was clear to them that Alexander was no poor farmer. They imagined him to be another wealthy pilgrim to the abbey, until Baliol shouted for his King.

"Your Highness," he yelled in a fluster, "This is unseemly! Let *us* help these people."

Owain and Eira ceased their efforts with held breaths. They stared stone-faced at their sovereign. The entire entourage was dismounted and observing.

Lindsay took one strong step to assist before Vanora grabbed his wrist and warned him, "Don't you dare."

Lindsay ordered the others back, and they all waited to see what would transpire. Owain and Eira bowed low. Owain shouted to his mother in a distant hut. An old woman responded in haste. Owain instructed his mother to make ready the table to receive the King.

Two weeks earlier, the words would have been unrecognizable to Alexander. As it was, he understood the gist and delighted in telling his dirty hosts, "I did not come here to be served by you, but to serve. Let us move this plow together."

Owain's mother ran back to the house to fetch refreshments for the travelers while Owain, Eira, and Alexander struggled against the reluctant mud. Lindsay forbade the others to assist. Owain's mother returned with dried meats and stale flatbread. Even the guards were repulsed by the offering, but to Owain and his family, it was the best they had, quite the royal feast.

The old woman went directly to her Queen and offered the bread. When Margaret accepted it with a grateful smile, the old woman swooned. She wept, dropped to her knees in the mud, and grasped at Margaret's dress. She was dirty from heel to scalp, and smudged and soiled Margaret's dress with her hands. The guards tried to intervene, but Margaret stopped them with a slight raise of her hand.

She did not see dirty hands or a muddy dress. She did not see a poor old woman. She saw a fellow-mother, a Scot, and a friend. She assisted the woman to her feet and embraced her tightly, seeming to take all of the woman's filth onto her own dress, hands, and face. The woman's embrace left a dark smudge of dirt on Margaret's cheek. Alexander looked at his wife and was reminded of the girl he knew and his first romantic attraction to her. This time, he did not wipe the dirt away with his thumb. It suited her better than any royal adornment, increasing her beauty in his eyes.

Poor Baliol shook inwardly at the impertinence, but he remained still and silent. Margaret joined Owain, Eira, and Alexander and pulled the plow from its clutching bog. When they freed themselves of the rope, Owain's mother awaited with provincial mugs filled with water from the nearby stream. As they refreshed themselves from their efforts, Vanora retrieved her book from her bag and scribbled a new passage.

Our Queen saw life
In the woman's soiled hands
She shed joy-filled tears
Gave no orders, made no demands

A faithful smile was drawn
By this woman of the soil
As they refreshed themselves as sisters
From the moment's sweat and toil

Many hours were spent with Owain and his gracious but impoverished family, and many of his rustic neighbors joined them. The lavish abbey teased and taunted Baliol. As the sun began to set, to his infinite delight, King

Alexander ordered him to the abbey to secure their lodgings for the night. After a provincial meal on a coarse wooden table, enriched to extravagance by fine, energetic, enthralling conversation, the royal entourage left the muddy village and received the lavish accommodations of the Cistercian Monks of Melrose.

Oh, Baliol was in his element! He hardly slept, but toured the abbey, perused the library, and engaged in conversations of the highest academic order. The abbey was a necessary visit. The Church was owed its due from the Crown. Much more than that, the royal couple needed the skills to relate easily with the very high and the very low. Vanora delighted in how seamlessly Alexander and Margaret transitioned from the company of peasant farmers to the pomp and circumstance of more prestigious hosts. And each source of her pride was well represented in verse, scratched from her very soul, directly into her journal.

They remained for four days in the abbey, making a few excursions to the surrounding people each day, then rolled forward again, continuing southwest, to the town of Ayr. Ayr would be another opportunity for Alexander to mingle with mixed company. It was the largest port on the west coast, filled with wealthy merchants, run by powerful barons, but populated also with dock workers, and surrounded by the farms that fed the town.

So near the border, Ayr clung tightly to its Scottish identity. When Princess Margaret was born in March of the previous year, the town began planning a celebration. They set the fair for September to note the successful end of the summer shipping season and the treasures it brought, but also to mark a treasure much dearer to them — the Royal Child, and the continuation of the Royal Line.

The first fair, in 1261, was understated and involved the efforts of a few prominent families. The royal entourage arrived in Ayr as preparations were being made for the second annual fair. They had no reason to expect a royal visit, which included the very Princess in whose honor the fair was celebrated, but it was no accident. Ayr was marked on Durward's map. He knew of the previous year's celebration, and he knew that a royal visit would sew tightly the loyalties of these prominent border merchants.

Lindsay and Durward rode ahead of the others to secure their lodgings and a royal welcome befitting the event. Ayr was all abuzz. The steady preparations turned feverish and four times as extravagant. When the four simple carriages rolled into town, the streets were already lined with Alexander and Margaret's loyal subjects. It was a parade like none ever seen on the west coast of Scotland.

The fair began two days later and lasted for another four. It featured samples of every foreign trinket and spice to travel the seas to Ayr. Spices from the Far East that had been carried along the Silk Road to Egypt, then sailed the Mediterranean to the Arab tribes of Morocco, and to Portugal, where they boarded a Scottish ship bound for Ayr, found their way to the tongue of the Scottish King. In attending the fair, Alexander saw much of the world and tasted its flavors.

In the midst of the crowded fair, Baliol pulled the King aside and gave a piece of understanding that only he could give. He was the master of traditions and a student of cultures.

He said, "There are three ways to know a people. Celebrate their holidays. That will tell you what they hold dear. Listen to their music. That is what carries their spirit. And eat their foods, for food is what binds it all together."

The fair in Ayr, that celebration of his daughter, offered him each of those things in samples just large enough to be savored. In the short week in Ayr, the King and Queen met nobles, who knew and observed every point of etiquette and decorum expected in the Royal

Presence. They also mingled with salty sailors, middle-class merchants, sweaty dock workers, and the mangy folk who scraped by with odd jobs and handouts. Bug-bane and Heather addressed them all equally, seeking the love of the lowest with no less effort than the highest. They felt an equal sense of kinship with them all, and by the time they left Ayr, all of Ayr felt the same. Each citizen of Ayr felt like Alexander and Margaret were their personal King and Queen, and Vanora had many proud verses to scribble into her journal.

An unprecedented blend of classes gathered elbow-to-elbow to see the royal entourage off. The four simple carriages headed north along the coast. They stopped for a few hours at a fishing settlement known by the locals as An t-Sròn. They bought from the local catch, observed with interest as an old resident instructed them on his technique of smoking and drying the fish, and left An t-Sròn with more food and less money.

They cut north through Corsehill, where Alexander met a great-aunt and several cousins. From there, they set their noses toward Glasgow. There was no nearer bridge over the River Clyde, and Glasgow offered much to distract them. If given his way, Baliol would have remained there until the following summer, which is why Lindsay spurred them onward after only two days. They left Glasgow on a sunny morning, heading northwest up the coast, and weaved a serpentine course inland and back to the sea. Along the way, they walked stone castles, dirty farmhouses, and wild land that had not hosted a human foot in centuries.

Exactly as they reached the border of Norwegian held land, the weather turned sour. If it was merely a coincidence, it was an uncanny one. The guards argued, two believing the weather change to be a warning from a Scottish sky that favored them, the other two seeing a Norwegian sky that threatened them. Whichever was the case, they heeded it. They cut inland along the border, into the sparse and rugged country that Alexander could still claim as his own. But only a few miles along, Vanora shouted the caravan to a halt.

She stepped from the carriage, walked beside Lindsay's horse, and spoke softly, "Here. We must go west from here."

Lindsay reminded her, "The lands west of here are held by a foreign power. It would be unwise to traipse our carriages —"

She interrupted him, "Not the carriages, not the others, only Alexander and Margaret, you and me."

There was a glossy glow in her eyes, one he had seen before. Whatever awaited them to the west was for Vanora to understand and for Alexander to discover. Lindsay had followed her like a child before, and he was willing to do so again. The rest of the entourage made camp in the wilderness. The Queen begrudgingly left her daughter in William's hands, and she, her husband, Vanora, and Lindsay rode west on two horses.

After an hour they rested and Vanora told them where they were going, "We have entered the ancient Kingdom of Dál Riata. This is their land, and the Kindred of Cenél Loairn are Alexander's people."

Alexander questioned, "Kindred?"

"Yes, my love, Cenél Loairn was a district of the Kingdom, a clan of sorts. Many boots have walked this land. Many soldiers have come and gone, but the land is still Dál Riata and the grass and soil are still Cenél Loairn."

In a tone of frustration, Alexander commented, "Tell that to the Norwegians."

"Oh, they will not be here long. They are not Cenél Loairn. The land will not accept them and, while you are still King, they will leave of their own accord."

In response to her prognostication, Vanora's lungs were the only ones to draw breath among them. The others stared at her, waiting for her next words.

She explained, "Imagine you are with a new friend who does not speak your language and refuses to learn. How long will you savor the silence before you yearn for communication? Miscommunication will strain the relationship, and the friendship will grow tiresome. The Norwegians do not speak the language of this land. They are not Cenél Loairn."

Alexander applied the metaphor to himself and, with itching apprehension, he said, "*I* speak no such language. The land says nothing to *me*."

"You will, my precious. That is why we are here. And when you speak to the Cenél Loairn, the land will belong to you, and you will belong to the land."

Alexander and Margaret's fresh young minds struggled to grasp the truth that stood just beyond their reach. Lindsay made no such effort. He was content to follow in faith, having learned the hard way that truth will seek out its own vessel, requiring nothing more than faith from the recipient.

With rested bodies and weary minds, Alexander and Margaret mounted a horse. Vanora and Lindsay took the other, and the rugged road to mystery unfurled before them.

They rode over hills, through forests, and around the lochs and firths, encountering nobody. A party of gulls trailed them, increasing in number with every mile, until the travelers were shadowed by the wings above them. Finally, they topped a hill and looked down on a large, flat valley. The sun was low and long shadows were cast across the grass by tall standing stones. The stones were still and lifeless, but their shadows seemed to waver and take on the form of men and women.

They rode into the center of the valley to a tall stone with a point at the top that directed the eyes upward. All four travelers dismounted and stood clustered in front of the pointed stone. The stone had a pattern of cup marks that resembled star constellations. Alexander pointed to the marks, then raised his finger upward to the point and farther still, until he pointed at the first few stars to shine through the dusk.

"No, no, no," Vanora corrected him, "Take your eyes downward. This has to do with the land, not the sky."

"But the stars," he began.

"Are you the King of the stars or the King of the land and people? This place has nothing to do with the sky!"

She extended a finger and placed it in one of the cup marks near the top, then traced a pattern from cup mark to cup mark. Chills ran through the others as Vanora began to mutter strange words in an unknown language. She seemed to speak to the stone — or speak *for* the stone. Alexander felt that she was speaking to him, instructing him in some urgent matter. But he could not understand her, and panic began to take him.

Vanora took his shaking hand, clenched his fingers into a fist, leaving only his index finger extended, and placed the tip of his finger into a cup mark on the stone. She dragged his fingertip from one mark to another, in a seemingly random pattern. It did not remain random for long, not to Alexander. He began to hear language from the stone, not in syllables into his ear, but in the rough pours of the stone, through his fingers, and directly into his heart.

Vanora released his hand. He continued the patterns on his own, and to the astonishment of Margaret and Lindsay, his lips began to mumble words in the same mysterious language. He giggled and he cried. He spoke and he listened, while continuing to trace patterns on the stone with his fingertip.

"For Heaven's sake, Vanora," Lindsay begged, "Tell me what is happening to our son."

"Hush David! He is learning. Watch our boy grow into the land and watch the Cenél Loairn root into him."

Lindsay's mind could only loosely grasp her meaning. But he took a step backward and observed. He reached for Margaret's hand and pulled her to stand beside him. As the valley began to glow with the strengthening starlight, the stones turned silvery. As Alexander's finger remained in contact with the stone, he shone with an identical glow. His mumbled words grew louder as the last remnants of the day's sunlight disappeared.

Vanora placed a hand on his shoulder and pulled him backward from the stone. She asked him, "What have they told you?"

Alexander turned to her to reveal cheeks shimmering with starlit tears. He smiled broadly, reached for the stones again, and translated the words.

In the absence of all
With the waiting of few
All has begun
As shadows bleed through

Send time to the sea
With many on hand
The few who stand near you
Will pass and disband

A gate waits to unlatch
Wings wait to dispatch
A new life will hatch
In your Castle of Sand

As he spoke the words, he scanned to his left and his right, in search of a castle of sand. He looked at the pattern of the standing stones and tried to visualize a grand structure around them. As he subconsciously stroked the stone with his fingers, his eyes went downward, and it struck him. The castle is beneath him, in the soil between his feet, in between the blades of grass, holding the roots of the trees, and rising up to form the hill to his right. That is the castle, and for a moment, he thought, "That is my castle."

As his wandering fingertip found another cup mark, the winged ring on his finger warmed by some unknown source, and the language of the Cenél Loairn poured into him again, and again found the air through the lips of Alexander.

Raise your hand and show it to all
The feathered crown
Was forged in the ground
And has always been bound
To the King and the Gull

Your story was told before it came true
You lived here before
And are bound at the core
To the hallway and door
Of the people you knew

The gulls flock near an empty throne
A space lies between
What is heard and is seen
For they cannot convene
With those who suffer alone

As he spoke for the stone, the weather seemed to respond in a language of its own. They nestled tightly to each other, leaning their backs against the stone. A bitter, biting wind gusted off the sea from the west. Their clothing was little guard against it. Lindsay led the two horses to the west side of the stone, where their large bodies blocked much of the wind from their human counterparts.

He pulled his cloak from his saddlebag and draped it over the others. Alexander was a stout young man, and Margaret was fearsome in her own right, yet they accepted his care like the children they once were, and huddled together beneath the Lindsay cloak. Lindsay sought no such protection. The sword at his hip, that blade pulsing with the blood of the slain, remained warm, as if it sat under the midday sun.

In the morning, they did not return to William and the others, but continued west under Vanora's leadership. Nobody asked where or why. Whatever they were to see, wherever they were to go, however they were to suffer, was for the best if Vanora brought them to it.

She led them to the shore of Loch Craignish. A boat waited for them, a boat and a man that Lindsay knew. It was the same boat and captain that had taken him to Skye. Oh, how Lindsay was flooded with memories, memories that slashed at him and bruised him, but that also gave him a sense of rightness.

Not a word was spoken to or by the captain. Vanora embarked and the others followed quickly behind. As the boat pushed from the shore, the horses whinnied and ran off to the east. In a sudden panic, Margaret grabbed Alexander by the sleeve, but before she could voice her concern, she noticed that Vanora and Lindsay paid the retreating horses no mind at all, but stabbed their focused eyes forward, to the west, to the sea.

They cleared the Slate Islands and found the open sea. Although the sky was bright and clear, and the breeze was light, the waves were rough. They churned as if stirred from beneath by an angry kraken. If there was some monster of deep intent upon sinking them, it was impotent against the skilled captain. Their boat seemed to sail in spite of the waves, not helplessly upon them. Margaret could not understand what her senses took in. The waves crashed loudly around them and splashed into the boat, yet it felt like she rode in a carriage, on a street of polished stone.

Vanora, again seeing more than was shown, stroked the back of the Queen's head three times and whispered in her ear, "Take your thoughts from what the eyes see, and place them on what the heart feels."

Suddenly, the waves meant nothing. Only the company of her loved ones mattered, and the strong sense of well-being their presence gave her.

They sailed around the southern tip of the Isle of Mull, then turned north, through a narrow channel with white beaches to their left. The white, sandy beaches — they captivated Alexander, despotically holding his attention. A figure appeared, strewn out upon the sand. At that distance, Alexander could not make it out. As the boat drew nearer, it appeared like a human figure, a lifeless figure. As they came nearer still, and Alexander strained his keen eyes, it appeared to be him. He stared at his own lifeless body on a bright sandy beach. His breath was taken. Every hair on his body stood erect, and chills waved across him with more fury than the sea around him.

The boat continued toward the sandy patch of beach. As it did, the nature of the figure took clearer form. It was not Alexander, nor any human body, but a tightly clustered flock of gulls. The small flock broke from their huddle and began to walk the beach like passers-by on a crowded city street. Their calls grew louder in Alexander's ears, only in Alexander's ears.

The squawking transitioned to a soft human voice, not his father's, not any he recognized, but in a *language* he recognized, in the language of the Cenél Loairn, and they spoke to him.

Alexander
Come with us
Follow our flight

Let me show you the Kingdom
From our point of sight

These are the trees
Of lands long ago
Learn from their roots
And know what they know

You are their keeper
As King of this land
Fly with our wings
From this beach of white sand

The flock silenced abruptly and took to the air. They flew along the channel, leading the boat through, into a pass of choppy sea, to the island of Staffa. It was a small island, no larger than some of the small villages they had passed on their tour. As they drew closer, they could see it was inhabited. It was a simple settlement. Small huts surrounded a central tower. Lindsay's heart jumped when he recognized the design of the buildings.

The exterior walls were made of vertical posts supporting thickly thatched roofs above. These were not Scottish buildings. They were Scandinavian. They were Norwegian. The peace was tenuous, if it could be called peace. Skirmishes along the border increased in number and violence, and there they were, pulling ashore on a Norwegian island. They all saw the wisdom of such a small party. The guards would have given the wrong impression. As it was, they were two men and two women, nothing more.

Lindsay prayed they could achieve whatever goal Vanora had in mind and leave the island unnoticed. Vanora had other plans. She led them up a path in the cliffs, not sneaking stealthily, but marching triumphantly, as if returning home. She led them up to the acropolis and into the village. It bustled modestly with people who, while speaking Norwegian, appeared like no Norwegians Lindsay had ever seen. Their dress was unique, made of strange blends of animal skins and brightly dyed textiles. It adorned people of flamboyantly good-nature. They inhabited a cold, harsh, wind-blown island, yet their complexions were soft, bright, and youthful, made brighter still by their welcoming smiles as their four guests walked among them.

In antiquated Norwegian, the travelers were greeted and invited to dine. Alexander's linguistic studies were put to the test, a test he passed admirably. His tongue volleyed his learned vocabulary, while his ears reveled in a different sound. During the course of the evening, Vanora spoke to their hosts in another language, or a blend of languages. Alexander caught a word here and there, while hearing amid them syllables that were as strange as they were beautiful. Whether his imagination painted the meaning colorfully in his head, or he had some hidden knowledge of a language he had never studied, he understood what was spoken, or believed he understood.

Vanora spoke to the leader of the village. They talked of a cave, of a man, of fire and smoke, and of a journey. They may as well have been humming some wordless lullaby for all Lindsay and Margaret could make of it. But Alexander understood, and as lovely as the melodic language sounded in his ears, it seeped deeply into him

with invasive darkness, filling him from bone to skin with
a scratching, squeezing sense of dread.

Words from soil
From stone and from men
Speak from a distance
The language of kin

Chapter Twenty-One:

Which Cloud Is You

Deeper and deeper
As dark as the night
The cave's solemn keeper
Reveals a new light

They all slept within the vertical posts of a Scandinavian hut, all four of them huddled tightly together. Heavy furs were piled upon them by their hosts, and the night passed warmly and restfully. In the morning, an elder from the community led them around to the southern edge of the island. From there, they were left alone to scale the cliff down to the narrow point of stony beach. Once soundly on the water's edge, they saw it — a cave.

It was like no cave they had ever seen. The entrance was framed by tall, dark, perfectly hexagonal columns, formed by the masterful hand of nature. It resembled the precise sculpting that adorns the ancient cities of the Mediterranean. The sea flowed into the cave entrance in steady strides forward, as if making a pilgrimage to a holy site. The site was indeed holy, of that there was no doubt. Whether from the pilgrim waves deep inside, or the local wildlife, or some other figure natural or unnatural, a strange, moaning, swooshing sound bellowed out from within.

The cave and its noises called to Alexander. Without consulting his thoughts, his feet took him several strides toward the mouth. He turned to beckon the others.

"No, love," Vanora instructed, "This is no standing stone. What awaits you in there calls to you alone, and you alone must face it."

Margaret shivered from toe to scalp, pushing a subtle whimper from her slightly parted lips. She was a stout-hearted young woman that had already faced and defeated terror and peril. But something about the cave, and in the tone of Vanora's voice, unnerved her to the core. Alexander felt no such apprehension. He kissed his wife twice on the forehead and two more times on the lips, ran his fingers through her hair, put his mouth to her ear, intending to whisper some encouraging words of faith, but nothing came out but a gentle exhale. It rolled around her ear and raised the fine hairs on her neck. Without another word or thought, Alexander turned his back on his dearest ones and walked the water's edge to the mouth of the cave.

It would have been easier to swim into the cave, for there was no path for walking in. The avenue into the cave was watery and deep, and although it appeared calm, it was not inviting. There was a dark and forbidding color to the water, as if it shared no relation to the bright sea from which it came. Alexander imagined that the water flowing into the cave was not of the shallows surrounding the island, but a pilgrim from the mysterious depths of the distant ocean, old, mean, and grumpy from a long voyage. He had no desire to ride its gentle current into the cave, or even alert it to his presence above.

He scaled the left wall of the entrance, finding few footholds of enough depth to linger long enough to take a stabilizing breath. Once he was out of the direct sunlight, there was an edge at the base, no wider than his foot. He could have relieved himself of much physical strain by lowering himself to the thin ledge, but he dared not. As the flowing water turned black, and its low and steady groan echoed more loudly in the distance, he was more frightened than ever of his fellow pilgrim.

Deeper and deeper he went, until the bright mouth of the cave appeared as small as his own thumb. It was the sunlight off of the sea that tried so desperately to dimly inject itself into the dark cave, but Alexander forgot all about the sun, and about the shallow sea surrounding the island. In his furiously scrambling mind, the thumb-sized light shone directly from his loved ones on the beach.

The thought of Margaret, Vanora, and Lindsay warmed him and muted the moaning lament of the inner-cave, distracting him until he lost his grip and slid down the damp natural columns. His heart plunged in a panic into the mean and icy water, but his body did not. His feet landed securely on hard ground beneath him. He let out three quick breaths, then a child-like giggle, before turning his head away from the light and deeper into the cave.

There was nothing to catch his eyes, only pure blackness, yet he stepped determinedly toward it. Hugging the wall, placing one foot at a time on the ground beneath him, pressing the sides of his feet against the wall, he pushed forward. Looking down, he could not see how wide of a ledge he stood upon. He could not see his own legs, so he made no attempt to focus downward. He kept his eyes forward, praying strenuously that whatever or whomever he was meant to encounter would soon reveal itself to his senses.

It might have been ten minutes or two hours that he crept his way precariously along the side wall of the cave. His sense of time became distorted in his head. His earliest childhood memories felt mere seconds into his past, while his entrance into the cave faded in his memory, as if buried beneath many active years. Battling the pesky midges outside of the hollowed trunk felt like half of an hour behind him. Snuggling within the vertical posts of a Scandinavian hut seemed to fall in the week between his father's death and the coronation.

Alexander's confusion was extreme, and he began to believe he had fallen into the water and drowned. That morbid notion was pierced and shattered by a speck of light coming from deep in the cave. It was not the bluish sunlight leaping in between the sky and sea. It was soft and warm, orange, like a candle flame. In contrast to his most recent thoughts, it was the warmest, most welcoming sight he could ever remember, beckoning him forward.

He forgot all about the watery curmudgeon to his right. He walked at pace toward the growing orange flicker. In violation of all he knew about space and dimension, the path into the cave felt like it sloped downward, each step sharply beneath the last, yet the light growing in the distance remained at the level of his eyes. Finally, his feet sensed a leveling out of the path, which invited his heart to increase his stride and pace. He rose to a full sprint until the nature of the light was apparent.

It was a fire, fueled by five or six logs, and rising waist-high to Alexander. It was a roaring blaze, but it lit nothing of the cave around it. How very wide the cave must have been. The bright fire illuminated no walls in any direction, no boulders, no features of the inner-cave at all. He strained his imagination to visualize the massive earthen cavity in which he stood. His heart jolted and ejected all such trivial thoughts when he became aware of a shadowed figure beside the fire.

It was a masculine figure, thick and burly, or heavily cloaked. Alexander could not tell, for this figure seemed more to absorb the light of the fire than reflect it. With a simple, slow, and subtle gesture of his arm, the man invited Alexander to join him by the fire. It was an invitation, not a command, yet one not to be declined. Alexander's obedience was not under his control. While his thoughts swirled in a chaotic stupor, his feet accepted the invitation, and he found himself standing nearly hip-to-hip with the only other occupant of the cave.

He was not forbidden to glance at his dimly lit host. He felt no fear to do so. But his eyes remained forward, into the flames. They did not appear as fire, as heat licking upward, but as something more substantial. He felt like he could reach forward and pull a flame from the fire, hold it without injury, and stroke its strange texture with his thumb.

He probably would have tried, had the man not spoken, "The fire... does it appear strange to you?"

Alexander nodded and answered, "It does. It moves like no fire I have seen..., slower, more intentional."

"You are right about that, my son. It is no random, haphazard pattern you watch. This fire knows where it reaches, and it does so with purpose."

Alexander strained his eyes to focus more clearly, then asked, "Is it fire, or is it something else?"

"It is light. It is vision."

With those words, the endless blackness of the inner cave evaporated like steam, revealing a breathtaking vision of snow-capped mountains in the far distance. He looked to the man beside him, whose image was suddenly as clear as day. He was bald and muscular, and dressed in animal hides. His scalp was decorated with intricate lines and patterns, painted directly onto him in colorful paints. In his right hand, he held a wooden pipe. Writing was carved into the pipe, sloping and swirling figures in the Pictish language.

Inexplicable to him, Alexander could read it. The writing wrapped around the pipe, and only a portion faced the King's eyes. What he could see, read, "The winged ring will find its—"

He could see no more of it. With the tip of his thumb, he stroked the band of his ring and wondered if this cave-dwelling hermit, deep beneath a distant island, could know of Alexander, and of the ring he had worn since he was a young child. Is it possible that the ring written about on the pipe could be the very ring on his finger?

He was starving to make the connection, desperate to change his angle and read the rest of the pipe, to maybe, just maybe, catch a glimpse of his own name and some hint at his destiny. He was no captive, yet he could not move. He was locked in a cage to which he held the key but dared not release himself.

The man reached the pipe over the fire, not near enough to ignite its contents, or even much warm his extended hand. The pipe began to smoke nevertheless. He returned it to his mouth and drew a deep inhale. He puffed a cloud directly in front of him. It held its place above the fire, unconcerned about the pulsing flames. The man pulled another draw from the pipe, turned his head to his right, and puffed another cloud. It too held its place and form. He put forth one more cloud, to his left, which hovered mere inches from Alexander's face.

The smoke carried a pungent aroma of old, musty bark with brighter hints of youthful flowers, beneath it all was a hint of baked bread and cooked meats. Alexander thought he heard muffled laughter from within the cloud in front of him, as if it held within it a tiny village of miniature people in celebration. From the tiny cloud next to it, he could hear yells of anguish and the clashing of swords. From the next, came soulful chanting, which turned to gasps, then the sound of coughing and choking.

As he stared at the small cloud of smoke in front of him, encased in an inquisitive trance, the man asked him, "Which cloud is you?"

Alexander did not understand the question. He had no idea how to begin a response. The man gestured around him, and Alexander became aware of many more hand-sized clouds of pungent pipe smoke.

"Which cloud is you?" the man repeated.

Alexander's confusion was easily read on his face. His eyes went from cloud to cloud, peering deeply into each, trying to recognize something, some shape or movement that might declare one of them his own. His darting eyes caught the man's.

They stared fixedly at each other, then the man looked at the fire as it crackled and sparked, and he said, "This fire represents *life* in its eternal form. All else is of the world and not of life... Let me explain. You see, when you

271

were born you came from this fire. This is your home. This will always be your home. As you dwell with others, you learn of rituals and routines, of languages and earthly communication, of pleasures and pains. All of this you do is of the body. It is of the *self*. You choose to speak. You choose to eat. You choose to grow and expand. This is what you do."

Alexander did a quick internal inventory of his most vivid memories, trying to stand them against the man's words. His thoughts were interrupted, "But, my child, you must understand. The *self* is only of *this* world. The fire that is your home is of *life* and is forever. You may understand only the self but you know that all is of the fire. The *self* seeks survival. Once survival is secured, it seeks pleasure, and when fully pleasured, it seeks power. But *life* needs not seek survival, nor pleasure, nor power, for it is infinite. Power is an illusion created by the self and is not true life."

Alexander's mind surged suddenly with thoughts of his father, and the prominent barons. He thought of Beolin Crymlyn, of the many clan wars that had been romanticized in song. The heroes of battle no longer seemed heroic, but the victims of terrible tragedy.

The man posed his challenge again, "Which cloud is you?"

"I am born of the fire, to rise like the clouds with everything else of the fire."

He pointed to one cloud and said, "I am that one."

His eyes drifted to another cloud, and his finger followed, as he said, "...and I am that one... We are all of the fire. We are, all of us, the clouds."

At that realization, the clouds came together as one and hovered over the fire, as if to pay homage to its mother. Alexander raised his hand, and the cloud rose out of sight. Not another word was spoken in the cave. The lessons of the day had planted healthy seeds, and Alexander's future would have to fertilize them.

The scene around him was still as it had been. The bright sky and crowning mountains, the lush field surrounding him, the stream that ran near the fire, still filled his senses. He still felt the open breeze on his skin, still smelled the verdurous field. Alexander walked in a small circle in order to take it in one more time, for he knew it would soon be gone. When his eyes caught the man again, the cave went black. The vision was gone.

The painted hermit escorted Alexander to a boat. Alexander sat down, and the boat began to move. He thought this peculiar, because the water had flowed *into* the cave. Now it carried him out. None of the anxiety that scorched his entrance accompanied his exit. There was far too much to ponder. He leaned back and fell asleep in the boat.

When Alexander regained awareness, he opened his eyes to find himself standing on the narrow beach near the entrance to the cave. From the cliff above, he heard the voice of his beloved Queen Heather, shouting down to him. Vanora and Lindsay quickly joined her, and the three of them made their way to Alexander.

Being the strongest and fastest of the three, and completely mindless of his feminine companions, Lindsay reached the King first.

"One more day...," he panted, "One more day and I would have gone after you, despite Vanora's assurances."

"One *more* day?" Alexander asked, "How long was I in there?"

"You entered the cave six days ago. What did you eat? What did you drink? How did you survive?"

Alexander lifted a subtle smile on one half of his mouth. He thought of his painted teacher, and he answered, "I am of the fire. I do not seek survival, nor pleasure, nor power, but to hold the clouds together as one."

The answer made no sense to Lindsay, but that mattered little. Alexander was there before him — healthy, vibrant, and no worse for wear.

The day was still young. They bid a slow and familiar farewell to their Norwegian hosts and left the Island of Staffa the same way they came. Alexander did not focus on patches of beach or treacherous rocks. He looked upward, to the clouds, and to the gulls that flew in and out of them.

Our King stares at the sky
Finding all beneath and within
As light takes hold
Let the journey begin

Chapter Twenty-Two:

Leave Dark in its Lair

The King led the voyage
With the cave on his mind
To a dangerous ideal
Both noble and blind

The four travelers made their way back to the royal entourage only to discover that two of its members were conspicuously absent. The two dearest, William Lindsay and Princess Margaret, were gone. The maids and guards battled with clumsy words that crashed together, each trying as calmly as possible to bring the panicked mother up to speed.

While camped in waiting, Princess Margaret had turned ill. It was nothing too concerning. Steady crying had turned to coughing, and when coughing went weaker and scratchy, William rushed the child toward Scone Palace, to be tended by physicians and recover in the comforts of a royal residence.

Lindsay's faith in his son was matched only by Alexander's faith in his childhood companion. Neither man was terribly concerned. Queen Margaret's maternal instincts gripped her in the natural way. She would not sit for a moment of recovery and refreshment. Alexander ordered two of their four guards to take Margaret and Vanora to Scone, while Lindsay and Alexander remained. There was one more estate Alexander insisted upon visiting — the home of Beolin Crymlyn, the very same castle in which he and his young wife had been held as prisoners.

"I must advise against it, "Lindsay warned, "I still hold Firbolg, but I am older now, and we do not know what sort of welcome to expect."

Alexander answered with the calm authority of a king, "It would not matter to me if you carried only a stick. This is a visit that must be paid."

Lindsay began another protest, but Alexander cut him short, continuing, "It is my will, my destiny, I believe, to end these ceaseless battles between the families. Too much blood has been shed for petty patches of ground. If I am to unite the families, I cannot remain at odds with one of them, especially not Crymlyn. They are an old and powerful family, and although I could rally the forces of the crown and remove every one of them from the country, what sort of king would I be?"

Lindsay saw the wisdom of the King's words, but that vision did nothing to alleviate his fears. With the two remaining guards and a few servants, they rode to Crymlyn Castle, towards those very halls that Lindsay had left lined with blood and corpses. The hatred was extreme, and it would take much more than wise words to mend the wounds of the past and return to the old good-humor once shared with the Crymlyns. Armed with little more than faith and goodwill, they rode directly for Crymlyn Castle, making no stops along the way, rallying no additional support, and placing them most precariously into the den of the beast.

As they entered the forest surrounding the Crymlyn estate, each subtle sound of nature startled Lindsay, who held the reins with one hand, while gripping tightly to Firbolg with the other. He watched the sky for any sign from above that might warn him against their planned visit. He saw nothing. He closed his eyes and listened for the voice of Scáthach. He heard nothing. In the absence of heavenly objection, he begrudgingly trotted beside his King with increasing uneasiness in his heart.

The walls of Crymlyn's castle seemed higher than last they saw them. The stones appeared darker, angrier, and more bitterly foreboding. Alexander approached with none of Lindsay's fears. A peaceful smile reflected the calm confidence within him.

It was an unusual and unexpected visit. It would have been an extraordinary circumstance for the King to arrive at the castle of a *friend* with such a small entourage, so scantily guarded. It was all the stranger at the door of an enemy. Crymlyn could make no sense of it. He assumed treachery, some sort of vengeful trap for the crimes of the past. Still, he had no choice. He could not refuse the visit. He opened his gate to the King, and to Lindsay, who had slain his clansmen.

Alexander gave no reason for the visit. He embraced Crymlyn like an old friend. He spoke kind words in dulcet tones. Such a trio they made — Crymlyn shaking and sweating nervously, Lindsay gripping the handle of his sword and staring with steely eyes, and Alexander smiling and speaking softly. Crymlyn invited them to dine. Failing to do so was not an option.

Before dinner, servants led the royal guests to private chambers to rest and refresh themselves. Alexander was given a separate chamber, the best in the house. Lindsay was loathe to leave his side, but Alexander wanted to be alone. He ordered Lindsay to his own room, and the loyal knight obeyed.

While Alexander rested, Lindsay did not. He could not. He had an inner room in the castle, with no window to the outside. Outside his door was a hallway he had walked before under very different circumstances. His memories of that dark and bloody night rushed vividly onto his inner-eye. He gripped Firbolg while pacing his small room, twitching with every violent recollection.

Firbolg grew hot and heavy against his leg. He drew the sword, and it seemed to glow. The room was brighter, and he waited for his teacher to speak to him. He did not wait long. The voice of Scáthach echoed, but whether off the walls of the room or the inside of his own skull, he could not tell.

What have you done?

You were warned of this path
Yet you returned
The King is in danger
Mind what you have learned

Tell him this truth
Leave dark in its lair
This is your charge
And your burden to bear

There was no uncertainty in the message. Scáthach had spoken. Crymlyn was still dangerous. Regardless of Alexander's noble intentions, they could not linger. Lindsay rehearsed his protest in whispers behind his closed door. Before he could address them to his King, a servant knocked on the door and invited him to the dining hall.

Lindsay followed the servant to a long but narrow room, with a low, arched ceiling, filled by an old, splintered, dark, and bulky table, surrounded by chairs of various ages and styles. Alexander was already seated across from Beolin Crymlyn. To Lindsay's relief, the room

278

was well lit. It would have been difficult for anyone to make a covert move on the King. It was not Crymlyn's plan to make a move, not yet. He served a feast of extravagant proportion, and he observed.

Alexander was intensely thoughtful and deeply introspective. With his dreamy eyes and wandering gaze, he was not the very portrait of a fierce warrior-king. Crymlyn sized him up scrutinizingly. He did not see a thoughtful student of ancient wisdom, but a weak boy, and long dormant ambition began to awaken.

Dreams and schemes that had been put to rest after his failed kidnapping bubbled and churned from his innermost being. His teeth clenched together in his mouth, as new, more vicious plots spawned silently within him. His teeth grinding was not the only outward signs of the stirring and tossing designs budding and blooming in his heart. Although his stomach was full from the feast, it rumbled. The hibernation of his gluttonous greed was ended, and it awakened with ravenous hunger.

Alexander was blind to the subtle signs. Lindsay was keen to them. He had seen much more of the world and its people, both in his physical ventures and in his visions at Dún Scáith. He became increasingly uneasy in their surroundings and with their dinner host. Bed chambers were offered, but Lindsay would sooner have flung himself and his King down a jagged-rocked cliff than sleep vulnerably under Crymlyn's roof after the warning given to him by Scáthach.

He sprang abruptly to his feet, and through a tightly clenched jaw, he thanked their host with as much counterfeit gratitude as his uneasy heart could muster. He gathered what remained of the royal entourage and fled Crymlyn's castle in the dark of the late evening, with no explanation for the hurried flight. There was such fierce determination in his words and manner that Alexander dared not question. He simply followed Lindsay like the boy he once was. They rode directly for Scone Palace.

They were scarcely two miles escaped when Alexander asked Lindsay to explain in their steady trot what he could not in their rushed exit. Knowing Alexander's deep desire for reconciliation, he could not bring himself to speak the truth, not with only the voice of Scáthach echoing within his own skull as the lone source of evidence.

He answered in factual words that omitted a larger truth, "You did as you set out to do. You paid your visit. There was no reason to remain, not while your wife tends to your ill daughter. Your place is at Scone, under the guard and care of the royal residence."

Alexander agreed, in part, but still feared what impression their hurried departure might leave. Scáthach knew what Alexander could not. The story of Crymlyn's treachery had not yet been written. The head of the once proud and influential Crymlyn family hardly slept that night, nor in the several nights that followed. In each moment of quiet and stillness, Beolin's mind tossed in an increasing rampage of ambition and fear.

It was no longer simply his designs on the throne that stirred him, but fear of retribution on himself and his clan. His ambition had only managed stealthy, distant plotting. When alloyed with fear, it spurred actions far more treasonous than a kidnapping. Plans that formed in the privacy of his thoughts turned to discussions at his table. Piece by piece, step by step, plans of the most sinister nature hardened within the walls of Crymlyn Castle.

Alexander reached his destination to find Scone Palace in a state of dueling emotions. Princess Margaret had shaken all signs of illness, but word reached Scone of troubles to the west. King Håkon of Norway, afraid of losing his grip on Western Scotland and the Isles, ordered the removal of all Scots from Norwegian held territory.

With Scotland so freshly in the hands of her young King, he seized the moment to secure his holdings, before a bolder man awakened within Alexander III of Scotland.

The reported treatment of the Western Scots was horrifying. Alexander had no room in his head for Beolin Crymlyn. His thoughts, his fears, all of his hopes and ambitions went west to his suffering countrymen. Within minutes of hearing the reports, he determined to continue what his father could not finish — returning all of Scotland to the Scots and securing the peace and prosperity of his people.

The scars of the past
Come forcefully true
As the King sees Scotland
From the gulls point of view

Chapter Twenty-Three:

Draw Your Sword and Send It Falling

The gulls of the sky
That gather and swarm
Unite with the Maiden
That calls out to the storm

A military response to the conflicts in the West was not an option, not immediately, not for Alexander. He attempted as his father had — to purchase peace with gold. He sent an envoy to Norway with an offer far more generous than the cost of the land. The entire country was on edge waiting for a response. King Håkon IV of Norway answered squarely in his nature. He refused the peace offering, imprisoned the Scottish envoy, and demanded a ransom for their lives.

Much of the money Alexander offered for the land was paid for the safe return of his diplomats. The prisoners were released and returned with a warning. King Håkon was launching an invasion. The news came to Alexander's ear on the same day as other news, sweeter news, news whispered into his ear by his dearest, his Queen Heather.

Margaret was pregnant again. The news raised a deluge of emotions that overtook him like the tide. The rising waters within him drowned his natural sensibilities, leaving little more than a barbaric need to protect his wife, children, friends, and countrymen.

In February of 1263, Alexander mustered a small army and marched with them to the western border. For more than a month they waited, making no moves against the Norwegians peacefully working the lands. The treasury felt the strain of encamping so many soldiers for so long. Alexander left the front and toured the estates of the Lowlands, raising funds for a military campaign he still hoped desperately to avoid.

120 Norwegian warships left Norway in June of 1263, stopped at Orkney to gather more soldiers, then made their way to Skye. Skye!! There was no more sacred setting in the mind of David Lindsay. He felt a swelling, surging desire to rush to the defense of Dún Scáith.

Vanora tried to calm him, reminding him, "Scáthach and her daughters are in no danger from Viking raiders. They are of the Shadows and the Mist. The night wind and the waves obey her. Håkon will possess Skye only so much as Scáthach wishes."

The assurance spoke clearly to Lindsay's mind, but his heart was deaf to reason. He joined Alexander in Ayr, pulling every able-bodied Scottish soldier in his wake. Vanora accompanied him, and her words were truer than she knew. The wind, the waves, and mists of Skye shook the warmth of the season and took on a biting, angry chill. Håkon took his army and armada and retreated south to the Isle of Arran, leaving sacred Skye to those peaceful Norwegians who had called it home for generations.

There they were, a massive Norwegian army on the Isle of Arran and Alexander, Lindsay, Vanora, and the bravely outnumbered Scots in Ayr, with only the narrow Firth of Clyde between them. Queen Margaret, with the swelling life within her, remained at Scone Palace, waking each night in sweats of terror for her husband's safety. Scone had not the bustle of Edinburgh, and loneliness was a poor state of mind in her condition. She wrote to Alexander every few hours, sometimes combining them into a single dispatch, other times dispatching multiple riders in a single day. In either case, the pages were stained with tears — sweet, cherished tears that Alexander held against his lips, kissing the paper last held by his wife.

Such moments of personal sentiment were sparse. Håkon's armada was easily seen on the eastern shore of Arran, yet he did not attack the weaker Scottish forces. He taunted Alexander, sending raiding parties from Arran to the peaceful Scottish villages scattered along the Hebrides and western coast of the mainland. The raids were brutal, intentionally so. They were clearly designed to bait a rash attack from Alexander.

Nothing could be done for the brutalized communities. Alexander did not have nearly enough soldiers to effectively patrol the area while maintaining a force large enough to withstand a direct assault. There was nothing he could do but weep and return Margaret's letters with stained paper of his own. Against the advice of those nearest to him, he rode out to console survivors, often sneaking away alone in the middle of the night.

One such night was a fateful ride north. In Håkon's most brazen attack, he had sent one hundred soldiers to the town of Irvine. It had once served as the capital. During the reign of Alexander's grandfather, Irvine was the military headquarters of the Scottish Army. It was a shell of its former glory, but its cultural significance remained, and having it defiled cut deeply. It was surely a trap, and Alexander took the bait.

He dared not travel the coast. But the inland roads, where they existed at all, were narrow, overgrown, and often heavily wooded. He got lost in the dark alone and never reached Irvine. The sun rose on the solitary King as his horse carried him into a field. There, in the center, was a tall, square standing stone. Alexander stared at the colorful dawn shining off the stone. His horse, as if directed by the King's eyes, walked him directly to it.

The four sides of the stone faced each of the cardinal directions. The eastern side took the rising sun most directly. The southern side was brushed by the infant daylight at such an angle as to boldly reveal the cup marks and etchings. Oh, how they sang to Alexander, called to him like a seductive siren. He dismounted, stood against the stone, ran his fingers along its markings, and heard, just as before, the words of his Cenél Loairn ancestors. As the words entered his heart, they were translated aloud by his lips.

Stretch the time, draw it long
Intoxicate them with your song
Then he with blood sword in his hand
Commune with water and with sand
To the Shadow Maiden he will demand
And weaken those who once stood strong

Alexander needed no lengthy pondering of the meaning. To him it was clear. He had to delay Håkon with negotiations and entertainment, while Lindsay, the holder of the blood sword, appealed to the Shadow Maiden who had trained him. Alexander mounted his horse in a single stride and rode back to Ayr. He set immediately to obey the stone prophecy, sending, not for a noble diplomat, but for a new, seductively diplomatic envoy. Such a company would hold no authority over the King of Norway. He sent for minstrels and storytellers, for those who held Scottish folk culture in their pockets, for beautiful village maidens with ragged dresses and golden voices. Within two weeks, he had assembled a party of nine that suited his aims perfectly. He simply called them The Nine.

The paltry Scottish forces continued to gather in Ayr, growing steadily, but still vastly outnumbered by the Norwegians on Arran. Alexander wrote a letter, appealing for a stop to the raids while negotiations commenced. He sent the letter with The Nine and a single unarmed escort. Håkon accepted the terms, and negotiations began.

It was unlike any suit for peace in history, recorded or otherwise. They were sung, and not by nervous, rigid nobles, but through beautifully blushing faces. They were spoken by rustics, woven into intriguing tales of local lore. Most importantly, they served their purpose. Håkon had no interest in imprisoning them and no desire to dismiss their company with a quick settlement. The Nine may not have been honored guests on Arran, but they were a diverting fascination, intoxicatingly entertaining to the Norwegian invaders, and serving their designed purpose of stalling until the numbers and the weather fell more in their King's favor. They sang, they danced, and they told enthralling tales of mysticism.

Lindsay made for Skye to fulfill his side of the stone's revelation. He was met on the shore of the Scottish mainland by eight Norwegian farmers. These were not soldiers of Håkon. They were stout men of the land. Skye had been theirs and their ancestors for as long as their oral history could remember. They loved the land, and the land loved them. Still, they were Norwegians and Norway was at war.

They met the Scottish noble with caution. They knew of David Lindsay. Word of his nobility and honor had long reverberated from every cliff and hill in the Western Isles. They asked him his business. Lindsay spoke openly about Dún Scáith, but stopped short of mentioning the Shadow maiden within. The Norwegians brought him on their own boat, across the sea to Skye. His sword was not welcome. His cautious hosts made him leave it on the Scottish shore. Lindsay drove Firbolg into the sand on the water's edge before boarding the boat.

On the shore of Skye, the Norwegians walked away from Lindsay without another word. Whatever he had planned on their island, the natives were contempt to leave it to him. He waited until they were out of sight, then made directly for Dún Scáith.

Again at the crumbling castle, with vivid memories of his training striking him like a heavy, pelting rain in his face, he called for his master. The day was not yet so aged. Light seeped into the castle, so it did not discourage Lindsay when the Shadow maiden did not answer him. He waited, leaning against the inner wall of the main chamber, much as he had years earlier. When the dusk came, his pulse elevated in proportion with the dwindling daylight.

When the stars could be seen through the hole in the ceiling, he whispered, "Scáthach."

He held his breath, afraid of drowning out any subtle response. He whispered again and again, elevating his voice with each recitation of his teacher's name.

Nothing.

Lindsay's mind began to drift. His pulse slowed. His eyelids went heavy. He slipped into a restless sleep, waking himself with sudden twitches of his stiff legs. Each time he awoke, he held his breath and listened. He scanned the inner walls for moving shadows.

Nothing.

Poor David Lindsay passed the most restless night he could remember since the last time he occupied that castle. But this visit bore no fruit. The sun rose with no word from Scáthach, no sight of her shadowy minions, no spraying mist forming into her silvery, warrior-daughters. It was just a sunrise. Even the local gulls were conspicuously absent. Lindsay stood for a moment, shouted for Scáthach one more time, fell back to a seat against the wall, buried his face in his hands, and cried.

His sobs beckoned no response from the absentee spirits of Skye. When the wells of his eyes ran dry, Lindsay took to his feet and marched slowly to the beach where the Norwegians had left him. They were again gathered there, as if waiting for their sad guest to return. They were gathered around a fire, singing and laughing. After only one long night, Lindsay looked like he had spent months at sea. The compassion of the Skye natives overflowed. They embraced him, fed him, and sang to him, but they asked him no questions.

Once he was reasonably refreshed, Lindsay boarded their boat, and they took him back to where they had found him. Firbolg stuck out of the sand where he had left it. The tide had come in, and the sea water rose nearly to the handle. Lindsay hopped from the boat, into water above his knees. With a grip on Firbolg's handle, he thanked his hosts and watched them sail away.

When they were gone from sight, he pulled on Firbolg. The legendary sword did not dislodge. He gripped it with both hands, grunted and yanked. The sand would not let go of the sword, or the sword would not let go of the sand.

In his imagination, he could hear Scáthach tell him, "Have you forgotten? The sword does not belong to you."

It was only his imagination. Scáthach made no sound. The gulls did not appear. Even the sea was silent and as smooth and placid as polished granite. Lindsay was at his wit's end. He released the sword that no longer obeyed him, and he walked from the water and sat on the shore. As he sat on the sand and stared at the sword, his sense of failure was sickening. Hours passed without food or water, with hardly a movement, until the tide had gone fully out and the sun lowered enough to stare him in his face.

Lindsay rose to his feet and walked to Firbolg. He touched the handle, not to grip and pull, but to tell it goodbye and wish it well. The sun was low in the west and cast the sword's shadow long across the sand. As Lindsay admired it, its form altered. The shadow of Firbolg softened, its rigid lines curving like the figure of a woman. The shadow of the handle turned to shoulders, the pommel to a head. This feminine figure was no stranger. It was Scáthach, the Shadowy One, taking form in the shadow of Firbolg.

Lindsay kneeled beside the sword, humble, obedient, and ready for whatever was to come. He caressed the handle with his thumb, the shadow of his hand appearing to hold the head of Scáthach. The water came back to life. Gulls circled above. The breeze returned to the land.

Scáthach spoke.

Why do you go
To the castle of stone
For I am of shadows
And light is my throne

Tell me your plight
Place it in my hand
This burden you bring
To this sword in the sand

Remaining on his knees, the sun sitting on the horizon, he pleaded the case of his King and his country. He spoke of the invaders, and of the injustices done by their hand to the Scottish people. He begged Scáthach to intervene on their behalf.

Dark shadows appeared on both sides of him. They were deeper and darker than any shadow cast by any object. They appeared as holes in the air beside him, like moving portals into nothingness. They seized him by the arms and lifted him to his feet, then dissipated, leaving only the last remnants of the day's sun and the voice of Scáthach.

She answered.

This King you fear from across the sea
Has won no gains, forced no decree
His countrymen live in peace with the land
They are kind to the water and good to the sand

I am not at war with them! Neither should you be
But if Firbolg is calling
And injustice is palling
The peace of rock and sand and tree
Then draw your sword and send it falling
Minding what you learned from me

In a voice that began defensive, but quickly softened into one of genuine, naive honesty, Lindsay replied, "I am not at war with the Norwegians who live in this land, nor is our King, nor our people. We are at war with the Norwegian King, a greedy, violent man who has rejected all of our entreaties for peace. He will disrupt the lives of all, even his own countrymen who live here in peace. Our King would have emptied his treasury to save one Scottish life. He would have paid as much to save one Norwegian husband from a Scottish sword. But Håkon rejected the money. He did not only want our land. He wanted it soaked in blood…, in our blood mixed with the blood of his own people. He wants war."

A long silence followed, then Scáthach's voice returned with a short and enigmatic answer, "Thank you."

"Thank you?" Lindsay questioned, "What does that mean? Will you intercede? Will you help us?"

With the sun completely submerged and its dark orange trail fading away, Lindsay stood alone. Scáthach had no more to say. Lindsay pulled Firbolg from the sand with ease. The sword was his again, and that was no small comfort. With that mild encouragement, he made his way back to Ayr with little to report to his awaiting King.

Alexander greeted Lindsay when he arrived and escorted him with urgency into his tent. He demanded a thorough report. Lindsay gave him every detail, every word he could remember from Scáthach. Alexander responded much as Lindsay had, asking, "Thank you? What does that mean? Will she help us?"

Vanora, who was seated in a shadowed corner, rose to her feet and embraced Alexander. Her smile was wide and widening still.

Seeing that Vanora held some knowledge that eluded him, he asked her, "What? What does she mean?"

Vanora laughed, pulled away from him, embraced Lindsay, took two steps back to face them both, and answered, "We have Scáthach. The Norwegian armada sits on the sea, and the sea is now on our side."

She let out a hearty laugh, which Alexander and Lindsay joined with nervous, uncertain giggles. As Vanora's laugh roared louder, her confidence consumed them, and their moods joined hers. Their spirits were encouraged enough to allow the soundest sleep any of them had in several weeks. They awoke ready to assume their place at Scáthach's side, wherever that happened to be.

News came early the next morning. Håkon was moving his army. By the time Alexander stood on the beach as witness, half of the Norwegian ships had already set sail. They were moving north, relocating to the island of Great Cumbrae. Only a narrow mile of sea separated the island from the town of Largs, on the Scottish mainland. The entertaining diplomatic envoy had succeeded in delaying an attack until the autumn had come. It was the last day of September, 1263, and the sea had shaken off the soft warmth and gentle currents of the summer. The sea was choppy. The wind was biting, and Scáthach was keen to their plight.

No longer daunted by their inferior numbers, Alexander rallied what forces he had and began a march north along the coast, toward Largs. On the first of October, Håkon had his entire fleet ready off the beach of Great Cumbrae, and a massive army ready to board. In preparation for the following day's attack, he ordered his army aboard the ships — a wise move were it not for the unforeseeable, for the fierce rage of Scáthach.

Early on the night of the first, the wind rose unnaturally. Waves lifted above the rails of the ships. The narrow swath of water between the Håkon ships and Largs churned like the deepest center of the sea. The Norwegian soldiers shook in terror. They had weathered storms at sea, but this was no natural storm. They prayed to their gods and cursed the witchcraft of the Scots.

Whatever effect their prayers were meant to have, they served only to anger Scáthach further. The tempest doubled in fury, blowing more than half of Håkon's ships off their anchors and pushing them to the open water without navigation.

Those unanchored ships had much more than wind and waves to contend with. Skilled sailors would have handled the storm. But Scáthach brought more than a storm. She brought her daughters to the fight. While the rain continued to pelt down, the sky above cleared, exposing the bright, silvery moon above. Waves crashed against the hulls, sending salty mist above the boards. Glowing from the moonlight, the mist formed into the fierce and feminine figures of Scáthach's daughters, lean, beautiful, baring their radiant flesh, and armed with watery blades.

Any soldier unfortunate to be near the rails when the mists rose was petrified by the paralyzing beauty rising above them, then pierced, sliced, and severed before they could blink their captivated eyes. Those who witnessed the carnage but escaped the blades crouched and trembled, abandoning their posts and leaving the ships to the whims of the storm.

The unanchored ships, with the few soldiers and sailors to survive Scáthach's daughters, were blown ashore on the beach of Largs. Håkon was left with less than half of his army, but still held greater numbers than Alexander. Early on the morning of October second, he sailed his remaining ships and army to Largs, to salvage what could be salvaged and rally his attack.

He was stunned by the wreckage. Oh, he had seen shattered ships, and he had seen battered and drowned men. Had that been the scene on the beach of Largs, his heart would have remained abominably stout. He found much more. The corpses strewn across the boards and tangled in the rigging had been slashed and pierced. There was no sign of an enemy boarding party, no slain Scots beside his own soldiers. The swords of his own dead soldiers remained sheathed at their hips. Looks of enamored terror remained locked on their lifeless faces. Nothing in the long and storied annals of Norwegian lore could explain the sights before the King.

Håkon was no child-King, not a man to be long distracted by the mythical and unearthly. He quickly regained his courage, and his ambition. He assembled the remnants of his army on the hill beyond the beach and prepared to meet the Scots in battle.

Alexander and his army continued to march north. They poised themselves on the opposite hill, with a small field separating the armies. There would be no negotiations, no envoys of dancers, singers, and storytellers. The battle was upon them, and each waited for the other to move.

Alexander, noting his inferior numbers, prepared his spirit for his likely demise. Resigned to perish for his country, he sat and wrote a letter to his wife.

My Dearest Queen Heather,

I fight soon for all that I love and all that I wish to endure. Our hearts have long been one, so it is unnecessary to write that you sit atop my passions, my greatest love, my dearest treasure, and an inseparable part of my very soul.

There is a part of me that begs to abandon everything but you, to take you in my arms and sail far from the concerns of this country. But I know that doing so would remove us both from who we are, and I would never diminish you in such a way. So I go to war. I draw my sword against the greatest warriors in Europe.

I do not know how this will end. At this moment it does not matter to me. All that matters is my love for you. Keep this letter as a treasure after my death. Kiss the pages that my hands now touch. Hold it against your breast and remember your Bug-bane. I cry now for one reason alone. I am away from you. But I will not be for long. I will haunt you after my death. I will lay beside you in bed. The breeze you feel across your skin will be my own fingers. I love you. I love you, and always will.

Yours Through Eternity,

Alexander Bug-bane

He dispatched the letter to Scone, donned his armor, mounted his horse, and took his place at the head of his army, with Lindsay at his side. He cut such a figure atop his horse. This was no child-king on a dwarfed pony, but a man to strike the chord of fevered patriotism in his men like a magical harp.

He turned to Lindsay and ordered, "I need your skills and your sword where the battle is thickest, not committed only to my protection. Promise you will fight for Scotland and not for me."

Lindsay shook his head and answered, "I will make no such promise, and I will follow no such order. I am allowed to hold Firbolg for one reason, the same reason it came to me years ago. I live my life for your protection, and the sword at my hip has the same objective. I draw my sword for you and for nothing else."

Alexander saw the futility in arguing with him. He determined to place himself in the thick of the battle. Where he was, Lindsay would be. Where he was in danger, Firbolg would be most furious. With steady minds, and their doubts and fears crusted deeply within the shell of their courage, they took the army onto the field below. Håkon advanced in kind, and the Battle of Largs began.

Horses whinnied, men hollered, swords crashed together, and men died. Håkon commanded superior numbers of better soldiers, but Scáthach was not finished. Icy rain, cold, biting, pelting rain, blew against the faces of her enemies, blinding them and slowing them. The efforts of the Shadow Maiden evened the battle, and both sides took equal losses.

Håkon remained at the rear of the fighting, watching his army fight the weather and the Scots. In the hours that the battle raged, more people joined the Scottish ranks from behind. Farmers and tradesmen with sticks and hoes bolstered the rear of the Scottish soldiers. Rising above the hideously chaotic noises of battle was the voice of David Lindsay. Each war cry from his mouth echoed off of Firbolg. Lindsay sounded like two warriors, side by side. He fought like twelve, and men fell at his feet like low grass being trampled by heavy boots.

Håkon had no reinforcements, no way to replenish his losses. At last he realized, even if he were to win the Battle of Largs, he could not hold the land with what remained of his army. He abandoned the effort and ordered the retreat.

When the battle was over and the Norwegians had sailed their remaining ships from Scotland, each side had lost a thousand men. Scáthach returned to her island. The weather calmed to more typical for the season. A warm October afternoon sun shone over a scene that was wretched in the extreme. More than two thousand bodies lay strewn across the battlefield, and Alexander walked among them. The moment was his. He had successfully fended off the invasion. He did not cheer, nor did any of his men cheer for him. Mothers, wives, and daughters trickled onto the battlefield, some reuniting with their triumphant loved ones, others searching body by body, until finding their beloved dead.

Alexander walked among the mourning. He stopped at every body he passed, Scottish and Norwegian alike, and he spoke to them. He wept for them. He prayed for them. And he asked for their forgiveness.

Exactly as Alexander surveyed the human calamity at Largs, a servant at Scone Palace entered the royal chamber and handed Queen Margaret a letter. She was five months into her pregnancy, and many miles from her husband.

As she read the first line, "I fight soon for all that I love," she drew a sharp gasp. She held that breath captive within her as she traced each stroke of the pen with her delicate fingertip. As she read her husband's letter, she understood that the coming battle he wrote of had probably already taken place, and her husband had either already survived it or was already dead.

When she finished the letter, and finally set free her held breath, it flew from her in the form of a hideous cry. Margaret was silenced by another knock at her door. The intruder was not a household servant, but a rider from the front. He held another letter.

Margaret's heart leaped into her throat, then plunged deep into her gut. She accepted the letter, and the rider departed without a word shared between them.

She gathered enough breath to mumble through her torment, though her intended audience had already left, "He is dead. My husband is dead, isn't he?"

She broke the seal, opened the letter, and in an instant recognized the penmanship and exquisite border art. It was a letter from Vanora. Her familiar hand gave comfort, enough for her welling eyes to read what she had written.

My Queen, My Margaret,

Keep the gulls in view
You may know what they know

And see what they are seeing
Blood will stain the dew
But the loss that you fear
Will not come into being

Spirits of Shadow and of Stone
Will lift the wind and raise the sea
And slice the flesh and crush the bone
And force the enemy to flee

Swords will crash and men will fall
And when mothers cry and widows call
Weeping loud but standing tall
There our loving King will be

Dutifully Yours,

Vanora

The letter said that and nothing more. Although it spoke of horrors, of broken lives and broken hearts, and of compassionate torment suffered by her dearest one, it told her that Alexander would live. Margaret believed her. She did not ask herself how Vanora could foresee the outcome of the battle, nor what powerful spirits would come to her husband's aid. She dared not consider such things. Vanora had written it. That was enough. How seamlessly the Queen's cries turned to giggles of delight and the faith-filled blush of a child.

With no immediate threat from the Norwegians, what remained of the Scottish army disbanded. They returned to their homes and their lives. Alexander, Vanora, and Lindsay returned to Ayr, where they secured a carriage to

Scone. It was a somber ride, hardly a parade of victors. Lindsay spoke of Firbolg, how heavily the sword carried with each man he killed at Largs. Alexander spoke of his experience after the battle. With rancid clarity, he described each dead face and each wailing mother. Vanora tied the two men together with moral reflections and ancient insights.

They arrived at Scone Palace almost two weeks after the battle. Lindsay rested for one hour, then took a horse and rode for Byres. Alexander went directly to Margaret. Vanora's letter had soothed her worst fears, but the passage of weeks had decayed her faith. The sight of her husband's face tingled her to the marrow.

Margaret could not control her laughter as they embraced around her swelling belly. Alexander did not laugh. He wept, and as Margaret sat him down and tried to soothe him, he told her of the feminine cries of wailing mothers and wives that still reverberated in his memory and haunted his every moment.

She felt his sorrow, and she felt the torment of the mothers and widows on that battlefield, but her heart was celebratory. How could it be otherwise? She cried with him. Oh, she wept profusely. But she did so through a constant giggle and widening smile that her flamboyant heart refused to hide. Her husband was alive. He was home in her arms, pressing against her and the child inside her.

The blood of the slain
Swam through his veins
But the touch of his lover
Softened the pain

Chapter Twenty-Four:

A Prince for Scotland

Our King and his Queen
And the gulls that guide them
Give Scotland a prince
To nestle beside them

King Håkon slithered aboard his battered navy, around the north shore of Scotland, to Orkney. He intended to replenish his stores there and return to his home, but he had made an enemy of Scáthach, and she was not finished with him. She drew a frosted wind from the north and set it directly upon the Norwegian flagship. While he slept, his ship froze. In the morning, that one ship, only the one ship among the many, was glistening white. The sails were torn, and every board was crusted over by a thick layer of ice.

Håkon awoke with a deep chill from which he would never warm. His extremities were frozen solid, his heart struggling to push icy blood through his body. He died the following day, along with his ambitions on Scotland. Christmas of 1263 brought a hope for peace to Western Scotland and the Isles, and the first month of the new year brought the promise of royal continuity.

On the twenty-first of January, Margaret gave birth to a prince. To the parents, he was a joy, a personal blessing to enrich their household. To the country, the child brought relief. A male heir diffused outside claims of succession and averted the civil wars that come with the end of a royal line. With that in mind, they named the child Alexander. He was the fourth of his name, a name the people had long come to love and trust. The birth of a fourth Alexander was a blow to the gut of Beolin Crymlyn.

Tremendous national pride abounded in the wake of the repelled invasion. The atmosphere was ripe for unity. Vanora found herself often caring for the Prince and Princess, not because their parents were neglectful, but because they were royal. The King and Queen were in almost constant tour of the kingdom, settling petty clan disputes, brokering marriage unions, and hosting those sorts of celebrations that bond strangers tightly together. Where they went, they went together — Bug-bane and Heather, united in all efforts, together in all things. Their unity was a shining symbol of everything they hoped to accomplish.

Where they were, hands shook readily, arms embraced, smiles lifted under their own power, and laughs rolled as beautifully as the Highland hills. They traveled simply, lodged humbly, and hobnobbed with the lowly and lofty alike. Their charismatic affection was contagious, and a golden age for Scotland followed behind them as they traveled.

Lindsay was no longer a regent of the Kingdom. He was not a teacher to the King. He was a friend, a husband, a father, and a grandfather, spending the bulk of his days in his own home, making up for his many years of absence in service to the Kingdom. He occasionally accompanied the King and Queen, but always with his wife. His mythical sword remained at his hip, but it grew lighter with every month it went undrawn.

Håkon's death had relieved immediate danger but replaced the sharp pain of fear with the dull ache of uncertainty. He was succeeded by his son, Magnus VI, a steady tempered, level-headed young King of a very different sort. He was pressed by the Norwegian tribes to resume his father's designs on Scotland. Little did they know that he and Alexander were in steady contact. Neither wanted war, but Magnus felt the pressure of his people.

He remembered the offer rejected by his father and hoped to renew it. In May of 1266, Magnus came to Orkney. He intended no violence. That is to say, he prayed to avoid it. But he would have been a fool to come without an army, and Magnus was no fool. He arrived with an armada nearly as big as his father's more than two years earlier. Alexander easily mustered a patriotic force to match and waited at the coastal village of Thorso. Had that narrow strip of sea separated two other men, two other kings, a grand scale of death would have followed.

Magnus came to Thurso with only a handful of guards and advisors. Alexander met them with only Durward and Baliol at his side. Lindsay commanded the army at an invisible distance. Firbolg would absorb no blood that day. Against advice from both sides, Alexander and Magnus rode alone together into a dense patch of forest to the southeast. The two men bonded as men have bonded since long before recorded history. They hunted the local game, collaborating in a primal way, and allowing the primal bonding that followed.

Five hours later, with anxious armies on both sides, the Kings returned on foot, side by side, dragging a stag behind their escorted horses, calling each other "brother". They gathered with their advisors and laid forth the peaceful arrangement they had made during the hunt. Alexander would pay 4,000 marks for the Hebrides, plus an annuity of 100 marks. Norway maintained control of

Orkney and Shetland. They had no wish for a single generation of peace. They wanted to bind their successors deep into the future. They agreed upon a 10,000 mark penalty to be paid by either side if the treaty were *ever* to be broken.

To keep the treaty unpolluted by political treachery, it was drawn up by the Church. A monk named Reginald of Melrose penned the document, while observers from both sides held it to the Kings' arrangement. It did not read like a peace treaty, nor like a business transaction, but like a moral treatise. It referred to Alexander and Magnus as "friends of peace and cultivators of justice", crediting them both for "warding off the dangers to life and shunning the slaughter of men." It was signed by Alexander and Magnus in an understated ceremony in Perth. The armies of Scotland and Norway have never raised swords in conflict since.

In the years that followed, Alexander's eye was free to focus inward. Petty clan disputes still bubbled into occasional violence. Alexander responded to each and left each with a sense of shared brotherhood and patriotism. He spent much of the year on tour, holding together a country, and sowing the seeds of a shared national identity.

A broader sense of unity came in July of 1270, when the long-planned crusade of Louis XIV of France finally embarked for the Holy Land. Battling lingering illness, King Henry of England could not go. He sent his son, Edward, Margaret's brother. Sailing beside him and whispering in his ear was Beolin Crymlyn. Crymlyn knew Henry was not long for the world. He set himself to be friend and confidant to Prince Edward, with distant designs on ambitions that had gone frustratingly stagnant while Henry lived.

Crymlyn was not the only Scottish baron to follow Edward. Pressure came from Rome, and many Highland homes were left without a master. The call came to David Lindsay, but he refused. Scáthach, Firbolg, Vanora — strong influences had taught him the value of life and the cost of killing. Although Lindsay was no longer a regent to the Crown, his place by the side of his King had never been more important. To keep him where he was needed, Alexander appointed him Lord High Chamberlain of Scotland, a position that required his domestic attention.

Queen Margaret split her time between the obligations of her household and her place beside her husband — until the summer of 1271, when they were blessed with another pregnancy. Alexander would have preferred to hunker down in a residential palace and be nothing more than a husband and father. Such could never be. The peace brokered to the north and west required constant fertilization. The relationship between native Norwegians on Scottish land and the Scots whose fields bordered theirs needed the constant caresses of the Scottish King. Clans that had long battled for plots of land needed his royal influence. Margaret would have spent her pregnancy with her family in England, if not for Henry's illness.

In the last month of her pregnancy, Margaret began suffering from intense, debilitating headaches. She usually awoke in the morning to strangely stiff and aching muscles. She was ordered to bed rest, again, like so many years earlier, a prisoner in her own palace. During that difficult time, Vanora had one duty alone. She was comprehensively Margaret's — her nurse, her servant, and her treasured companion.

There were many loose political threads in Scotland, which would have unraveled if not perpetually sewn and knotted by the King. Alexander tried to accomplish his duties from his wife's bedside, dispatching letters and decrees. But that would not do, and there was too much to lose. So, his mind and his body took to the roads, the narrow, forgotten paths, and sometimes the untouched wilderness, while his heart remained where it belonged, entrenched in his wife's bed.

"Thank God for David Lindsay! Thank the Lord for him!"

Alexander spoke that prayer daily, for Lindsay was forced to be four men at once. He rode beside Alexander and offered his priceless counsel. In the name of the King, he made excursions of his own, sowing peace and unity when multiple crises would arise. Every time Alexander surged with panic for his wife's condition, he sent Lindsay in hurried rides to check on her. In the few precious moments left over, David committed his love to his own household.

On the twentieth of March, 1272, a new Prince was born to Scotland. Not having consulted each other, Queen Margaret, Alexander, and Vanora all began calling the child by the same name. They called him David. They could imagine no more appropriate name. In a rare lull in their frenzied lives, Margaret, Alexander, Vanora, and Lindsay were all gathered together for the Prince's christening. By the authority of the Bishop of St. Andrews, the child was called David, while Lindsay held his namesake, standing as godfather to the child.

Lindsay, Baliol, and Durward were granted royal authority for the next several months. Alexander detached himself from all matters of state and ensconced himself fully in his growing family. It was the happiest he ever remembered being. He had his wife and children. He had Vanora. The political concerns of his country — well, they were no more dire to him than the game of marbles he had played with Margaret in York Castle many years before.

During the day, he was another child among his own children. During the night, he was the most passionately devoted lover any woman has ever had beside her in bed. Alexander and Margaret were like two trees planted side by side when they were saplings, which had grown into each other, knotting their roots and wrapping their trunks, so that they could hardly be distinguished from one another. It was a love for the ages, one that put every romance ever written about before to diminished shame.

It was no surprise to either of them that by the beginning of August, Margaret was pregnant again. The growing seed inside of her was the product of the purest sort of love, at the height of its divinity. But the duties of the King could not be paused indefinitely, and it struck Alexander with acute anguish to saddle his horse again and put miles between his own body and his heart.

In September, King Henry's illness turned grave. He sent for his son. Crymlyn was beside Edward when the order arrived in the Holy Land. He saw that his ambitions were in peril. He convinced Edward to ignore the order and remain with the Crusade. He knew which of Edward's heartstrings to pull, swelling his thirst for valor and glory. Through Beolin's influence, Edward stayed, driving a wedge between himself and the Royal Family back home, between his household and his sister's. When Henry died on the sixteenth of November, the separation was complete. Edward was King of England, and Crymlyn had finally succeeded in wrapping the fingers of influence around the English Crown.

Henry's death devastated poor Margaret. She was a full five months pregnant, and the voyage to London would have been perilous. Her pregnancy was not the only complication to her wishes. With Henry dead and Edward in the Holy Land, political snakes slithered across the entire island. Margaret could not travel, not without an entire army as escort. Everybody knew Crymlyn stood beside Edward in the Holy Land. The Crymlyn influence on the English Crown was not some whispered rumor, but a well-known fact that turned loyal Scottish eyes defensively to the south.

Alexander could not be with his wife, neither could the Lord High Chamberlain. The death of the English King had the same result all royal deaths have, complicated further by the absence of the new King from the country. The political hands of Scotland were in constant motion, staving off the ambitions, fears, and violence that such uncertainty brings. Thank God for Vanora. Thank the Great Creator for her. She was mother, nurse, friend, and counselor to Margaret, holding her weeping head and stroking her swelling belly.

But Vanora's comforts could not cease all pains, nor shield all treachery. On the first of December, at Scone Palace, Margaret awoke early to a cold, bright morning. She headed for the kitchen. The servants were not yet awake. The household was still, yet a torch was lit in the stairwell, recently lit, but by whom?

Margaret made her way wearily to it, then looked down and noticed the wet stairs. Lamp oil drenched the passage, and a torch blazed above it. Margaret was a single fallen ember from being incinerated where she stood. In a rabid panic, she turned and ran up the stairs. A few steps into her ascent, she slipped on the oily step. Her right foot slid behind her, and she smashed her shin on the sharp edge of the step. She howled in pain, waking the entire palace.

Vanora arrived quickly at the top of the stairs, just in time to watch her dear Queen tumble like a child's toy down the stairs, rolling, bouncing, and battering in a violent descent. She ran in pursuit. When she noticed the oily floor and the threatening flame, she quickly doused the torch within her own clothing, scorching herself to blisters. The pain meant nothing to her. Her focus was on Margaret, who lay at the bottom of the stairs, writhing, and moaning, and calling for her by name.

Vanora was a full five steps from the bottom when the extent of the damage had already become clear to her.

Margaret's knee was twisted to an unnatural angle. She bled from the face and elbows. But the moaning had another source, one more tragic than any cut or sprain. She held to her belly, crying, not for the pain of her body, but the torture on her soul.

The child!

There, lying awkwardly at the bottom of the stairs, bleeding and unable to stand, contractions began. These were not like the contractions of her other births. These were wrong. They were strange, as if her body was trying to evict an intruder. Vanora delivered the child there. It was a girl — a sweet, beautiful, tiny, dead girl.

Vanora and Margaret held the child tightly between them and wept and prayed, until the suspiciousness of the circumstances dawned upon them. Vanora called for guards and servants. As painful as it was to move, Margaret was lifted and jostled, and thrown with haste into a carriage, still clutching the dead child. The palace was searched thoroughly. All inside were interrogated. Whoever had oiled the stairs and lit the torch was gone.

Four soldiers escorted Queen Margaret on a bumpy, rugged, cruel road, all the way, without pause, to Edinburgh Castle, while four others were sent in each cardinal direction to find the King and call him home.

Tears from the Queen
Fall from the clouds of treason
Warning the land
Of a treacherous season

Chapter Twenty-Five:

The Ocean of Your Eyes

The sight of a man
With trust in his eye
Fills the land with darkness
Bringing thunder to sky

The Crusade in the Holy Land ended without the glory Edward prayed for. That is to say, it ceased to rage and rather rolled, with petty skirmishes breaking up long weeks of placid encampment. It could not have played better for Crymlyn. He saw enough action beside Edward to develop the sort of brotherly bond that only combat can foster, while having long hours of leisure laughing, storytelling, and manipulation. Edward responded so well to Crymlyn's charms that the traitor's designs on his own country's crown swelled into grander ambitions.

There was still one great impediment, one nemesis that struck terror in his heart. Reports reached him constantly of the heroism of David Lindsay. Letters sent weeks apart arrived in his hands simultaneously, each detailing some effort of Lindsay's on behalf of the Scottish King. He seemed to be in all corners of Scotland at once. Those exaggerated reports coupled with the memories of his attack on Crymlyn Castle and his masterful wielding of a mythical sword, giving Lindsay the appearance of god-like abilities. No move could be made against Alexander while Lindsay was in Scotland.

Crymlyn's forked tongue licked Edward's ear with its signature venom. There were still Crusader fortresses and Crusader cities to hold. History breaks the Christian efforts in the Holy Land into a series of individual wars, with clean chronological borders. The reality is very different. It was one long, drawn-out conflict, covering centuries, with phases of renewed vigor, but never a true cease in the violence. Crymlyn convinced Edward to remain, and to call on the legendary sword of David Lindsay to aid him and serve as his personal protector.

Edward wrote to his sister, appealing to her familial love. Margaret, having lost her father and her unborn child, could suffer no more losses. Rather than appealing to her husband, she spoke directly to Lindsay and begged him to stand at her brother's side. There was strong political reasoning in support of the request. If Edward was to die in the Holy Land, the instability in England would drag Scotland down with it. Lindsay's affection for his Queen coupled with his strong patriotism to overcome his better instincts. With Alexander's reluctant blessing, Lindsay left Scotland, his duties, his home, his family and friends, and his King.

Lindsay's ship stopped for two weeks in France and another three in Cyprus. By the time he arrived in Acre, King Edward was gone. He had returned home, but not without the poison of Crymlyn's ambition still coursing through his veins. It was Crymlyn himself who greeted Lindsay at the docks of Acre. Beolin had aged. To Lindsay, he resembled more closely Beolin's father, a man he trusted and supported, than the young Beolin Crymlyn he encountered in the forest as he sought the rescue of young Bug-bane and Heather.

Crymlyn's face had weathered to the very likeness of his noble father, and he greeted Lindsay with an artificial version of the same charm.

Over their first shared meal, Crymlyn told Lindsay, "This war has changed me. Here, in the Holy Land, drawing my father's sword alongside my fellow Christians, fighting for our shared faith and the safety of our Christian pilgrims, I have become what I should have been all along."

Lindsay's lonely heart needed companionship. His skepticism stood on shaky legs.

Crymlyn continued, "I shudder to think of how I have behaved, what I thought I wanted, and the sins I was willing to commit. I ask for your forgiveness, my brother, and for a return to the old good-humor our families have long shared."

Lindsay was an intelligent man, a seasoned warrior and politician. He was not entirely blind to deception. But if there is one weakness shared by the truly noble, it is that their hearts are lonely. They long to connect with people of their own extraordinary excellence of character. Having been pulled so suddenly from such people, and having traveled for months beside people of coarser character and depraved virtue, poor Lindsay favored his desires over his reason. He willingly accepted Crymlyn's apology on behalf of Scotland and its King.

Crymlyn entertained Lindsay in Acre for days, occupying an otherwise curious mind with brotherly charm. Finally, Lindsay asked to see King Edward, holding out a letter from Queen Margaret. When Crymlyn told him that Edward was back in England, and had been for several weeks, Lindsay was furious.

"Word could have been sent to me in Cyprus!" he thundered, "I am the Lord High Chamberlain of Scotland. I abandoned those duties and the service of my King so I could stand beside Edward in the Holy Land. Why am I here?"

Crymlyn calmly placed a hand on Lindsay's shoulder and answered, "Come with me. I will show you why you are here."

Lindsay's skepticism found its legs again. He followed Crymlyn down the streets of Acre, but with one fist gripping Firbolg's handle.

Crymlyn led him to the heart of Acre, to the Hospital of Saint John, where sick pilgrims and bloodied knights crowded the rooms on shared beds. Crymlyn did not have to say a word. He was not a noble-hearted man, but he came from a noble family, and he knew how their hearts worked. Crymlyn and Lindsay toured the hospital, hearing the horrid tales of knights and soldiers from every Christian kingdom between Scotland and Croatia.

When they left the hospital several hours later, Lindsay embraced Crymlyn and told him, "Thank you, my brother. You have shown me why I am here and how I may serve my King and country so far from my home."

Crymlyn knew that the fighting in the Holy Land would never end. He had done what he had for so long attempted but failed. David Lindsay, the great shield of the Scottish crown, was removed indefinitely from his post. The spies and traitors under his influence were able to maneuver freely through Scotland.

Crymlyn and Lindsay joined the Knights Hospitaller on Pharaoh's Island, a Red Sea island castle off the eastern coast of Egypt. From there, they aided in the light battles and petty skirmishes north of the town of Safaga. There was no real danger to Lindsay or his fellow knights, not with Firbolg among them. But the action was steady enough for Lindsay to believe he was fulfilling some higher calling — and he remained in Egypt, bonding more tightly each week with the artificial affection of Beolin Crymlyn, his "brother-at-arms".

Word of Lindsay's exploits in Egypt reached Scotland, finding loving ears that were desperate for word of him. David had written many letters, each carried by Crymlyn and hand-delivered to the flame. Without Lindsay's firsthand accounts, Edinburgh and Byres had to satisfy their need for him with the morsels that came from the desert on the lips of returning Crusaders. National pride in Scotland's Lord High Chamberlain swelled beyond the walls of every castle, home, and hut.

William Lindsay filled his father's shoes admirably. As often as he could, he was by Alexander's side, but when the King named him Deputy Lord High Chamberlain, the duties of his father's post took William to all corners of the Kingdom. He was away from Edinburgh, away from his mother at Byres, away from his lifelong friend and King. Queen Margaret was still bogged in a mire of mourning. Margaret Lindsay ached for fear of her husband's safety. The noblest hearts of this story were separated from one another and in need of something to unite and bolster them.

Vanora hatched a plan. The heroics of David Lindsay were the talk of the country. If he could not be in Scotland to bring their spirits together, they could unite in the name of his spirit. Vanora began planning a celebration, a celebration of Lindsay, of all he had done for them and all he meant to them. The proposal was enthusiastically accepted by all. They set it for the 26th of February, David Lindsay's birthday. The heads of every prestigious household in Scotland were invited to attend.

Vanora hoped to serve two purposes — to raise the spirits of her dearest ones, and to bring the barons of Scotland together in the name of the King and in honor of the King's most loyal subject. Had Vanora a keener eye for treachery, had she heard the slithering of the snakes that crawled just beneath the surface, she would never have had such a thought. She set the King's table for a den of vipers.

In February of 1275, preparations began for the largest gathering of lords the grand city of Edinburgh had ever seen. The castle was decked to the rafters in the Lindsay family colors. Musicians were gathered. A feast was prepared. Boats and carriages came in from every direction. And a pair of horses rode away.

A dispute between a Norse farming community and a Scottish village threatened violence on the northwestern coast. Alexander rode in haste with William Lindsay. They settled the dispute within days and returned to Edinburgh. They arrived in the evening on the 26th of February. They could hear the music of the celebration pouring from every window of the castle.

In her husband's absence, Queen Margaret took the duties of host. Her health had been weakened by the tragedies of the previous years, and by the steady absence of her lover. Oh, but she hid it well that night. She shined like a blazing chandelier, illuminating the deep corners and crevices of every room she entered.

Just as Alexander and William trotted to the gate, the activity of the party caught up with Margaret. A mild cough of no great concern nagged her every proclamation. Vanora ordered her to bed and appointed Baliol as the new host, a position he accepted with more grandeur than was intended.

Margaret was in her room for no more than a few minutes when there was a knock on her door. She let in a middle-aged man with kind, gentle features. He carried a purse of vials and bottles.

"Vanora has sent me to you," the man said meekly, "She recommends an elixir I happen to carry with me."

"Dear wo… woman," Margaret replied through a cough, "She finds a way to be every place at once."

Margaret took the elixir, and the man left quietly without being dismissed. The itch in her throat swelled, and her coughs struggled to push through. A pain arose suddenly in her stomach — a knotting, gripping, squeezing, wrenching, breath-taking pain. A mindless panic overtook her as she grasped at her throat and belly. She collapsed onto the bed and writhed on her back. The pain and suffocation continued to climb, but she went suddenly still. A moment of realization struck her with dark, horrid terror, and with aching, hollow sadness. She felt herself fading. She knew she was dying.

She gave no thought to what was killing her. She held no anger, pondered no blame, dwelled on no regrets. She only wanted her husband by her side one last time, while she could still hear his voice and feel his touch.

Lying stone-still on the bed, with her eyes turning glossy, locked fixedly to the ceiling above her, her lips began to move, as she struggled to push sound from her seizing throat, "Alexander... Alexander."

She heard footsteps coming, his footsteps. In a different moment of a different day, her mind would have been filled with all the things that fill an opulent mind, and she would not have been able to identify those steps as Alexander's. But in this moment, there was nothing on her mind but her husband. She knew he was near, and she so desperately wanted to sense him before the world went black and silent.

She continued, in increasing faintness, "Alexander... Alexander."

He heard her whisper and stood behind the door, hoping to spy on her intimate thoughts. As the sound of her whisper faded like the sun behind the horizon, there seemed something urgent about it. He cut into the room just as she exhaled her last slow, drawn, wheezing breath.

It sounded to him like a dreamy sigh. He sat on the bed beside her and looked at her wide eyes. She appeared frozen in deep contemplation. Those eyes he had so long admired — the same color, the same size and shape, yet there was something strikingly different about them. In one sudden and terrible moment, he identified the difference. There was no life behind them, none of the brilliant joy and fragrant love that had captivated him since the moment she stepped out of her carriage at York, many years earlier.

His Queen Heather was dead, and the realization bludgeoned him in the head. The pain surged down his throat and seized his stomach. He did not cry out at first, but simply whimpered, as he laid his head upon her chest. Her body still held the warmth of life. The tiny hairs across her skin stood erect, like they did when a cool breeze would brush her, or when he would run his fingertips softly across her skin.

He held greedily to the sensation. He savored it, as he whispered his love to her. As he told her all that she meant to him, his voice grew louder, more sorrowful, more desperate. While he spoke, the full truth clutched him tyrannically. He spoke to ears that could not hear him. His effusions of love would never elicit another blush of her cheeks. His words of admiration, devotion, and regret rose to a hoarse scream, sobbing in morbid conversation with his dead wife.

William heard him and ran toward the bedroom. When he crossed the threshold and saw his friend and King crying over the corpse of the dearest, loveliest, most benevolent queen to ever rule beside a king, his face reddened, his cheeks shook, and he knew someone was to blame. But he could not run in pursuit. He would not have known whom to pursue. Even if he had, his focus was on Alexander, who sat up, looked at his old friend, and broke into child-like sobs, with eyes begging for an embrace. William ran to him and held him like the childhood friend he once was.

William pinched his eyes tightly closed and squeezed Alexander, as if trying to nestle him securely between his heart and his lungs. He opened his eyes and saw his beautiful Queen with a horrid final look on her face. It was not a look of peace, not the picture of a young woman dancing with the angels. It was an expression that begged for one more moment — one more moment of life to laugh, cry, and sigh with the only man she ever loved.

William's thoughts left his king and leaped to justice, to revenge.

He growled through his clenched teeth, "Father, where are you now? Why aren't you here?"

He ran to the Queen's window and saw a lone, shadowy rider hurrying south from the castle. He yelled for the soldiers, but before the echo of his voice died, the galloping figure was lost to the darkness of the night. The Queen had been murdered, and there was nobody left to pursue, nobody to arrest, not that night, not at that moment. William's attention returned to where it belonged, where it could be of service. He kissed his friend on the head, gave a gentle stroke of his dead Queen's arm, then left the room, gathered the soldiers, and locked down the castle with everyone who remained inside.

Word of Margaret's death spread in whispers across the castle. United outrage swelled and pushed against the inner walls of the castle with an almost tangible force. William Lindsay, Durward, and Baliol led an immediate investigation. The guests of the celebration were kept awake and unfed until the middle of the next day. After each had been spoken to, they were no nearer an explanation for the tragedy. They unlocked the castle gate and the guests went home. As the horses and carriages thundered away, Alexander remained as he had been all night, holding the corpse of his sweet Heather, alternating between incoherent mumbling and the most wretched, wailing cries ever to come from the tear-drenched face of a heart-broken husband.

William, Durward, and Baliol each leaped to the place where their hearts and minds took them. William's mind clung to the wider investigation, considering in detail every face he saw and every voice he heard since he and Alexander rode through the gate. Baliol began planning a funeral befitting a beloved queen. Durward began composing letters, beginning with a gingerly worded letter to London.

Vanora was what she had been since the day Alexander was born — entirely focused on her son. He needed every bit of her guidance and more. With each hour, Alexander became visibly weaker, and his wits left him with the expulsion of each tear from his eyes. By the day of the funeral, he was nothing that resembled a man. He did not speak. He hardly lifted his eyes from his own feet. He had to be carried from room to room and force-fed by servants.

He would have no memory of Margaret's funeral. It is unlikely he realized where he was. When the chanting stopped, and the body of the Queen was sealed away in stone, Durward went to Vanora.

"You must do something about the King," he demanded, "We cannot go on this way."

"We?" Vanora questioned.

"Listen to me," Durward demanded, "and see with wider eyes. King Edward is not what his father was. His sister has died suspiciously, and now the King of Scotland is no better than a babbling infant in our hands. The country is in danger. We are all in danger, nobody more than our King. You are as a mother to him. Do something!"

"I am his mother," she answered calmly, "and you are right, Alan. I must do something."

She ordered Alexander to be lifted and carried to a carriage. Durward saw to it that nobody doubted, nobody questioned, and nobody interfered. Servants carried the King as ordered. Vanora gave the driver directions to her home, and she held her darling child for a rugged ride, while she sang in a half-vocalized whisper for the full day and half a night it took to get to her homestead.

It was a gamble. Placing Alexander in the field where he and Margaret played as children, along the stream where he was first struck by her feminine beauty, and in the house where they first shared a bed, could have adhered his broken pieces together or scattered them to the wind. They arrived late in the night. The driver helped carry Alexander to the same bed he had shared with Margaret. Vanora dismissed the driver and fell asleep on a chair.

The early morning light through the window already revealed improvements. Vanora awoke to find Alexander standing against a window, staring into the open field in front of the house. It was the first time he stood under his own power in many days. He even turned to face her when she greeted him. He still said nothing. He showed no expression on his face. And he was shaky from lack of nutrition.

She took him by the hand and led him to the table. It was clear he understood where he was. Vanora was not sure he understood *when* he was. He spontaneously turned his head to an empty part of the room and giggled, as if reliving a past moment. He took the food she offered and he ate it. By midday, he was very much improved, answering her simple questions and walking about the house on his own.

In the afternoon, he told Vanora he was going outside. In the middle of the field, on the way to the stream, he picked up a stick and waved it in the air like a sword, then he dropped it and continued toward the stream. He found the hollowed trunk of the same old tree. But he was no child at play with his friend. He was a man in the throes of unspeakable mourning. He huddled his much larger body into the trunk and sat, remaining there until the sun began to set. Vanora found him where she knew he would be, and she led him inside.

Again at the table, she asked him, "Have you spoken to her?"

"Have I... spo...ken?"

"Yes, my son, have you told her that you miss her, that you love her and always will? Have you invited her to be with you?"

Alexander swooned in spiritual confusion, and he stammered, "I... She... She..."

"Your Queen Heather has not disappeared into oblivion. She is as real as ever, and as near to you as you invite her to be. Now speak to her, for Heaven's sake. Tell her how you feel."

He stuttered a few more half sentences, each word lodging in his throat and only being shoved out by the force of the words behind it.

"Take your time," she instructed, "Think of her. Let her surround you. Let her enter you. Then the words will come. A love like yours cannot be coughed out in simple syllables."

Alexander obeyed. He walked slowly to the bedroom and closed the door. The progress, though slow and painful to observe, was steady and promising. Vanora contented herself to rest on the chair and sleep. The following morning, Alexander was not out of the room. She opened the door and found him standing in the middle of the room, facing away from her.

He turned with moistened cheeks and sobbed, "I can't."

"Now, now," she calmed him, "Perhaps these words are not ready for the air. They might take more kindly to paper."

She sat him down, handed him a pen, a well of ink, and a few pieces of expensive paper. She suggested that he write her a letter he can read aloud to her later. She left him in peace to write to his wife. A half hour later, she heard him calling for her.

She entered the room and asked calmly, "Yes, my love, what can I do for you?"

He held a paper stained from top to bottom in inked words, as he whimpered, "I cannot speak to her."

Vanora turned on her heels and left the room, returning within seconds with a small box.

"This is a gift from me," she told him, "from me to Margaret. This is her box. When you place your letter inside, it is Margaret's letter. She has it."

Alexander grinned widely while Vanora placed the box on a small table. Before he put the letter in the box, he asked Vanora to read it.

"I have written to her, written how I feel. She would want you to know."

He handed Vanora the letter. With no endearment at the top, no "My Dear Wife" or "My Precious Lover", it read,

Your eyes were like the ocean portioned into sips
With waves that roll and crash but make no sound
Like the ocean, they were capable of holding giant
ships
It is in those ships my spirit may be found
For when I found the circumstance
Of falling in that deep expanse
With just a slight and passing glance
I lost all fondness for the ground

Your ocean conveyed my soul with remarkable
speed
To locations that my flesh will never know

To valleys free from anger and islands free from
greed
And hills capped with cold and contemplative
snow
It is there I wish to stop and lie
To sigh an everlasting sigh
And fix my thoughts upon the sky
Which, like your ocean, seems to grow

But I must tear myself from the mystery
That seems to draw me ceaselessly
In my desire to be lost at sea
Within the ocean of your eyes

When she was finished reading, he placed his hand over hers, and together, they opened the box and gave the letter to Margaret.

An anxious Edinburgh awaited their return, unsure if their King would ever recover. They would have to wait a little longer. Alexander had more letters to write before he could assume his place on the throne, more things to tell his wife, and more time to spend with his mother.

The mist in the wind
Shares tears from the land
Sorrow falling to the knees
Weeping quietly in the sand

Chapter Twenty-Six:

Like the King He Hoped to Be

As evil finds it's hold
And terror makes a path
Our King seeks the truth
Letting light conquer wrath

Word of Queen Margaret's death reached Pharaoh's Island, but made it into the wrong hands. Had Lindsay read the dispatch, he would have made immediately for Scotland, swimming the length of the journey if need be. Crymlyn received the letter sealed with the crest of the Durward. The report both delighted and terrified him. He could not let Lindsay know. Within one breath of the final line, Crymlyn had torn the letter into tiny pieces.

It had to be kept a secret from Lindsay. But how could he? News of that nature would soon travel every circle in Europe and well beyond. The Hospitallers would talk of it. Lindsay would leave, and everything Crymlyn had worked for would be for naught. He hatched a scheme he needed to implement immediately.

At dawn the next morning, he rallied the entire castle, "My friends, my brothers, we must act without delay! The Templars, our Christian brothers-at-arms, they have been ambushed and captured!"

He proceeded to spin a tale sure to rally the heroism inside of them, detailing inhuman treatment, satanic rituals of torture and torment, and of unthinkably bloody executions. Oh, he was a masterfully dynamic speaker! The knights of Pharaoh's Island boiled from within and gave no thought to evidence or explanation. Within an hour they were armed and armored and ready to ride into the desert.

Crymlyn did not yet know how it would happen, but he was certain of one thing — David Lindsay must not return with the others. He must not return to Scotland, ever.

The heroic band crossed the strip of sea and rode west, blindly following Crymlyn. After a day of ceaseless riding, they camped. It was then, only then, that they began to question their mission.

"Who captured our brothers?"

"Where are they being held?"

"Beolin, do you know where you are leading us?"

He was quick-witted in his deceit. It was a skill long sharpened by excessive practice. He answered without pause, "The Fatimid Caliphate has taken them. Those vile sinners will not only mortify their flesh. They have ungodly rituals, magic enchantments that will deliver the souls of our brothers directly to Satan."

One tall, deep-voiced knight stood tall above the others and asked, "Why then do we camp? Are we to sleep while Christian soldiers are delivered to Hell?"

Beolin replied quickly, "Your courage and valor are beyond reproach, but this is no time to be impetuous. We have much worse to fear than the sword. Would you have us all ensnared? No, no, we require a subtler plan."

Lindsay, torn down the middle between faith and suspicion, placed one hand on Crymlyn's shoulder and asked, "What do you recommend?"

"I will ride out tonight," Crymlyn answered with mock fear in his voice, "We need not risk more than one man. I will ride out and find their camp, report what I have seen, then we can devise a plan. If I am not back at dawn, I am lost. Return to Pharaoh's Island and pray for our souls."

All agreed with the plan, all but Lindsay, who demanded to ride with him.

Crymlyn's artificial fear put on a cloak of shimmering friendship, as he spoke softly, "I would not, nor could I ever, place your life in danger for my sake. You are the Lord High Chamberlain. Our King needs you. Our country needs you, and when you are finished with the Lord's work in the Holy Land, you must return to Scotland in safety."

There were no more words on the matter. Crymlyn saddled his horse, and the knights of the expedition saw him off with earnest prayers and well-wishes.

Crymlyn did as he said he would. He rode west to the nearest settlement of the Fatimid Caliphate. There were no evil rituals, no captured Crusaders, but a band of men as faithful and war-weary as any Christian in any Crusader castle. Crymlyn startled their guards, woke their entire camp, and brought them all into a frenzy. They bound him and held him until their translator was up, dressed, and ready to speak.

Crymlyn's skills of dramatic deceit were at their finest. He gave them a grave warning, about a band of rogue Crusaders, Knights Hospitaller ready to defy the mandates of the treaties and the orders of their superiors, blood-thirsty killers bent on the death and defilement of their enemies.

"Are you not one of them?" the leader asked.

"I am one of them, but I am not with them. The tenuous peace stands on a thin pane of glass. There is much to lose for us all. If they have their way, the wars would be ceaseless, the killing absolute, until you are all with your God and we are all with ours."

He promised to lead them to the Crusader camp, asking only that his own life be spared. Within an hour, and well before dawn, a band of Fatimid soldiers twice the number of the isolated Crusaders was in the open desert, within sight of Lindsay and the others.

As promised, Crymlyn returned at dawn, pulling death in his wake, death for all but himself. The lives of the Hospitallers were a petty price to pay for the demise of David Lindsay. Crymlyn alerted those standing guard, who woke the others and gathered for Crymlyn's report.

"They are near on my trail, my friends, but we need not fear. Our numbers and arms are superior. I watched them circle to the south. It is from that direction they will attack us. But we will be ready, and we will prevail. We will rescue our brothers, and they will sing songs of you all."

As directed by Crymlyn, the Fatimid circled around to the north. In the dim, pink light of the infant day, they attacked. The numbers, the surprise direction, it should have been a one-sided slaughter. It was indeed a one-sided battle, but not as Crymlyn had planned. In their many battles, the Fatimid had never seen the likes of Firbolg, nor that of the man who wielded it.

As the sun lifted higher, bringing brightness to the land, Lindsay was like a shadow. Firbolg had taken a dozen lives before any of his fellow Crusaders had clashed a sword. But the cost to his heart was severe. He did not fight with a Crusader's zeal, for each life he took was absorbed by Firbolg, and with each life he extinguished that morning, he was shown images of the lives, the love, the families, the hopes and dreams of the men who fell at his feet.

Firbolg grew very heavy. By the time the battle ended, Lindsay had killed two thirds of the attackers by his own hand. Only two Hospitallers had fallen, and another three were wounded. Lindsay had saved them. He had saved almost all of them, but *he* did not save Crymlyn. Crymlyn's life was the only one certain to survive the day. But his treacherous scheme lie dead among the fallen Fatimid.

When the battle was over, and they had piled the bodies of the fallen enemies, Lindsay demanded they ride out in rescue of the Templars.

"It is too late for that, my dear brother," Crymlyn told him, "I saw for myself. They are already lost. It is best we return and report what we know."

It was agreed. They would return to Pharaoh's Island, but not that day. They decided to remain in camp, bury the dead Fatimid, dress the wounds of their own, celebrate their unlikely success in battle, and return in the morning. When the urgent and mournful had been attended to, they placed their hearts and minds on the celebratory. They wrote songs for David Lindsay, and for Firbolg, the sword they all credited for their own continued lives.

When the uproarious gratitude of his brothers-at-arms died down, Lindsay walked from the camp, into the open desert. He dropped to his knees in grateful homage to the tutor who had prepared him for the days victory, to the unearthly benefactor who blessed him with Firbolg.

"Scáthach," he spoke loudly to the sky, "whatever blessing might fall on you from the gratitude of a humble knight, I send with a full heart. We were attacked by cowardly shadows, by treachery without honor. You took many lives today, and you saved many lives. I will be forever your student and devotee."

There were no gulls to carry her response to him, but that did not matter. It was enough for him to imagine she heard him and basked in his adoration.

When he rose to his feet, a sharp pain pinched at his back, followed by a strange seizing of his breath. He looked down to see the sharp edge of a sword protruding forward from his chest. It disappeared back into him as it was withdrawn from his back. He turned and saw Beolin Crymlyn holding the sword. The crimson-coated steel dripped with Lindsay blood, while its wielder gloated with a sinister grin. Lindsay's knees gave out and he fell to his back. As the parched sand beneath him drank his spilling blood, Lindsay asked him, "Why, my brother?"

Crymlyn stood over him and confessed, "I do not give a damn about this desert, about Jerusalem or this war. I am here for you, and you were brought here for me. I will have the Scottish Crown. I have killed the King's wife, and I will kill his children, but I cannot get to the King, not while you live. You will be dead before my next meal, then nothing will be between me and the neck of our foolish King."

Lindsay tried to beg for Alexander's life, but all that came from his mouth was a gurgle of blood.

As the world around him faded, Lindsay heard Crymlyn say, "I wanted you to know as you die, I am the one who will end the King's line, and my descendants will sit with strength on... the... —"

All went black and silent. David Lindsay was dead.

The moment the last flicker of life was extinguished, Crymlyn reached for the sword at Lindsay's hip. What he pulled from the sheath was something unexpected. It was not the glamorous sword he saw in heroic action that day, not at all the sword described to him by the lone survivor of the King and Queen's rescue. It was a bent, rusty, old blade in some antiquated design. Crymlyn hollered and hurled the useless antique into the sandy expanse in front of him.

His yell drew the attention of the Hospitallers, who quickly surrounded him. They stared at Lindsay in grieved disbelief. Crymlyn expected to be pierced by Crusader swords from every direction. Instead, he was peppered with questions.

"What happened here?"

"Beolin, who did this?"

"Tell us brother, who has slain Lindsay?"

Crymlyn's reddening face was authentic, as was his sweating brow. Fear for his own life brought it on, but he sold it to the others as grief. He dropped to his knees and embraced the body. He loudly cursed their enemies, then stood again and told a tale of assassins.

"I arrived as they fled," he told them, "and I watched my old friend fall."

"Where is his sword? Where is Firbolg?" one of them asked.

"They took it, "Crymlyn answered in a wavering voice, "They took my dear brother's life, then ran away with his sword. Firbolg is in the hands of our enemies. We should return without delay to the safety of our fortress."

They silently buried David Lindsay in a shallow, sandy grave, without eulogy, without songs of his deeds, without prayers for his soul. They packed as quickly and quietly as they could, and rode east to the sea.

The following morning, from the safety of Pharaoh's Island, Beolin Crymlyn excused himself from the Crusader Knights.

"It should be I and no other to bring the tragic news to Lindsay's family and to the King," he told them with a lowered head and somber tone.

They arranged his passage and outfitted him lavishly for his journey home. They gave the vile villain a hero's send off, and Crymlyn took it all in like a king — like the King he hoped he soon would be.

> *The fall of the father*
> *The grief of a nation*
> *The bubbling greed*
> *Of vile elation*

Chapter Twenty-Seven:

The Stars to Keep

The gulls above
Weep in the sky
As all take a knee
And silently cry

It is no surprise that Crymlyn did not march directly to Byres or Edinburgh with the news of Lindsay's death. He *marched* nowhere, but rather slinked and slithered. Only his most trusted clansmen knew he had returned. He had two great advantages he was loath to release. Scotland believed him still in the Holy Land, and David Lindsay was no longer an impediment to his ambitions.

Word of Lindsay's death crept across land and sea at the rate of a rumor. The Hospitallers told their fellow knights, who spoke the sad news to tradesmen. Tradesmen told their wives, who spoke to friends. Friends told travelers, and word reached Alexander, not in a dispatch sealed with wax, but by the illiterate mouth of a servant. When the mumbling fool delivered the news, with no ceremonious compassion, William stood near. He learned as Alexander did.

Alexander wrote immediately to Acre and waited three miserable months for a response. He dared not tell Margaret Lindsay until he knew for certain. When the commander of Acre replied, confirming the truth, Alexander, William, and Vanora went directly to Byres.

There was nobody better suited to give the news to Margaret than Alexander. He still mourned the loss of his dear Heather. William was severely cut up by the tragedy, but not all losses are equal. There is no pain suffered by our species like the loss of such a spouse. Alexander knew that pain all too well. Vanora had suffered it many years earlier. But it was Alexander who broke the news. They sat together for hours and wept in each other's shared misery and compassion.

From Edinburgh and Byres, word of Lindsay's death spread quickly. Crymlyn was not the only enemy of the Crown. The gate had fallen. It was open season on Alexander and his faithful. The danger was real and immediate, and it was Durward who rose to fill Lindsay's boots as well as he was able. It was Alan Durward, short-sighted, single-minded, but noble and fiercely loyal Durward. He was the keeper of the King's property, and there was no more precious property than the King's life and that of his children.

The dear man did not know a peaceful moment, not a second of restful contemplation. He never left the King's side. He ate in nibbles and rarely slept. Vanora, that servant woman who had so long confounded him, who, to his anxious frustration over the years, had assumed influence above her station, was almost as precious a royal commodity as the King himself. Durward kept her under constant guard, never allowing her a moment of solitude.

Many months went on in this way. Seasons passed with no overt action against the Crown. All traitorous scheming occurred behind walls, never in the open. Crymlyn rekindled his friendship with King Edward of England, commiserating the loss of Edward's sister, and blaming Alexander for her death.

No attempts on Alexander *could* be overt. Enemies had to slither in the shadows, for Alexander was a popular King, the most beloved in a century. He had brought peace. Peace brought unity. Unity ushered in prosperity, and happiness followed. To the people of Scotland, it was a golden age. To the King and his nearest, it was a wretched time, filled with sorrow and fear.

King Edward was convinced of the lies told to him. His rage demanded an invasion of Scotland, but his better sense prevailed. With such support from his people, Alexander could not be easily defeated. There was more. Alexander's friendship with the powerful King of Norway was well known. Any plans to take Scotland must also account for Norwegian involvement. Edward bided his time. Crymlyn could not. He set the wheels in motion to eliminate the Royal Family and their supporters one at a time.

Durward, narrow as his thinking could be, was no fool. He fully understood the dangers surrounding the Royal Family. It was early March of 1281. Prince David was almost nine years old. Prince Alexander was seventeen and training in warfare. Princess Margaret had just turned twenty-one. She was of age to marry, of age to produce a child. But to whom could she be married? There was no place in Scotland, no castle beyond the walls of Edinburgh where she could be safe.

The answer was obvious, and occurred first to Durward. King Magnus of Norway had a son of his own. Prince Erik of Norway was a full seven years younger than Princess Margaret. Nevertheless, Alexander wrote to his old friend. The arrangement was made, and Princess Margaret sailed for Norway, to live with Magnus and her young betrothed.

A treaty was drawn between the Kings. Alexander gave several Scottish estates as the dowry. Most importantly, it stipulated that the first child of Erik and Margaret would succeed to the throne of Scotland, not Prince Alexander or Prince David. Crymlyn had no reach in Norway. The treaty with Magnus relieved the dangers to Alexander's boys — or it should have. Durward was pleased with the effort and greatly relieved by its assurances. Vanora was not. She still shivered with fears she could not put into words.

A locked chamber under guard was no place for Vanora. She needed to consult with her ancestors. Through the narrow window of her chamber, her only view of the outside, she scanned the tiny strip of sky for the gulls. None appeared to her. None shouted their guiding squawk from the unseen distances. Vanora needed out. She needed the words of her parents. She needed the sacred Druid Den of Dunino, where the voices of her parents had descended upon her.

She spoke to Durward with such gravity in her voice, and an expression of fear on her face that he had never seen on her before. She could not explain her fears to him in words he would comprehend. She did not need to. It was enough for him that she felt them. How very far he had come with regards to her. In their many shared years in the life of Alexander, he had come to accept what he could not understand.

Lindsay's death had shaken him severely. Until then, he had not realized how much he leaned upon Lindsay, how much he trusted him. And Lindsay trusted Vanora. He yielded to her request and allowed her to leave the castle for her home. Alexander wanted to accompany her.

"Under no circumstances!" Durward roared before remembering himself, "I am sorry, my King. I was out of place. It is only that I believe it unwise for you to travel together."

Highly debated planning went into the excursion. She had to pass for any ordinary woman, so she could not travel alone. The best disguise was as a traveling family, a man and a woman, perhaps a child. It was decided. One soldier would travel with her, dressed as a farmer, and one child to pass as their own. But which child would go, whose child?

The intimate circle of knowledge must remain minute. Vanora asked to take Prince David. The child was almost nine, and he had learned so little of what his father had learned by that age. Durward protested, but Alexander gave in. The next morning, Vanora and Prince David left Edinburgh for Dunino Den with a single escort, passing as a simple family returning home.

The plan was poorly considered before being put into action. Crymlyn knew well of Vanora. He knew of her home, where his own men had kidnapped the King and Queen as children. Within four hours of her departure, Durward thought better of it. He took a dozen soldiers and set out in pursuit.

Vanora wasted no time preparing David for what he would see. She told him many stories of his parents, and many stories of hers. He learned of his own ancient lineage, and of hers. By the last mile, he understood why he was there, and what was to be gained.

They were so engrossed in their conversation, trotting side by side, they had forgotten all about their escort. Vanora stopped suddenly when she realized she could only hear the steps of two horses. She looked in all directions. They were alone. Their fellow rider was gone. Her heart leaped into her throat.

"This is a trap," she warned the Prince, "We are in danger. **RIDE!**"

They sped away in the same direction, but did not approach the house. They circled around, through the thick woods that entombed the old Druid Den. The house was well known. The Den was not. They found the sacred stones exactly as she had last seen them, quiet, shielded by thick foliage, and as welcoming as ever.

Vanora and David dismounted and walked reverently to the central stone pit. Vanora kneeled, and David imitated her. She closed her eyes tightly and prayed in words long forgotten by the world. She called to her parents and asked for their Heavenly guidance. Two doves flew into the circle from above and landed together on a branch. "Mother, Father, speak to me," she begged, "Tell me what is to come."

Their voices came down from the direction of the doves, but not only for Vanora. David heard them too, and he stared upward in astonishment as they said,

Our daughter, oh dear, sweet child
You have done so much and so very well
You have freed what was caged and tamed what
was wild
Your ancestors ring in you like a bell

Take the child in your arm, hold him and sing
Your arm and his will transform to a wing
You join us today
As your flesh is the prey
Of those who convey the traitorous sting

But please do not fear, not for you nor for him
The blades will be painful but quickly turn dim
You both soon will fly
With us in the sky
As your spirits comply with the Heavenly hymn

Vanora had no need to see or hear who approached. The message from her parents was clear enough. She obeyed them, taking Prince David tightly in one arm and singing a song of eternal love. They appeared from all sides, thrusting and slashing through maid and Prince alike, leaving the bleeding bodies to wet the sacred stones beneath them.

The Crymlyn clansmen stared with self-congratulatory postures over their victims, but they did not see, they could not have seen, the powerful spirits their violence had freed from the mortal world. Their attention was drawn by the calm, peaceful call of an owl, a deep-brown, majestic bird that seemed to radiate its own light. They were spellbound by its presence. It nodded its head with a disapproving eye and flew away.

"It is a bad omen, I tell you!" one of them shouted to the others, "We will pay for this crime."

"Nonsense," said another, "It is only a bird. Unless you are a mouse, you have nothing to fear."

The words were brave, but the owl *was* a bad omen, and this particular owl seemed to communicate as much. Crymlyn's men left the sacred site with no cheers for their success, but in silent chills they went back to their homes.

Durward and his soldiers rode quickly, but not quickly enough. He came across a lone rider and recognized him right away as the soldier he had sent to escort Vanora and the Prince. When the rider saw Durward and his band of armed men, he turned sharply to the south, into the woods. Durward spurred his horse forward, shouting for the man to stop. The rider was too skilled. They lost him.

Durward's mind put the pieces together. He rode at full speed to Vanora's home. He and his soldiers arrived to an empty, still, and silent house. They inspected every inch of the property, around the perimeter and along the brook. There was not a suspicious sight or sound until a soldier heard the distant whinny of a horse. He called to his master, and the lot of them ran to the sound.

They entered the Den, Durward leading the way, where they found the slain bodies of Vanora and David. Unlike the final expression of Queen Margaret, or the pleading expression frozen to David Lindsay's face as he died, Vanora appeared at peace. Her eyelids were slightly parted, as if enjoying something pleasant, and a slight smile lifted the edges of her lips. The child still held tightly in one of her arms had eyes peacefully shut, like a baby that has just been sung to sleep. If not for the vicious, mortal wounds on them both, and the blood that pooled around Durward's feet, it would have been a sight of pure bliss.

But there was nothing blissful about the truth before him. If Lindsay's death was like the protective walls of a castle crumbling down, Vanora's was like the castle itself being removed, leaving its inhabitants to the chill of the open air. His own temperature seemed to drop at the sight. He had never felt so vulnerable, never like such a failure. He did the only thing he could think to do.

"Go to Edinburgh," he ordered, "Double your numbers and bring the King here. Do not tell him what has happened. This is my failure. I must tell him. I must show him."

The soldiers all stood as they were, until Durward yelled sternly, "GO! LEAVE ME!"

They obeyed, all returning to the house where they had left their horses. Ten departed for Edinburgh as ordered. Two remained behind to protect Durward, but kept their distance, approaching just near enough to hear the poor man's wailing. How he shamed himself — cursed and shamed himself.

The soldiers were true to their orders. They did not tell the King what he demanded to know. They did not have to. By the time they approached Dunino Den, Alexander knew he was riding toward terrible news. He was riding to mourn, but whom would he be mourning?

They arrived in the night, twenty-two soldiers and the King, a thunderous herd of horses, whose rapid galloping could have been heard from a half mile away. To Durward, who stood under the dim light of a half-moon heavily filtered by the branches and leaves above him, it sounded so much nearer, like twice as many horses ran across the top of his skull.

When Alexander dismounted, only one set of steps thundered. Alexander caught sight of them all at the same time, his son, his mother, and his former teacher. Many words ran through Durward's mind as they locked eyes, but nothing could escape the lips he bit tightly together with his teeth.

Alexander walked nose to nose with him, took a fistful of hair on the back of Durward's head, kissed him on his forehead, and whispered, "This is not your fault. This is mine."

He released Durward's hair, turned to his son and mother, dropped to his knees, and began the weak and whimpering cry of a sickly child. It was such a mournful sight, this strong King crying on his knees, that it spread to the soldiers surrounding him. Cries, sniffs, and whimpers orchestrated around him, like sad and pathetic applause in a full amphitheater.

A single noise came from above, one heard only by Alexander. He shushed the others, and the scene suddenly silenced. They all waited with held breath and darting eyes to hear what he had heard. It came again — the lone hoot of a single owl. They all looked up together to see the same deep brown bird that had frightened the attackers. It flapped its large wings and descended onto Vanora's bloody shoulder. The winged ring on Alexander's finger surged with heat.

Durward lunged at the owl in a rage, yelling, "Get off of her. Go! Go!"

He swung his fist toward it, but Alexander caught him. The owl did not flinch.

"No, no, Alan. It is all right," the King said softly through his tears, "This bird is no scavenger. It is not here for a meal."

He turned toward the owl, which remained perched on Vanora's shoulder, and he told it, "Speak to me. I am listening."

The owl made no sound. It blinked a few times rapidly while maintaining a fixed stare into Alexander's eyes.

"Speak," Alexander ordered again, "I beg you. Tell me what you have come to tell me."

The owl flapped its wings and flew up to the nearest branch above him. It kept its eyes fixed on his. As he stared back at the owl, a small circle in the center of his chest grew as hot as the ring on his finger. The warmth surged outward, filling him entirely, filling him with a memory of a moment long forgotten. The recollection was as vivid as the moment it happened, a song in Vanora's voice. It was the song she sang to him when he was seven years old, on the day he learned his father had died, as she sat beside him and rubbed his little head.

The warm memory continued to swell and could no longer be contained. It poured through his lips in Vanora's words and melody.

Rest your head
On my breast
Let the world beyond go to sleep

Safe and warm
Dream little one
Your cares are the stars' to keep

Under the sinking moonlight, they buried Vanora in front of her own house. They marked the grave with the sign that had hung above the door for decades.

Welcome to our home built of pure love

Surrounded with light with hands from above

No eulogy was given. Vanora's life could not be summed up with words, nor could Alexander's affection for her. Durward composed some words in his head, but he did not speak them. They gave her a moment of reverent silence, then left for Edinburgh, taking Prince David's body to be buried beside his mother.

When they arrived at the castle, the Prince's body was cleaned and laid in state. But no visitors would come. The castle was locked down, allowing only the mandatory comings and goings of supplies and payments, and to allow a single messenger to leave. Alexander dispatched a letter to Magnus, begging an end to the betrothal and the immediate marriage of his daughter to young Erik. He begged Magnus' pardon for his absence from the ceremony, but implored him to see it done as soon as appropriate arrangements could be made.

He included a letter to Princess Margaret, his first child.

My Sweet Girl,

You are a woman now, and a much greater woman than I could ever have hoped you would be. Of course you are. You are your mother's. Someday you will learn why I rush your wedding, and why I cannot attend. These are not concerns for you now, not today. You need only know that you are loved. Your mother is with you. Of this I am certain. Look to her. Listen to the gulls. And know that I have no possession more precious to me than your happiness. I am and will always be gratefully,

> Your Father,
>
> Alexander III,
>
> King of Scotland

Chapter Twenty-Eight:
The Path of the King

The scars of pain
Render through
A bond takes form
And loves shines anew

King Magnus did as he was asked. Erik and Margaret were married the very morning after Alexander's request arrived in Norway. It was a simple and rushed ceremony, with no more guests than were already in the castle, and no more of a feast than what the cooks could prepare in a few hours. Margaret would have had it no other way. The letter from her father diminished all extravagance in her eyes and illuminated the simplicity of love and family.

She did not know her husband. Her reluctant heart married him for duty to her father and country. But her vision of marriage came from her childhood, from her mother and father, and the deep, selfless, impassioned husband and wife that they were. The moment she was declared to be Erik's wife, her devotion to him echoed her parents' love.

Margaret and Erik were quite safe in Norway. Crymlyn had no reach there. Edward of England was little more than a name thrown scarcely around the political discussions. In Scotland, it was altogether different. Alexander's reign had never been on shakier ground. By his own sunken heart and the mandates of his advisors, he hunkered in place. He did not tour his kingdom, breaking bread with his countrymen. He did not ride out to settle petty clan disputes.

The stitches he had sewn with his wife over the years of peace were tight and strong, but needed upkeep. Without Alexander's attention, those stitches came loose and began to unravel. A slow and subtle fracturing of Scottish unity coincided with the chisels that worked against it. Crymlyn worked subtly and quietly, with a devious word here and a planted conspiracy there. King Edward, on the other hand, was much more overt. The remaining Prince and Princess of Scotland were his niece and nephew, the grandchildren of his own father. He claimed the right that King Henry would not.

Although Edward claimed Scotland as his own, naming himself dual-monarch, it was in words only. There was no practical way to exercise his claim, not while Alexander had living heirs. He recalled his old friend, Beolin Crymlyn, to London, where the greedy, venomous tongue of Alexander's greatest enemy served as Royal Advisor to the mighty King of England.

Erik and Margaret were a slight thought. They were in Norway, and not relevant to the ambitious designs of Edward and Crymlyn. Alexander's remaining son however, young Alexander IV, was the next impediment to be kicked down and demolished. Young Alex was eighteen years old, strong and intelligent. Like his father, he had been trained by David Lindsay, and by William after David's death. He was schooled by Baliol and nurtured by Vanora, loved by his mother and admired by his father. He was tall and beautiful, kind and charismatic. His would be a powerful reign, were it to ever come into being, one not easily dislodged.

As important as it was to protect Alex from the traitorous hands of treachery, he could not be bound within the walls of a royal palace. The people loved him. He had too much of his mother in him. He wanted to shake dirty, callused hands, and dine at worn, splintered tables.

Alex wrote regularly to his sister in Norway. Her letters in return were the fuel that kept him moving. In their shared correspondence, they created a blissful bubble, one which they alone shared. It was in stark contrast to the reality of the Royal Household. But brightness came to all in the form of a dispatch from Magnus. Princess Margaret was pregnant. A grandchild of the King would do much to secure the continuity of the Royal Line.

King Alexander had few with whom to share his ecstasy. His wife was gone. Lindsay and Vanora were gone. His son was often away. Oh, he was delighted with the news, but quite lonely in his joy. He had William Lindsay, and he had Alan Durward. Those two men were rarely far from his side.

"This is exactly what we need," William told him from the dark corner of a dimly candle-lit room, "We will prepare a celebration. The people will want to join you in your happiness. When the child is born, we will fill Edinburgh with celebrants."

"Yes!" Durward agreed, "England will see how they rally to you, and to your children and grandchild. Edward will sit and brood, but he will not dare move against us. Just think, the grandchild of our King and of Magnus of Norway!"

William and Prince Alex were sent with an entourage to spread the good news from Ayr to Inverness. They traveled ceaselessly, but the clamorous reception of every town, village, and castle propelled them with tremendous energy.

It was late in the afternoon, as they rode through a forest east of Loch Ness, when the messenger reached them. The child of Erik and Margaret was born. The anticipation of a coming birth was replaced with the news of a royal birth.

"I should be with my father," Alex told William, "He will need family to celebrate family, and I am all he has."

He ordered William to ride on and spread the word, while he returned with the messenger to Edinburgh. William was leery, but as Alex pointed out, the clans were united in the news they had spread. Loyal patriotism flowed from every household, be it made of stone or sticks. Alex turned south, while William continued north.

East of Drummond, Alex turned east, into the mountains. His destination was Creag Choinnich, where his father's old friend, Sir Colban, was now a very old man, still ruling his Highland estate with the same spit and vinegar.

They did not reach Creag Choinnich. The messenger stopped sharply and told him, "Your Highness, there is more to the news I have brought, what is meant for your ears alone."

"What is it?" Alex demanded, "Is my father unwell?"

"He is as well as he can be, bearing the news I must share with you. It is of your sister. Her child is healthy, but Princess Margaret, I am afraid, is not."

"What is wrong with my sister? Why do you delay? Tell me now!"

"Your sister is dead. She died giving birth to the child, and with your death, the King will have no children."

With those words, the messenger drew his sword and struck Alex on the side of the head with the blunt side, knocking him unconscious and sending him to the ground. The traitor pulled a rope from his bag looped it around Alex's neck, and strung him to a tree. He wrote a note of despair and farewells, and signed it with the Prince's name. He left Alex hanging from the tree and took the counterfeit note to Creag Choinnich. He delivered it to Sir Colban.

"How did you allow this?" Colban roared with the furious vigor of a man half his age.

"I sleep too soundly, My Lord. The news of his sister's death was more venomous than I could foresee. When I awoke, I found the Prince..., and his note."

The messenger was dismissed. He left Creag Choinnich knowing that the news of Alex's death would soon spread to Edinburgh, to London, and beyond.

The messenger told lies and he told truths. Princess Margaret had indeed died soon after giving birth. There was no treachery involved, just a strong Norwegian child fighting a little too forcefully to enter the world.

King Alexander was broken into pieces, as he sat in his room in Edinburgh, mourning the death of his first child, with no familial shoulder to cry upon. He wanted his son. He wanted Alex, and just as he cried his son's name aloud, word came from Creag Choinnich. Prince Alex was dead. Sir Colban, old as he was, made the journey himself, and delivered the forged note.

"This is not my son's hand," he growled, "Alex did not take his own life. He was murdered, killed by the same man who delivered this forgery."

"I had him!" Colban spoke through a roar, "The man was in my hands, and I sent him away."

As Colban spoke, Alexander's thought left the messenger and turned to his son, "Alex, my son," he moaned, "where is he now?"

"My friend and King," Colban answered, "do not think I would leave him like that. He is in my home, lying in peace on my own bed."

"I want his body brought here immediately!"

"The arrangements have already been made."

Alexander called for Durward and Baliol to join them and the four of them wept together. But within their tears, they all knew how perilous was the state of the monarchy, and each began to weave a plan.

Before any of them could speak what was in their heads, Alexander spoke, "The matter of succession must be firmly fixed, or there will be fighting among the clans. I have only one living heir, one child with my father's blood."

"Yes," Durward followed, "The child of Margaret and Erik, the heir to your throne, is safe where she is and must remain there."

It was agreed by all. The child must not come to Scotland. Alexander wrote to Magnus, with the other three in the room dictating their contributions to the wording. They drew up a contract, signed by King Alexander III of Scotland, reaffirming the daughter of Margaret and Erik to be the heir to the throne of Scotland.

Durward, ever practical, remarked, "This decree will do much to settle disputes while you live, but when the terrible day should come, and your crown is ready for the child's head, it will be another matter. She will be seen as Norwegian, as an outsider, inviting the very contention we now seek to avoid."

"So you had better not die," Sir Colban added, "not until you remarry and produce another heir..., a male heir that is raised here in Scotland..., no, not here, in the Highlands. Let him be a coarse, rugged Highlander, a man of the people."

"Easy now, Colban," Durward ordered, "You speak of a child from a marriage we have not yet arranged."

Baliol spoke up, "That is my duty. I keep the family lines, and I will find our new Queen."

Logistically, it all made good sense, but the thought of remarrying spun Alexander's heart within his chest. He had known only one wife, only one lover, one he had married when he was still a child. His head agreed with the plan, while his heart protested by beating indignantly against his ribs.

It was King Edward's unveiled, brazen political moves on Scotland that convinced Alexander's heart of what his head knew must be. Edward sent a message to Magnus, asking for the hand of Erik's daughter to be given to the son of Edward. Alexander was left entirely out of the affair. Although Magnus would have never agreed, holding too dearly his affection for Alexander, the move from London gave a distinct expedience to Alexander's need to remarry.

The image of a wedding night with some strange woman, some faceless new lover, deeply impregnated Alexander's dark musings. It grew in him, wrestling with all that was inside him. What else could be done? The King's romantic heart was placed on a sacrificial altar to be bloodied and demolished for the sake of his people.

In February of 1285, an emissary was sent to France. Yes, it had to be France. Marriage to a French noblewoman, or perhaps a French royal, would erect a barrier against England much taller and stouter than Hadrian's Wall. They settled on a young woman with whom Alexander shared common heritage. Yolande of Dreux had Coucy blood, distantly connected to Alexander through his bitterly estranged mother, the dowager queen mother, Maria de Coucy. Maria would have sabotaged the union, had she still lived. But she was many years dead, and had no say in the matter.

Yolande was twenty-two years old, not much older than Alexander's late son. How could they relate to each other? She had been long coddled in lavish splendor. He had been dragged through betrayal, loss, and torment since he was a young child. He had known the truest sort of love, and lost that love in the most wretched form of loss. Yolande's bedchamber was still decorated with her childhood dolls. Yet this unlikely pair would be placed into a shared bed for the production of a new life.

Yolande's lower relations were the Scottish barons of Kinghorn. Her ship landed there, where she spent three days and nights being prepared for a Scottish husband, learning the proper phrases to please, the behavioral expectations of a Scottish Queen, and just enough of the local history to strike terror into her bones.

For the next several months, Yolande was paraded by her French entourage from one Scottish palace to another, shielding her from the sort of squalor that had drawn Queen Margaret's compassion, and giving her a polished, however inaccurate, vision of her new home. Her tour of castles and monasteries took her from Sterling to Scone in a calculated but meandering tour, until, in October, they arrived at Jedburgh Abbey.

The site of the marriage was chosen by Durward. Jedburgh was deep in the south of Scotland, near the border with England. It was very intentional flaunting and taunting in the face of their English neighbors. Jedburgh filled with French nobles of the highest order. As tempted as Edward might have been to disrupt the wedding, he dared not.

On the fourteenth of October, on the evening before the wedding, Alexander met his young bride. She was a striking beauty. Not even his battered heart could deny it. She had been bred and groomed for that very day, and she glowed like the sun under the dark, clouded, Scottish night.

It was a brief introduction, cordial and heavily chaperoned. She was elegant and refined, speaking the right words in the best manner, just charming enough, while not too bold of a presence. But she was so young, and she shared none of the experiences that made Alexander who he was. He gave her a tiny kiss on the cheek, one that was more like that of an older relation than a betrothed lover. He bid her welcome to her new country

349

in a tone of voice that resembled a condolence, and he excused himself and went to bed.

This wedding, this taunting show in the face of England, was everything one would expect from a French wedding. The area was cleared of the poor and dirty. They turned Jedburgh into a French palatial estate. It was not Scottish in any way. It was not Alexander. Yet he performed his duty admirably. The ceremony was in Latin with French responses. Alexander answered in exquisite French, impressing his stranger-bride and her relations.

In the moment before Alexander's vows, the abbey turned dark, like the large, stained-glass windows were suddenly shuttered up tightly. The doors of the abbey were closed, yet a chilling wind rushed through the attendees, raising the hairs of each and dragging across their skin like icy fingernails. It was carried on the back of a high-pitched, wicked, scornful, malevolent, shrieking, howl, that at once expressed its own pain and its desire for the pain of others.

All eyes turned to the windows, in wonder of the sudden darkness, then to the rafters above, where the horrid howl seemed to come from. A deep purple glow drew their attention to the altar. Inside of the glow, mere feet from Alexander and Yolande, was a gaunt skeletal figure, human in its proportions, but unearthly, with eyes radiating like two small, brownish-red, angrily churning and swirling storms.

Hung about the apparition was a transparent gown, a French burial gown that the intruder tried miserably to throw off with her waving arms. Nobody in the abbey could make sense of the scene before them. They closed their eyes to the terror and shielded their ears from her ceaseless howl. Alexander did not shield his senses. He stared. Something about the figure struck him as familiar. It was not the proportions, nor the wretched voice, but the hatred and the anger. It was his mother, Maria de Coucy.

Her body rested in burial in France, but it seemed her spirit was doomed to the country she despised, overlooking the son she resented.

The howling ceased suddenly. The guests opened their eyes and unblocked their ears, but the wicked apparition was not gone. Maria de Coucy walked the three steps to reach Alexander and Yolande. She reached her ghostly hands forward and took them both by the shoulder. Yolande teetered on the brink of fainting, but a firm squeeze of her hand by Alexander awoke her and drew her eyes to Alexander. He stared forward with bold defiance, and in that look, Yolande too stood stout.

Maria's cold, specter fingers began to sink into Alexander and Yolande, and they both felt their blood turning cold and stabbing. Maria let out another screech, riding on another gusting wind. The large, stained-glass window behind them blew out in a loud crash. The moment it did, another uninvited guest entered through the shards, uninvited, but not unwelcome. It was an owl, a deep-brown, majestic owl with a stern and protective scowl.

"Vanora," Alexander whispered in his weakened breath.

At the mention of the name, Maria de Coucy withdrew her phantom fingers from Alexander and Yolande and stared her stormy eyes at the owl. The owl flew at the ghost, uninhibited by the wind and sound that rushed at it. It flew through the skeletal figure and landed on the head of a statue of Saint Andrew. The apparition dissipated with a mournful scream. The purple glow faded, and the natural light of the sun returned through the large windows.

The owl, still perched on the statue, began to open and close its beak and nodding its head, as if in conversation. No sound came from the owl. Instead, words came from

Alexander, not a message *from* him, but *to* him, from his mouth, in a voice higher than his own.

The path of the King, the King of the Gulls
Is paved with tears, with bones and skulls
It is not of his making
But of the centuries aching
Of faith scared and shaking
And walk it he must

Do not look down to witness his throne
It is not made of skulls, not made of bone
It was fashioned in Spring
By the Heavenly Wing
And awaits its King
On a ship made of dust

Absolute silence followed the words, until it was broken by the flap of the owl's wings. It flew from the statue and left the abbey through the same broken window it had entered. The verses spoken by Alexander had expelled all of his breath. He drew a sudden and violent inhale. His knees buckled beneath him, and he fell to the floor.

Durward ran to him and helped him to his feet. When Alexander regained himself enough to look around him, all eyes in the building were locked on him. Frightened, helpless faces begged in their frozen expressions for guidance and reassurance.

Alexander announced with loud authority, "We will finish the ceremony, and go on with our lives as they are prescribed to us."

With shaken nerves and faltering voices, the ceremony resumed. Alexander and Yolande were married in the strangest atmosphere ever to fill a wedding venue.

When the ceremony was over, the newlyweds were escorted by her father to nearby Fernieherst manor, directly to the bedchamber. They would have stripped her themselves and hand-placed her into Alexander's arms if he would have allowed it. But this was *his* new bride, his wedding day, his country. He sent them away, closed the door, sat Yolande down on a chair, and talked to her. They spoke nothing of the ghostly events of the day. For different reasons, it was a topic neither would raise to the other. They were well into their wedding night, still stitched tightly into their wedding attire, learning the minute details of her sheltered life, and the grand and often gruesome truths of his.

By the wee hours before dawn, the seedling of a friendship had sprouted its first soft, tiny stem. It was enough, it had to be enough. Alexander undressed his bride and took her to bed. It was an act of patriotism, not of romantic passion, but their conversation had given them just enough understanding of the other. The act was ensconced in mutual respect, and in a shared hope that greater affection would develop.

A marriage is formed
A stranger's debut
As evil moves on
And shadows pass through

Chapter Twenty-Nine:

A War of One Against Many

Silence prevails
The King honors true love
A new family grows
The gulls guide from above

Yolande was quite taken by Alexander. Her heart thumped at the thought of him. It is fair to say she was in love. He could not be in love. A man like him can only be in love once, and never can recover from that love. He knew he could never love Yolande as he loved Margaret, and she soon realized the same. Still, he came quickly to care for her, to truly care, and she recognized his efforts to be all he could be for her. Although it was the romantic nobility of his faithful heart that prevented him from being in love with her, it was the same traits that made her fall so deeply for him.

Alexander had all of the concerns of a middle-aged king of a troubled country. Even if he were able to develop a husband's bond with Yolande, time would never permit it. He would not cage her in Edinburgh or Scone, leaving her to wallow in isolation while the man she loved traipsed the Highlands and Lowlands. He established a royal residence in Kinghorn, a mere country walk from her relations. She remained under guard there, where her lonely hours could be occupied by loved ones.

Alexander spent as much time in Kinghorn as his schedule would allow. While he was with her, he gave her all the love and attention that was his to give away. Her ardent affections were resplendent. She did not hide them well, and would not have if she could, which only made him feel guiltier for his inability to return her love.

They shared their bed in Kinghorn only four times between their wedding and the end of January 1286. The third time placed a child inside of her. The fourth time, she told him. His affections for her had indeed grown. He did not realize how much until he learned of her pregnancy and surged with protective zeal. It would have been very good for the country to know of the baby, but very dangerous for Yolande. She had told nobody but him, and he intended to keep it that way.

She was forbidden to leave the residence, even under guard. Her local relations were informed and sworn to secrecy. Alexander wanted to remain at her side, more out of fear than love. Oh, how he pitied her! She had married into circumstances she could not have foreseen, but as she told him, even with the clarity of hindsight, she would have chosen him all the same. She was a young woman with a tremendous capacity for love, and she filled her copious heart with love for her husband.

As much as he wanted to, Alexander could not remain by her side. Less than a full day after hearing of the child growing inside of his wife, he was away again, on a boat, sailing for Edinburgh.

As Yolande's birthday approached, she yearned more than ever for social interaction. Her Kinghorn relations began planning a large, very French birthday soiree. But how could such a thing take place? She could no longer hide her swollen condition. They could not afford to expose her, not to anyone beyond her intimate circle of servants and family. So the twentieth of March came and went, and Yolande's twenty-third birthday passed just like the day before.

On the day after, she wrote to Alexander. He was in Glasgow when the letter reached him. It read,

My Dear, Noble Husband,

As our child grows within me, other things swell in equal proportion. Thoughts and feelings aggrandize, nearly bursting me from within. Of these, none stand in comparison to my thoughts and feelings for you. You have forbidden my birthday celebration, and I understand why. I love you all the more for it. I do not need parties. I desire no guests toasting my health, no singers or dancers to entertain me, if I could only mark the occasion with you. That would be enough. It would be much more than enough. It would be Heaven to me.

Please come to me as soon as you can. Please come. I ask only one thing for my birthday, that you place one hand on my face and one on my belly, so that all that is most precious to me may be united in touch. I do not fear the dangerous shadows around us. I do not fear treachery or treason. But I am terrorized by every hour without you. Please, please come to me.

Ever Faithfully Yours,

In the Purest of God's Love,

Yolande, Queen of Scotland

There was much to attend in Glasgow. It all went uncompleted. Alexander left immediately for Edinburgh. He planned a birthday celebration for Yolande, minute in scale but tremendous in thoughtfulness. It had to be within the confines of the Kinghorn residence, and include only their most intimately trusted circle. With Durward, Baliol, and William Lindsay, he assembled a list of necessaries. His personal cook studied French recipes. Baliol himself would arrange and provide the decorations. William chose his own Lindsay cousins to stand as guards.

It was scheduled for one month after Yolande's birthday, the twentieth of April, 1286. Yolande's Kinghorn relations abandoned their homes a week before the party and took up residence with her. On the morning of Thursday, the eighteenth, a humble carriage was filled. But it could not depart Edinburgh. A storm had come upon Eastern Scotland, and it threatened to get worse. Durward, Baliol, and William approached the King in his study.

"The party must be delayed," Durward declared, "We cannot travel in this storm."

"Alan," Alexander answered, "the Queen and her family are gathered already. We will be there as promised."

"Have you seen the storm?" Durward protested, "You would be unable to see your horse's head from the saddle. It is too dangerous."

"I am going, if I must ride alone, I will be there as promised."

"I do not understand this resolution. The Queen can wait for the sake of the King's safety."

Alexander slouched back in a chair and covered his face with his hands.

Durward placed a firm, brotherly hand on his shoulder and said, "I understand what pains you. You cannot love Yolande as you wish you could, and you compensate how you can. But please keep your head. You have no reason for shame. She will get over it."

"Will she? Will she forgive me? She is so young. She loves me so deeply, much more than I can love her. Worst of all, she knows it."

"She needs only provide you an heir. Nobody expects you to love her."

Alexander turned his head sharply and yelled in a fierce tone that stunned and frightened Durward, "She deserves to be loved!"

He turned his head from Durward to the floor, shook it subtly and echoed softly, "She deserves to be loved. The poor girl."

"Poor?!" Durward exclaimed defensively, "She has married the King, left that fish market town in France, and come here. Now she carries a king inside of her."

"She has been taken forcibly from her home and family and united irreversibly to a man who cannot..."

His thoughts were dark, too dark and too difficult to speak. He locked his eyes steely to Durward and continued, "She is caged in a simple residence, with none of the palace pleasures we have here. She remained locked in that cage for her birthday. Now she asks only for me. I have promised her a party with her husband, and I will give it to her as promised."

After a moment of floor-staring contemplation, he added, "I *will* love her as she deserves to be loved, whatever it might cost me, and I will begin in three days, when I celebrate her birthday at her side."

After a cold and steely silence, Alexander asked Durward, "Alan, what have you done this week?"

Durward began dutifully listing all the things he had accomplished in the King's name.

Alexander rolled his eyes upward and interrupted, dreamily and more to himself, "Not one thing that will be anchored to the memory by the heart."

Baliol and William listened and understood the King's point. Their philosophical minds quickly acknowledged and applied the lesson. Durward did not. His mind struggled to imagine how he could have been more dutiful, more industrious, and more faithfully present. Alexander declared that their business for their King was concluded, that they all had pressing personal matters to attend. Baliol and William left the room, and turned their thoughts toward long-neglected domestic matters. Durward did not. He lingered with sweat beading on his troubled brow.

Durward's thoughts were distant, but not where they should have been, not where Alexander tried to direct them. He began a stumbling blend of excuses and promises, oaths of loyalty and protestations of concern.

Alexander interrupted him, "Go home, Alan."

"Are you dismissing me? Have I displeased you?"

"No, my old friend, you have not. You have pleased me and you have pleased Scotland, and now it is time to please yourself and your family. Go home. Take a month.

Be a husband, a father, a grandfather. Be with your family. I am going to be with mine."

Durward stepped gently onto a tender subject, "My dear King, you have lost them. Your family is all gone."

Durward was never a spiritual man, yet he would have sworn that Alexander gazed through his eyes and directly into his soul, as he responded, "I am a husband. I have a wife. I have a child not yet born in Kinghorn. You have a wife, rooted to you by decades of devotion."

Durward could not have looked away if he wished to. The King's eyes held his with a clenching grip.

"But you —" Alan began.

"Forget me!" the King shouted. He softened in tone and posture, then continued, "For Heaven's sake, for a while, forget me. Forget your country. Your whole world is within the walls of your family home. For a short while, live in *your* world. I am going to live in *mine*."

Durward felt like a child being taught something that remained just above his head. He thought of David Lindsay and wondered silently, "What would David have said?"

Alexander spoke, "Lindsay lived within his world. He carried it wherever he went. His love for his wife, his children, me, you, his country, we were always with him. Even in the desert, he carried us with him."

Durward was struck dumb by Alexander's penetrating vision. For the first time, he saw his former student not as a king, but as a sage, one whose wisdom was not to be refuted. Alexander would leave for Kinghorn, through any obstacle nature could throw at him. But the lesson was not fully absorbed. Durward did not turn his eyes to his own heart. They remained on his King. If Alexander was to ride to Kinghorn. Durward would see him there safely!

Alexander did not wish to endanger anyone but himself, yet he knew he could not dissuade Durward. Still

William's superior, Durward ordered him to take the men he had gathered and meet him at the gate of Edinburgh Castle. It was a small party, Alexander, Durward, William, and a handful of Lindsay cousins. Their greatest advantage — an ambush was unlikely, for who else would go out in such a storm?

The moment their heads were exposed to the air, their peril was apparent. A heavy, freezing, malevolent, spiteful, pelting rain struck them from the side, carried at that unnatural angle by a ferociously angry wind. It was as if nature had withheld its hatred for every offense of mankind through the ages, then released all of its pent-up fury at once, all on Eastern Scotland.

The King and his faithful rode at a snail's pace, along the southern shore of the Firth of Forth, one labored yard at a time, until, late in the afternoon, they reached the home of the ferryman. His name was Eaun, a thick-bearded, stout man in his mid-thirties. He had recently assumed the post from his father, who stood at the door beside him, equally astonished to receive the King to their humble home.

Alexander demanded immediate passage across the firth.

"I... I... I...," Eaun stammered, "The..., have you seen the storm?"

Eaun's father pushed his son aside and welcomed the travelers in, then slapped Eaun on the shoulder and said, "Have they seen the storm? Stupid boy! They have been riding in it."

Alexander interrupted the family argument, turning to Eaun and asking, "I am sorry we cannot accept your hospitality. We must get across the firth immediately. Can you ferry us?"

"Of course he can," the father answered proudly, "look at him. I did not feed him so well so he could serve refreshments. Go boy, ferry your King across the water."

Eaun looked truly terrified, and for good reason. This was no time to be on the water, not for the most skilled ferryman. But he was given no option to refuse. He led the travelers to the ferry, loaded it with its passengers, men and horses alike, and set them all into choppy water.

They were all soaked to the bone with freezing rain, but that was not the reason for the chills that shook them. The ferry was tossed. Waves swatted at it like it was an annoying little bug buzzing around the face of the firth. They could not see where they were going, and on several occasions, were certain that that very moment was their last, all but Alexander. It was duty that drove him, not love. But it was his duty *to* love that kept his mind on Kinghorn, while others focused on the angry, icy water.

It took them two hours to get across. Once on the other side, Eaun dropped unconscious to the ground. The Lindsay clansmen carried him to the north side ferry house and left him to recover by his own means. They pushed forward, often walking beside their horses rather than riding, so the bodies of the beasts could protect them from the wind.

They reached Dunfermline Abbey in the early evening. It was a commonly used royal residence. The unannounced arrival of the King would have been no surprise on any normal evening. They kept it in readiness. This was no normal evening. The staff was already in bed, trying to shield themselves from the historic storm with as many layers of stone, wood, blanket, and clothing as possible.

They roused quickly and received their King, arranging accommodation for each of their guests.

"We thank you," Alexander told them, "but we are not staying the night. We stop here only to warm, and to dry our clothes by the fire. As soon as we are fed and dry, we leave for Kinghorn."

"No, no!" Durward spoke loudly, much more like the teacher of the past than like the servant of the present.

William supported him, "I agree with Durward. We were nearly done in by the day. How do you think we would fare with the night? No, no, my old friend, I owe you much more than my obedience. I owe you my judgment, and if I must chain you to your bedpost, you will remain in this abbey until morning."

Now, it was a matter little spoken of, that Alexander, since he was a young child, kept the same three stones gifted to him at his coronation by the old sage always in his pocket. He donned them habitually each morning, usually without thought, like putting on any other article. He gave them little consideration, yet there they had always been, the three silent sisters, waiting for some purpose long-promised but never shown.

Alexander suddenly became aware of a clicking sound at his side. Once his attention was drawn to it, he realized he was fiddling with the stones, clicking them rapidly against his winged ring. Nobody else seemed to hear it over the protest of the advisors. Now that he thought of it, Alexander heard nothing else. In the frenzied clicking, he heard the voice of Yolande, "Please come to me."

In the middle of some demand of William's, one he could not have later recalled, Alexander turned from his friends and walked to the royal chamber. He seemed convinced. He appeared resigned to follow the advice of Durward and William. He shut his door behind him without another word. Durward assigned twelve of the abbey soldiers to stand guard outside of the King's door. Content with themselves, Durward, William, and all of the Lindsays retreated to their assigned quarters.

After an hour of silent contemplation, Alexander went to a narrow window in his room. It could not open, yet he spoke through it just the same, "Vanora, my dear mother, David, father in all but name, where have you been? You taught me to see more than my eyes and hear more than my ears. Why can I not see you or hear you now? Can your gulls not handle a storm?"

He took a step back from the window, looked downward, and spoke in a whisper to himself, "Of course they can handle a storm, but I am not in the storm. I am behind stone. The gulls spoke to me in the storm. Yes, I remember, at sea, in a storm like this. The gulls were there."

A resolute decision seized control of him. He swung open his chamber door and walked through with the bold authority of his crown. He tapped the first six soldiers on the shoulder and ordered, "Follow me."

They obeyed him, and the seven of them walked with steady, unrushed steps, out of the abbey to the stable. The storm had calmed slightly, as though it drew a slow brief breath between shouts of anger. Alexander and his six escorts rode in the dark, under wind and rain, eastward, toward Kinghorn.

They rode with speed from the abbey, while they remained on the roads. But in the dark and rain, the roads disappeared. There was nothing in the sky to mark their way. The distant landmarks could not be seen. It had rained for a full day. Fields became marshes. Streams snuck beneath them. Within two miles, each of the soldiers had been tossed from their horses at one point or another, and were lucky to remount.

When the marshy field gave way to a bog, thick and sticky, with clinging, gripping mud that held to the hooves of the horses like misers to a coin, they were slowed to a crawl. The only thing that moved more slowly than them was the night. Day had no interest in taking its place in the sky. It too wanted to hide from the storm.

Six of the abbey soldiers assigned to the King's chamber had gone with them. Six had been left behind.

Alexander had given no thought to the other six until he heard a noise in the distance.

"Here they are," he said, "They have come for me."

He was right. Horses rode for him. But it was not the soldiers of Dunfermline Abbey. There was a spy in the abbey, and word got quickly to Alexander's enemies. Darkly cloaked and hooded riders, ten, twelve, maybe twenty rode through the King's party. There were too many to see or count in the darkness. They scattered the soldiers. Some left in pursuit of the assailants as they rode by and fled. One fell from his horse and chased the animal into the dark distance. In the chaos of the moment, Alexander was knocked from his horse. Whether by friend or foe, he could not tell.

The remaining soldiers and dark riders all scattered. Where and why, he did not know. All Alexander knew was they were gone. Sloshing, splashing and yelling faded in every direction until he was alone. His horse was gone. He and he alone remained, sunken halfway to his knees in the thick, smelly bog. It was a wretched smell, but not like any bog he had experienced. It smelled old, like old death, and yet young, like fresh death.

Alexander dropped to his knees and sank to his waist. He looked up. There were no gulls above, no voice of his father or Vanora, no bird squawk to transform into the voice of David Lindsay. A voice did come to him, but not from above. It howled at him with the wind from the east and stopped the rain as it flew by, as if it shut a giant window.

The voice in the wind — it was not Vanora's or Lindsay's, not Margaret's nor anyone else he had loved and lost. It was a strange voice, or a concert of many voices that shared the same thoughts and feelings. They were mournful voices. They spoke to him in a harmonized howl of many notes, high and low.

The incessant attack of disjointed sensations
By mere misfortune, they tighten their grip
The winds and the waves, who share no relations
Convene in communion to capsize the ship
Fortune can raise you to the peak of elation
Then tear through the flesh, like the slave master's
whip

How can it happen that heaven is courting
The heart with gorgeous and glorious gifts
Then to your sweet praise you find heaven retorting
And love's solemn sanction suddenly shifts
Then the clouds upon which you walk stop supporting
The weight of a king burnt and burdened by rifts

Then like a war of one against many
You find yourself staring at enemy eyes
Hatred hangs heavy but costs just a penny
And is purchased by all who curse and despise
They will feed on the heart if the flesh is too skinny
Then run away dripping with the blood of their prize

Now as a carcass sucked dry to the marrow
You lay lacerated and linger alone
Your spirit scrawls with the point of an arrow
A gruesome gospel engraved in your bone
Then whisks away on the wings of a sparrow
A fluttering flicker, searching for home

There was such a lamentful tone in the voices, but
whether they lamented for him or for themselves,
Alexander could not tell. The words seemed to describe
him, his life, his tragedies.

"But then," he spoke aloud, still kneeling in the sticky bog, "mine is not the only tragic life. I am not the first to mourn beloved dead."

He thought of David Lindsay, of his dear Vanora, of his children, and of his most precious Queen Heather. His heart broke all over again, but not for his sorrow alone. The haunting lament of the phantom voices remained in him, and he mourned for them. He wept for all who had suffered as he had, and he felt a powerful urge to act. What could he do for the lost and mourning? He was alone in the bog, the King of a country in peril, scant of allies and rich with enemies, in a world that seemed to conspire against him.

The words of the wind echoed in his head, "How can it happen that heaven is courting the heart with gorgeous and glorious gifts?"

Vanora often spoke of Heaven. If there was such a place, it was surely far away. Alexander was chilled to the bone, with a far more biting chill gnawing at his heart. He sat back onto his heels, half content to die.

Kneeling alone
To his hip in the mud
Hearing the voices
Of long-vanquished blood

Chapter Thirty:

Searching for Heaven

Holding the captives
The victims of hate
The trees are the cages
The King is the gate

Alexander stood. What hope or fear, what hunger motivated him, he did not know. The storm that had subsided raged again. Lightening cracked nearby, illuminating his surroundings for the length of a heartbeat. It was not the warm light of midday, though just as bright. It was an unwelcoming light, like a nightmare, and the world around him was hideous and hateful.

In that flash, he thought he saw the dark riders. In the still silence between the lightning and the thunderclap, there was nothing but darkness. He was still alone. The thunder that followed grabbed Alexander by the skull and shook him. There were no dark riders, yet he heard them in the thunder. He felt them in his troubled memory, real and violent, as if they rode against him again. He fell again to his knees, then nothing, nothing but the swelling storm.

A gust of wind howled by him again. He heard it. He saw its effect on the bog around him, but he did not feel it. It was as if the wind wanted to get his attention, but dared not touch him. In it, he heard the same concert of voices, not in words as before, but a pleading howl that struck his compassion while avoiding his flesh. Another flash of lightning and another clap of thunder frightened the wind away, like the ambush of dark riders. The thunder sounding like the crack of a rider's reins.

Alexander looked angrily to the sky and shouted upward,

Be still the thunder of old, with horses too few
Among the reins that crack does sorrow pass
through
Shadows on horseback charge while others flee
Starlight! Oh starlight! please bring light to me

Over the mountains in darkness and fear
Searching the forest for that presence so near
Yet out of my view
Cold and damp as the dew

Show me your wares!
Disclose your pain!
As scars from the ages
Assume their reign
And hunt the light
I shiver in fright
Searching for Heaven
With weak, earthly sight

The moment he spoke the last word, a dark, deep brown owl flew over his head, nearly within his reach. It followed the retreating wind. Alexander watched it diminish in the darkness, but before it left his vision, it looked back to him.

"Vanora!" he shouted.

He stood as quickly as he could and fought his way east through the bog. Within a hundred steps, the mud became shallow. Higher and higher he walked upon the wet earth, until he stood again on solid ground, at the entrance of a forest. The owl sat perched on the nearest tree. It locked eyes with him for a moment, then flew into the forest. Alexander followed with the same energy that had propelled his younger legs up Creag Choinnich.

He thought of that day as he ran in pursuit. He thought of the tree he had rested against, and of the voices he heard coming from it. He remembered the words clearly.

Your feet tread the path
Your hand holds the tree
That speak to you now
Through the rock and the bough
Of what you must be
Both the seed and the plow

Propelled by some force beyond him, he pushed forward through the trees, hearing words from them, either in his ears or only in his imagination. He came to a clearing, and there, on the lowest branch of a tree at the far end, was the owl. Alexander felt great relief at seeing the owl, but that moment of well-being was shattered when he realized that a solitary figure stood before him. It was a man, standing perfectly still. Alexander stepped nearer and saw plainly. It was Beolin Crymlyn.

It was Crymlyn, no doubt.

Alexander gazed at him and asked, "Crymlyn, how are you here?"

Crymlyn smiled at him with devilish eyes.

Alexander demanded, "I am no child in the woods, I warn you. Tell me now. Why are you here?"

Crymlyn answered calmly, "Finally, my victory is almost in my hand. I have taken almost everything from you. There is only one thing left to take."

With no patience for a greedy baron, he told him, "You have taken nothing from me. My own pitiful fate has robbed me of all I have loved."

"Yes, your fate," Crymlyn returned, "which I have held in my hand. It was I who brought you down. I killed your children. I poisoned your wife. It was my sword in my hand that pierced the heart of David Lindsay and spilled his blood onto the desert sand. Now, at the end, I want you to know it was I."

Alexander stared into Crymlyn's eyes, as he had once stared into clouds of pipe smoke in a cave, trying to see into them, at what truth could be found. There was an abundance of viciousness in those envious, green eyes. There was greed, feverish ambition, but no deceit. Crymlyn spoke the truth. Each of the most horridly torturous moments of Alexander's life had been brought down on him by the figure in front of him.

In a breath shaken by erupting emotion, Alexander whimpered, "Why?"

"I took no lives unnecessarily. I killed your children to end the claim of your blood on the throne. I killed your wife to anger her brother and bring England against you. And I could never have killed you while Lindsay still held a sword."

"You fool!" Alexander shouted, "Don't you see what you have done? You bring England against *us*, against Scotland. You too will lose."

"No, I have already won, or will have, with one more swing of the sword. You will see your family soon in Heaven."

Crymlyn raised his sword and leaned forward. Alexander thought nothing of survival, not of pleasure nor of power. Rage swelled in him, not toward Beolin

Crymlyn. It was a fury not associated with his slaughtered loved ones. He was angry at the world, the whole world, with all of its violent greed and ambition, with its weeping widows, with every glossy, dead eye that would see no more sunsets, with every man slaughtered to gain a tiny patch of useless ground.

Crymlyn lifted his leg to take a step toward Alexander. Before his foot hit the floor of the forest, Alexander had closed on him with a mindless lunge. Before Beolin Crymlyn could release his next breath, the Lindsay sword, gifted to Alexander at his coronation, thrusted under Crymlyn's chin and found the forest air again through the back of his skull.

The slayed villain released his last breath, which gurgled and bubbled around the blade. He died with his last thought plastered onto his face. It was not greed or ambition. It was fearful regret. Truth finally dawned on Crymlyn in his final second, and that was the lifeless expression staring back at Alexander.

Crymlyn's legs went limp beneath him. He dropped to his knees and was held upright by the Lindsay sword still gripped tightly by Alexander. Blood ran down the handle and onto Alexander's hand. It was still warm, so recently from the living, but now serving no purpose but to haunt the King with another tragedy.

Alexander withdrew the sword from its victim. Crymlyn's kneeling body fell forward to lean against Alexander's legs. This sword, this honored gift of his childhood, given to him by the most honorable man he had ever known, held in his hand as a bloody reminder of its nature.

"This is no treasure," he said aloud, "This is vile!"

He sheathed the sword with disgust, then wrapped both arms around Crymlyn's bloody head and wept.

Crymlyn's last words echoed in the King's head, "You will see your family soon in Heaven."

Alexander looked up to the forest canopy above him. The owl sat on a higher branch. He laid Crymlyn's body with gentle care and walked away, toward the owl. When he was directly under it, he shouted upward, "Where have you led me, to what destiny, to what Heaven?"

The owl gave no response, but stood perched like a statue. It was only an owl, not a mother or sage, not a guide, only an owl. Alexander felt as abandoned as ever. All that he had lost ran through his mind, each of their faces and each of their voices, and the cause of all his loss was right in front of him.

Crymlyn was dead at his feet. This man, this enemy, this murdering thief of all of Alexander's happiness, lay lifeless on the forest floor, oozing from his wound and staring upward with vacant, glossy, half-opened eyes. But it was not enough. He was not dead enough for Alexander, as the blame for so much sorrow rested painlessly on the ground.

Alexander unsheathed and raised his sword. Fury clenched his entire body. His cheeks shook, and his face contorted into twisted rage. In the last moment before releasing his blade on the corpse, he heard a whisper from behind him. He turned defensively and swung his sword at the open air.

The whisper came again, in a soft, feminine, familiar voice, "Bug-bane, release it."

The remnant wind of the storm through the trees conspired with his imagination. He turned again to Crymlyn and raised his sword to mutilate the body in a berserker frenzy.

The voice came again, undoubtedly the whisper of his Queen Heather, "Bug-bane, let it go."

Alexander crept forward to investigate. The soft and subtle breaths of his dear Queen Margaret pulsed from a nearby tree. Every hair on his body stood erect. He crept forward to the tree, and there, in the deep recesses of the bark, was an eye looking back at him. It was not any eye, but the deep-blue, ocean eye of his only true lover.

"My God," he shouted, "You are in there!"

He banged on the side of the tree with the handle of the sword, while scratching at the bark in front of him with his other hand, yelling in desperation, "My Heather, my Margaret, my love!"

As if awakened by the violence against the tree, other eyes appeared in the bark, eyes of various sizes and color, some clear and some bloodshot, some dry and some crying tears that ran down the tree to the ground.

Startled, Alexander took one quick step backward, and he yelled, "Margaret, you are not alone. Who is in there with you? Leave her alone! Let her be!"

"My love," came Margaret's dulcet voice calmly back to him, "we have no enemies here. Put it down. Release it."

Other voices, from other eyes, echoed, "Release it. Release us."

"Who is in there with you?" he demanded more sternly.

Margaret answered, "Not only here, but in that tree behind you, and the ones around you, in every tree in Scotland."

"Who are they, and why are you with them?"

"We are all those who died too young, who died in war."

"But my love, you were not killed in war."

"Wasn't I?"

With a surge of renewed determination and a desperation that was fueled by rage for all he had lost, Alexander lifted his sword and began hacking at the tree, speaking in a trance-like mantra, "I will free you. I will free you."

The whispers of the caged came at him in concert, but he could not understand them, as he continued hacking, and speaking in a rising voice, "I will free you. I will free you all."

He was brought to sudden stillness and silence when he felt the brush of a bird's wing on his head. The owl, the very same owl, landed and perched on the lowest branch of the tree. Alexander stared at the owl, then back to the lone eye of his dead wife.

Margaret's voice came again from the tree, but in melodic concert with another. It was Vanora's voice joining Margaret's from some unknown direction.

Not like that, not in that way
Not with the fury that enslaved us
Not with a sword but with a golden ray
Leave the violence that has haunted and depraved us

Release it now, let it go
Encase it deep in ice and snow
Give it to the cold below
It is time to be the one that Heaven gave us

Voices from within the many trees around him, and the hundreds more beyond, repeated in haunting, chaotic concert, "Release it now, let it go."

They all suddenly hushed, and Queen Heather's voice echoed alone, "Release it now, let it go."

Alexander's shoulders lowered. His hands fell to his sides. The twisted expression of vengeance on his face melted into the sadly innocent, doe-eyed look of a child.

One more time, Margaret whispered, "Let it go."

Alexander looked to his right hand, which still tight-fistedly squeezed the Lindsay sword. He relaxed his hand one finger at a time, until the sword fell to the ground. He stared at it, this sword that had meant so much to him. He fixed his attention on the noble Lindsay crest on the pommel. There could have been no better reminder of all that had been lost.

With one long exhale, Alexander released his anger, his vengeance, and every clingy, sticky piece of hatred that was adhered to his pain. The hand that had held the sword was in his pocket, holding the three stones. He pulled them out and laid them on the forest floor with held breath. When he expelled the last of that held breath, the sound of his exhale continued. It did not come from his own mouth, but from the trees. He looked at Margaret's tree. The bark was only bark. There were no eyes and no voices.

A swooshing sound of jubilant voices blew past him and through him, to the east. In the ghostly breeze, he could smell the scents of all who had been encased in the trees. He distinctly picked up the scent of his dear Queen Heather. It was a scent that had long left her personal possessions. It had long left the physical world, and had existed in Alexander's memory with increasing faintness.

Oh, but it was vivid in that moment, and it dragged in its wake a flood of precious memories.

As it blew past him, he panicked. He was not ready to lose such a physical connection to his childhood lover. He chased the escaping gust, running east behind it, to the forest's edge. There, silhouetted in front of the horizon's brush of morning color, was the old man. It was the same old sage who had served as a timeless interpreter of his destiny since he was seven years old.

Following voices
That gust like a wind
To the edge of a new day
And a mysterious friend

Chapter Thirty-One:
To Cover the Soil of Bloodshed

A wounded king
With scars unseen
Will walk with the sage
And carry the ring

Had the encounter at the forest's edge with the old man happened several years earlier, it would have borne a very different air. But Alexander was broken in every way a man can break. He did not see a wise teacher with petty nuggets of ancient wisdom to pass in enigmatic verse. He saw a father-figure, a sanctuary, and he ran the several paces between them. He did not ask why the old man was there, standing in the wilderness in the middle of a storm. He ran like a child with childlike needs.

In contrast to Alexander's frantic state, the old sage stood still, calm, and patient, with a subtle smile that pushed wrinkles against his eyes. Alexander stumbled to him and dropped to his knees. Without a word, the old man took Alexander's hand and helped him to his feet, threw an arm around his shoulder, turned him eastward, and began walking.

The storm traveled west, revealing hints of a calm blue sky on the eastern horizon.

"Hmmmm," the man hummed blissfully, "Heavenly."

Alexander stopped sharply, his mind buzzing with all he had experienced that night and the many wretched nights before. He turned to the man, and spoke in a cracking voice, gushing verses in a breathless torrent.

What is this heaven, where does it lie?
How do I find it? Do I look to the sky?
Can it be seen from the stations of life?
Can it be heard through the pain and the strife?
How can it guide the actions of men
Can it see where we are going, does it know where we've been

This plague all around us, this illness of greed
Taking all that they want and more than they need
With all of this near me, how can I see
The power of God, the power to be
All that Vanora said I would be?

Alexander's eyes were fixed on the sage's, while he waited for a response.

An answer came, but not in full, "That is the right question, my son, and I will do my best to answer it for you, but first may I tend to your scars?"

"Scars?" Alexander asked, "Which scars?"

He expected some ethereal answer in puzzling verse, some hint to an inner truth. But the man gestured downward to Alexander's shoulder, then farther down to his knee. Alexander followed the man's hand and saw the physical wounds he had not known were there. Blood ran from under his shoulder plate. That was clear to see. He became aware of the pain in his knee. It was not seen, but felt by Alexander alone. Somehow, the old man knew.

The rain had slowed to a light sprinkle, and they sat together. A piercing, reaching whistle came from the old man's weathered lips. A horse responded from some unknown distance, trotting calmly but obediently to its old master. The man stood and removed from a satchel affixed to the saddle an old piece of cloth, some horse hair, and a vial of some strong and pungent elixir. He removed Alexander's shoulder plate, revealing an oozing gash. He cleaned it with the cloth and applied the elixir directly to the wound.

It stung the wound and the nose alike, but just as the sting faded into a warm sense of well-being, the biting aroma sweetened. The old man threaded the horse hairs through a needle and sewed the wound shut.

Alexander lifted the leg of his trousers, revealing a deeply bruised knee with a displaced kneecap.

"That looks very bad as well," the old man commented with confident gravity.

With a hand on Alexander's ankle and the other on his knee, the old man pulled and shifted the knee back into place. With what was left of the cloth, he wrapped the knee, and to Alexander's surprise, told him to drink the rest of the pungent elixir. The King did not question. He was little more than a child in this man's care. He sipped down the rest of the concoction, which heated the mouth and stung the throat. As the heat radiated throughout his body, the pain in the knee subsided.

Surging with new energy, Alexander stood and tested his knee, bouncing up and down a few times in disbelief. Once certain of his ability to move, he demanded, "I must go now. There is little time."

"Time?" the old man answered, "Hmmm, time."

He placed his hands palm down on Alexander's shoulders, gazed deeply through his eyes, and spoke in a melodic chant.

This time you speak of, what is it you see?
Is it measured with numbers or does it run free?

Does it come from the Heavens, or was it drawn by
a hand?
Does it stand by you now and give a command?

You choose to live inside it
While the Eternal have denied it
For the spirits have untied it
From their tether to the land

Alexander's antsy, eager muscles relaxed, gaining just
enough patience to ask for more. The old man responded.

Close your eyes
Look with your heart
What do you see?
All that is and forever will be
Heaven is there! and will always be seen
What is, and what was, and that light in between!

The pain of the living
Is felt by the dead
But the chord that connects them
Has worn thin as a thread

Walk ahead
Seek the light
Reach and find
You must hear for the deaf and see for the blind
Not with foggy eyes or muted ears
Through the walls of the prison of worldly fears

Alexander stared in amazement. He understood
enough for the truth to burrow under his skin and cause
an insatiable itch, but not deeply enough to provide the
guidance he desired.

He asked, "Please sir, where do I go? What do I seek?" The morning slowly brightened, but the clouds had cleared enough to reveal a moon that was not ready to follow the night. It shone pink in the sky in the minutes before the sun breached the horizon.

The man looked to the moon, then pointed to the horizon and said, "Can you see that hill up above the trees, with the moon shining on its crest? On the other side of that hill lies the sea. You have something to say, son."

In a chant, he finished,

Go tell the sea!
Go and tell the sea!

They both looked to the east. As they each placed their synchronized step in that direction, the new day's sun broke the horizon. The storm behind them still churned. The thunder that continued to roll angrily to the west of them seemed only paces behind them, as if the sunny day ahead and the stormy night behind fought, pushing against each other for control of the sky above Alexander's head.

Alexander and the old man walked with steady, matching paces toward the sun, toward the shore, toward Kinghorn.

"Kinghorn!" Alexander exclaimed as the thought entered his head, "My wife awaits me there."

"Yes," his companion answered, "your wife awaits you there. You have freed her, as you have freed them all. Now they await you at the shore."

Still matching the old man's paces, Alexander remembered the encounter in the forest, Margaret's eye, her voice in the tree, all the voices.

"You speak of my first wife, Margaret, my Queen Heather."

"*You* speak of her, my son. *You* think of her."

"So it *was* my Heather in the tree. Where is she now?"

"She is where they all are, where you must go. They need you."

"Need me?" Alexander asked incredulously, "How could I possibly be of service to them?"

"They need their King, and they cannot be what they must be without him."

"Then I will go to them and guide them in any way I can."

The sun continued to rise in the east ahead of them, but it did not overtake the night, nor did it push away the storm that still hollered its battle cry behind them. Alexander and the old man were the line between night and day, between storm and calm. The ageless volley of night and day fought its nature, ceasing its perpetual march from east to west. It moved steadily from west to east, keeping pace with Alexander, each fighting to overtake him.

The dark rain poured just behind them, remaining on their heels as they walked. Alexander felt a strong urge to run forward, away from the stormy night and toward the bright day, but he knew it would do no good. He knew the night would follow. It was attached to him, and he pulled it with him into the day.

Alexander's thoughts were heavy, mired in a thick internal bog, but the old sage had a lightness about him that gave a certain buoyancy to Alexander's spirits. While the King thought of the perils of his Kingdom, of his departed wife and his living wife, of the blood spilled by his own hand, and the blood of his dearest ones, which soaked sand and stone, the old man spoke of lighter topics, of pleasant things. He talked of the sun and the breeze, of thistle blossoms and the smell of pine.

As he continued to list the pleasures of nature, he mentioned the gulls, and his tone turned grave.

"The gulls, my son, are like ships without passengers, like horses without riders. For now, they can only speak for the sacred few."

In the somber moment that followed, the storm behind appeared to gain strength and push more forcefully against its bright opponent.

In a sudden return to lightness, he added, "How could they do better? The King of the Gulls is away. But he will soon take his throne and connect the sky and the earth."

Alexander had seen enough. He had overheard and been taught. He knew himself to be the King the old man spoke of, which only frustrated him further.

He thought to himself, "I do not have Vanora's vision, nor this man's wisdom. I cannot simply remove my shoes, grip the soil with my toes, and speak to my ancestors."

In a response of penetrating vision, the old man replied to his silent thoughts, "Can you not? The gulls have spoken to you."

Alexander argued, "They come to me by their own will and in their own time. I do not command them."

"Not when you called with your mortal voice, but when your spirit commanded them, they obeyed."

As Alexander searched his memory, looking for truth in the man's words, they came to the land's end. They stood on the edge of a cliff, south of Kinghorn. To their left were the buildings of the town. Beyond them was the royal residence, with its captive Queen. Beneath them was a strip of sandy beach, brilliantly reflecting the eastern sun. Mere feet behind them was the incessant roar of pouring rain, the relentless clap of thunder, and the darkness of midnight.

The old man repeated his instruction, "You are here, my son. Tell it to the sea."

Alexander closed his eyes and cleared his mind. His face felt the warm sun in front of him. The back of his neck felt the dark chill behind him. His ears — his ears again heard the voices from the trees, Queen Margaret and the others from the forest, and many, many more, too many to make sense of. The voices had the sound of desperate sorrow, but with a lining of excited anticipation.

The thunder behind him took on the sound of clashing swords. The pouring rain sounded like thundering hooves and cries of anguish. But the voices came from the sea. Alexander dropped to his knees but did not feel the ground. He squeezed his eyes more tightly shut and grinded his teeth together. He lost all sense of direction. There was no up nor down. He could hear the squawk of gulls beneath him, then to his left, then right.

In a gradual realization, he felt soft warmth on his left side. He opened his eyes and found himself lying on the sand at the water's edge. The sun off the sand and water was almost unbearably bright. Once his eyes adjusted, and his mind could go elsewhere, he noticed that the sound of thunder was gone. There was no darkness overhead or anywhere.

The old man's horse was lying beside Alexander, broken, mangled, and dead. Alexander looked up to the top of the cliff, then down to the broken horse. The fall from the cliff had been violent to the poor beast, but Alexander stood tall and in one piece.

The old man spoke from behind him, "He was a good horse."

Alexander gestured to the top of the cliff, then down his own body, and he stuttered, "The cliff… the fall…, and the storm. Where has the storm gone?"

"My King—," the old man began before Alexander interrupted.

"Your King? You have never called me your King."

"That is because you were not yet my King."

"I was and I am," Alexander argued, "I am the King of Scotland!"

The old man answered calmly, "You *were* the King of Scotland, not anymore. Now you are *my* King."

The old man walked around to face him squarely. He placed both hands on Alexander's shoulders and said,

The war has now ended, may the whisperer cease!
The warrior inside has muted the beast!
The spirit surrounds to bring forth it's glow
And show you the way to the water we know

The trees will return with their majestic reign
To cover the soil of bloodshed and pain
For life is our child
So free and so wild
But often beguiled and bitterly slain

Now all are your subjects to love and to lead
With the voices of gulls, through the pain and the need

He pulled his right hand from Alexander's shoulder and pointed out to sea. There was a ship off the shore. It was gold, then silver, then white, as if the sunlight it reflected came from varying directions. There were hundreds of people on the deck, perhaps thousands. They stood perfectly still, staring at Alexander on the beach. The voices he had followed out of the forest returned to his ears, but clearly and distinctly. They all spoke simultaneously, yet he heard and understood each individually. They all had things to say, important messages to give to their loved ones, and it seemed they awaited Alexander's permission.

"Go to them, my King," the old man suggested.

Without a thought of the water's depth, Alexander walked toward the ship. It felt like an upward climb, like the gradual incline of a gently sloping hill. The ship grew larger in his vision until he was upon it. He stood at the rail, while the hands of the passengers reached for him. They helped him aboard. He looked up to thank the nearest of them. It was a face he knew well. Staring back at him was the smiling, lovingly paternal face of David Lindsay.

"Welcome aboard, my King," Lindsay said in a half-giggle.

Alexander knew he no longer lived, not as he had before. He shook his head and answered, "I am no longer the King of Scotland."

"No, my treasure," came the voice of Vanora as she walked up beside him, "You are the King of the Gulls."

As he heard the words, he felt the winged ring on his finger turn hot, then disappear. It was replaced by a warmth and a weight on his brow. It was a crown — a deep-black circle with the wing of a gull. Alexander threw his arms tightly around her. As he squeezed her, he felt a tug on his shoulder. He released Vanora and turned to see his precious Margaret, his Queen Heather, radiantly aglow with a beaming smile. Framing her from behind were his lost children, each in the bloom of perfect wellness.

"My one and only lover," Margaret told him, "We have so much to do. There are thousands here, each looking downward from the rails, unable to reach those below. Call for the gulls. They are yours to command. Send our voices to those who cry out for us."

Alexander finally understood. He leaned over the deck rail and scanned the world below. He turned back to Lindsay and pointed down from the ship, saying, "I will begin with you, my very dear friend. Your wife calls out in need of you."

He called for the gulls, placed Lindsay's voice within them, then whisked them away toward Byres. He sent the gulls, with the voices of the loving departed, to all who looked to the sky for guidance. He does so still. Some listen. Some do not. But the King of the Gulls hears them, and he sends the voices of Heaven to guide them.

The golden ship rose higher, and its master, its captain, the captain and King of the Gulls, ran his hands tenderly along the rail, and declared to the world,

> With mist surrounding
> And always so near
> Our presence prevails
> And welcomes no fear
>
> This way!
> This way!
> As the gulls surround
> Onward to Heaven
> With the Heavenly crowned
>
> The wind blows through
> This ethereal veil
> Showing its force
> And power to the sail
>
> Moving with a wonder
> Questioned only by time
> To gaze at this beauty
> And blend with this chime

Epilogue

It was late in the day on the beach of Kinghorn. The old seanchai had spoken all day with the passionate fire of truth. Yet he was not weary from the effort. He stood tall and powerful among the townsfolk. They too were briskly alert. The story of King Alexander III was told, not one of them moved. They hardly drew breath. They awaited more, not more of the story, but instruction, guidance.

The old storyteller walked one slow lap among them and returned to where he had stood. Each eye on the beach was fixed implacably to him. He raised his hands high, and he spoke.

Do not look to me, turn your eyes wider
To the gulls in the sky, to the web and the spider
Hear the wind in the reeds and the break of the waves
Seek the warrior maidens and the men in the caves

Hear your mothers and fathers and the ones before
them
Find their love in the soil and the rose on the stem
No one is gone, nor will ever leave you
They will speak from beyond and will never deceive
you

They share your laughter, they hear each cry
With the *King of the Gulls*, from his ship in the sky

The seanchai hoisted a young child from the lap of a nearby mother, kissed the yellow locks of her head through a rolling giggle, returned the child to her mother's arms, and walked from the beach. They watched him until he was out of sight. Then they followed his parting advice.

They looked to the sky, and to the gulls walking on the sand. They heard all of the natural sounds around them with hearts open to a deeper message. They listened for the loving words of those who had come before them, words dispatched from a shining ship they could not see, but they knew was there. In their faith, they heard the voices, and they gave thanks to God for the King of the Gulls.

The End